S. R. Keightley

Heronford

S. R. Keightley

Heronford

ISBN/EAN: 9783337186708

Printed in Europe, USA, Canada, Australia, Japan

Cover: Foto ©Andreas Hilbeck / pixelio.de

More available books at **www.hansebooks.com**

Heronford

By

S. R. Keightley

Author of

"The Crimson Sign," "The Cavaliers," "The Silver Cross," etc.

New York

DODD, MEAD & COMPANY
1899

INSCRIPTION

My dear Philip Russell,

It cannot be denied that you have the right taste in Romance. Unlike other critics, however accomplished, your own moods never interfere with your clear judgment and perfect faculty of enjoyment. At every hour your ears are open to the ringing of the horns of Elfland, and your heart is responsive to the wooing of the Fairy who has a constant seat at your fireside. Your young feet have not yet trodden far upon the strange and devious paths of life; but you are now learning, without knowing the fine truth, that there is refuge and sanctuary from care and trouble and pain in the fair house of which Imagination is the builder—a house that, though unsubstantial as a dream, abides for ever, and is full of joy and all delights. We have spent many happy hours together in the wonderland of Youth. On that future day when you come to read this book, it is my hope that you may find in its pages some faint reflection—alas! you will be older then—of that sweetness and joy that we have found together in the Cave of Aladdin and the Garden of the Caliph of Bagdad.

CONTENTS

HERONFORD

CHAPTER I

THE WAY I FIRST CAME TO HERONFORD

IT cannot be questioned that there was and is a wild strain in the Cassilis blood—a wildness that disappeared in this generation or in that—but invariably and inevitably reasserted itself after a slumbrous interval in the headstrong men and beautiful women who drew their birth from the first Cassilis of Heronford. There was a lonely child of whom I shall have much to say, who used to ponder with all the fascination of terror over the tragic chronicles of this family, and who was wont to watch in the evening shadows of the great hall the long line of warriors and knights, statesmen and priests, boisterous cavaliers, sour-visaged Puritans and beautiful women (these for the most part with the same proud high air, but some with a look of pain and fear eloquent in their splendid eyes)—the lad, I say, would watch that visionary cavalcade pass before him with its burden of reckless mirth and tragic despair—pass to the same dark and miserable doom. In the solitude of his young life these ghostly shapes stepping from their canvas peopled his dreams asleep and waking with an awful reality, and even yet sometimes appear to him as shadowy visitants

from the gloom and sorrow of the past. The whole
history of the house was written for the precocious child
in the sombre portraits that lined the long and rambling
corridor at the head of the great staircase, and he found
a certain companionship in the awe and fear inspired by
their silent faces. His mind was filled with their wild
and stormy history; he knew the name and history of
every splendid gentleman and haughty lady in that long,
illustrious line. He felt that in some curious, inexplicable way his young life was a part of that strange assem-
bly, and that each had a message for him.

Who shall explain the strange, unmeasurable working
of a child's mind? More than once the boy was caught
in his little nightshirt with a candle in his hand, standing
before the portrait of the Grey Countess,* his eyes fixed
in terror and his little heart beating wildly in his breast.
I remember how the passionate disdain of those haughty
lips was wont to hold him with a complete fascination,
and the cold denial of her cruel eyes would send him
back in childish terror—of what he could not tell—to
his solitary chamber to shut out the sight of his tear-
stained pillow. I cannot remember that anyone had ever
told him—I think it must have been his own thought and
the result of his own imaginative and morbid dreams—
but he never doubted that the evil spirit, and the dark
fate that followed as its shadow, entered the house for
the first time when that awful woman crossed its threshold as a bride. From that time the same eyes and lips
and the little frown between the brows were repeated in

---

* This lady was a widow when she intermarried with the fourth Lord
Cassilis, there never being an earldom in the family.

a hundred canvasses, and in every case the history was the same—wild riot and inevitable despair, or a still darker tale of crime and punishment.

Is it possible that the child sees more and further than the man? I cannot say, but I know that in my graver years here and there in that line of portraits I have caught a fancied resemblance to the Grey Countess of tradition, but of that spiritual sympathy and inward likeness I have seen nothing or nothing of which I could speak with assurance.

As in most great houses looking back to a remote past here also there was the story of a ghost, and it was said—there were few who did not believe it—that the awful shadow of the Grey Countess passed through the great hall to the chamber which she had occupied in life when any misfortune was about to befall the family at whose door she had laid the atonement of her crime. It may be that this wild and foolish story had first awakened the boy's imagination, and led him to trace those baleful features in the wayward and unfortunate among her descendants; but it is certain that for many years, in the languid and feeble hours of midnight the lad would lie listening for the rustle of her sweeping garments, and the solemn tread of her pitiless feet with the blood stains fresh upon them. In any case that great grey house with its slumbrous galleries and lonely chambers, and all about it the sweep and swell of the sea, moaning ceaselessly in calm, or roaring in the stress and thunder of the storm, seemed not unfitted to become the birthplace and cradle of a race wayward and ungovernable as that of Cassilis.

The late lord was an old man when I first remember him and it is with him that this story begins, though I shall not have much to say regarding him. He was then more than sixty, but I can still call to mind the brightness of his eyes, the stately dignity of his carriage, and the ungovernable temper that not unfrequently burst into a tempest of oaths, shocking beyond description. I speak now not merely from my boyish recollection, but from what I have subsequently learned, and I am sure that if the Grey Countess bequeathed her spirit to any of her descendants, to none she gave a larger portion than to John Cassilis, twelfth Baron Heronford.

And yet of all the gentlemen I have ever known his manners were the most perfect, his courtesy the most distinguished, and his quiet gaiety the most winning and charming. There was no one of whom I ever stood in such dread and terror; I would tremble at the sound of his voice, and shrink when I heard his footstep and the tap of his stick upon the floor. His venerable white head, his shining eyes whose brightness age had not in the slightest degree dimmed, his ceremonious manner, were, so to speak, merely the mask to my youthful eyes that concealed the waiting fury that burst forth from time to time in fits of wrath and passion. At such times he was entirely transformed, and as I have since thought, his actions were completely beyond his control. His servants did not venture to enter into his presence, and he lived almost altogether in solitude until the mood passed and his volcanic passion had spent its force.

They still point out the path along the cliffs where in one of these wild paroxysms he urged the famous white horse he was used to ride—a mere sheep track climbing in broken leaps along the side of the cliff that ran sheer down to the white surf and the shining grey rocks below —a path on which the cragsman would need to exercise all his skill and coolness. As I shall have to tell hereafter I climbed that path once, and all the way along that dizzy verge I heard the ringing clatter of the hoofs and the old man's labouring breath as he swung in his hunting saddle, and I felt that men do not altogether die when they are laid in the quiet churchyard and a stately monument is reared over their mouldering bones.

John, twelfth Lord Heronford, was twice married. His first wife died within ten months of becoming a bride, but his second wife lived long enough to bring three children into the world, and then quietly, and I am afraid not unwillingly, went to rest with the wives of the house of Cassilis in the shadow of the church. From this time, I have been told, the old lord's temper became more and more ungovernable, and his actions less amenable to reason. It was said he had treated the mother of his children with great harshness (a faded beauty with sorrowful eyes whose portrait you may still see), and it was supposed that his unkindness broke her heart. However, whether it was due to remorse or whatever other cause, from this time he was in the habit of making prolonged sojourns in Paris and London, and lived among the rakes and bloods of that period with the same audacious recklessness he had done at home. During his long minority the estate had recovered itself and he had been the master of a large, not to say a splendid fortune, but a few years of cards and dice sufficed to empty his purse,

and in the days when I first remember him my lord was
a poor man with a desire to save and a touch of avarice.
His career as a prodigal had lasted for fifteen years,
and when he finally returned home, having drunk the
cup of pleasure and sin to its poisonous dregs, he found
his sons already grown up and his daughter a beautiful
girl blossoming into her first womanhood.

It has been said, but I think unjustly, that my lord had
no heart. It was, perhaps, hard to find and when found
hard to touch, but in any case there was never any love
and sympathy between my lord and his family. From
the first there was an impassable gulf of fear and distrust
between them, and finally, at any rate in the case of his
eldest son (my friend and patron), a fierce and irreconcilable quarrel which lasted till his death. At all events,
my lord was soon left as completely alone as if his pale,
heart-broken wife had died childless, and the man, old in
heart and grey in experience, lived his own life solitary
and forgotten.

His daughter, toward whom her father had never
shown the least affection, had found a home with Lady
Ashtown, her mother's sister, and passed her time between that fine lady's Yorkshire house and the gaieties
of Bath; a haughty and fashionable beauty of whom no
less a judge than Mr. Steele wrote with warmth in his
Tattler, and who found many admirers, though none
with sufficient courage to make her his wife. She wrote
once a year to her father, a letter proper in tone and duti-
ful in expression; and there all intercourse between them
ended, for the old man, having read the filial epistle with
a smile, put it in the fire and returned no answer.

My lord's two sons were of a very different disposition. The elder (my own lord of whom I shall have so much to say) being quick, impatient, and high-spirited; while his brother was little more than a boor and a sot, finding his chief companionship in the tavern and his highest pleasure in the stable. Whatever cause for quarrel my lord had with his eldest son he was never unmindful of the dignity of the family, nor did he once, then or at any time, permit his personal feelings to interfere with what he looked upon as his duty toward the family honour and the reputation of his name. Even after the bitter and irreconcilable quarrel between the father and son had arisen the young man was always supplied with the means to support his rank, and I am sure all my lord's scraping and savings found their way in the long run into the pockets of the prodigal. Nor did he look for any recompense in thanks or return in gratitude, which he certainly never got. It was merely the form which his pride—perhaps his madness—assumed, and he was satisfied that his eldest son should cut a figure in the great world which he himself had abandoned. If this was his ambition it was certainly satisfied to the fullest extent, for from the time that Richard Cassilis left his father's house till the time that he returned after his father's funeral, there was no more brilliant and audacious figure in the society of his time.

The story of his extravagance had reached even the village of Cassilis, and the villagers discussed his doings with a feeling which was partly awe and partly admiration. They spoke with a lowering of the voice of the enormous sums he had won and lost at cards with the same easy indifference, of the duels he had fought and the skill and success with which he fought them, of his career of gallantry and the broken reputations carried off as spoils by the victor; in short, a multitude of traditions grew up round his name which are even yet repeated round the cottage firesides of a winter evening long after Richard Cassilis, Lord Heronford, has passed to his rest. It is likely the bright, audacious boy had won the hearts of his people, and when he passed from their sight into the great world they found an excuse for his sins and excesses in the harshness and severity with which he had been treated by his father.

Be this as it may, for a number of years the old man lived completely alone, Will Cassilis, the second son, being the only member of the family who ever visited the Hall, and then altogether without his father's knowledge or even approval. These secret visits were no doubt the result of necessity, and this younger son of a great house lived on terms of equality among his father's grooms and servants because there was no other refuge open to him. It was not, indeed, that he felt out of place in the pantry or the servants' hall, for Will Cassilis had early developed vicious habits, and more willingly chose his companions among jockeys and broken gamesters than among those of his own rank and degree. But the sums of money with which his brother and sister periodically supplied him were speedily dissipated in the tavern or on the racecourse, and he was compelled to lie hidden till his purse was again filled, and the means were supplied to follow the courses he best loved.

In this way, separated from his family and indifferent

to the world, the old lord lived like a hermit and a madman, keeping his own accounts, playing the tyrant over
his tenants and dependants, turning the night into day,
and giving matter for daily wonder to his neighbours by
his solitary freaks and extravagances of conduct. He had
furnished for himself a little room in the western tower,
which it was only possible to reach by a movable stair or
drawbridge, and here he would shut himself up for a fortnight at a time, admitting no one to his presence and re-
fusing to see even his domestics. But for some reason
during these periods of retirement the light burned night
and day in his window. It was said he never slept or
rested, and that I can almost believe. As a child I have,
indeed, often wondered whether his conduct was due to
remorse and spiritual fear. He never sat down to his
solitary meals, he never retired to his lonely pillow, without his drawn rapier placed upon the table or laid upon
the coverlet of his bed close to his hand.

For some years no change took place in his moody,
retired life, and then an event happened in which I myself had some interest, and which was not without its
effect on the fortunes of the family. It happened about
six months after the marriage of Richard Cassilis. That
prodigal (and with all his great faults no one possessed a
kinder heart or more generous disposition), having sorely
tried his father's patience and made tremendous inroads
on the already impoverished family estates, thought to
mend his fortunes with a rich wife, and married in the
June of that year Alicia, widow of the Honourable
Nicholas Carteret, with a fortune of sixty thousand
pounds, as I have seen stated in the *Gentleman's Magazine*.

I have no doubt that my lord, his father, was rejoiced that his son should have given promise of amendment in his life, and was still more delighted that there was a prospect in the future of keeping in his own hands the rents and profits which till now had rattled through the dice-box. Indeed, for many reasons he must have been more than pleased. I have myself seen a letter—almost the only one he ever wrote—addressed to his son on the occasion of his marriage, and congratulating him, though with a somewhat sarcastic humour, upon this happy and fortunate event.

For a time the reconciliation was quite complete, for though they could never agree when they met, in his own way my lord was proud of his eldest son. In any event the bitterness between them was so far abated that there was some talk of the newly-wedded pair paying a visit to Heronford, and arrangements had actually been made for their reception when the incident occurred of which I have spoken, and father and son never saw each other alive. The marriage took place, as I have said, in June; the winter following was severe almost beyond precedent, and from the middle of November till some time in February the roads were almost impassable by reason of the tremendous snowfall and continual frost. This may have been the cause of the visit being postponed, but in any case his necessity must have been urgent and his case pressing who visited Heronford during that time.

On the evening of the twenty-third December my lord was dining, as was his general custom at all seasons of the year, in the great hall, though now close by the north fireplace, and altogether alone. You know the great hall at Heronford—that gloomy, high-vaulted chamber, even during the daylight filled with melancholy shadows and cold silences. At night I can still hardly enter it without a shudder. Yet my lord loved it better than any other room but his little refuge in the west tower, and here he sat, the table lighted by many candles, and the other end of that spacious apartment dark almost as night.

He leaned back in his chair and cracked his walnuts, with a bottle of his favourite port at his right hand. It is easy for me to picture him on this evening—his cold eyes settled on the gloomy shadows before him, his white head resting against the back of the black oak-chair, and his hand, the fingers covered with brilliants—this being one of his weaknesses—playing with the stem of his wine-glass; a solitary, morose old man who even in his pleasures saw in life not a caress but a struggle. The four servants had retired—for this was the number that always waited on him when he dined alone—and only John Osborne stood behind my lord's chair and closer to the fire. I used to think that the two understood one another without words; certainly there never was a servant more faithful, observant, and devoted, and though neither ever for a moment crossed the formal line that rank demands, I know my lord had always an affectionate regard for his old servant beyond any living person, even his own children.

John's duty ended for the day only when the last bottle was finished and he had seen his master safely to bed, which he did regularly at the one hour. To-night, however, my lord had sat longer than usual, and had drunk less and with more deliberation than was his custom. It was past ten o'clock and there was still a bottle warming in the hearth where the fire played among the great logs and went roaring up the wide chimney. John walked to and fro behind his master's chair, while my lord sat in gloomy silence and shivered a little. At the further end of the hall the moon was shining through the great window, and the glowing circle of light filled the room with shadows.

"John."

"Yes, my lord."

"'Tis a fine night."

"A fine night, my lord."

"You are not a man; you are only a parrot."

"Yes, my lord."

"A very old bird."

"Neither of us is as young as we were, my lord," John answered cheerfully.

"I know that, you fool," cries my lord moodily. "'Tis a damnable world, Osborne. There is no room for old men; good wine won't warm their dry bones. There is nothing before them but the churchyard."

"If the Lord pleases, my lord."

Heronford laughed drily.

"And the heir—I must not forget my importunate heir who is waiting to bury me. I have kept him waiting long enough, Osborne."

"If God permit——"

"God does not enter into the matter. Heronford has always managed its own affairs. Bring a glass, sir. You must drink to the health of him who will turn you out of doors when I am gone—to him and my lady, his wife. 'Tis good wine at any rate, and the toast will not spoil it."

Without a word Osborne brought a glass and placed it before his master, who poured out the wine with a steady hand and with a face perfectly grave. Then the latter rose to his feet.

"We will drink to my son, Richard Cassilis, the future Lord Heronford, unruly child, reckless boy, and godless man. I give you his health, my servant and friend. May his friends love him as mine have loved me; may his children honour him as mine have honoured me; may—in the devil's name what is that?"

The two men, both old and white, stood facing one another with their glasses suspended in their hands, while the fire leaped in the great hearth and the rows of candles in the silver candlesticks burned feebly round their long wicks. There was a prolonged silence; then Osborne laid down his glass.

"'Tis the judgment of heaven, my lord," he said feebly. "You must not ask me to drink that toast."

But before Lord Heronford could answer the knocking which they had heard was repeated with a clamorous insistence, awakening the echoes of the empty house, and it may be filling them both with a sense of its desolateness.

Lord Heronford put his glass untasted from his lips and sat down with a quiet smile.

"It may be the devil come for me at last, Osborne. You had better go and ask him to wait till I have finished the bottle."

"But, my lord ——"

"Do not be a fool.   Go and see who wants me at this hour of the night.   And remember, I will not see an angel from heaven."

My lord watched his servant pass waveringly down the hall, and then emptying his glass sat for some time with his hands resting upon the table, the tips of his fingers pressed tightly together according to his custom.   Then he rose from his chair and went over to the hearth, standing with his back to the fire.   He was of a very tall figure and not in the least bent by his age.   I have often seen him standing in this way—his favourite attitude— his brows drawn, his eyes fixed, and if at such times he did not affect me with fear he always impressed me with awe.

A long time passed—nearly a quarter of an hour—and he began to grow impatient, for he never could bear delay.

Then the door opened and Osborne reappeared.

"Have you been asleep, sirrah?   What is the matter?   Have you seen a ghost?"

"As I am a sinner, my lord, I do not know."

"Pooh! you are a fool.   What is it?"

"I am not sure that ——"

"Hell and the devil!   I must see myself.   Get out of my way, you addle-headed ass."

"Your lordship must not do that."

"I must not walk in my own house!   This is not language that I will tolerate, sirrah."

"But, my lord ——"

"Let me have no more 'buts.'   Speak out plainly."

"It is a woman."

"The devil!"

"A woman and a child."

" Pooh ! " said my lord, returning to his seat and possessed at once by irritation and a certain humour. " I thought you had more sense, Osborne. 'Twas only a stone in the horse-pond after all. Times have changed, John ; times have changed. I am too old for the baggage to come trapesing after me. 'Tis a hard night ; let them give her a bed and a crust and see her to the parish in the morning. Let me hear no more about it."

" It is not my fault, my lord, but ——"

" Well ? "

" I doubt but you must hear more. The creature seems dazed-like, but is soft-spoken and well-mannered. She says she has come from London to see your lordship."

" You are an idiot, John Osborne. I will see no living woman in this house. I know what has happened —oh ! I know very well what has happened. I will gather no crop of wild oats for any son of mine. 'Death, man, don't stand glowering at me like the jackanapes you are. Let the trull have a bed and show her to the door in the morning."

Osborne came close behind his master's chair. Then he did what he had never done before in his life ; he laid his hand upon his arm.

" I think your lordship must see this woman."

Lord Heronford was so much taken by surprise and so possessed by anger that for the moment he was unable to answer a word. His domestics, as much from habit as from fear of his wild and terrible fits of passionate wrath, never ventured to question his commands for an instant. He sat erect and speechless, his eyes flashing, his lips white, and his long, thin fingers trembling upon the arms of his chair. But the servant was evidently as much moved as his master, and from whatever cause seemed possessed by a fear greater than any the latter could inspire.

"I think your lordship must see this woman."

Then he leaned forward and whispered some words in a low tone in my lord's ear.

It was characteristic of the man that he should act as he did. He had been swaying on the verge of a paroxysm of passion—of a wild uncontrollable outburst which yielded to no persuasion and admitted of no pause until it had worn itself out through mere exhaustion, but now in an instant he was cold as ice, and only in the tightening of his white lips was there evidence of his inward agitation.

"An impostor or a dupe, Osborne," he said calmly and with stern composure. "But I will see the woman. Bring her here alone, and stay—you said there was a child, let her bring the child."

He rose from his chair and resumed his place by the hearth, standing with his hands behind his back and his eyes looking straight down the great room with a fixed gaze, almost like that of a man walking in his sleep. But his lips were still white and his brows were gathered in a frown. He never moved nor stirred a foot from the time that Osborne left the room until he returned followed by a woman clad in a cloak that concealed her face and figure, and carrying a child in her arms. Even when she came close to where he was standing he did not look at her; he only drew his snuff-box—a thing he seldom used—from his pocket and leisurely took a pinch of snuff.

"Give the lady a chair, Osborne. You desired to see me, madam. I am Lord Heronford."

As I have said, whatever were his faults and his vices there never was any man more courteous and full of dignity, but that of a nature that rather repelled than attracted, and now his manner was cold beyond measure though full of formal courtesy. At the sound of his voice the woman raised her eyes to his face and then sank with an air of extreme exhaustion into the chair which Osborne made haste to offer her. She was quite young, hardly more than a girl, and to say that she was beautiful is to speak with a halting appreciation. I have in my possession—a sacred treasure, a holy memorial—a little miniature of this forlorn wanderer, and I am sure the sweet innocence of girlhood, the frank joy and freshness of youth, was never wedded to a beauty more subtle and ravishing. But now there was no trace of timidity in her manner, and the look she bent on my lord's face was not one of appeal or entreaty, but of strong purpose and courage. I think her face and eyes and the way she regarded him won upon my lord, for his voice was softer when he spoke again. That was his way—you could never tell whither his feelings would lead him a moment before.

"It is a hard world, madam. I think I know your story."

She looked at him with a fixed, bright look, and their eyes met; she held the child more tightly clasped in her arms.

"I cannot—I dare not believe that."

"No? You are young, very young, and I am old. I have heard a good many stories in my time. I think I have heard yours among them. My poor child, 'tis a common tale."

" I am sure that mine is not a common tale."

" My son Richard? Ah! I thought as much; his brother's tastes are different, but both — Good God! madam, I will hear nothing more. I have done with both of them."

" I have walked seven miles, my lord, and never thought I should reach your house living. Do you know what gave me strength? It was my child—my child and his. For my boy's sake you must hear what I have to tell you; if you refuse to hear me I must tell the world. I cannot leave my boy without a name, I cannot—I dare not die and leave it unspoken. I owe that to my baby."

There was an undercurrent of passionate despair in her voice, but there was something more—the insistent assertion of a right which gave her strength and courage, and the old man, unaccustomed to such language, started at the threat contained in her words. For a moment he seemed swayed by contending emotions, and it seemed to his servant, who knew his way better than any living person, that he was about to order her from his presence. But he suddenly changed his mind. He went to the table, and lifting a candlestick with a steady hand came over to where she was seated.

" Let me see your child," he said in a hard, measured voice.

Without a word she opened the cloak that she still kept gathered closely round her, and the streaming light fell on the face of the sleeping child. The old man looked at it for a long time and with a smile that was almost a sneer playing about his lips. Then he silently returned to the table, set the candlestick in its place, and resumed his place by the hearth.

"I am satisfied," he said. "Heronford is true to its traditions. Osborne, you may leave us now. Madam, I will hear your story."

From that hour till the day of his death they say my lord was a changed man. Whatever the story may have been he heard that night his strong and wayward spirit seemed broken, and a haunting, watchful fear seemed to possess him at all times. Nor was he ever known to mention his children either in anger or contempt as he was used to do, but having once written to his eldest son, which he did shortly after this, he removed his portrait from the wall of the gallery and burned the canvas with his own hand.

Upon this particular night it was more than an hour before he rang for Osborne. His servant found him in such a condition as he had never seen him before, his hands trembling, his voice thin with emotion, and his head bowed like one struck down by misfortune.

"This lady will remain at Heronford," he said shortly. "Have the rooms in the east wing prepared for her and the child, and look you, John Osborne, if I hear a whisper—you know what I mean—before heaven I will break your neck and fling you into the moat."

With that my lord drew himself up, and with all his fine courtesy bowed to the lady whose hand he kissed; then walking unsteadily down the long chamber—a shadow among the shadows—he passed through the door and went unattended to his room.

CHAPTER II

THE child who was brought in this way to Heronford has now no recollection of his mother. The lamp of memory sheds no light on that sweet, innocent face. He cannot withdraw the curtain that has fallen upon the past, but he can remember when little more than a child sitting on the grassy mound by the churchyard wall, his boyish heart full of uncontrollable grief, and beating, as it were, with his young hands upon the unmoving gates of death.

He was four years old when he lost his mother, and though as I have said, her face has passed wholly from his memory, he can still remember the day on which she was buried. There still remains in his mind the indistinct, shadowy picture of an open grave, the parson in his cassock, and Lord Heronford standing with his white head uncovered in the pouring rain. Of this scene he can see nothing else through the mists and shadows of the past, and perhaps at the time these things impressed him most. I have, indeed, sometimes wondered whether this scene, so faint and vague, was not the creation of my own fancy, for the child, living for the most part solitary and alone in that grey, desolate house, early became the subject of a thousand waking dreams. I lived altogether in a world of ideas; I moved in a land of strange and grotesque imaginings. It is true that I was clothed and fed and treated without harshness, but I had no companionship: I lived altogether alone. The servants permitted the strange, uncompanionable child to go his own way and to indulge undisturbed in the solitude he seemed to love.

And in this manner, shut out from all other company, I came to build my own house of dreams and to retire thither, unloved and unpitied, a waif who had no business in that great house. As for my lord, till I was ten years old he never spoke to me, nor so much as noticed my presence in the house. Not once but frequently he passed me on the staircase as though I had no existence, and at such times my heart would stand still in my bosom. For of all my childish terrors there was none so great and so overpowering as my fear of that old man with his white face and tall, unbending figure. I cannot remember what awakened that dread first, but certainly it was the great and absorbing passion of my childhood. It was unreasoning, as a child's fear always is, and it was unfounded, but I always trembled at his approach and stood breathless till he had passed me.

That he was not altogether unmindful of me is clear from the fact that by his orders I was sent every day to the Vicarage, where for two hours Mr. Ballard assumed to direct my studies, though I fear neither the master nor the pupil was much in love with the task. But at any rate I learned to read, and was soon able to open up for myself a new world of which I was not slow to take possession. There is a room in Heronford that I shall always love—the Book Room, that looks out upon the pleasance and the grey cliffs beyond the swelling downs.

Here I found contentment; here I lost my haunting sense of terror. Crossing the threshold of this chamber the grey shadows and shapes that possessed the dim corridors melted into the sunshine, and the lad who an hour before had been listening for the rustling robe of the Grey Countess went hand in hand with Una, or swaggered in the tavern with Tom Jones and Parson Adams. My books were a strange company—poets, dramatists, novelists—and though I found much in them that I did not understand, still there was life and action, and a great, unknown world in which I was able to lose myself.

That I was a child grave and precocious beyond my years is undoubted, but I do not remember ever wondering how I came to live at Heronford or why I passed my life alone. That I accepted as a simple fact; I was part of this old house as much as my lord or John Osborne, who never was my friend, and who treated me always with a coldness and distant respect that I could never overcome.

I think I must have been about ten years old when an event happened which created a deep impression upon my mind, and opened up a new field of speculation and wonder. It must be remembered there is nothing trivial or unimportant in a child's life—his petty sorrows are tragedies, his little daily incidents the adventures of romance. And this was especially the case with the solitary child whose existence was an unbroken round of dreams and musings, and who passed his life from day to day without companionship.

It was the first time my lord ever spoke to me, and that fact alone, with the circumstances attending it, combined to make the impression deeper and more abiding. On the afternoon of a winter day—indeed I can hardly remember any summer in my childhood—I was standing in the round window of the Book Room, as was usual, altogether oblivious of the present, and following the curious voyages of Sir John Mandeville in a folio I had lately discovered. I had not heard the door open, nor had I heard the footsteps upon the floor, but I was roused from my dreams by my lord's voice, and looked up to find him watching me with a strange expression on his face. It was not anger, for his lips were smiling, nor was it love, for his eyes were hard and cold. I can, perhaps, understand his feelings better now and the strange interest he displayed, but then I was altogether overcome, and would have made my escape had it been possible. But he stood between me and the door, and never took his eyes off my face.

Then he spoke, and I started at the sound of his hard voice —

"Come here, boy."

In an instant the book which I had been holding fell with a crash to the floor. For a minute I stood trembling, and then walked with a certain fascination close to where he was standing. He took my chin in his hand that was cold as ice, and with the same unchanged look about his eyes and lips read my face as one would read a book. But with a curious reaction I had ceased to fear him, and I met his eyes boldly. He withdrew his hand and did not speak for a minute. I found myself counting the rings on his thin white fingers. Then what I have always accounted one of his strangest fancies seized upon him—a fancy so grotesque and terrible that its full force, awful as it was, did not impress my childish mind, but has often recurred to me since with a certain added horror.

"There is an heirship of the body and the spirit," he said as though speaking to himself. "Come with me, child, and I will show you your future and your past."

With his hand resting on my shoulder, and with a certain gentleness that was almost affectionate, we left the room together and went slowly toward the portrait gallery. It was a curious picture—the tall old man, with his white head erect and proud and his eyes lighted with a strange fire, and the sedate, solemn child full of awe and wonder, and neither of them speaking a word.

The afternoon light was streaming through the western windows with a mellow glow, and the long rows of portraits had caught the soft light. I had been afraid of these pictures before, but never so much as now. Three times we walked up and down the long gallery, stopping here and there in silence, until that long line of silent faces seemed to me to be alive, and the eloquent eyes filled me with a nameless fear. Then Lord Heronford stopped before that portrait painted by Jannsen; the portrait of a boy little older than myself, in the dress of a royal page.

"You have now seen your inheritance," he said slowly. "There is your past and your future. These worshipful gentlemen are working in your blood as they have wrought in mine. I have heard their footsteps behind me all my life. The world says they are dead. That is a lie; they are living—every one of them—

living in me and in you.   Not yet, perhaps they are sleeping, but by-and-bye you will hear them whispering in your ear; you will feel them pulling at your heart. Look, the master has already painted you," and he pointed to the portrait of the page, "the same eyes and lips and forehead; you have already taken your place among your ancestors.   Perhaps a man's soul comes back and lives again in the body of his descendants; if so, 'tis a good omen, and you should thank God.   That was a good man, a happy, brave, and fortunate man, John Cassilis, Governor of the Virginias.   I could show you your father's face, painted a hundred years before he was born —and mine.   I had finished my life before I began to live at all.   But I will join them presently, and then ———"

He turned away and left me abruptly, and I stood there lost in amazement.   But though at that time I did not understand all that he said, nor, indeed, till long afterward when his meaning became clearer, there was part of his language that I was able to follow.   From that time the thoughtful face of the youth became like the face of a friend, or rather, like the presentment of my better self, and I searched industriously among the records in the Book Room for memorials of that honourable and fortunate personage.   I think that happy resemblance was not without its effect upon myself.   It opened up an avenue of hope and light among these shadowy paths in which I had begun to travel, and though I dwelt upon my lord's words till I had them by heart, they rather encouraged than depressed me.

I kept my own counsel regarding this strange interview, and though Osborne questioned me in his indirect and ambiguous manner, I answered him with that discretion and, perhaps, evasiveness that I had early learned. But from this time forward my lord noticed me with increasing friendliness, and more than once had me to dine with him in the great hall, where we sat in chilling and depressing state. On such occasions he never spoke a word, but neither did he relax in that kindliness with which he henceforward treated me. He not unfrequently broke out in abuse of the servants, but his anger never vented itself upon me, and though I still held him in the same awe, my fear was in a great degree abated.

There was no change in the life we led. The solitude of Heronford remained unbroken, and my lord ceased altogether to have any communication with the world beyond his own estate. Besides his own servants the only person he ever saw was the Vicar, and him he regarded with good-natured contempt and only as a boon companion. Perhaps once or twice in the week Mr. Ballard was carried from the Hall to the Vicarage in a pitiable condition, my lord, who had drank glass for glass with him, lighting him to the door, and walking as steadily as though he had not tasted a drop. But as time went on this happened less frequently, for it was evident to everyone that my lord was failing fast, and age was making rapid inroads upon the vast fund of health and vigour he had formerly enjoyed.

These signs of decay, however, never touched the strength of his mind or his indomitable spirit. Even when he was able to cross the hall only with the aid of a stick, and his head and hands both shook with that senile tremor that speaks so eloquently of change, the fibre of his understanding had not relaxed, his memory had not weakened, nor the fire of his temper, so swift and flashing, abated in the least degree. Osborne, indeed, was of opinion that the end was at hand, but for a reason of his own. My lord had begun to read—though it seemed to me fitfully and always with impatience—a manual of devotion which he now carried continually under his arm, but from what cause or for what reason no one ever knew. It had certainly no effect upon his conduct or the wild intemperance of his language, and I am sure Osborne welcomed such outbursts as a sign that his master had still some years to live.

But the end came, and that in a way as appalling and terrible as it was sudden and unexpected, though, perhaps, it formed a fitting conclusion to a life so wayward and tempestuous. I was then about fourteen years of age, a period when events leave a deep impression upon the mind, and there is nothing that stands out so clearly in my memory as the events of the fortnight preceding Lord Heronford's decease. In a moment you will, perhaps, understand why that should be the case, and though you may hardly credit the story I am about to relate, yet I set it down with sober and veracious faithfulness. I can offer no explanation; I merely chronicle the events as they occurred.

It was one of those rare evenings when my lord had me to dine with him in the great hall. Throughout the entire meal he had not spoken a word nor had I ventured to address him, a thing I seldom did. I saw nothing unusual in his appearance; there was certainly nothing observable in his manner beyond the common. We had not quite finished when suddenly he laid down his wine-glass and sat for some time, his eyes fixed and bright, and his head turned a little aside as though listening. Then he moved in his chair —

"Osborne—John Osborne."

"My lord?"

"What day of the week is this?"

"Friday, my lord."

"And what day of the month?"

"The 21st September."

"Ah! very well. This day fortnight—remember, this day fortnight—I shall be in Hades."

Only he used a stronger word.

I sat and gazed at him in speechless astonishment, and the servants who had distinctly heard his words did not dare to move where they stood. He intended no jest; he meant every word he said. I think he was pleased at our consternation, but he only wiped his lips with his napkin, and folded his hands before him. It was merely my fancy, but it seemed to me as I looked at him that he was already dead, and that the lips which were speaking were no longer living lips. For I was now quivering with horror; I could almost have cried out in my fear. At any time such words were sufficiently terrible, but the tone in which they were spoken, and the look which accompanied them, intensified their effect a thousandfold.

Osborne tottered to the table and leaned against it for support, his face blanched and his hands trembling.

"My lord—my dear lord—" he cried.

"Do not be a fool, sirrah. Every man must die sometime—I as well as the rest. A little sooner or later—what matter? I had as lief die as live. Osborne, listen to me, you dolt."

"Oh! my lord."

"This day fortnight. Did I ever break my word, blockhead? John Cassilis can keep his tryst with death as well as with the puppets who march at his bidding. It is not every man who sees his own obsequies. I must prepare for mine."

At this I thought, perhaps, he only jested in his own peculiar way, but I was very much mistaken. If it was a jest it was carried out with a humour such as I hope never again to witness.

At the beginning of the week a great oak coffin very richly mounted was brought into the hall, and placed upon a table in the centre of the chamber. Upon the silver shield that was fastened on the lid some words were engraved that at first I had not the courage to read. But stealing into the room in the afternoon when there was no one present I satisfied myself upon the point, and crept away possessed by such feelings as you can imagine. These were the words that I read—

JOHN CASSILIS,
12TH BARON HERONFORD,
BORN JULY 13TH, 17—,
DIED OCTOBER 5TH, 17—.

During the entire week these words kept a sort of rhythmic dance in my head, and never left my mind for a moment. Death seemed to have already entered the house, and the domestics moved about with the noiseless feet of those who seem fearful to awaken one sleeping his last sleep in the same house. But my lord was altogether unchanged, and in no respect departed from his daily routine. He even dined as usual in the hall with that awful memento of mortality before his eyes, and walked past it as he went to his room with the same unmoved countenance. From the evening when he first made the announcement till the fatal Friday he did not again revert to the subject, or allude to it in the most distant way. Perhaps he was a little less restless and spoke with less insistence than was his custom, but there was no other change, and that hardly perceptible.

Upon the Friday night, however, for the first time I observed that an alteration had taken place in him. There was a cheerfulness and alacrity in his demeanour such as I had not noticed for a long time—a gaiety and almost a softness which were quite foreign to his character. Nor did he speak in that high tone which he always used, but in a low and level voice, which seemed quite strange to me when I heard it. For the first time also in my life he spoke to me with a show of affection, and I thought more than once he was about to impose some confidence regarding matters of a personal nature. But on each occasion he changed the subject, and finally dismissed me with both his hands resting upon my shoulders.

I had returned to my own room, and was sitting considering what would happen when Osborne, who was quite distracted with grief and terror, came to tell me that I was wanted. I did not delay a moment, but putting on my shoes which I had removed I went down with him into the hall, where I found all the household servants assembled.

My lord was standing at the door of the dining-hall with a book in one hand and a candle in the other. As soon as we came down he motioned to Osborne to come to him, and handed him the candle. Then with his hand resting on the shoulder of his trembling servant he turned and walked slowly up the great hall, the servants and myself following behind. As he advanced he began to read in a steady, unbroken voice, and so soon as I heard the first words I knew to what I was about to listen —

"*I am the Resurrection and the Life*——"

It was the burial service, and surely never since those beautiful words were written did they form part of a ceremony so tragic and terrible. Lord Heronford turned at the foot of the table, and till he had finished the concluding "Amen" an awful silence filled the room and oppressed our hearts. It was ghastly beyond description, and as we rose from our knees there was no face in the room but that of my lord that was not stamped with a panic fear. It seems to me wonderful now that no one ventured to say a word or to protest against a ceremony so unnatural and appalling, but my lord's influence was such that, even at this time, no one dared to oppose his will. The domestics cowered together like a flock of sheep, and I was no bolder than the rest.

When he had finished we found ourselves at the door almost without knowing how, and my lord bowing in his stately manner as though we had been his equals.

"Good-night, my friends. I am tired and have to make a long journey. You need not call me early, Osborne."

With that he closed the door and we heard the great bolt shot behind us. I cannot now remember how we passed the night, for it is only a confused dream, but I very well remember how the door was forced open in the morning. We found my lord seated quite upright in his chair, his hands resting upon its arms, and a serene, almost a triumphant, look on his face. But he had finished his long journey, and it was in this way that John Cassilis, twelfth Lord Heronford, went to his own place.

CHAPTER III

MR. WILLIAM CASSILIS was the only member of Lord Heronford's family who was present at his funeral. He had been in the neighbourhood—indeed, I might almost say in the house—when my lord died. In any case he appeared on the morning following, his face swollen and flushed, his eyes red and his hands trembling like one just emerging from a prolonged debauch; and at once, and with a great show of authority, took the direction of everything into his own hands, and prepared to celebrate his father's funeral in the manner that seemed to him most fitting. Certainly death is the soundest of all sleeps or my lord had arisen in anger and indignation from the oak coffin in which he was lying, and had driven the intruder from his house. The wine and ale were flowing all day long; the tables were spread continually as though the occasion was a festival; the doors were thrown open, and all the world of idlers, topers, and jockeys flocked like hungry birds to the good cheer.

Mr. Will did not, indeed, show himself much in public but sat in his late father's room, surrounded by a select crowd of boon companions, drinking early and late, and playing at cards without intermission. You cannot imagine a greater change than that which took place in the short space of four-and-twenty hours. Formerly we had spoken only in whispers, and silence had filled the darkened rooms and corridors; now the chambers were brilliantly lighted, the doors were swinging continually, and the sound of tipsy laughter sounded like mockery—as indeed it was—in the ears of death.

It is true that I had not loved my lord during his life, but it was natural that I should feel some grief at the death of the only protector I had ever known, and I remained alone in my own room, more lonely than I had ever known myself, a prey to my grief, and filled with an unmeasured indignation which I could not put into words. No one troubled himself regarding me; I remained forgotten and unnoticed, and I shrank with a peculiar sensitiveness from the crowd that filled the rooms and passages. I was not present at my lord's funeral, nor did I witness the closing scene, though I would willingly have done so.

On the afternoon of the following Monday I saw through the early snow that was falling in large infrequent flakes the coffin being borne down the drive toward Heronford Church and Mr. Will following some dozen paces behind, wrapped to the chin in his horseman's cloak and walking very unsteadily. Then there came a great crowd of hangers-on and dependants, who displayed gaiety rather than grief, but there were none of the old lord's acquaintances or equals present, and the procession was rather a comedy than the closing scene of another human tragedy. Perhaps the lonely youth looking from the window, and remembering the last kindly words and the affectionate pressure of the old hands upon his shoulders, dropped some regretful tears, but for all that, it remains to be said that John Cassilis went to his grave unloved and unmourned, and followed by the laughter and jests of the crowd he hated and despised.

It was not to be hoped that there would be any change in the new order after the funeral, for Will Cassilis found his temporary authority too pleasant to relinquish almost at the moment of his taking it up. After all his years of the lean kine he had now, at least for a brief period, an uncontrolled opportunity to gratify his vicious tastes in his own manner. I do not know whether Heronford had ever seen anything like his reign before, but I am sure it will never forget that brief tempestuous despotism. Comus and his revellers filled the house with the sound of their swinish merriment, and turned the night into day with a thousand excesses which I am unwilling to describe, as I was pained and shocked to witness them. A few of the old servants still remained, astonished and bewildered by the new order, and among them my lord's faithful servant Osborne, who had almost seemed to himself and to me as much a part of Heronford as the grey stone lions at the main door. I think Mr. Will was afraid to meddle with him, though he did not spare his old legs, and cracked his jokes upon him in his clownish, insolent way till the old man found himself seeking my company, whom he had always coldly avoided, with his eyes streaming and his heart well-nigh broken. He needed some confidant into whose ears he might pour the story of his wrongs; there was at least repose and quiet in the little chamber at the head of the staircase, and sympathy in the eyes of its occupant.

"Listen to them," he would say. "I found that runagate, Dick Scattergood, sitting in my lord's chair and drinking his favourite tokay out of a tankard as if it had been common ale.   And that painted Jezebel wanted me to dance with her, who have been in the house man and boy for fifty years !   And my lord hardly cold yet ! Oh, he can never rest through these wild doings !   They are bringing down the judgment, and some night soon they will have my lord coming into them fresh from the churchyard and all the old Heronfords behind him. They were always a proud, stiff-necked race, alive and dead, and my dead lord won't stand the Hall being turned into a tavern."

I am certain he believed this and looked confidently for some supernatural visitation as the result of Mr. Will's riotous and vicious conduct.

As yet the latter and myself had never met, and I need scarcely say I shrank from the thought of such an encounter.   That he must have known very well of my presence in the house there could be little doubt, but it is likely that more pleasant and congenial occupations prevented him for the time from disturbing my solitude. I can write of him now without bitterness, but at that time I endured the agony of a shy and sensitive lad when I heard his voice at a distance, and trembled when I heard a footstep on the stair.   I must confess also that I shared Osborne's superstitious fears, for these had grown with me as a part of my life, and I watched for the tall figure and listened for the heavy step, as though the old lord were returning from a journey, long after the lights had gone out and silence had closed on the sacrilegious merriment.

One forenoon, thinking that I was not likely to be disturbed, I had stolen to the Book Room, almost the first time that I had ventured thither since my lord's death. Having gathered those volumes that I intended to carry with me to my own chamber, I stood looking down upon the deserted pleasance lost in the contemplation of that dreary winter scene. I must have stood there for some time when the door flew open and Will Cassilis came noisily in, his riding-whip in his hand, and his face, naturally red, more deeply flushed with his exercise. For a moment he seemed surprised to find me here, and then burst into a loud, unpleasant laugh that seemed to come in part from ill-nature and in part from amusement.

"Ho! ho!" he cried, "I have smoked out the young fox at last. The whelp ran very shy of me. This is your lair, then?"

I made no answer but stood looking at him almost in consternation. Even though it was still early in the day he had already made his libations to Bacchus, but as I looked at him I could plainly see a change coming over his countenance, only to be compared with that of a man who suddenly and unexpectedly meets a well-known face in a crowd.

"By—'tis true as the gospel. Is it Dick or —— ?"

Then he stopped and looked at me curiously, but the smile had now gone from his lips.

"Do you know who I am, my young Jesuit?"

I answered that I knew him to be Mr. William Cassilis.

"As you will learn some day 'tis a wise son knows his own father, but 'tis like enough we are twigs of the same tree. I have heard a whisper of this before, and upon my soul I believe it now.   You are growing too old for Heronford."

I answered that I had been there all my life, thinking at the time that drink made a man talk curiously.

"Then you never have heard much good of me, I will take my oath."

I said I had never heard anything about him, good or bad, and at that he laughed and shook his head with a knowing look.

"Ay, ay, he rode a high horse, and it carried him to the last fence.   Dick favours him at odd times, and has the same cursed trick of temper, but he can't stay.   I was always a jolly fellow and loved a jolly fellow.   Dick won't have you in the house; you are too cursedly like the family portraits for that; he won't stand them sitting down at the table with him, especially when they come in on the wrong side, d'ye understand?   You will have to march.   For me I don't mind—not a damn.   I like my friends about me—the more the better cheer.   But Dick is master here.   Lord!   I can see his face when he hears how I have warmed the house for him.   We must both make the most of our time, lad.   When the piper has changed the tune it will be time enough for us to change our dancing."

Though upon the whole the interview was not of that unpleasant nature that I had feared and anticipated it caused me a good deal of disquietude, and I began to look forward to the coming of the new lord with a certain anxious foreboding.   That Will Cassilis was in his own way afraid of his brother I could very well see, and what hope was there, I thought, for one quite unknown and friendless like myself, in the house of one upon whom I could have no claim and who could only regard me as an intruder, or at the most a claimant upon his charity. That the late Lord Heronford had some personal reason for his kindness I had now come to think, though in a vague way; and if, as youth is prone to do, I indulged in any dreams regarding my birth, they were sure to end in a blush of shame and a feeling of humbled pride. I was sure that in some way I was connected with my late lord's family, though such association brought me no advantage and conferred no honour. Rather it was a thing, if possible, to be concealed, and this thought added to the solitude and isolation in which I was placed.

Will Cassilis did not again intrude upon me; it is quite possible that he forgot my very existence. He certainly made the most of his brief hour of power and enjoyed himself to the fullest while his sun shone. But that suffered from an early eclipse, and so suddenly that his day ended in the midst of his festivity.

Perhaps I was the only one who saw the chaise and pair of horses being driven up the avenue, and a tall gentleman clad from head to foot in black leisurely descending, standing to give instructions to his single servant, and walking to the door with an air which was strangely familiar to me. I knew in a moment that the new master of Heronford had arrived, and those fears which Will Cassilis had awakened were by no means allayed as I watched the stern dark figure walking slowly to the door. I knew that he was lately a widower, but I had expected to find him younger. He seemed to me to be already an old man, and I could see that his hair was almost grey.

He was as tall as the late lord and bore himself with the same erectness.

I do not know what occurred upon his arrival, but whatever happened, his action must have been prompt and decisive. In a quarter of an hour Mr. Will's boon companions, with many oaths I have no doubt, were seeking other quarters, and with as great haste as they had ever shewed in their lives; the cards and song-books were thrown into the fire, and the litter of glass which had been permitted to accumulate in the hall was swept into the dust-heap. In a shorter time than I can tell you every trace of the late saturnalia was carefully removed. What passed between the two brothers will never be known, but for some time Mr. Will treated the new lord with a deference which showed that he had learned where his interest lay. Indeed, as you will see, no two men were ever more different, and if Mr. Will usually got his own way it was because his brother was too indolent or careless to interfere.

My farthest hope was that I myself might escape observation, and I was certainly very far from expecting what eventually occurred. I never dreamt for a moment that I could have any interest for my lord, or that upon the very day of his arrival we should be placed upon that footing upon which we stood till the day of his death. I believe that Mr. Will in their first altercation had referred in plain terms to my presence in the house, and that my lord had immediately silenced him with a threat which the latter had no desire should be put into execution. In any case my lord was perfectly aware of my presence in the house and the position I had occupied in his father's time. Indeed, I found that he knew more than this, but of that I shall write later.

It was some way on in the evening when my lord paid me his first visit. I had lighted my little lamp and was seated before my books far away in a sunny dreamland, solitary no longer nor touching earth at all. But I heard my lord's hand upon the door, and as he came in I rose up, making a respectful bow and closing my book. He looked quite pale and worn, and his eyes had a weary and melancholy look, but were full of kindliness. Indeed, with the quick instinct of a child, I had no sooner seen his face than I felt that I had found a friend, and the fear that had tightened about my heart relaxed in a moment. Without speaking he took a chair near me, and folding his hands upon the table—the very attitude that was customary with his father—he looked at me out of his kind, weary eyes.

Then he spoke in his low, pleasant voice.

"I am the new Lord Heronford. What is your name, my boy?"

"I am called John Cassilis, but—" I hesitated.

"Ah!"

"I do not know that I have any right to that name, my lord," I said, flushing hotly and with a sudden courage.

"Who said you had no right to be called by that name?" he said sharply.

"I have only thought that," I answered, hanging down my head. "I do not know."

"There are things of more importance than a man's name," he said slowly, "but a good name is not to be despised.   You need not blush for your name; but there are reasons—remember there are good reasons—why you should not know more than that.   Some day you will know but not yet.   Do not think it matters much.   I am not a good man, but I am your friend."

He held out his hand to me across the table, and I placed mine in his hot palm.

"I have never had a friend," I said.   "I am glad your lordship will be my friend."

"Your eyes are like your mother's!   I knew your mother, my child."

Here was a new bond between us, for that name (alas! it was only a name and not even a memory) always touched my heart like a note of sweet music.

"I should like to hear something about my mother," I said, looking up at him with a sudden appeal, but he seemed to shrink at my words, and let my hand fall which he had continued to hold.

"It was a long time ago—almost before you were born —and she was only a girl, a beautiful girl, with the finest spirit, and the sweetest, strongest heart.   It is strange that you and I should sit talking about her here, and that to-morrow, perhaps, we should visit her grave together. And I knew your father "—he paused and then went on with a sudden change in his voice—" but of him you must never speak."

"Why, my lord?" I cried impulsively.

"Because he broke the best, the truest, and most faithful heart in the world; because he broke every law of God and man, and because he is dead and buried.   The world never knew.   She was an angel of God."

There was a long pause ; I could see that he was deeply moved.

"The world thought your father a splendid gentleman, John, but it never saw his heart. Even the wife who slept in his bosom, and who came to hate him before she died, never knew his suffering. He came to be a very old man before—before he died."

" Dead !" I said, with a feeling of relief.

" Dead—yes, dead, soul and spirit, mind and body, dead and buried. We need not weep for your father."

" I am glad that he is dead," I said firmly.

" He was not a good man," said my lord gravely, "but he has had his reward and his works have followed him. We must be friends if only for your mother's sake."

There was something in his voice and manner that affected me exceedingly. Altogether unaccustomed to the language of tenderness, I caught hold of his hand and kissed it passionately. He did not at first prevent me, but then he slowly withdrew it and placed it upon my head.

CHAPTER IV

It was not long before the domestic life of Heronford began to flow in that quiet and monotonous stream which continued undisturbed and unruffled for some years. Madam Cassilis had arrived from London and had taken up the government of her brother's house with that high hand and imperious will which distinguished her beyond most women, and had it been possible for any living being to move my lord she at least might have accomplished it. But we were not long in discovering that my lord, with all his quiet ways and air of settled melancholy, having once made up his mind, was not to be moved by any influence or argument, and presented on all sides a passive resistance, which was inexpugnable. From the first he refused to see any company, and every attempt that was made to overcome that resolution was met by a quiet smile more eloquent than the strongest negation.

"I have seen too much of the world," he would say, "and have grown in love with solitude. I have had my time and must now pay for it; I cannot be tempted. Will has his friends, choice spirits, noble wits who flourish in the alehouse, and is esteemed a fine companion, but I—I am too much in love with myself, Judith, to spend my time upon others."

In this way it came about that Heronford was almost as solitary as it had been in the late lord's time, and the neighbouring gentry, who had hoped to find a change, were not long in discovering that they were unwelcome visitors, and soon altogether ceased to trouble us. Mr. Will entertained his friends abroad, and usually returned home late at night from the " Heronford Arms," very unsteady on his legs and inarticulate in his speech, to sleep off his debauch in his own room. He had come to regard me with suspicion and dislike, and watched my lord's increasing familiarity and friendship with a jealousy which, never openly manifested, showed itself in a thousand trivial ways.

I found that my lord's first proffer and promise of friendship was not a mere idle form of speech, but that his first kindness grew and ripened into affection and tenderness. This was never shown in public, for then he displayed toward me some reserve and coldness, but in the privacy of his own room his real nature opened and expanded. I say his real nature, though I should not err if I were to write his better nature, for indeed my lord seemed as various as the chameleon and the creature of as many whims and changes. At all periods solitary and reserved, there were times when he would not utter a word for days together, but sat in black and settled gloom, the victim of I know not what dark and despondent thoughts. But when this mood passed, which it did as suddenly and unexpectedly as it had come, his speech was full of a cynical yet kindly humour at once removed from gaiety and levity.

There are men like my lord who see in life only the play—tragedy and comedy—of marionettes; they see the wooden figures and the cunning strings that move them; they are familiar with the oft-repeated story, yet all the time they are touched to kindly yet distant sympathy by the good-humoured laughter and the wonder, admiration, and pity of the open-mouthed spectators.

This was my lord's attitude in his lighter moments, but indeed it was never quite possible to see the working of his mind, for, as I have said, there never was any man more reserved and less used to give expression to his feelings and sentiments. Of his own past he never spoke by any chance; even the friends and acquaintances he had left behind him in the great world he had quitted he never once mentioned. Whether he had suffered an injury or inflicted one I did not know, but I was sure my lord shrank in pain from the recollection of his past life, and would willingly have forgotten it in the employments of the present.

I came to be admitted at all times into his presence, and very soon learned the nature of his moods and the manner in which to treat him. I found that he soon discovered this, and would call me with a smile his little confessor, though I had no other feeling than that of affectionate regard. Indeed, I came very early to love my lord almost as a son loves his father. I am sure it pleased him to see my young affection, and he took pains to cultivate it. He would suffer no one to come between us, and when Madam Cassilis in her masculine way would have had me sent into the world, as she said, to become a man, he answered with his quiet smile that she, at least, might teach me that but not too roughly. I had long since sounded the depths of Mr. Ballard's learning, and had taught him to fear me more as a pupil than I had ever reverenced him as a master.

It was now that my lord himself took up the direction of my studies, and we spent many pleasant evenings together in my old playground, the Book Room. It was now that he first named me his young secretary—a title which he bestowed upon me in jest, but it was not very long before I came to fill that position in earnest, and was soon initiated into the management of the estate, the affairs of which had become complicated almost beyond unravelling. My lord was pleased to say that I had a good head for business—he himself could never understand figures—but at least I was willing to be useful to my patron, and I think the efforts I made were not without some success. His deceased wife's fortune had either been dissipated or had proved to be merely visionary—I could never rightly tell which—and the late lord, with all his desire to save in trifles, had allowed his larger interests to remain completely neglected. With all, my Lord Heronford was a poor man and had never a large supply of ready money, though sufficient for his limited expenditure. I knew that these things never troubled him, and he met my fears with the same easy smile with which he would have met his final ruin.

No brother was certainly ever more generous, and while himself practising the most modest economy Mr. Will had always enough, perhaps a superfluity, to indulge those tastes and habits which distinguished him. As a patron of the prize ring and a frequenter of racecourses he was not unfrequently absent from home, an absence that no one regretted, for at Heronford the pigeon and the dupe became merely the bully and the sot. There never was a greater contrast than that presented by these two brothers, who hardly seemed to be sons of the same house—the one boisterous, rough, and unlettered, the other of the most easy manner and most perfect courtesy ; the one eager in the pursuit of his desires, the other apparently regardless of all the pleasures of the world, and having no outlook beyond the dull circuit of his daily life.

So long as his own privacy was undisturbed he gave Mr. Will his own way and liberally provided him with means.   One thing, however, he would not tolerate, his brother's friends and companions found no footing at Heronford, and the one occasion on which I saw him moved to anger was on his finding Mr. Weston of Langston, had been brought to supper at the Hall.   I own that I was astonished at the vehemence of my lord's lauguage, and I think his brother was nearly as much surprised as myself.

Though his guest was not very sober he had treated him with a chilling courtesy throughout the meal, and upon its conclusion, but with perfect politeness, had informed him that his horse was at the door, and they were accustomed to keep early hours.

" We do not see many strangers," he had said, " and are, perhaps, the more anxious for their safety.   The roads are dangerous, and there is a fine moon.   I have no doubt that you will forgive me that I do not press you to stay with us longer, but it is now past our usual hour and I am sure you are anxious to be upon your road."

Mr. Weston, who had settled himself down for a long night, and who had been hoping, I have no doubt, that Lord Heronford himself was about to retire, had risen up astonished, but did not dare to question his dismissal, and left his unfinished bottle with no very good grace. It was only when he had gone, and we heard the clattering hoofs ringing on the gravel, that my lord gave expression to the feeling he had repressed while his unwelcome guest was present.

" Perhaps," he said, "you are sober enough to listen to me. If you are not I shall wait till the morning, for I will never speak again. I have given you a home here; I have fed and clothed you; I have given you means to live your swinish life; I have indulged you almost out of my poverty; I know you give me no thanks; I expect no gratitude. You think I am only a fool for my kindness. Do not mistake me, sir, or rather, do not mistake me twice. This is my house; this is my table; there is no will here but mine. Take your boon companions to the tavern; drink with them in the bagnio or the booth; play the fool as you please in your own haunts, but before heaven, if you ever intrude one of them upon me again you have crossed my threshold for the last time."

He stood with his eyes flashing, and though he hardly spoke beyond his quiet tone there was something in his manner—I can hardly describe it—that his brother cowered before as though he had been struck.

This happened nearly five years before those events occurred of which I purpose to write more fully, but from that time Will Cassilis took care never to transgress in the same way. Mr. Weston, indeed, gave his own version of the story, a version very far from correct, for I was present and saw what occurred, but he would have ridden a long distance before he would again have stalled his horse in my lord's stable or ventured to sit down at his table.

It was, perhaps, a curious thing but Madam Cassilis generally took her younger brother's part, though in her high proud way she herself did not spare him, but she never understood my lord. It may be their nature was too nearly allied for perfect agreement, but between the two there never was the least sympathy or confidence. It is possible that a spoiled beauty may make a good wife, but it is certain that she never makes a sweet old maid, nor was Madam Cassilis any exception to this rule. The intercourse between my lord and herself was like the friendly play of a pair of foils that brighten one another by the contract—a game of thrust and parry in which her womanly quickness gave her all the advantage. And certainly if my lord did not openly exhibit that family pride which was yet the strongest passion in his heart, his sister asserted her position with a cold arrogance it is impossible to describe. Myself she always treated as a mere servant and dependant, though not unkindly, and this more especially in her brother's presence, when she met his eye with a look of defiant inquiry to which he never made any answer. I had grown so used to my position that such treatment had ceased to pain me, but my lord never failed on such occasions to atone for her asperity by his own increased friendliness and affection. I had come to think that he felt for me more than I felt myself, and perhaps I was not far wrong in this; in any case no man ever had a kinder friend, a more patient teacher, a more generous protector.

CHAPTER V

THE events which I am about to relate seem naturally to begin with the coming of Mr. Earnshaw to Heronford. Before that time there is little to chronicle; our uneventful daily life presented no feature of interest; time slipped past, leaving no memorial to mark its flight, yet preparing us imperceptibly for those tragic scenes which brought sorrow to the house I loved. But with Mr. Earnshaw's arrival a new element was introduced into our dull and uniform existence. He seemed to have brought with him a new atmosphere, a new spirit. We had grown grey with lethargy and melancholy, but at once he introduced into our quiet household the gaiety, bustle, and activity of the great world, the inimitable touch of youth, the breath of merriment. We had lived isolated and apart from the world; we now seemed to hear its joyous laughter and to touch it with our hands. I could not have believed after so many years of solitude and seclusion any one could have moved my lord from his settled life, but with the coming of his guest he seemed to have caught the infection of his gaiety, and to have awakened from his spiritual catalepsy.

I remember when Mr. Earnshaw had first proposed to visit his kinsman, being then in the immediate neighbourhood, my lord opposed the idea very strenuously, and only consented to receive him after considerable resistance and upon express conditions. But almost immediately on his arrival he was drawn from his reserve and surrendered almost at the first challenge. It was like the renewal of his own splendid and prosperous days—his guest brought with him the laughter and *bon-mots* of the wits, the news of Almacks', the gossip of the Court. His courteous indifference was first quickened into curiosity, and that, finally, into a fresh and vivid interest. Mr. Earnshaw, I could observe, exercised all his arts, and I was pleased to see my lord drawn from his moody self-seclusion. But this visit, which at the outset was to have lasted four days, lengthened into a fortnight, and finally the guest ceased to talk of his immediate departure. There could be no doubt my lord enjoyed his society beyond anything I had known; they were very equally matched in knowledge of the world, and each capped the other's story without pause.

To hear them talk was to myself the introduction to a new world. At first my lord would retire after dinner, as he had been in the habit of doing, but in a short time they got into the habit of sitting over their wine, and afterwards of taking a hand at cards, when I was seldom present. How these came to be first introduced I do not know, but the fascination they had always exercised over Lord Heronford appeared to revive, though he would not admit so much to himself. It was very like him to trifle with this temptation. I have seen him sitting out while his brother and Mr. Earnshaw were playing, and toying with his book that he was pretending to read. However, though he played frequently he lost no large sums of money, though I do not think he won, and the players were pretty equally matched. But Earnshaw was a gentleman of very large means, and the stakes for which they played appeared to me quite disproportionate to my lord's limited fortune.

Upon a certain afternoon we had been dining with more than our customary conviviality, Lord Heronford being, in what for him were very high spirits. Mr. Will and the Vicar, the only stranger who ever joined the party, were, I remember, engaged in an animated discussion over the merits of a horse which the former had sold the day before, and they both agreed with some humour that there were surprises in store for the purchaser. Mr. Earnshaw and my lord occasionally joined in this conversation, but for the most part laughed and chatted very pleasantly by themselves, relating certain recollections of the prize ring of which Lord Heronford had been an enthusiastic patron. It was a matter of such unusual occurrence to hear my lord refer to the past that I listened with great attention to their talk, and thought it a very good sign to see him so bright and cheerful.

Taking no part myself in the conversation I watched him as he sat at the head of the table, and I said to myself, looking at his fine face, his pleasant smile, and the pose of his noble head, that never was a man kinder and handsomer than my dear master. On this occasion his animation had brought a flush to his cheeks, and his eyes were quite bright and sparkling. Mr. Earnshaw certainly had the happy knack of drawing him out, and I am sure took some pleasure, as he felt some pride, in breaking down the barrier of reserve behind which he had taken refuge.

Having upon this afternoon an errand of my own, and seeing that the gentlemen were likely to sit a long time over their wine, I slipped quietly and unobserved from the table and ran to my own room. Then I went through the little door into the south garden, and ran down the walk toward the wicket that leads upon the cliffs.

I closed the gate behind me and walked rapidly along the cliffs, the little book that I had gone for carried under my arm. The sea that lay in almost a summer calm had caught a hundred lights from the setting sun, and broke in a long, plaintive murmur on the sands far below me. From the top of the downs where the cliffs broke I could see Carnforth and the captain's house, with its red roof, high chimneys, and tangle of enclosed garden; and I thought once I could catch a glimpse of a white figure among the walnut trees. It was not the first time coming from Heronford that I had waved my handkerchief as a signal here, and had caught the answer from the distant garden, but this afternoon I looked in vain for a response.

My way led down the broken cliffs, along the deep, dry sands on which walking was not easy, and then upon a stretch of short sea grass that ended with the little river and a wooden bridge across it. Here, a hundred paces away and backed by a little hill covered with firs and poplars, was an old house set in the heart of a garden that grew almost in wild and unrestrained luxuriance. 'Tis hard to draw in words any picture of this house, builded apparently upon no definite plan or design, with its offshoots of little gables and long red chimneys; its half a dozen separate roofs of different heights; its quaint porches leading through low-browed doors, and its windows opened without any thought of effect or appearance. A great hedge of copper beeches higher than the height of a tall man ran all round the garden, in the centre of which was a fine smooth lawn and a sun-dial set upon a twisted column. By the door, or rather by the main door, for there were several, were two small ship's guns mounted upon painted carriages, and in a little arbour on the left as you came up you could see the figure-head of a noble vessel, all green and gold and a shameless carmine on the cheeks—the *Saucy Arethusa's* self.

As I opened the gate there was an air of sleepy quiet all about the place, but coming nearer the house I heard a ripple of silver laughter, that, let me own it with an open mind, brought a flush to my face. I went round by the west side and then stopped short, thinking I had never seen a prettier picture in my life. Upon the path stood a slim figure in a white dress, a broad hat set upon the shining curls, and a bit of colour, blue —what I do not know—about the waist and bosom. She was feeding the pigeons that fluttered about her feet and flew in little broken circles round her, so absorbed in her task that she did not notice my approach. But when she heard my feet upon the gravel she looked up with a demure smile, but never pausing, while I stood bareheaded with my hat held in my hand.

"Sit down on the seat, Jack, under the laburnum. I have a great deal to say to you this evening, but I must give my pets their supper first."

I did as she bade me, and for some time sat watching

the pleasant picture that she made, till having shaken the last grain out of the basket, she came over and sat down upon the seat with me, though quite at the other end.

She had taken off her hat, which she held by its silk strings, swinging it slowly as she watched her favourites —white and blue and brown—running, fluttering, jostling in their eagerness.

Then she turned to me, who had been watching her alone, with a mock defiance in her eyes and a tone of simulated reproof in her voice.

" Now, sir."

" Now, Mistress Victory," I said, coming a little nearer and trying to take her hand. " I am glad you have so much to say to me."

" You have no reason to be glad. Do you know what day this is ? "

" I am sure it is Friday," I said, smiling.

" That is five days since Monday. You must sit where you are, Jack. It is five days since you sat beside me last, and that shows ——"

" It has seemed like twelve months, Victory."

" Jack ! " She held up her forefinger menacingly. " I have ceased to believe you, sir."

" Since when ? " I asked.

" Since I have come to know the world. And oh ! I had so much to tell you."

" I will listen for a week. What has your wonderful knowledge of the world to do with me ? "

" All men are the same—there is no difference between them."

"Then I may go back to Heronford, and I thought, Victory ——"

"But you must not think—you have no right to think. Listen, Jack. It is a great secret."

"I will keep it better than I keep my own."

"I did not know that you had any secrets. But this is—awful."

She was smiling—half-playful, half-serious—as was her custom in a mood like this.

"I hope it will not frighten me," I said. "What is this awful secret?"

"Jack," she whispered, "I have got a—lover."

"But that is no secret; I have known that since the first day I saw you. I have never forgotten it for a moment."

"But I do not mean you, I mean a real lover."

I thought my dear sweetheart was mocking me in the playful way that became her so well, and I answered lightly —

"Yes, I know—a real lover. As he walks the birds say— 'I love her, I love her; the wind ——' "

"But, indeed, Jack, this is serious. I do not mean you." And she came a little nearer me.

"Victory!" I cried now for the first time, seeing that beneath her smiles and laughter there lay a sober earnestness.

"You see I did not think he meant anything—that he rode over to see my father, and, Jack—he frightened me."

I rose to my feet and held out my hands to her.

"Tell me all about it," I said.

"It was on Wednesday, when I had been expecting

you all day. When he came in I was quite alone and he told me he loved me, and, Jack—I hate him."

" But I do not understand, dear," I said. " Who did this ? "

" Mr. Weston, of Langston."

" Why, he is old enough to be your father ! " I cried indignantly.

Then I remember that I had met him here more than once and that his visits had been growing in frequency, but I had never for a moment had any suspicion regarding their object, though now when I came to think of it I wondered that I had been so blind. Who was there who could see my sweet mistress and not instantly love her ? Who could withstand the arch and radiant innocence that gave her beauty the charm and freshness of an opening flower ? Who that saw the dawn of sweet womanliness in her eyes would not long to possess the full day of sweetness and tenderness disclosed there ? I remembered the first day I had seen her in Heronford Church, her sweet face hidden by her bonnet and her eyes bent soberly upon her book. From that hour the world had changed for me ; a new song beating to a new, undreamt-of melody had filled the pauses of my life and mingled with my dreams; a new interest had awakened in the breast of the solitary lad and a new sense of the largeness and joy of life. I do not know whether others have experienced the same feeling—with my discovery there came the sense of sweet possession, a feeling of proprietorship growing out of the perfect assurance of my love.

And now, when for the first time I learned that others saw with the same eyes and were moved in the same way,

I had a feeling of consternation almost as much as of jealousy. But I had another feeling. To think of Weston of Langston, Will Cassilis' boon companion, who passed for a jolly fellow, with his hard living, hard riding, hard drinking ways, with his oaths and rough manners, with his coarse, red face and cruel eyes—it was little wonder that I stood with a sense of anger and indignation in my heart. And my sweetheart's face puzzled me.

"You say nothing, Victory," I cried, trying in vain to read her eyes.

"What am I to say, Jack?"

"Say! Say that nothing will ever come between us; say that your heart is mine; that——"

"You were always a foolish boy. How can I say that—and Mr. Weston is——"

"Oh!" I cried bitterly. "I know all you would say. It is true that he can give you a fine mansion and I—I can give you nothing but myself and my love. I have nothing—less than nothing. I do not even know certainly that my name is my own—John Cassilis, son of nobody and master of nothing but himself. But, indeed, I loved you, Victory. I could not help myself. I loved you long before I knew I loved you. I was wrong and you are right; I am not fit even to be your servant. It was a dream—a pleasant dream. I will waken by-and-bye."

I do not know what other wild, ungenerous words I spoke, and I am glad to think I do not remember them, but my heart was tossed in such a sea of passion and doubt and unreasoning jealousy that I was for the moment quite beyond myself. As I stood up, flinging out my bitter words, she lost the arch and playful manner that till now she had been wearing, and looked at me with a tender seriousness that stopped me in my tempestuous speech. She only spoke one word —

"Jack!"

But that one word was more eloquent than a thousand. In an instant my base suspicions, my selfish fears, my first and last doubt, passed like a flying shadow, and in an agony of self-reproach I caught her to my heart, and kissed her a hundred times. For a moment she submitted to my embrace and then gently released herself.

"I am wiser than you are, John Cassilis."

"Wiser and better a thousand times!"

"I think women are wiser than men; at least they do not lose their faith so easily, and perhaps—perhaps they think more of these things. Now sit down and let us talk seriously."

"You have forgiven me, Victory?"

"I have forgotten," she said simply; "that is better. I have been thinking, and I have thought—you are listening, Jack?—that we cannot live always this boy-and-girl life. Some day the world must come in—Lord Heronford, Mr. Weston, who can tell what? The world makes a difference."

"It can make no difference," I cried.

"Ah! you think so, but it does. It was pleasant to have our world all to ourselves, a little undiscovered world of love and happiness, but ——"

"I am listening, dear."

"We must tell my father, Jack."

"Yes," I said, "it is right that we should tell him; perhaps we should have told him long ago. But you do

not know what he will do, Victory ?   Do you know what
he should do ?   He should rise up and say, 'Mr. Cassilis,
or Mr. Whatever is your name, you have no right to
love my little girl.   She is set far as the sky above you ;
she is a rose for a prince's garden.   What have you to
do with her—you a poor dependant, a nameless pauper
—at best a drudging, poor relation ?   You are a good
fellow—at least he will say that for he likes me, Victory
—but you are not for my little girl.   I will not give her
to an admiral of the blue.'   And then he should bundle
me out of his house and I should never see you again.
Perhaps—I cannot give you up, Victory."

    " If my father should say that——"

    " What would you do ? " I cried.

    " I should know he did not mean a word of it.   Let
us go and hear what he does say, Jack."

    Then she took my hand with a bright, confident look
in her steadfast eyes and a smile of hope and happiness on
her tender lips, and we went together toward the house.

    It was now more than six years since Captain Blythe
had carried his household gods to Carnforth—that quiet
port in which he had resolved to moor his storm-tossed
bark after thirty-five years spent in the service of a not
ungrateful country.   Thither he had carried his models,
his guns, his wooden leg, and his fine, fighting spirit, in
sight and sound of the sea he loved ; to talk of the great
captains, to fight over again the old glorious fights, and,
as he hoped, to make ready for the last voyage that all
men must take when the Master Death comes quietly on
the quarter-deck.   I had first seen him from above the
high oak rail of my pew staggering like a ship under a

press of canvas down the aisle of Heronford Church.
Then, indeed, I had noticed the shining, red face, the
blue eyes with the light of the sea in them, and the faded
uniform which he always wore, but it was only when the
service—the coldest, dreariest service in the world—began that I looked up curiously. His voice rang out like
a storm-trumpet, till at last his was the only voice that I
could hear. From the beginning to the end—from the
first solemn words till the last Amen—that deep voice
thundered in response—a voice of fearless faith and earnest piety. It amazed the sparse congregation; it dis-
composed the vicar; the clerk suspended his office in
bewildered indignation, but the new worshipper saw
nothing, heard nothing, felt nothing but the mystery and
solemnity of his devotions. Then when the church dis-
persed, taking the tall, slim girl with the sweet face by
the arm, he trudged sturdily down the aisle with his head
held erect and the iron ring of his wooden limb echoing
on the pavement.

That was the first occasion on which I saw him, but
it was not long before I was made welcome in the captain's parlour and drank in his stories with the fine enthusiasm of youth. Perhaps that enthusiasm first insured
my welcome. I never tired hearing how the *Belle Marie*
was cut out at Brest; how single-handed the *Wasp*
fought three frigates for the length of a whole summer
day, with forty men dead on the decks and nearly as
many more dead or wounded below; how the might and
majesty of England had made the sea her own glorious
heritage, and men like my old captain won her imperish-
able renown. Then I am sure for some reason he came

to like me for my own sake, and looked eagerly for my coming.   It was impossible not to love and admire him; his fine contempt for all form, his irresistible mirth breaking forth in loud chuckles of laughter, his innocence of the world, and his unconscious pride in himself and all that belonged to him.   He had offered me his friendship without question, though at first with prudent reserve, and I was certain that no consideration but personal affection ever entered into our friendship.   He had made no enquiry regarding me or my condition, and I am sure no thought of doing so had ever once occurred to him.

But now the case was altered, the situation was completely changed.   Never for one moment had he imagined that my boyish friendship for his daughter had ripened into love.   He had seen nothing; he had understood nothing; such an idea must have appeared to him impossible and absurd, and I knew how different a thing it was to receive me as a friend and to welcome me as a lover; and I felt now that I had almost betrayed his trust, though heaven knows with no will of my own. The growth of that tender love had been so spontaneous and unconscious that I cannot remember the first moment of its revelation, or the time when that sweet confidence and mutual knowledge sprang to life.   That might to some degree excuse my offence, but the offence remained, and I knew that I had no excuse to offer in my own justification.

Victory halted for a moment on the threshold, and turning round looked at me with a bright, high look that flashed like an inspiration.

" Courage, Jack," she whispered, and then led me into the room where the captain sat dozing by his table, with a chart spread open before him and an old newspaper at his elbow. We came up the room together—I can see that picture yet—and stood at the other side of the table for a minute without a word. The old man drew himself up with a start, and looked at us with a puzzled expression on his cheerful face. Victory was the first to speak.

" We have come to report, Captain Blythe," she said, with a brave smile, and then her courage failed her, and I felt her hand trembling in my own. There was another pause. I own as yet I could not put my thoughts into words, but I was now full of courage.

" God bless my soul!" cried the captain, " what is the matter?"

" I hope sir," I said, " nothing is the matter, but ——"

" Then you hang confoundedly long in stays," cried the captain cheerfully. " Take a pull on your weather braces and you will move ahead."

But while I was still considering how I should put the matter, it not being an easy one, nor I having had much practice, Victory quitting my hand, went round the table quietly and knelt down at her father's knee —

" Father," she said, " we have something to tell you."

" 'Tis a monstrous long story, little girl. Have those contraband rascals from Carnforth ——"

" Not that, sir, but something ——"

" It is right that I should tell my father; it is all said in a moment. Father, Jack has told me that he loves me and I have told Jack that I—I love him."

Then she hid her shining face on her father's knees, and the sobs, which she had resolutely repressed, broke out uncontrolled.

"God bless my soul!" cried the captain, half rising from the table and reaching for his pipe, as he always did when greatly agitated. I did not like the symptom, knowing it of old, but I kept my heart up, and began as bravely as I could ——

"It is all my fault, sir; I only am to blame. I could not help loving Victory; I have loved her from the first day I saw her, and I am sorry ——"

"If anyone should be sorry it is I, man. What the devil have you to be sorry about?"

"I am sorry, sir, that I am not worthy of her—sorry that I have nothing to offer her but my love."

"It is a damned poor outfit for a long voyage, sir," cried the captain, now purple in his agitation. "Wait till you get into the doldrums. Oh! this is news with a vengeance."

"I have kept it back too long," I said; "it is right that you should know. If I had done wrong ——"

"For God's sake let me hear no more—not another word—I want to think it out."

He rose up, leaving Victory still kneeling by his chair, and paced up and down the room with his short broken strides, and making a curious blowing noise with his mouth. At every two or three turns he would stop short in his walk, look first at Victory and then at me, and then with a smothered "God bless my soul!" resume his uneasy march. I had never seen him so much moved, but I could not tell with what feelings—whether anger, dismay, or astonishment—he was regarding our sudden announcement. We did not venture to disturb his tempestuous meditations, but watched him almost with a guilty look upon our faces. Then he stopped abruptly —

"You say you love him, my lass?" he cried in his deep, strong voice.

But Victory did not falter in her sweet courage.

"I cannot help it, father. I love Jack."

Again the captain resumed his walk, and again he blew out his lips like the fine, old grampus that he was.

I do not know how long he continued to walk in this way—it seemed like an age almost—but at last he stopped, and coming over to the chair he had quitted sat down in it with a sigh. Then he laid his hand on Victory's head, and sat for a while without speaking a word, his great hand resting among the shining curls.

"We can't help it," he said, as though speaking to himself; "'tis the great law—aye, the law of God, and no man can say it nay. The woman must quit her father and mother. God knows, Victory, I thought you were only a little girl."

"Nineteen is a great age, father."

"Ay, ay, Methuselah's sister. And you, John Cassilis, you silent dog, what have you to say for yourself?"

"Only, sir, that I love Victory with all my heart."

"And let me tell you there are worse things than love if it will but wash and wear. I won't deny I have been infernally upset. 'Tis no easy thing to be turned out into the cold at a moment's notice and without as much as by your leave. But it's according to nature. I did it myself and never thought of what I was doing. Yet I never thought my lass would leave me."

"I will never leave you, sir."

"Hearken to that, my gay rover.   But I know better, and will only keep you while I can.   Come here, sir."

His voice was hard and strong, but his eyes were shining with a kindly light, and I laid my hand in his with a swift pulse of hope throbbing in my heart.

"I thought it was I who was sailing this ship," he said, "but I find I have made a mistake.   We won't cry over that; we'll try and make the best of it, and look you, sir, we must see that we don't break her heart between us.   I have known you lad and man for six years, John Cassilis, and maybe, after all is said and done, I had rather see her leave me in your convoy than anybody else's.   You are a good fellow, Jack, an honest fellow, and I hope God will bless both of you."

I am not wronging his honest memory when I say that he brushed the tears from his eyes with his hand, and looked up at me as through a mist of autumnal rain. His voice was shaking and his lips trembling.   But, indeed, my own eyes were not dry, for in the midst of my own happiness I read his kind old heart as though it had been a book.   Then Victory flung her arms round his neck and kissed him passionately.

"There, there, my lass," he said gently, "it is all over and we are going to be happy again.   We will have a bowl of punch, and Jack and I will drink prosperity to a long voyage and a fair wind all the way.   And look you, John Cassilis, here am I at sixty years, having worn the King's uniform and fought his battles; and I started my voyage with nothing in the world but hope and an empty sea-chest.   'Tis a stout heart and a clear conscience that helps us to drum the French and beat the devil all the world over. Now, lass, dry your tears and let us have the punch. And—Jack—Jack Cassilis—I don't mind if you—kiss my little girl."

I can remember no evening so pleasant in my life—the new-risen sun of love shining on the future without a shadow, and all discord lost in that new sweet music.

It was like the captain to think of nothing but his daughter's happiness. He refused to permit me to discuss my own hopes or prospects—that might be done in the future if it must be done at all—but at present we should make the most of the shining hour. The fiddlers were striking up and the jolly mariners were dancing; to-morrow the winds might blow and the seas might storm, but to-night love was playing her melody, and our hearts must keep time to that bewitching tune.

I shall never forget that evening, nor the moon against the western sky, and the vast glory of starlight, as I walked home across the cliffs and listened to the ripple of the tide almost below the shadow of Heronford.

CHAPTER VI

WHEN I got home, it being then about eleven o'clock, I found Mr. Ballard gone, and my lord and the two gentlemen in the Book Room together. Will Cassilis and Mr. Earnshaw were playing at cards—the one flushed and excited, the other cool and sedate, but both very quiet—and my lord was seated by the hearth with a book open upon his knees and his head resting upon his hand. He had not been playing at all, pleading a headache, with which he was often troubled, but I wondered to see him sitting there at this hour, for it was a thing quite contrary to his custom.

As I came in he looked up and merely nodded to me, but in such a way that I could not tell whether he was not displeased to see me. For the other two gentlemen, neither of them paid any attention to my entrance, both being too much absorbed in their game. I walked over and stood for a minute or two behind Will Cassilis' chair, till I saw that he disliked being overlooked in this way; but before I went I noticed that his hands shook and that the stakes were out of all reason for one of his means. I own I could not help finding some fault with my lord, who after all would have to pay the reckoning, that he permitted his good nature to carry him so far in the indulgence of this criminal recklessness, for a word from him might have prevented this folly. But that word my lord would never speak. Upon the subject of his poverty his pride carried him to a point I could never understand, and I am sure even Mr. Earnshaw never knew how deeply even his moderate winnings had involved his host. Whatever it might cost I knew my lord would not now interfere, and I knew also that he would discharge his brother's indebtedness with the same punctilious exactness and outward suavity that he would discharge his own. I had myself, feeling it to be my duty, spoken to him more than once upon the subject, and had so far prevailed upon him that he had remonstrated with his brother, who as usual had promised amendment and gone on as before.

As a rule Will Cassilis was the most unlucky player in the world, but to-night his ill fortune had deserted him, and by the time I came in he had won a considerable sum. I noticed that he had by no means drunk so much as usual, and with a permissible laxity of speech might be called perfectly sober—a condition of affairs which never improved his temper. Nor had I been in the room very long before I saw that my lord was for some reason very unquiet in his mind, and was far more interested in the play and the players than he desired to appear. He would from time to time turn over the leaves of the book upon his knee, but his eyes hardly rested upon the printed page, and reading his face as I was always able to do, I knew that he was agitated and troubled to no common degree. For this I was unable to account, but looking for an explanation it occurred to me that possibly as a kind of self-imposed penance he was resisting that temptation which had been and still was the strongest in his life. For my lord was naturally a gambler, and could never withstand, at least till lately, the allurements of the cards and dice.

I came over to the hearth and stood with my back to the fireplace.

"What is the night like out-of-doors?" my lord asked, like one speaking mechanically.

"'Tis a fine moonlight night and quite warm."

"Ah! And nearly bed-time for all quiet folk."

He said no more but I knew that this was more than a hint, and I was about to leave the room when an incident occurred which held me fixed in astonishment. The two gentlemen at the table had been playing almost in perfect silence—only now and then we heard a word spoken in an undertone and the shuffling of the cards, but nothing more. Then suddenly and without warning Mr. Earnshaw pushed back his chair and struck the table sharply with his hand.

"This has gone on long enough, sir. You are a common cheat."

The two gentlemen—my lord and his brother—at the same instant leapt to their feet and stood looking at the speaker, one in an agony of horror and dismay, the other scowling and defiant. At first neither of them appeared able to say a word, my lord's white face showing very ghastly in the candlelight. But Mr. Earnshaw retained his perfect self-possession, not raising his voice in the least nor showing the slightest display of temper. He even went so far—but I thought at the time this was merely a piece of acting to cover his agitation—as to snuff the candle nearest to him before he spoke again.

"You must remember, sir, you were not playing with

a schoolboy. I have been watching you for some time. It was a common trick but very clumsy."

I still remember the easy contempt of his tone and the fine manner with which he tossed his hand of cards on the table. At this Will Cassilis began to swear and bluster, but my lord stood very still and with a white face in the place where he had risen. Indeed, I thought he would have fallen, and I instinctively moved a little nearer to him.

" 'Tis very well," Will cried with an oath. " We should have heard nothing of this had I not won your money. You must not think to come over me in this way, sir; I have seen it done before. By —— if I did not remember the roof you were under you should give me satisfaction for this here and now."

Earnshaw smiled.

" Whenever and wherever may suit the convenience of Mr. Cassilis."

" By —— no man will call me cheat twice," Will cried in his blustering manner. " But I don't forget whose guest you are."

" I am quite prepared to stand over my words, sir, and repeat them if necessary."

Then I saw my lord's face harden, and he came forward to the table.

" I think," he said, " you have both forgotten me, gentlemen."

Earnshaw rose from his chair and bowed gravely.

" I have spoken, my lord," he said, " in the heat of the moment, but I cannot withdraw my words. I regret that for my own sake and yours."

"It is a grave charge," my lord said slowly; "a serious accusation that no honourable man would make lightly. But Mr. Earnshaw must remember that my brother's honour is mine."

"I know none of your lordship's friends who would agree with you. I cannot."

"Sir!"

"Lord Heronford's honour is beyond suspicion as it is beyond praise."

"At least no man ever ventured to question it. Your words imply, sir, what has never been said before in my presence, nor will I permit them to pass now. You know what you have said, Mr. Earnshaw?"

"Lord Heronford does not desire me to repeat my words?"

"They have been spoken once too often—that under my roof, at my table, and in my presence you have been cheated by a member of my family."

"That is an unpleasant way of putting an unpleasant truth."

"I beg your pardon," my lord said, turning to his brother, who till now had been silent. "I am the master in this house. Mr. Earnshaw himself must see that for my own sake I cannot permit this to go further."

"Perhaps," Earnshaw answered, "your lordship will see what the cards themselves say?"

"I will see nothing, sir; I will hear nothing; and relying on my own unquestioned honour and integrity in this way I answer your accusation."

He lifted the pack of cards from the table and, walking slowly over to the fireplace, flung them into the grate

and stamped upon them with his heel. Then he turned
round, his tall figure drawn up to its full height.

"I cannot now speak more plainly than I have done
by my action. I do not forget that you are my guest,
but there are higher claims than the claims of hospitality.
The honour of Heronford is in my hands; I will not
stand here and see it called in question. Now, Mr.
Earnshaw, there is only one of two ways out of this
difficulty: either that you withdraw your words, which I
have no doubt you spoke honestly, but labouring under
a terrible mistake ——"

"That with your lordship's permission I cannot do."

"Then you accept the other alternative?"

"If you mean, my lord, that you will take the matter
upon your own shoulders, I have sufficient courage to
refuse that alternative also. There is no power on earth
will make me cross swords with you in this vulgar brawl.
Your brother and yourself are two very different persons."

"In this matter, sir, we are one. I recognise no difference, and I cannot permit his character and reputation
to be impugned any more than I would my own. And
you forget, sir, at my table, in my presence, almost under
my very eyes ——"

"I forget nothing, my lord, and least of all do I forget
the pain my words must cause you. I esteem the honour
of your friendship, and it is not my least regret that this
incident should cause a breach between us. But even
that cannot deter me from speaking the truth and standing by my words. At the same time I trust you will
pardon me when I say the position taken by your lordship is one no sensible man ever would have anticipated."

"I beg your pardon, sir."

"There was a time when you would have acted differently. Living here ——"

"You have already insulted me and my household, Mr. Earnshaw, but I will not further permit you to criticise my views and my conduct. Besides, that is altogether beyond the question. Am I then to understand that you refuse to uphold your words in that manner customary among gentlemen?"

"Even that taunt will not tempt me. In the same manner that your lordship destroyed the proof," and he pointed to the fireplace, "I will take the high ground and refuse to quarrel with you upon any terms. But if Mr. Cassilis desires to go further I am always at his service, and he knows where I am to be found."

I own that at that moment my heart was sore for my dear master, for I knew that every word that had been spoken had lacerated his heart and caused him infinite suffering. Knowing him as I did, in his strength and weakness, from the beginning I had seen his mind laid open before me. I felt that he did not doubt the truth of the charge to which he had listened—that he was convinced in his own mind the fact was as Mr. Earnshaw had stated—but I knew there was hardly anything he would not do to keep that knowledge from the world and cover the disgrace. The longer he had lived in the retirement of Heronford the deeper and more absorbing his pride had grown, till it seemed to have become the dominant note and passion of his life. It grew to a pass that was almost incomprehensible; it swayed him with a tyranny that was absolute; it interfered with the promptings of the kindest heart in the world, and warped his judgment till right and wrong seemed to me quite confounded.

" The Honour of Heronford " ; the phrase was continually upon his lips till I had almost come to dread it. It centred in himself; he was the guardian of the family name, the upholder and champion of the family honour. For this reason he had pinched to pay his brother's debts, he had indulged while he had screened his libertinism, and now for the same reason and no other he had placed himself in a wholly false position. He knew that his own character was above suspicion and his own honour undoubted, and he imagined that in taking up his brother's cause that in itself was sufficient to avert scandal and save the situation. I do not seek to justify him or to excuse his conduct. The course which he adopted was the only one that occurred to him to avert a disgrace that had far more terror for him than death, and having once adopted it he clung to it regardless of all consequences. Perhaps it might have succeeded with another person than Mr. Earnshaw, whose manner and conduct I must admit I could not help admiring from beginning to end. I felt, so to speak, that he knew the cards in my lord's hand and sympathised with him in the difficult game he was endeavouring to play. But, notwithstanding, he was not to be drawn from the position he had taken up, and while he did not conceal his contempt for the detected cheat, his manner toward my lord, while always firm, was full of courteous respect and regard. I saw that my lord perceived he had failed, and that knowledge added a thousandfold to his pain. The comedy, that to him was all tragedy, was only too apparent, and the sooner it was brought to an end the better.

"We have now spoken the last word, Mr. Earnshaw," he said. "I cannot doubt for a moment you believe you are right—so much at least I owe you. But wiser men have been mistaken, and who can doubt you are mistaken here? If you please you can speak the story anywhere, but I shall expect you will tell the whole story, omitting nothing, and above all that I took and still take my brother's part."

"Permit me to say, my lord, that I never admired you more than at this moment—even when you tell me I am wrong. I might have held my tongue—I almost wish I had. But you may be certain that our discussion of to-night will not be repeated by me."

"On that head, sir, you will be pleased to exercise your judgment. I regret that I shall be unable to see you before you leave in the morning."

"I assure you the regret is mutual."

With that the two gentlemen bowed courteously but with great coldness to one another, and my lord followed his guest to the door, where he bowed to him again.

When the door was closed he walked up the room with his hands behind his back, his lips trembling, and his eyes shining with an intense, inward fire. At the hearth he turned and stood looking at his brother with a look I had never seen him wear before. I cannot quite say what I felt, for the face was certainly not that of my dear master. I could not have believed that such a change was possible, so terrible in its sudden transformation, so ghastly in its abandonment of despair, so hard in its indignant pride. I could see that he was fighting with his tumultuous feelings that surged to find expression, and it was a good while before he was calm enough to trust himself to speak. Then he spoke in a cold, hard voice.

" Well, sir ? "

" By —— you let him off too easily, Richard," Will answered with an uneasy shrug, for there was something in his brother's voice he did not like.

" Is that all you have to say ? "

" I'll say anything you like—I don't care a damn what. What would you have me say ? You don't mean that you believe Earnshaw's cock-and-bull story about the cards ? Upon my soul 'tis bad enough to hear another man —— "

" You miserable cheat and liar ! " cried my lord, with slow, deliberate emphasis and with every word seeming to drag out his heart.

" Hey ! This is Mr. Facing-both-Ways with a vengeance."

" Yes, sir. I, Richard Cassilis, Lord Heronford, have trifled with my honour to screen your dishonour. Do you think you deceived me any more than you deceived that fine gentleman who now pities me as much as he despises you ? A cheat ! A lying rogue ! The scandal of the country ! A bye-word among men ! Do you think, I say, you deceived me ? Oh ! not for a moment. By heaven ! I read it in your face and the very motion of your hands. You have soiled me with the filth of your dishonour ; you have made me a partner in your shame. While I sat here in silence and agony I prayed that you might not be discovered, and the devil would not hear my

prayer.   And my hands were tied; my mouth was closed!
I could not rise and say, 'My brother, of my own blood
and name, sitting at my table and playing under my eyes,
is cheating his guest in the house of Cassilis.   Our kindness is the hospitality of rogues; we rob you while you
sleep; we drug your wine and pick your pockets!'"

"And then," cried Will, with a laugh, "we offer to
cut your throat."

It was a cruel stab; I could have struck him on the
face for that blow.   My lord caught a deep breath, and
with his left hand over his heart stood looking at his
brother in speechless horror.

"You are right," he said slowly and after a long pause;
"you have spoken the truth.   To save your name—my
name—from the disgrace, I think I would even have
killed my friend.   I did not see it in that way."

"Oh!   It is a hundred to one you would have made
daylight in him.   No man ever I saw could stand up
against you with the foils."

Strong in his passions as he was infirm in his judgment, my lord always lived at the extremity of his emotions, and now when his brother's brutal words had
placed his conduct in the strongest light he was plunged
in an agony of shame and contrition.

"It is true," he wailed; "I am judged even out of
your mouth.   My dishonour is as great as yours."

"There is not much to choose between us.   Between
us we shall keep up the reputation of the family; 'tis a
good thing it has little to lose."

"I have borne with you a good many years, and no man
can say that I have not shown you as much kindness as

you deserve. You have already tried me beyond endurance; I will stand it no longer. Another word ——"

"I did not begin the sermon—I don't want to end it," Will added with a significant look at me. "I would remind your lordship that I am not responsible for the congregation. Mr. Secretary stands to your credit in the house."

For the first time Lord Heronford seemed to become aware of my presence; till now he had wholly forgotten that I was in the room, and at these last words he looked round at me almost with a look of fear in his face. Moved by a sudden impulse and touched by his look of suffering I came forward and held out my hand. But he either did not see or disregarded the gesture I made.

"I am sorry," he said, "that you should have been present at this painful scene. I should have wished to spare you. But you are in some sort a member of the family, and everything that touches its honour must have concern and interest for you. And it has its lessons— hard lessons, bitter lessons, the lesson that a man gathers in his after years, the crop of what he has sowed in his youth, that he gathers it at his own fireside and in his own house. And not himself alone, but if he has children, then his sons and his sons' sons after him. He can't step aside from fate. I have something to say to my brother, and he alone must hear it. You will see Mr. Earnshaw before he leaves Heronford in the morning, and tell him I do not know ——"

" I will say, my lord, that your kind heart wishes him a prosperous journey, and that you never esteemed him

more than when you last parted from him "; and my eyes
met those of Will Cassilis'.

" God knows that is true," said my lord with a sigh.

" You have a fine gift of words, Mr. Secretary," Will
said, but I did not answer him.   Then I silently withdrew and left the brothers alone.

I do not know what happened after I was gone, but
nearly an hour afterwards I heard the door opened and
closed, and the sound of footsteps echoing along the corridor.   But my lord had never gone to bed at all.   He
had spent the night in the Book Room, and in the morning, before anyone was astir, had gone out in the first
grey light along the cliffs.

I was the only one of the household present at Mr.
Earnshaw's departure, and I gave him my lord's message
in such terms as I was able to command.   He was
standing with his foot upon the step and his hand resting
on the window of the chaise, almost hoping, I think, that
at the last moment my lord would put in an appearance.

" Lord Heronford could not have said more, Mr.
Cassilis," he said, when I had finished, " and he could
not have put it better.   I have had a night to think upon
it, and I feel that I should not have spoken at all.   I may
have been mistaken, and now dismiss the matter from my
memory for ever.   In your ear I tell you Lord Heronford is the finest gentleman I know, but I have known
gentlemen commit an indiscretion in the blindness of their
family pride.   It was natural that he should stand by his
brother, who also is a gentleman, but living too much
alone is apt to make a man quixotic.   Convey to my lord
my warm regard and sincere regrets ; I am still his friend.

And for yourself, do not live too long at Heronford ; the light is too dim. Come up to town, see the world, and do not forget there is one gentleman there will make you welcome."

Then the door was shut, the postilions cracked their whips, and I watched the chaise lumbering down the drive till it was lost to view in the bend of the road. But I could not help feeling that Mr. Earnshaw's visit and the manner of his going had in many ways altered the life at Heronford.

CHAPTER VII

I HAVE said I never knew what passed between Lord Heronford and his brother when I left them together in the Book Room, nor did my lord ever approach the subject in my presence even in the remotest way. This was altogether like him, and quite natural to the man. With a feminine sensitiveness he always avoided a painful subject, and however much it might possess his own mind and poison his own thoughts, he never could be induced, even remotely, to touch upon it in conversation. But I knew this subject engrossed him wholly; the entire transaction was one now only personal to himself, and he brooded upon it with a persistence which seemed to me childish because it was wholly unreasonable. It grew like a shadow from the darkness of which he was never able to move, and which drove him more and more to seek that solitude which only increased his morbid thoughts.

From that day he was quite changed; the little gleam of playful humour that used to light up his conversation like rifts of sunshine entirely disappeared. His interest in matters of the household, always distant, seemed wholly gone, and he avoided my society, which he had hitherto welcomed, till I began to look for some cause of offence in my own conduct. At another time I might have felt it more, but if love is free and generous it also possesses a certain selfishness, and in my own happiness I almost forgot my lord's distress. Perhaps it was natural that I should endeavour to escape from the gloom and shadow of the house in which I lived, into the sunshine and beauty of the new world that lay before me. The sweetness of the present, the delicious promise of the future, possessed me, as it still possesses youth, to the exclusion of everything else.

Morning and evening I found myself (what long, sweet days they were!) in the captain's house, in the beech wood at the back of the hill, on the cliffs, on the sea-kissed sands, the distilled sweetness of the world walking at my side. Were the violets of that spring larger and more fragrant than they ever have been since, the skies bluer, the days balmier, and the long evenings tremulous with a more delicate moonrise? Oh! love makes its own world, and I suppose made my world for me, an earth newly fashioned, and skies with the first morning and evening glow in them.

It will give you some idea of the seclusion in which we lived when I say that none of the family at Heronford knew anything, or appeared to know anything, regarding his neighbours. Certainly as far as I know they had never once been mentioned, nor had my lord or any member of his household ever called on them. This fact had never troubled the captain, nor, so far as I remember, had he ever remarked upon it, but I felt that the present state of affairs could not long continue. My own position was sufficiently ambiguous and embarrassing, and my long absences, open as they were, could not fail to be observed. So far as my lord himself was concerned these might have been continued indefinitely without exciting either notice or comment, but in my calculations I had to reckon with Madam Cassilis, who had never shown me any sympathy or kindness, but who had always regarded me with suspicion and dislike almost openly avowed.

One morning Lord Heronford and myself were seated over our accounts (since Mr. Earnshaw's visit the balance had been deeply weighted upon the wrong side), my lord with his brows drawn, and myself in vain endeavouring to deduce some prospect of hope from the inexorable figures. The windows of the Book Room were lying open, the air was sweet and warm, and the martins flew in dips and circles about the pleasance. Presently Madam Cassilis came in, and my lord rose and bowed to her, for he invariably treated her with the same punctilious courtesy that he would have showed a stranger. She returned him a sweeping courtesy, though with some disdain in it, that being the way she always affected to treat him, and came over to the table where I was still seated with my pen in my hand. She had been, as I have said, a great beauty in her youth, and her figure must always have been very striking, but her cheeks had now grown thin, her lips hard, and her eyes had lost their softness and only retained their fire. I own there was a time when I was afraid of her, and I still preserved something of my boyish shrinking in her presence, for she treated all alike, and her swift, incisive speech always seemed to me to cut like a whip. I often think that Nature had done her a great wrong in not making her a man.

"I am very busy, Judith," said my lord, resuming his seat. "I must finish these accounts this afternoon."

"You are always busy when I have anything to say.

You do not seem to get much comfort from your books."

" There is not much comfort in them. They speak a very hard truth."

" Well, that is one comfort. What do they say ? "

" That I am a poor man."

" Do they say it is your own fault ? "

" Not in so many words, but I do not require to be reminded of that fact. I do not forget it."

" You have the knack of remembering unpleasant things, but you don't profit by the experience. If I were in your place ——"

" I wish to heaven you were."

" I would burn my books, look after my affairs, and —discharge my secretary."

My lord looked up at her with a swift look and a sudden flush upon his face. I could very well see that for the moment he was so astonished that he did not quite know what answer to make. Then he recovered himself.

" I suppose I have given you the right to say these things. I have indulged you so long. But there is still one matter in which I will not permit you to interfere ——"

" I have no wish to interfere."

" Then we need not continue the subject."

This was the way in which these altercations always ended, my lord's listless coldness and apparent apathy presenting no weak point for attack, but on this occasion I was not wrong in imagining that Madam Cassilis had found a new weapon which she intended to use.

She made a little gesture of impatience.

" You are the master in your own house, but at least

it is your duty to look after the welfare and the morals of your family. I am glad that you blush, Mr. Secretary. I thought you had ceased to blush, but I am not quite so blind as my lord. I have no desire to interfere, but at least the amours of Lord Heronford's secretary should be conducted with some outward regard to decorum."

" Madam ! " I said, rising to my feet.

" Sit down," my lord said quietly, and almost, as I thought, with a feeling of relief. " It is best that we should hear the last word upon this subject; at least it can do no harm."

" And I fear 'tis too late to do very much good," madam cried in her high imperious way. " Ask this gentleman where he spent yesterday and the day before and every day for the last week past."

" I do not think it necessary to put that question," he said with a grave smile. " I know already, and I am sure he spent them more pleasantly than either you or I."

I do not know whether madam or myself was the more astonished.

" Then you know your dependant's low intrigue ? " she cried; " it has gone on with your permission and authority ? I was ready to believe anything, but I could not have believed that."

" Hardly with my permission, for that never was asked, and scarcely with my authority, for I have not ventured to interfere. But "— here my lord smiled gravely—"you must admit the lady does credit to my secretary's taste."

" A brazen baggage with red curls and a milkmaid's cheeks," madam cried indignantly; " a saucy, giggling dairymaid. 'Tis the talk of the country."

"If we listen to the talk of the country I am afraid we must begin to put our house in order in more ways than one. My dear Judith, do not let us forget our own youth."

"You are pleased to insult me, my lord."

"Pardon me, I had forgotten. At least let me remember mine. My secretary is still young enough to be happy."

"And old enough to bring discredit on the family."

"Even if it were as you say the family would not suffer much—it would not add the burden of another straw. Have you anything more to say?"

"Will you bring her home to Heronford? Shall I prepare the bride's rooms in the west wing and send in my own harpsichord that she may sing you ballads? I'm told she sings like a nightingale."

"I have sat long enough," I cried indignantly. "I have listened to words ——"

"'Tis well to follow the proverb in a case like this," said my lord. "The storm is over."

"At any rate I have done my duty, and given you warning. I know it has fallen upon deaf ears, but I thought at least you took enough interest in your *protégé* to keep him from making a fool of himself."

With that she flung out of the room in her high tragedy manner and left my lord and me alone together.

There is no speech that can cut and sting like the speech of a woman. You can answer a man with a blow or a word, but it is one of the privileges of a woman to strike, and to strike where it hurts most and wounds deepest without fear of retaliation or power of redress. When Madam Cassilis was speaking I felt that I had no power to reply, and while every word she spoke added to my indignation and anger, I felt that my lord was right, and that the wiser course had been to say nothing. But the insulting bitterness with which she had treated me, the cruel wrong she had done my dear love, gave me now the courage that I needed, and I made up my mind to tell my lord my story from beginning to end. But he, so soon as Madam Cassilis was gone, reached over and took up the pen that he had laid down.

"We have already lost too much time," he said in his quiet voice. "We must go through this account again, John."

"There is first something that I would like to say if you will hear me."

"Upon the subject of which I have just heard?"

"Yes, upon that subject."

"Remember, I am quite satisfied. Are you sure you wish to speak under no feeling of compulsion or restraint?"

My dear master laid down his pen, leaned his arms upon the table, and looked at me with a soft and kindly look in his eyes.

"I was wrong," I said, "not to speak of it before. I have been burning to tell you, and if you will listen I will tell you now."

"I am glad you think it right to tell me," he said, closing the book that was lying open before him. "You had better begin at the beginning."

I do not well remember what I said nor how I said it, but I am sure I forgot everything but my subject as I went on in my narrative, pouring out my whole heart in the abandonment of my love. I drew such a picture of

my sweet mistress, of her beauty, her courage, her innocence, as only the painter Love can draw. I described
her father with his heroic heart and honourable wounds
received in the service of his country; how my love had
first sprung to life and grown in depth and fulness every
day, till now it meant all the world and involved all my
happiness. I omitted nothing, and when I had finished
I had laid open my whole heart, as we only do in youth
and perhaps can only do once.

As I ended my lord drew a deep sigh.

"Ah! if a man were always young—oh! happy three-
and-twenty. 'Tis a pretty story, John—a fairy tale with
a lilt of music in it, but ——"

"Ah! my lord," I said, "that is it, but ——"

"But what?"

"Sometimes my love seems altogether beyond my
reach; for what can I offer? What am I? Nothing
but the poor dependent on the best master in the world.
I have nothing; I have neither means nor hope of
means, birth ——"

"Who spoke of your birth?" he asked sharply.

"I have never heard it spoken of but by yourself, and
then—then I learned nothing. But I cannot remember
the time when I have not been reproached with it. It
used to hurt me, my lord; it used to cut me deeply, and
perhaps it still does, but I have grown more reconciled
to what I could not help. When I was a child the hints
of the servants used to send me to my bed weeping, and
later ——"

"Later?" queried my lord.

"Later, when I saw the footing on which I was treated

by the family—I mean by all but your lordship—I knew that I had no right to the shelter of this roof but by your kindness."

" A man should never forget his mother, sir. To doubt his birth is to dishonour that mother's memory. I told you once I knew your mother. She was no man's mistress. She was a bad man's wife both before God and man."

I never doubted my lord's words—not for an instant. Only the man who has lived for years under the shadow of disgrace and brooded upon it till he has felt it nearly every hour of his life with poignant shame; only the man who has seen that shadow pass away and feels that he no longer rests under it, can realise what I felt at that moment. I could not keep back the hot blood that flowed to my face.

" The time is coming," my lord went on, " when you will hear your mother's history and the story of your birth. But, my dear lad, 'tis a sad history, and for one man a disgraceful story. There are grave reasons why I alone was made the depository of that history, though your— the late Lord Heronford was aware of all the facts. The same reasons which compelled me to silence also restrained him. But now I think there is another who guesses the secret, and it must be told perhaps sooner than I expected. Wait "—my lord laid his hand on my arm—" I have something more to say. I could not take your father's place nor could I ask you for that affection which a son naturally yields, but I have not been a harsh guardian, John, and—and I think you have some regard for me."

" There is no man in the world I love and respect as I love and respect your lordship."

" You can understand that only the strongest reasons have kept me silent—reasons that affect a man who was once my friend, and the honour of a great and noble house—but no reason that affects your mother or you. Your birth is as clear and honourable as my own, but "—he paused and looked at me gravely—" when I speak, when the world hears the story, the man to whom you owe your birth—if he were alive—would be compelled to suffer the punishment of his crime. He would have no refuge but in death."

" I do not understand ———"

" The time has not yet come for me to speak more plainly. It is a law we cannot alter—the children must suffer for the transgressions of their fathers, and I have seen the same law working in this house and in myself. You must bear a little longer, my dear lad, without questioning."

I saw that he was almost overcome, and there was a look in his eyes I did not understand—love and entreaty —but the memory of which dwelt with me long afterwards. There were many questions upon my tongue, but at that look I instantly checked them.

" I have implicit faith in your goodness," I said ; " I will wait patiently till you think it time to speak."

" That is well," he said, laying his hand upon mine, and letting it rest there for some time ; " it is something that we are able to trust one another. Ah ! a great wrong has been done you. A great wrong, an unpardonable sin. It was not a little thing for a child to grow up among these shadows and in this loneliness. It was a hard lot for a child, and I have watched how you bore it."

"I have always felt that I had one friend."

"A bitter, disappointed man, John, whose heart is buried in the grave of the past. But I can still remember. It was because I saw my own life—the life that might have been—in this new life of yours that I have said nothing. But I loved you too well altogether to close my eyes, and "—my lord smiled sadly—"if I could not recall the rapture of love, at least I could hear the fluttering of his wings. It was something to see that you were happy, and I felt that the past owed you some recompense that the future could afford to pay. I suppose you are happy?"

"My lord!"

"Ah! there is no cloud in the springtime of love. She is a beautiful girl, John, with eyes that remind me of a woman—a good woman—I once knew."

"I know whom you mean," I cried. "I have seen the resemblance myself."

Lord Heronford looked at me in amazement.

"She I mean died when you were only a child," he said slowly.

"Four years old," I said. "My mother had the same eyes."

I always wore my little miniature round my neck like a charm, as indeed it was, and almost without thinking what I did I opened my vest and placed the little gold case in his hand. But I was not prepared for his agitation. He sat gazing at it in perfect silence and with a stony look, and then rising walked to the window, where he stood looking at it with his back to me. I felt that it must have recalled some very painful memory; when he turned round his lips were quite white.

"I remember the time that was painted," he said. "Your father was a villain, John, though he was my friend.   He broke her heart."

"Do not let us speak of him," I said.

"No, it is better that we should not speak of him. You are right; there is some resemblance here, but your sweetheart is not so beautiful as your mother was.   Good God! how those sweet lips used to laugh!   And she died broken-hearted at two-and-twenty, and sacrificed herself for the man who killed her.   Sometimes we should pity the living more than the dead.   Well, you must see that you do not walk in your father's footsteps."

"God forbid!" I cried, almost with a feeling of horror.

"Amen!" said my lord; "we both pray the same prayer.   Take back your relic and pray that the world may never warp and poison your heart as it has poisoned his, till he forgot his love, his honour, and his name, and found himself a criminal listening for years for the foot-steps of justice."

Then my lord gave a little cry, tottered forward a step or two, and fell in a swoon across the table.

CHAPTER VIII

My lord's illness was more serious than we at first supposed, and I think he never regained his original health in its entire vigour. The doctor who had come flying at the first imperative summons pronounced that he was suffering from a kind of stroke, and he remained unconscious till the middle of the next day, when his mind came back, though without the power of speech, which only returned slowly and after nearly a week. During all this time I remained constantly at his bedside, for he seemed unwilling that I should leave the room, and distressed when I was absent.

I had a little bed brought into my lord's dressing-room, where I used to lie listening to him tossing uneasily, and after he had recovered his speech, talking with a broken and passionate utterance, though it was impossible to piece his rambling words together, or draw a coherent meaning from them. In justice to myself I must say that I had no desire to gather my lord's secrets from his unconscious wanderings, and I as resolutely shut my ears against them, but it was impossible at the end not to find myself driven to the conclusion that he had lived and was living under the shadow of a great fear. What the mainspring or cause of this terror was I did not know, for always at this point he seemed to stop aghast and returned upon the path he had travelled, repeating the same phrases, and dwelling on them with an iteration of horror.

There were times when I thought he would like to have taken me into his confidence, and once he had actually made me sit down beside him, but it was evident that at the last moment his courage failed him. As he grew stronger (and he now began to mend rapidly) this desire seemed to pass away, though his dreams were still broken and his sleep disturbed. But it was a very great relief to myself when he became perfectly convalescent and no longer required my attendance, and he was able to resume his old habits without any change or interruption.

During all these last days I had spent in this way with my lord he had never once returned to the subject of our conversation, though I afterwards found he had kept the matter in his mind and had by no means forgotten it. It was after he had recovered so far as to be able to sit out in the sunshine upon the terrace that he returned to the subject. Sitting here under the south wall one can see the vast girdle of sand that clasps the waves of Carnforth Bay in its silver folds, and the green swell of the hill that rises above Carnforth Cottage. I suppose my lord had seen how my eyes had followed my heart—that they could not outrun—beyond the cliffs and across the bay; he had been watching me as he sat wrapped in a great cloak, for the day though bright was not warm, and never speaking a word. At last he sighed, and at that moment I turned to him.

"It has grown cold," I said, "your lordship had better go indoors."

"No, it is not that. I have been thinking what Pisgah views there are from the hills of youth; the vineyards that need no husbandry, the cornlands that are still ripening to the harvest, the streams flowing with milk and honey, the life that never withers and the hearts that never grow old. Ah, that is a golden prospect. But there is another. Ah, there is another. The old man at the end of his journey looks back upon the wilderness he has travelled, the long track of desert strewed with the wrecks of faith and love and the promise of wasted years—with desires and unfulfilled ambition—with memories that gather like ghosts and ghosts that are more than memories. Of all those who quitted the House of Bondage how many were there that entered the Land of Promise, John?"

"My lord, there were reasons," I answered gravely.

"Still it seems a pity they should have come so far; it was a long journey for nothing. But there were reasons —that is the answer, the last word, and Faith is silent with the question on her lips. Still, you did not tell me the name of your sweetheart, John?"

"Victory, my lord."

"Ah, I suppose a sailor's curious fancy, but a very good name for a woman—a beautiful name on the lips of a lover."

"A beautiful name anywhere," I cried. "She was born on the day that Rodney chased the French at Finisterre, and Captain Blythe fought the three-decker *Sanspareil*. You should hear him tell the story, my lord. You would think he saw every incident in the fight, from the time they grappled with the enemy till they ran up the English colours and gave three cheers for the fighting captain."

"Yes," said my lord, "I have been told he was a good sailor, and with a little more luck might have been an admiral. I am satisfied that he is a gentleman—a little rough but still a gentleman. You thought the eye of the schoolmaster was not on you when you were playing truant, and spending your days at the other side of the bay with love in idleness. You were mistaken, my dear lad. It was my duty to see that you made no mistake, and I am satisfied. You might have done better, but you might have done a great deal worse."

"I could have done no better," I said, " my love is the best woman, the sweetest and tenderest, and she loves me altogether for myself."

"Ah," said my lord gravely, " the love that only gives is excellent, but the love that receives is perfect. I suppose since the world began there never was a sweetheart yet who had not all the graces. I should like to see your sweetheart, my boy."

"Then come with me to Carnforth," I said. " I should like you to see her with your own eyes."

I confess that I had no hope that I could induce my lord to take this visit, his reluctance to passing beyond his own rooms, and the strip of cliff where he was used to exercise, being excessive, and his dislike to meeting strangers amounting to a passion. But I did not altogether despair, since I had already succeeded so far, and since the wish that he had expressed showed that he had no ordinary interest in the affair. I did not immediately press him, but neither did I let the matter drop, and after a good many efforts I ultimately succeeded in inducing him to name a day for his visit to Carnforth. But even then he would have temporised and endeavoured to excuse himself upon some trivial grounds, and I am quite sure he regretted his promise.

When I announced his approaching visit, Captain

Blythe for the first time realised that there were more interests in the world than he imagined, and his excitement
increased as the day fixed for the interview approached.
In common with the rest of the neighbourhood he had
formed the most extraordinary ideas regarding Lord
Heronford's character, which nothing that I could say
shook in the slightest, and a visit from a person so inscrutable and mysterious was a visit of no ordinary occurrence. At first he was—as his phrase ran—inclined
to cut his cable and run, but his natural courage came to
his aid, and he began to prepare for the interview in much
the same way and spirit as he would have prepared for a
general engagement with a superior force. A day or two
before he had laid out his glorious blue coat that he had
worn on the high day of Porto Rico, and paced up and
down his garden walk as he would have paced the quarter-
deck waiting for the enemy to come in sight—a little
irascible and quick of temper but full of a noble courage.
He had carefully prepared his speech—double-shotted his
guns—and given directions as to the way in which my
lord was to be received ; but as it turned out his calculations were entirely upset, and the introduction was of the
most informal description.

My lord and myself were nearly an hour early, and
taking advantage of the familiar footing on which I stood
with the household, I had ushered him somewhat un-
ceremoniously into the captain's sanctum. It was a fine,
warm day, and the window looking out on the garden was
thrown open. The captain, divested of his coat, which
lay beside him, was seated at the table, stealing, as I suspect, Dutch courage from the case-bottle at his elbow,

and resting, as was usual with him, his wooden leg upon
a chair. As we came in he hastily drew himself bolt upright, his face very red, and showing unmistakable signs
of consternation. But I will do him the justice to say
his perturbation passed very quickly, and when he had
gained his feet he came forward dressed as he was, and
held out his hand with a heroic squareness of figure.

"I fought the crew of a French privateer in my nightshirt once, my lord."

"And I am sure you gave them a sound drubbing too."

"I gave them as warm a welcome as they could have
wished, but 'tis not the way I like to go into action."

"We will imagine," says my lord, taking his hand, "that
the drums have beaten to quarters, if you please, and the
colours are flying, but I hope you will treat me as a friend."

"God forbid that I should treat you as anything else.
It is allowable to hate the French, though I allow there
are fine fellows among them, but I have done with fighting for the rest of my life. I am glad to see your lordship under my roof."

There was never a finer gentleman in the world, and
though his language smacked of the salt water and his
headlong life, his manner was altogether perfect, clothing
him with his natural character—frank, generous, and full
of fitting self-respect and simple dignity. My lord's
manner, though altogether different, being stately and
ceremonious, was not more admirable, and if upon occasion there broke forth a certain rough hilarity in the captain's conversation, it was only a strong breeze that
stirred you to congenial laughter. You never for a moment forgot that he was a gentleman in that full and

splendid sense which implies a simple heart, a noble sense of baseness, a generous sympathy, and unfailing loyalty to truth.

I must own that I had looked forward with some anxiety to this meeting between Lord Heronford and the captain, for I knew how fastidious my lord always was, and I knew how closely the result might affect my own future. But in a very few minutes my fears were laid completely at rest. Without the least thought to impress his visitor favourably, or draw him from the cold reserve he generally maintained, the captain won my lord's sympathy completely, and inspired him with a real interest. To me who knew Lord Heronford intimately that would not appear an easy thing to do, for his mind had been so warped and narrowed by his secluded life that few things touched him with pleasure, and though proud beyond reason he had become as shy and diffident as a young girl in the presence of strangers. It may seem a curious thing to say this of one who had seen so much of the great world and taken so large a part in its follies and gaiety, but there were in my lord two men and two natures so different that they never coalesced, and so distinct that they were the antipodes of each other. For the most part the one was now only a memory; the other was the kind, retiring master with whom I spent my life.

In a very short time my lord was completely at his ease; I could see that he was willing to draw his host out, which was never a difficult thing to do. Once you carried the captain back to the quarter-deck he forgot everything else; the fighting blood of the old seaman mounted to his brain, he seemed to hear the thunder of the broadsides, the ringing cheer of boarders, and the call of his old comrades from their places of renown. He never wearied in relating that splendid history of thirty years with its fine, heroic passages, when England was at war with all the world and kept her right hand firm on her goodly heritage, the sea. I had often heard his story myself, but it was new to my lord, to whom it came like the salt, quickening breath of ocean. The captain had forgotten his shirt sleeves and his blue coat lying beside him ; he had forgotten his forebodings, everything but the look of interest on my lord's face and the memories that had been awakened.

" By heaven, you are right, my Lord Heronford. Rodney is the finest fellow in the world—a hero every inch of him from keel to truck. I have sailed with him myself, and should know him if ever man knew another. It was a sight worth seeing how he took us into action with the wind blowing half a gale from the south'ard—sixteen ships of the line and half the men down with the scurvy. Upon my honour, my lord, this useless timber leg of mine gets up and walks when I think of the way that gallant fellow (God bless him !) sailed his ship that Wednesday morning, and came up on the starboard side of the French Admiral with a rousing English cheer."

" It must have been a fine sight," says my lord.

"There never was such another in the world. Here," cries the captain, rising to his feet and breaking a piece off the stem of his churchwarden, " here was the *Terrible*, Captain Jennings—Daddy Jennings we used to call him till he was drowned off the Goodwins, but a good man and a fine fellow always—and here was the *Hecate* coming up with her foremast gone by the board."

I need not follow the gallant old gentleman through the details of this glorious day, but when he had finished the churchwarden had lost its stem, and the fragments laid upon the table had changed their position a hundred times with the varying fortunes of the fight. In his excitement he had risen to his feet, his face glowing, his blue eyes gleaming with enthusiasm. The panorama of that heroic sea-fight lay before him; he was standing again on his own quarter-deck, and his heart was filled with the clamorous call of battle. At such times he needed only a sympathetic listener, and having now no doubt that he had such an audience in my lord I slipped quietly out and left them alone together. I was anxious that my lord should not be restrained by my presence in any communication he might see fit to make, and what, perhaps, was more to the purpose, I had seen through the open window a dainty figure in white crossing the bridge and passing up the lane.

When I came out Victory was standing hesitating at the gate.

"Jack!" she cried.

I came down through the laurels and held out both my hands.

"Oh, Jack! what have you done?"

"I have brought my lord to see my dear sweetheart, as I promised. That is all."

"I saw you coming across the sands. I knew my father did not expect you for an hour, and I am sure he was ——"

"My dear," I said, seeing now what troubled her, "you can hear the thunder of the guns through the window yonder. The famous blue coat is nailed to the main-mast, and Lord Heronford is watching the fight off Finisterre. They have forgotten you and me."

"You are sure Lord Heronford will not care?"

"Not the very least in the world. There is not a gentleman in England like the captain."

"I am sure there is not, and for that reason—but you do not understand."

"Only a woman can understand."

"Do you think——"

"I think Lord Heronford will say there is no rose in the garden like the roses on your lips, and that John Cassilis has had more luck than he deserves in this world."

"He may not see with your foolish eyes, Jack."

"I would have him see with his own. Come and hear what he will say, Victory."

I did not then think how formidable this meeting must have seemed to my dear love, or with how much trepidation she had looked forward to this interview, but she placed her hand in mine without a word, and we went into the house together.

My lord sat in his chair in the attitude in which I had left him, and the captain, who had not yet finished his narrative, had just swept the fragments of the church-warden into a heap, which I suppose represented the conclusion of the engagement.

"'Twas a good day's work," the captain was saying, "and deserved the thanks of Parliament—nine ships of the line brought into Plymouth Sound——"

My lord rose and came forward, holding out his hand.

"I need not ask your name, my dear," he said in his

grave, friendly way, " I have heard it so often that we are friends already—if you will permit me to be your friend."

From that moment I had no fears regarding the result, if at any time I had doubted. I could now understand how my lord had been so great a favourite in his younger days, and with what art he had won so many hearts and gained so many friends. Though I knew him so intimately, I had never yet seen the same gentle and winning courtesy in his manner, the same gracious openness and absence of reserve. It was done without an effort ; it was quite natural and spontaneous ; and if it surprised me, who knew him so well, it overcame my dear mistress, who was quite unprepared for a reception so frank and unceremonious. But, indeed, it was not wonderful after all. Looking back across that long stretch of time and changing fortunes, after many happy years, I can still see my dear love bowing before my lord with the modest roses on her cheeks, clad in the beauty of her youth and innocence, a picture still fresh and glowing. What heart could have failed to respond to that magic witchery ? Who would not have yielded at the first summons and laid their hearts at her feet ? Certainly my lord was entirely captured and yielded at the first word.

CHAPTER IX

ONE morning Transome, the bailiff, and myself rode over to Fareham on some business connected with the estate—I think chiefly to see my lord's attorney regarding a mortgage, as to which some difficulty had arisen. At any rate, the matter was one of some importance and required immediate attention, and I was anxious that it should be settled without delay, for Lord Heronford was the worst man of business in the world, and now generally left these things in my hands.

When I got to Fareham I found a great stir of people in the streets, it being market day, and Mr. Stone, the attorney, so busy that it was some time before we had satisfactorily finished the business on which I had come, if it was satisfactorily finished, as to which my memory is not clear. At any rate, I had a long interview with the little man in a back office overlooking a yard that was full of country life, and no doubt lost my temper over the meaningless forms and unending delays which seem incidental and natural to our English law. Mr. Stone was quite an honest man for an attorney—I think there are more rogues in that profession than elsewhere—and had managed the Heronford business so long as I remember. If his advice had been followed upon many occasions my own labours would have been less difficult, but his assistance was most frequently sought after the step had been taken, and it was necessary to provide for the consequences.

He had been good enough more than once to tell me in his dry, caustic manner that it was to be regretted I had not been at Lord Heronford's elbow twenty years before, and that for one who bore the name of Cassilis I had some faint ideas of business. But we were always on quite friendly terms, and I have no doubt he preferred to transact matters of this kind with me to dealing with my lord, who usually flung into a passion and ended the interview abruptly.

Whatever the business was on which I had come that was at length settled, and he was gathering up the papers. As he tied them he looked up at me under his brows as you have seen an attorney do.

"I have always found you a sensible man, Mr. Cassilis. I can speak plainly with you?"

"I hope I have merited your good opinion," I said. "I do not object to plain speech."

"'Tis the short way—the safe way. What I have to say is for your ears alone and altogether outside our business."

I prepared myself to listen to him patiently.

"I do not know how intimately you are acquainted with Lord Heronford's affairs—I mean his private history before he succeeded to the title."

"I know nothing, Mr. Stone," I said with some heat; "I desire to know nothing."

"That is exactly my own position, sir; I have too many concerns already to be troubled much by curiosity, but ——"

"Is it necessary to pursue the subject?"

"I hope the necessity may never arise. I accept the assurance that you know nothing and have heard nothing —I am right in going so far?—that would be likely to cause him any uneasiness in the present or fear in the future. I am now speaking with more freedom than I am in the habit of using, but I trust you implicitly, and have some confidence in your judgment. The stories which travelled to Fareham years ago, magnified I have no doubt by rumour, were the idle tales that follow a foolish young man of the town, intrigue, debt, drink, play—wasted wealth and wasted hours—but nothing dishonourable, disgraceful, or—criminal."

"I cannot discuss the matter, sir, for it is impossible."

"Pardon me, I am afraid we must, and I can only deal with it in my own way. I remember Lord Heronford in his youth. I have seen few handsomer young men, with fine high spirits and an unfailing fund of gaiety, but he was ridden at the first with too tight a curb, and perhaps there was something in the blood—pardon me, I have the highest regard for his lordship. I must own, however, that after he returned to Heronford upon the death of his father, I was surprised beyond measure at the change that had taken place in him. It was not the same man; I should not have recognised him."

"Time changes most men. Even we do not grow younger."

"It was not that—not that. Mr. Cassilis, besides yourself there is no stranger living who has the honour and welfare of Heronford and its owner as much at heart as myself. Will you be plain with me, for such plainness may assist us all—does my lord live in fear of his brother?"

I looked at him in amazement.

" Fear ! " I cried.

" I see," he answered, " that my question surprises you, but I am perfectly serious.   Then they are still on terms of friendship ? "

" There have been differences between them," I said, " but only on matters perfectly within my knowledge. So far as I know my lord has no cause for fear."

" I hope that may prove to be the case.   It may be a mare's nest, but—I am not sure."

" What do you mean ? " I said, with a foreboding that I would not have expressed for the world.

" There is no man living," he went on quietly, " for whom I have less respect than for Mr. William Cassilis. Boy and man he, at least, has not altered, and the most that I can say for him is that he deserves the character that he bears—a bad man, Mr. Cassilis, a vicious man, an unfeeling and heartless man ; a man who would willingly injure his best friend."

" That supposes he possesses the power."

" That is the very point.   I have no ambition to possess a client in this gentleman ; I have no desire to see him in my office or in my house, nor to bow to him upon the public street.   Even an attorney may possess some self-respect, Mr. Cassilis.   But this gentleman was good enough to visit me some time since on a very curious business."

" I presume he was quite sober ? " I said with some scorn.

" Perfectly sober, and which is more to the point, perfectly serious.   He was sitting in that chair, Mr. Cassilis, when he opened his business, and I must say there was a fine directness in the way in which he dispensed with preliminaries. There was no preface or apology or expression of regret. A bad man, sir; a very bad man."

"May I ask what was his business?"

"Surely, that is exactly what I have set out to tell you. It is monstrous, incredible; I could hardly believe my ears. He was anxious to know how in the event of his brother, my lord, having committed a felony he would stand in relation to the title and the estates."

"A felony!" I cried, rising to my feet in astonishment. "You are not serious?"

"Oh, perfectly serious! I have used almost his very words, omitting only the unnecessary adjectives and interjections, without which no speech of his would be complete or perfect."

"And what was the offence with which he charged Lord Heronford?"

"Men in my profession at least acquire patience, Mr. Cassilis, but perhaps even the best of us have still something to learn to attain perfection. I may have been wanting in tact; I may have shown some disgust or indignation, I cannot say, but though I exercised all the art of which I am possessed, I could not draw him an inch toward committing himself. He merely wanted an answer to his question and refused to move beyond this."

"You answered his question?"

"Yes, I answered his question—" Mr. Stone rubbed his hands—"but I do not think it probable he will repeat the language I used or seek another interview with me for some time to come. It is not often that men of tape and wax have the pleasure of ordering a gentleman out of their house, but really it afforded me some satisfaction. A bad man, sir; a very dangerous man."

"A sot and a bully!" I cried indignantly.

"Admitted all the way, but such persons are usually troublesome, and especially—well, especially when they have found, or imagine they have found, something which may turn to their own advantage. Now suppose——"

"Mr. Stone, I will suppose nothing."

"Again admitted, but that is evidently not his brother's opinion. Very well. I have hesitated whether I should make this communication, but I have come to the conclusion that I owe a clear duty to Lord Heronford in this matter, and that the best way I could discharge this duty was to warn you. As yet there is no open trouble, nor, so far as you have learned, any private claim, but my experience tells me we shall hear more of this. The question then is, what steps you are to take to anticipate him, if any."

"I am so confident of my lord's rectitude and honour that I have no fear for the result, but I own I have not the courage to tell Lord Heronford the story you have told me. I have eaten his bread; I have lived in his house for years, and I have seen with my own eyes the generous kindness with which he has treated his brother, and born with his follies almost beyond endurance. No other man in the world would have done it—not one. It is incredible."

"That is merely a figure of speech—there is nothing incredible in human nature. But you have now been warned and placed upon your guard. As a member of

the family, so to speak, I know that you are concerned
for its honour and welfare, and should you see fit to consult me hereafter I shall be very willing to give you what
advice I can. I admit I do not like the complexion of
affairs, and it is possible, as I have said, we have not
heard the end."

I had taken up a very natural position during this interview, and in my attitude of indignant protest I gave
expression to my natural feelings, but behind and beyond
this sentiment of anger there was a feeling of dismay,
doubt, and foreboding as yet too vague to put into words.
My knowledge of Lord Heronford's character, from the
time I had first known him—his pride, that keeps most
men from meanness and wrong, his scrupulous honour
and veracity, his generous heart, cried out upon such a
charge as incredible and impossible. But there were many
things—trivial incidents, chance and vagrant words, that
I could not forget, and above all those unconscious con-
fessions to which I had been an unwilling listener, and
which had caused me so much pain. I had been driven
to the conclusion that there was a secret in my lord's life
—a secret with fear and terror at the heart of it—but
it had never occurred to me, nor could I now bring myself to believe, that this secret was of such a nature as his
brother indicated and supposed. It was likely, I had
thought, that he had done some rash and unconsidered
wrong, upon which he had meditated and brooded until
his nature, naturally sensitive, had been changed and
warped, and his conscience had been charged with a burden
too heavy for his pride and self-regard to support. But
that my lord—my kind, proud master—had at any time

been guilty of a crime was beyond belief, and though I was staggered and bewildered at what I had heard, I was yet clear and confident.

On one matter, however, I had expressed my real feeling to Mr. Stone—whatever the consequences, I could not bring myself to disclose to my lord the lawyer's confidences. There was nothing for me to do but to exercise a watchful vigilance, and to wait upon events which I had a dull presentiment were about to follow. Latterly, Will Cassilis had spent little time at Heronford, and when he appeared there it was with a sour, discontented look and an apparent desire to keep only his own company, which I had not regretted. For the most part he had, I learned, been staying with Mr. Weston at Langston, with whom he had long had a close friendship, and who was in every way fitted to be his intimate friend and congenial companion, for their tastes and pursuits were identical. His attitude toward myself had entirely changed; whereas formerly he was in the habit of treating me with a coarse and contemptuous pleasantry, now he took no pains to conceal his dislike or even some stronger feeling, and scarcely spoke to me when we met by accident. That I did not mind, but I could not now help thinking that his change toward myself was in some way connected with the wicked design he was harbouring. However, 'tis always better to have a bad man for an enemy than for a friend, since he is less likely to prove dangerous at arm's length, and I was quite contented that he should treat me in this way.

When I left Mr. Stone's office I returned to "The Little Green Man" where I had put up my horse, in-

tending to dine there, as I usually did before I returned
to Heronford. There was always a great charm for me in
the square at Fareham upon market days, in the activity,
varied life, and humours of that miniature world. I liked
to see the open red faces puckered into cautious shrewd-
ness or expanded in hilarity, and to listen to the babel that
rolled and swelled over the price of pigs or the points of
a horse. I touched a life that was for the most part remote and distant from my own, and felt a kindly sympathy
in a world from which chance and circumstances had
shut me out.

"The Little Green Man" was overflowing when I
came in, and I hardly ever remember when that benignant
and prosperous person had more guests under his roof. I
found a place at the table with some difficulty between
two neighbours who had a difference, and so left more
room between them than would otherwise have been the
case. What a continual uproar of boisterous, side-shak-
ing laughter ! What a clatter of knives and forks, and
what an endless succession of foaming tankards, the pledge
of good fellowship and loosener of tongues ! I own I like
to see men happy, contented and prosperous, and blessed
with a good appetite, and I enjoyed the spectacle almost
as a child enjoys a lively piece of acting in a theatre.

It consequently turned out that the afternoon was
growing when I went to look for Transome, whom I
found very comfortable in the bar, and after I had bidden
him see my horse brought round I went to the door,
where I stood watching the little busy groups now slowly
disappearing. I had already delayed too long and was
anxious to return home, for I remembered I had some

business to which it was necessary I should attend. Besides, Transome was in that condition in which men act with a judicial slowness of movement, and I was myself about to walk round to the stables, when I heard a sudden and startling clatter of flying hoofs at the upper end of the market square. Two horsemen came thundering down the street—one mounted on a strong, grey horse, and the other on a handsome bay—and both pulled up opposite the inn door with a reckless promptitude. I recognised them immediately I had seen them, and from the way that Mr. Cassilis sat in his saddle I could see that he had been drinking. He flung the reins on his horse's neck and slid heavily to the ground.

" Here, you——" he cried to me; " come and take my horse."

I made no answer, but stood looking at him quietly with some thought of returning into the house, for I had no desire for a public scene and perhaps a public quarrel, and I saw that he was quite prepared for either.

" Do you hear me, you——? " and he repeated the opprobrious epithet. " I mean to put an end to your fine airs, Mr. Secretary Cassilis."

" Try the horsewhip, Will," said Mr. Weston, who had by this time given his horse to the ostler; " try the horsewhip, and put a little movement into the legs of his reverence. There is nothing like the horsewhip."

" I'll take my own way to make him dance," says Will moodily. " Here, Tom, take my nag, for my man won't."

He let go the bridle and came up the steps to where I was standing, his face inflamed with passion and his eyes bloodshot. I felt that my position was a delicate one, for he was determined to push me into a quarrel, though at the same time I knew him sufficiently well to know that he would stop short of actual violence, for bully as he was, he was also a coward. But I was firm that if I answered him at all it would be with that soft answer which turns away wrath, and that nothing he might say would lead me into an angry altercation.

He came up close to me with his riding-whip held threateningly in his hand.

"What fool's errand brought you to Farcham?" he said.

"That is my business, Mr. Cassilis," I said, looking at him quietly and squarely. "We had better not continue this conversation at present."

"Tilly vally!" he cried contemptuously. "You are going to teach me manners next, damn me, and give me a lesson in etiquette. I am not to speak to his lordship, George!"

"Take his advice," said Mr. Weston. "Try the other way about."

"I have had enough of your fine words and high looks, and I am going to put up with them no longer. You think you are snug and warm and comfortable. But some fine morning you will waken up and find you have made a mistake. Go back to your damned books and make up your figures, for you are come to the end of your rope."

He had raised his voice in his drunken anger, for a knot of idlers had gathered round and were enjoying the quarrel in which we were engaged, though I am sure the sympathy was upon my side, for neither Mr. Weston nor Will Cassilis was a great favourite. I need hardly say that I did not enjoy the position in which I was placed, and I was now more than pleased to see my nag being brought round.

" We will not quarrel, Mr. Cassilis," I said. " With your permission I will ride home."

" You have my permission to ride to the devil."

I pushed quietly past him pleased at the self-restraint I had exercised, and walked leisurely down the steps. As I passed Mr. Weston, that gentleman wearing a contemptuous smile, tapped me on the shoulder with his heavy riding-whip. At the touch my blood that had been flowing with a cool and even pulse leapt in my veins, and the anger that I had hitherto kept in check now entirely overmastered me. I halted on the instant and turned to face him.

" A word with you, sir."

" What have you to say to me ? " I asked.

" Mr. Cassilis is not quite sober, but I am."

" I am sorry to think there is one of you sober," I said.

" Hey ! you had rather I was drunk too, you ———"

I will not write the word he used, but I had already heard it twice before within the last five minutes. Perhaps I should have been wiser to have taken no notice of the insult, but those considerations which had before restrained me were not now so pressing, and my temper was beyond my control. I only saw his mocking face and heard the disgraceful taunt, and almost without thinking of what I did I struck him with my closed hand fairly on the mouth. The blow was so violent that he went down like a log and lay at my feet for a minute without stirring. Then he gathered himself up and stood scowling at me, but the fight had all gone out of him.

"If you ever dare to address me again," I cried, "I will horsewhip you like the cur you are, and if you desire satisfaction you will know where to find me. Good-afternoon."

I turned upon my heel and made my way through the crowd of spectators, who respectfully made a path for me, and who seemed disappointed that our altercation had come to a termination so abrupt and ignominious. I thought I knew what Mr. Weston had desired to say, and I was not sorry to think I had prevented him from dragging into this vulgar brawl a subject which beyond all others was dear and sacred to me.

CHAPTER X

I HAD made up my mind to say nothing to Lord Heronford regarding what had occurred at Fareham, but by some means it came to his knowledge—probably through Transome—and he was very angry and indignant. I am not sure that he did not attach some blame to myself, though even when my blood had got time to cool I was at a loss to see how I could have acted otherwise than I had done, and felt that under the circumstances I had exercised some moderation and restraint. But while he only hinted his displeasure at my action, he declared that he would no longer tolerate his brother's conduct, and repeated with great bitterness that he should no longer make that house his home.

For the first time he took me to some extent into his confidence, and showed me how much he had suffered by his brother's conduct, which gave no sign or promise of amendment. Till this time he had never said one word to me upon the subject, nor, except upon the two occasions to which I have referred, had I ever heard one angry or passionate word pass between them—at least upon my lord's part. During all the years I had seen them together I had never heard his voice raised in anger or even in friendly remonstrance, but whether it was that his patience had now been tried to the point of breaking, or some new element had been introduced of which I knew nothing, he had suddenly become very hot and bitter. In this new state of affairs Madam Cassilis entirely sided with her younger brother. I could not remember the time when she had not inveighed against him and called upon my lord to prevent the disgrace his conduct brought upon the house of Heronford, and now, as usual when my lord at length set down his foot, she went over to the weaker side and took his part with acrimonious energy. There were some frequent and painful scenes between herself and my lord, though I was never present at any of them, and I have reason to believe that she frequently saw Mr. Will, and even gave him a lodging in the house without his brother's knowledge.

My own position was by no means an enviable one, for she showed me in a hundred ways that she attributed to me or to my influence the rupture which had taken place, and endeavoured to make me feel that I was now only tolerated as a dependant because I made myself useful. I am sure I should not have cared for that, since I was too long accustomed to indifference and contemptuous treatment, though never so openly displayed, but I knew that Lord Heronford was pained by these outbursts and was more than once on the point of interfering. Certainly at this time there was not a more divided or unhappy household in the world, and, but for the hopes I cherished and my love for my lord, I am sure I could not have continued to live there longer.

"I suppose there is light at the end of the passage," my lord would say wearily, "but it is a long journey in the dark—altogether in the dark. I have heard someone say a man's worst foes are those who sit at his own table and lie in his own bosom.   Not always—there is worse than they ——"

"I can think of none worse," I said, "if they are foes, but ——"

"But there is—worse—much worse.   A man may be his own deadly enemy.   The world thinks mine an enviable lot, John?"

"You would find many men to change places with you, my lord."

"And if they knew! if they knew!   You see how happy I am and how much there is to make me happy. And I cannot stir hand or foot; I am bound under the wheel, and it must go on grinding till—till I am ground out.   My father believed it was in the blood, and he may have been right—bad blood—tainted blood, seven centuries old—a noble retrospect.   Does a man make his own life, or has it already been made for him before he comes into the world at all?   I don't know, I cannot tell; but I know this—one false step leads a man either to hell or paradise—one false step taken in the folly and wildness of unripe youth.   I hope you may never know what it is to live under the shadow of sin through the best years of your manhood—sin—shame, and—fear."

"My lord," I cried, full of pity, "you know I love you like a son, as indeed I should, for you have been more than a father to me.   Can I help you?"

"There is no one can help me; I must stand alone— at least, not yet.   Some day you will hear everything, and, John—listen and promise—the world must not know—I should not rest in my grave if I thought the world knew.   And yet ——"

"Will you tell me one thing?" I said with sudden boldness; "I do not ask or desire to know more. Has your brother guessed or learned what you have now hinted at?"

He rose to his feet and looked at me with a white face. "You have some reason for asking that question," he said. "Tell me the truth—tell me everything. Has he spoken to you?"

"He has said nothing to me, but ——"

"To whom has he spoken? I can read it in your eyes—you have heard everything."

"I have heard nothing," I said.

"Then why did you ask the question? You would not ask without some cause."

"It is only that he now seems to act as though he had some claim upon you."

"Ah!" said my lord with a sigh of relief. "He would not spare me at whatever cost to myself, or to the honour of Heronford. I think—I hope, he does not know or I should have heard—a brother's help—a brother's sympathy. I have been a good brother to him."

"You have been at least an indulgent one."

"Could I be otherwise? What am I that I should judge him—I who was the rock, and am now only the broken wave? But he would not spare me."

I never forgot this conversation, not so much for what was said, though in that there was enough for thought, but for my lord's manner, which showed me how far he had drifted into the shoals of despair and wretchedness. In my own mind two things were now clear to me as noonday —the first that my lord had something to conceal, the revelation of which menaced him with disgrace and perhaps with ruin; the second, that whatever the secret might be his brother held the clue in his hands and was bent upon following it to complete discovery. I felt that I had not been entirely open and frank in the conversation which I have just narrated, but I felt also that I had some excuse. I could not bring myself to add to my lord's misery, and I saw that the relation of what I had learned from Mr. Stone at Fareham could do little good. I had, however, no doubt that a catastrophe was impending, vague and indefinite as yet, but shaping to fulfilment.

Nothing worthy of remark happened for some weeks, and, outwardly at least, we continued to lead the same dull and colourless life, unbroken by incident and undisturbed by change. It happened, however, during this very time that a serious affray, in which two lives had been lost, had broken out between the Revenue officers and the lawless free traders who lived round Carnforth and ran their cargoes of silk, lace, and spirits into the sheltered bay on the other side of the headlands. As long as I remember this trade had been carried on, and the deep-sea fishers had been accustomed to land their commodities with impunity, snapping their fingers at the law, and hardly waiting for the dark to come ashore. We had drunk their French brandy ourselves, and Madam Cassilis had worn their laces without question. Now, however, there was a cruiser off the coast and a sloop in Carnforth Bay, and the Preventive officers were continually on the alert upon the cliffs.

Captain Blythe had taken part in the quarrel with his headlong enthusiasm, and declared the coat he wore and the commission he carried compelled him to take the King's side and fight his enemies ashore and afloat, whether French, Spanish, or English. He had gained some ill-will by the attitude he had taken up, though he had done little more than talk and bluster, and I was afraid that some attempt at retaliation might be made either on himself or his household. This fear brought me very often to Carnforth, and I frequently stayed there till late at night, walking home in the broad moonlight, and gaining my bedchamber by the little hidden door in the west wing. I do not think anyone in Heronford, except perhaps Madam Cassilis, whose vigilance was lynx-eyed, knew anything regarding these nocturnal wanderings, but even she made no remark upon them. I own I liked that quiet moonlight walk with the soft shimmer of light in the throbbing sea, and silent cliffs, and undulating downs, and more than once I have lain down on the heath under the silver braid of stars with a thousand hopes and dreams flowing through my heart.

I remember that fateful night very well. I remember every trivial word and incident, and I shall never forget them while I remember anything. The captain and myself had sat talking later than usual, for the dog had been barking viciously during the evening, and we had thought we heard the sound of footsteps under the window. But whatever it might have been, nothing had happened, and about midnight I had set out on my way home.

What a night that was! The great orb of the moon hung over the tremulous expanse of sea; the vast depths of heaven were sown with stars; there was not a breath of wind, and the languid waves broke one by one, each with a separate note, on the shining beach.   I had crossed the sands of Carnforth Bay, taking my time as I went, and had now the heather and soft turf that carpeted the cliffs under my feet.   I was not anxious to get home—the beauty of the scene had laid hold upon me—and after a while I lay down in the shelter of a great boulder with my face to the sea and the soft stream of silver light that rained upon the water.   The music of the breaking waves came up from far below, and now and then from some-where on the downs I heard the bleat of wandering sheep.

The night was quite warm, and I sat here a good while, half dreaming, half waking, till I was hardly con-scious of the scene before me.

Then I suddenly became quite awake and sat up to listen, for I had distinctly heard the sound of voices in the soft, still air.   I was unwilling to expose myself to view, for the free traders had a bad reputation; and lift-ing myself cautiously till I had a clear view of the stretch of cliffs, I saw the outlines of the speakers about a hun-dred yards away.   When I first saw them they were standing apart, but it was altogether impossible for me either to hear the words which were spoken or to recog-nise the forms.   But I was sure of this—the voices that I had first heard were voices raised in anger.   The place where they stood was the highest point of the cliffs, and near the spot where the Grey Man's Path, of which I have already spoken, begins its tortuous and terrible descent.

They were standing quite close to the verge, and I was sure that from where they stood it was impossible for them to discover myself.   I never for a moment doubted they were either Revenue officers or Carnforth men, but in either case I was unwilling that I should be discovered here at this hour of the night; and I was about to return to the shelter of the boulder when the terrible tragedy occurred.

It seemed to me almost to take place in a moment—a moment of incredulous terror. They were still standing apart when I heard a voice raised with a throb of anger in it, and one of the two men stepped forward with his arm raised as if to strike a blow. Whether he struck I could not tell—upon my solemn oath I could not tell— and at the same instant the other stepped back as if to avoid the attack. There rose into the night a great ringing scream of fear and agony, and then—merciful God ! the man with his arm still raised stood alone upon the cliffs.

It was all over; the tragedy was completed. I had seen it all, and yet failed to realise it. I leaped to my feet unable to move or speak, and while I still stood fixed and fascinated, the murderer—if, indeed, he was a murderer—stepped to the extreme edge of the cliff. Then he threw up both his arms, and with a cry—rather with a scream which I shall never forget—he set off running, and was almost immediately lost to my view.

It hardly occurred to me till afterwards that I should have followed the fugitive, but for the moment I was so thrilled with horror and chilled by a blind unreasoning fear, due, I suppose, as much to the suddenness of the episode, as to the darkness, silence, and solitude, that I remained standing motionless for a considerable time. You can understand that, though you may never have experienced my feelings. It is not a little matter to be awakened in an instant out of a pleasant dream and find yourself standing face to face with a tragedy, grim with the issues of life and death, and a cry of agony ringing in your ears.

At least I found it so, and then hardly knowing what I did, but with the horror of it still clinging to me, I ran to the verge of the cliff and gazed down that dark and yawning gulf. I held my breath to listen as with a sort of instinct; I could hear nothing but the murmur of the sea and the occasional cry of the distant sheep. Then hardly trusting my voice I called aloud—once, twice— and listened with no hope of an answer. A minute passed filled with the beating of my heart as with the tolling of a minster bell. Surely I heard something, a cry, a moan, or was it only fancy? And then I called again, but only the sea throbbing in the silence answered me, and I knew that I had heard nothing.

There was a fascination in the spot and I could hardly drag myself away, halting, as I went, to listen, and turn- ing on my steps at every sound. I knew that I could do nothing; I felt that I could lend no help; and yet I was unwilling to quit the scene. Indeed, the wild thought occurred to me to make my way down the cliff, but I knew how arduous and dangerous that was even in the day- light, and at last I set out almost running for Heronford.

I found the gate in the sea wall open, though it was usually locked, and closing it after me, I came at last to the winter garden and so reached the angle of the west wing. It had now grown much darker, and I was about to push open my little door, when I heard the sound of footsteps, and saw a man carrying a lantern, and running at some speed, but stealthily, in the direction where I stood. I drew further into the shadow of the door till he came close to where I was, and then I leaped out.

"Who is that?" I cried, for I could not see his face.

He stopped short at the sound of my voice as though overcome by surprise, but made no answer.

I again repeated my question, but hardly had I spoken than I saw it was my lord, bareheaded and with a heavy cloak about his shoulders.

"My lord!" I cried in astonishment.

"Yes, it is I. My God! You have heard it too."

"Heard what?"

"That awful cry. I cannot get it out of my ears. It has been ringing in them for half an hour. It was my brother's voice, John."

"I hope to God it was not."

"There was murder in the voice. You have heard it too?"

"My lord, I saw it all."

The lantern fell from his hand with a crash to the ground; he staggered forward and caught me by the shoulder. Never in my life had I seen him so agitated. His breath came in deep, swift respirations and his hands were trembling.

"You! what did you see? Tell me what you saw."

I told him briefly all that I had witnessed and as clearly as my own agitation would permit. When I had finished he dropped his hand from my shoulder.

"Then you could not see the faces? You did not recognise the voice?"

"I could see nothing more than I have told you. I am sorry that I could not now."

" He cannot hide his crime—it was an awful deed. But perhaps he did not strike; perhaps he did not even intend to strike.   You could not see that."

" I think he did not, but I am not sure."

" God knows that, but it was a sudden, awful death. And he was a bad man, John; my brother was a wicked man, cut off in his sins.   But he was my brother."

" I do not think it was his voice I heard," I said.

" I know it was; I heard it here; I shall never forget it.   He had wronged and tortured some poor soul past endurance and—but he was my brother.   We must find his body, John.   There is no doubt—none."

" If you think that I will take the servants," I said; " you must not come."

" I could not rest—though he did not love me he is calling for me now.   Listen !   Do you hear him calling ? "

" My lord, this will not do," I said firmly.   " Mr. William Cassilis is still a living man and ——"

" I am a dreamer dreaming dreams.   Come with me and you will see."

Before I could answer him he set out almost running down the path, and I, filled with amazement, for I had not yet had time to think, followed him closely.   If I thought at all I believed he was the victim of a terrible hallucination, for I could not believe that at this distance he had heard the cry that had so thrilled myself.   And yet it was, after all, possible that the voice was that of William Cassilis—nay, the more I considered it there seemed something familiar in the sound, until I brought my mind to believe that I had recognised the tone.

As we went my lord never spoke a word to me, but I

could hear him breathing heavily in front of me, pausing now and again as though to listen, and his face as white as the face of death. But I asked myself, What could we do? What assistance could we render? What discovery even could we make? Even at dead water at this point it was impossible to reach the foot of the cliffs but by a boat or by the Grey Man's Path, and I never for a moment thought that either my lord or myself would essay this perilous route at this hour that was darkening toward the dawn.

I could not tell what he had in his mind, but he went on silently and quickly, and at length stopped on the very spot where the fatal quarrel had taken place. He turned round and waited till I came up, for I had fallen a little behind.

"It was here, I think." He spoke in a voice that was little more than a raised whisper.

"Just where you stand," I answered. "He slipped back with his arms raised and fell over there."

He shivered a little, and then stepped forward till his feet rested on the dizzy brink, and I involuntarily moved forward to catch him. But he waved me back with his hand.

"Listen! Can you hear anything?"

We both stood perfectly still.

Then I answered, "Nothing."

"Nothing, and I can see nothing, but he is lying below there. I must go down to him. The path leads past this very spot where we are standing. I remember it when—when we were boys."

"My lord," I said, now thoroughly alarmed, "you

must and will do nothing of the kind. It is madness to think of it. Before you had gone a dozen yards you would have made your last step. I know the path and I know its danger."

" You do not understand. I care nothing for danger."

" I understand this, that I will not let you go. My love gives me the right to prevent you."

" There is nothing will prevent me. I should never rest again."

I saw that he was terribly in earnest—so firmly fixed and resolved in his purpose that it would be impossible for me either to restrain him or dissuade him from his mad attempt, and almost without thinking what I did I cried out passionately —

" If anyone goes I shall go. I am sure that I could do it, but for you it is certain death—that is, if either of us need go, but ——"

" I must find him," he wailed. " He must not lie bruised and mangled. I should go mad to think of it."

" Then you must wait here till I return. If the body can be found I shall find it."

He sat down upon a boulder and wiped his white face with a handkerchief.

" You will not be long, John. Perhaps—he may still be alive."

" I shall not be long," I answered. " Do not move till I return."

In the long and varied history of my life I can remember no scene like this. It was only when I had set my feet on that narrow, broken path that ran zigzag along the black and frowning cliffs, and looked down into the depths below, that I realised fully the perils of my task. The moon had disappeared and the stars were dying one by one, while the cold morning wind had risen and the first faint silver streak of dawn was lightening in the east. Below me was the hollow roar of the sea breaking on the jagged rocks ; round me rose the startled sea-mews fluttering with angry wings. Here and there I seemed to hang on the air without foothold or room to stir, the path broken and terminating at my feet. Once or twice looking down into that black depth I grew so giddy that the cliff seemed to sway with me, and I clung with a cold, sickening terror at my heart.

But this was hardly the worst—there were other terrors fiercer and more turbulent than these, terrors begotten in my own mind and created, as I now know, by my own imagination. The hundred legends of my youth took form and shape, and there, on that awful path, the ghosts of Heronford rose mocking round me with their eyes and voices. The two brothers of that fratricidal story whispered the tale of that old crime in my ears, and whispered —it was too terrible for thought—that the crime was alive again under the stars, and cried blood-guiltily from the earth. And even at that moment—I do not ask for your belief—I heard the clink-clank of a horse's hoofs ringing on the rock behind me—clink-clank—I could hear the steps behind me and the stones go rolling into the chasm below as the iron struck them. I could have cried out I was so full of panic, and I would have given the world to turn my head but dared not.

I shall never know how that journey was accomplished, but at length I stood at the foot of the cliffs, where there was a narrow fringe of rock and sand covered by tangled sea-weed, and wiped the cold perspiration from my forehead. I was for the moment too weak to prosecute my search, and sat down for a while to recover. The dawn was growing clearer and broader, and I could now see the line of coast lifting through the greyness of the morning. It was very cold—that early cold that takes away one's courage—and I felt very miserable and depressed. But I knew with what anxiety my lord was waiting my return—at that moment I felt a traitor toward him—and I rose up to pursue my search.

I walked backward and forward a dozen times; I searched everywhere but I could find nothing. Certainly the body of the man had not fallen to the bottom; of that there was not the least doubt. It was possible that it might have been caught in its descent by some projecting crag, but I did not think it likely, and looking up that frowning bastion I could see nothing that would lead me to that couclusion. Yet, unless I had been dreaming— dreaming awake and with my eyes open—that must have happened or I should have found him here at my feet. It was altogether inexplicable; nothing suggested itself that would in any way account for his disappearance, and I could not think what I should say to my lord when I ascended.

All the time that I climbed up the path on my way back my thoughts were busy rather with the living than with the dead; I was beset by a host of suggestions and suspicions that made my master and benefactor the centre of a tragedy as terrible as any in the legendary annals of his house.

My lord had heard my footsteps as I ascended and was waiting for me at the head of the path.

"You have found him?" he cried. "He is dead?"

"I do not know," I answered. "There is no trace of the body anywhere. I have searched everywhere and could find nothing."

"You dare not trifle with me. You think I cannot bear to hear the truth. You were accustomed to speak the truth."

"I am speaking the sober truth. I cannot understand it, but there is not the slightest sign. I must have been dreaming."

"Good God! What a dream! I tell you, you have not searched. I can see him lying there with his up-braiding eyes wide open and his blood crying like the blood—I will go myself."

"Not one step," I cried, placing myself before him. "If you are not satisfied with what I have done—and I have done my best—we will bring the boat round and you can satisfy yourself. And, indeed, my lord, we have more than that to think of—we must consider——"

"What?" he cried.

"Who could have done this dreadful deed, and what was the cause of its doing."

"Ah! What, indeed? My heart has gone out of me. John, we will go home."

He suffered me to lead him home without showing any trace of that strong, insurgent excitement which had possessed him so short a time before, and appeared alto-gether listless and apathetic. He had changed so far in the course of an hour or two that instead of desiring to prosecute his search he showed the utmost reluctance to proceeding further, and it was only by a supreme effort that he at length consented to resume it.

But though we continued our labour the whole day we made no discovery; our search was entirely unproductive of results; and the matter appeared to me to become more and more deeply enshrouded in mystery.

In another direction also our enquiries were equally without result—of William Cassilis we could learn nothing. He had completely disappeared. He was seen in none of his old haunts, and none of his old friends who were accustomed to see him most frequently professed to know anything regarding him.

CHAPTER XI

MR. WILLIAM CASSILIS had disappeared as completely as if he had in reality been the victim of the tragedy which I have described in the last chapter. But if he had met his death upon the cliffs his body must unfailingly have been discovered, for there was no inch of ground that had not been thoroughly examined, and there was nothing found which yielded us the slightest clue or offered the merest indication. There was not even the trace of a struggle at that point upon the cliffs where I had seen the shadowy drama enacted. There was no trace of a footprint upon the virgin turf; not a stone that we could see had been overturned; no whisper of the secret could be won from the inviolate cliffs. In another direction also my investigation was barren of results. There was no one missing along the coast, a fact which could not well have been kept hidden for any length of time, and upon this particular night the Preventive men had been engaged upon a dangerous service on a distant part of the coast.

The matter was so completely involved in mystery that I could now form no opinion or theory, and had it not been for the strangeness of my lord's language and conduct in regard to it, I am certain I should not have dwelt upon the scene with the intensity and persistence which I did. But strive as I might *that* fastened upon me like a vice, and with a hideous and fertile suggestiveness poisoned all my waking thoughts. It lay in wait for me at every turn, it rose at every instant, and in the end so affected my free intercourse with him that I am not sure what was in my mind. But though these horrible suspicions attacked me with clamorous insistence I still clung loyally to my belief in his innocence, and though it may appear strange to say it I think I loved him better and with a deeper sympathy at this period than I had ever done before.

Though he did not utter a word of complaint, it was easy to see that he suffered beyond expression. His cheeks had grown wasted and haggard, his eyes dry and bright with want of sleep and the nervous fever that follows upon extreme wakefulness; he could not rest for a minute together in the same position, and flitted from occupation to occupation with a feverish aimlessness. One question was always upon his lips—"Is there any news?"—and I do not know whether he received the invariable answer with a feeling of relief or of despair. He wrote a good deal shut up in his own room that he sometimes used as a study, but I could form no idea of the subject of his thoughts, and though usually careless in these matters beyond the common he now carefully locked up his papers in the armoire of which he carried the key. I am not sure, however, that any one saw the change which had taken place in him but myself. In manner he was still the fine gentleman we had always known—courteous and considerate with his dependants, uncomplaining and easily satisfied, and bearing himself outwardly with his usual urbane dignity.

For a week I had carried on my fruitless and unavailing search, and had exhausted every means of enquiry within my reach; no one had seen or heard of Mr. William Cassilis, and the general opinion seemed to be that this was merely one of his frequent disappearances, and that he would return shortly a shade more disreputable and more bloated than he had left. I should add that in pursuing these enquiries I had been guarded in the extreme, and I was certain that besides Lord Heronford and myself no one knew what I had seen upon the cliffs, or had any idea of what had taken place there. For several reasons I shrank from making this disclosure; it could not help me in my investigations, and—for this was after all the real reason that I did not even confess to myself—it might entail consequences that I did not dare to contemplate. I felt certain that my early suspicions were shut up in my own breast, and that I alone had any grounds for forming them.

Even during my visits to Carnforth I had been as reserved as elsewhere, and if Victory had seen anything in my manner—I am certain the captain did not—she made no remark upon it, for which I was thankful at the time. But here also I had another cause for anxiety. Mr. Weston, who for some time had ceased in his attentions, had begun to renew his visits with a frequency that gave me cause for alarm, and seemed to have won over the captain by a display of good nature and hilarity which he could sometimes assume. He could tell a very good story with a natural turn of humour, and when he cared to hide his coarseness had the art of proving a very entertaining companion. I felt that neither Victory nor her father had any suspicion of his real character, and my own pride prevented me from saying anything to the detriment of one whom I looked upon as a possible rival.   It was not that I doubted the faith and affection of my sweetheart—that I never did—but I felt that he disliked and hated me, and took no pains to conceal his feelings, and in a thousand little ways slighted or ignored me.   In any other place or time I should not have borne with this treatment, but here, where it was a hundredfold more intolerable, I had not the means or the power to resent it without provoking an open quarrel.   There was no apparent deliberateness in these petty slights and insults; they seemed spontaneous and natural, and the free outcome of that superiority with which he assumed to regard me.

Yet, notwithstanding, I knew that he acted upon a set purpose, and knowing the position which I occupied, imagined that contempt was the best weapon he could use against me.   I suppose I was too proud to remark upon it, but it pained me to think that Victory should have stood by and showed no indignation or perhaps a certain indulgent tolerance.   But at that time I knew little of the working of a woman's mind, or of those subtle feminine arguments by which a woman's heart can justify her conduct in aiding those whom she may love. She could not fail to read wonder and remonstrance in my face, but only once she spoke to me of her visitor.

"I am going to school with Mr. Weston, Jack, and hope to learn a great many useful lessons before we have done.   He knows so much and is not nearly so stupid as you imagine.   When he has completed my education I shall be able to tell you ——"

"What, Victory?"

"Some things you would very much like to know."

And with that I had to be content.

This was the third evening I found Mr. Weston installed at Carnforth. I found his horse tied at the gate when I came up and himself lolling in the captain's chair with a churchwarden in his hand, and a bottle of port almost empty before him. When I entered there was an almost imperceptible halt of embarrassment, and I thought for a moment that I had been the subject of the conversation, especially as I did not see Victory in the room. But her voice was the first to welcome me from where she was seated in the embrasure of the window and quite hidden by the drapery of the curtains.

"Sit down quietly, Jack, and do not interrupt the story. My father and Mr. Weston are seeing ghosts, and you will break the charm."

The captain gave me his hand silently and with a rather shamefaced look on his honest countenance, and again turned uneasily to his visitor, who sat on his chair and looked at me darkly.

"Oh! Mr. Cassilis may as well hear the history, perhaps 'twill interest him. You see," Mr. Weston went on, "his name was Steen—Jan van Steen, and he had lived with the devil so long that they were a good deal more than speaking acquaintances. And the devil took care of him, as the devil always does, Mr. Cassilis—very good care. For fifteen years his lugger ran her cargo as regularly as a mail-coach, and Van Steen's dollars would almost have satisfied a Jew. But he was voracious, insatiable, a perfect leech. The more ankers of Nantes that he ran ashore

the more he wanted to run, and he came to think his calling as lawful as a parson's, and a good deal more useful.
He grew crazy on that head, and he worked his men like
so many negroes. Worked them? I should think he did,
but only with his eye and his hand, and never a word did
he speak from one year's end to the other. For ten years
I don't think there was a word spoken on board the *Frau
of Haarlem*, but Jan van Steen's eye was worth all the
oaths that were ever sworn. His men trembled before it
open and shut, and used to declare that the devil was plain
to be seen when he looked at them. One man went overboard, another had his throat cut, a third was found
strangled in his berth; but the devil was a silent devil,
and nobody cried out over the mystery. When a man
once entered that vessel he never left her again—alive at
any rate—and there never was a crew that grumbled less
and worked harder. Oh! Jan van Steen was a rare
captain.

" Now I should tell you that Jan, besides the devil, had
one friend—an excellent friend, as silent as himself and
quite as fond of the brandy they ran ashore. The year
out and in they drank and played cards together, sitting
in the little cabin with never a word between them, and
what the stakes were nobody ever knew more than myself.
But while Jan grew thinner and more ghastly the mate
grew fatter and rosier, and the crew began to think the
dollars were changing hands, but they couldn't tell with
any certainty. No man dared to look through the sky-
light or listen at the door, but the ship sailed, and the
players played, and the devil was sitting by them all the
time. Well, things might have gone on in the same way

still, but the mate said something Jan did not care to hear, and no man dared to cross Van Steen twice.

" They were lying at the time in Fairford Bay, an ill-named, awful spot, with a narrow path up the cliffs and the devil of a sea among the breakers, where the tide runs like a mill-race. That night Jan and the mate had business on the cliffs—what their business was no one knew but themselves, and Jan had business the mate knew nothing about. The crew saw them landing in the cove and going up the cliffs together, the mate first with a bag upon his back, and Jan behind with his head sunk between his shoulders, and his cap drawn down over his eyes. I am the only one who knows what happened there, Mr. Cassilis, and I don't ask you to believe me unless you like.

" When they got to the top of the cliffs they were both tired and sat down to rest, for it is a stiff climb and the mate had been carrying a heavy load. They didn't speak a word to each other, but the mate was whistling all the time, for, as it turned out, he had had the best of the bargain—very much the best of the bargain. Jan eyed him evilly, but the mate did not care, for he had either grown accustomed to his look or had something in him of the same nature himself, though with more humour in it. I don't know how long they sat, but at last the mate got up and lifted the bundle upon his back.

" ' It has come to good-bye, shipmate,' he said. ' We have sailed together for a long spell.'

" ' Ten years and better,' Jan groaned.

" ' Better and worse; I am the better, you are the worse. But we have had a merry time.'

" ' I am a beggar.'

" ' You have the ship and the crew; I have the dollars. That is all. All's not gone by the board yet. Put to sea again, get a few more of these shining boys together, and I'll come and sail with you. Ugh, we have had a fine time, you and I.'

" Then the devil spoke in Jan van Steen's ear and he got up.

" ' We must shake hands before we part at any rate.'

" The mate grew afraid of him and stepped back till one foot hung over the chasm.

" ' I don't like that black look, Jan van Steen. Don't come near me.'

" But Jan had made up his mind that he should not work for twenty years and die a beggar at the end of it. Before the mate could raise his hand Jan had taken him by the throat and squeezed the life out of him. His eyes started from his head, his black tongue lolled out of his mouth, and the choking rattle sounded in his throat. When Van Steen saw that he was dead he gave him a little shake, such as a terrier gives a rat, and flung him backward over the cliffs, crashing headlong to the rocks four hundred feet below. Jan straightened himself and wiped the perspiration from his brows. It was an ugly thing to do with the man he had lived with so long, but Jan was glad when it was done. The money was safe at any rate.

" Jan lifted the bundle where it had fallen, and walking back to the edge of the precipice looked down at the black spot lying on the rocks with two arms spread out like a cross. All at once he started back with a cry and dropped his bundle. He could hardly trust his eyes—*the thing was moving*. There was no doubt of it. His eyes were glued upon that awful object that writhed and twisted into a hundred fantastic shapes, and turned its white face and staring eyes continually toward him. Jan van Steen was no coward, but he shivered and covered his face with his hands. Then he looked again, and he saw that the mate had risen to his feet and was beckoning to him to come down. He even thought he could hear him calling to him —'Jan van Steen, Jan van Steen.' Jan resisted that awful invitation as long as he was able and then his fears got the better of him, and leaving his savings of twenty years lying there like so much dirt he began to go down. He was shaking so much that he could hardly draw one leg after another, and he hung back like a whipt boy, but every time he stopped he could hear 'Jan van Steen, Jan van Steen,' called by that awful voice.

" When he got to the bottom he walked straight to the spot where the thing was lying, and found that it lay lifeless and motionless. He had the courage left to turn it over, and he could not understand it at all—that shapeless, broken mass that had once been a man had surely never moved. There was no life there—there had been none from the moment he relaxed his hold on the cliffs above. Jan's eyes were not in the habit of playing him tricks like these and he was angry with himself.

" ' Der Teuffel!' cried Jan, invoking his best friend, ' I will soon settle you.'

" Then he found a deep, narrow gully in the rocks, a sort of natural grave, above the reach of the tide at high water, and without more ado he dragged the body here and thrust it deep into this ready-made sarcophagus. After that Jan was a busy man for half an hour. He collected a vast quantity of stones and piled them up upon the mate till the hole was quite filled up and they rose level with the top of the rocks. He thought he could never gather enough nor bury his old friend deep enough. The more the better; the heavier the better. And when he had finished he wiped his forehead and shook his head.

"'Please God, you will not rise out of that, my friend.'

"But you will see.

"When Jan came back to the boat where the men were waiting he did not expect they would ask him any questions, and when he threw his bundle into the stern-sheets, and sat down beside it, they pushed off and nobody said a word. This was what was always done, for Jan encouraged no familiarities; but after a while he began to think he must lay some ground to account for the mate's disappearance, and so he said carelessly —

"'You will have to go back for Mr. Munday in an hour, my lads.'

"The men looked at him in surprise, and one of them whistled under his breath, for he thought the skipper had been drinking. But none of them dared to contradict him.

"'Ay, ay, sir!' And then the man added, 'If you please, sir, Mr. Munday has come aboard half an hour ago.'

"Jan turned deadly sick for a moment and then he began to swear, a thing he never did, until the men thought he had taken leave of his senses altogether, and perhaps they were not so very far wrong. But Jan thought the men were attempting to trifle with him, and it looked very like it, for when they got to the lugger the mate was not to be found on board, and nobody knew anything about him. But the men were positive they had rowed him aboard before Captain van Steen had appeared, and upon the one side and the other no one knew very well what to think. Only Jan had thoughts of his own.

"But as to one thing he had made up his mind—nothing under the heavens would keep him another hour in Fairford Bay, and so they got the mainsail on the lugger and slid out past the surf into the dark, with a storm coming up into the hot night and the thunder already beginning to mutter and growl, with distant flakes of blue lightning to give it edge. Though they had a lee shore and a bad coast under them Jan did not care a straw. He wanted his cabin and his bottle, and the quiet of his own companionship. But he wanted what he was never to get again. The lamp was lighted, the case-bottle was set out, and Jan seated himself at the swinging table to look the events of the last hour in the face. At first he was not very comfortable, but by the time the bottle was half empty he was entirely himself again and had recovered his self-possession. He even dozed a little, but would waken with a start and look round him with a kind of expectation. Then he would rally himself on his fears.

"'Ho! ho!' he thought, 'and they rowed Tom Munday—honest Tom—aboard, did they? I think not, Tom. I have made you very comfortable in Fairford Bay with a stone blanket and pillow, and we'll meet at the resurrection, honest Tom.'

"After that, with a smile of satisfaction, he dozed again, and for the first time he confessed to himself now he was honestly frightened when he was told the mate

had been rowed to the lugger.   But he had discovered
that was impossible, and every minute and with every
plunge of the *Frau of Haarlem* he was getting further
from the spot.   He was rising to fetch another bottle
when he sank back into his chair with a gasp, and the
cold sweat stood out on his forehead in separate drops,
his lank black hair was lifted on end in his fright, and his
eyes bulged out from their sockets.   The mate had come
back.   There he sat as he had sat any time these ten
years past at the other side of the table, shuffling the
cards and dealing them with his slow, deliberate habit.
He was not changed in the slightest, or if changed only
more sinister and diabolic.   First he dealt a card to himself,
then a card to Jan, and when he had exhausted the pack
he gathered up his cards and began to sort them in his
hand.   His eyes frightened Jan as much as anything
else.   There was such a look there and a yellow light in
them that scorched Jan's heart like a flame.   And the
worst of it was that Jan could not help looking at them.

"The gale was rising and the *Frau of Haarlem* went
staggering like a drunken man, but Jan never heeded.

"'Mein Gott!' he gasped at last, 'you are not dead
then.'

"'You are wrong, Mynheer van Steen,' said the mate,
still calmly arranging his cards.   'I am dead and my
soul is in hell these three hours.   But my body has come
back, and you have some reason for fear, Jan van Steen.'

"'In Heaven's name what do you want with me?'

"'You murdered your friend; you robbed the dead;
but you forgot that he might come back for his own.
And I have come back.'

"'Take everything then,' wailed the captain, 'and leave me in peace.'

"I shall never leave you again, Jan van Steen, as long as you live. We will play cards together while the sternpost and the keel of the *Frau of Haarlem* hold together, and after that we will go on playing to eternity. Oh! 'twill be a fine game for a poor stake, Jan.'

"'What stake?'

"'Your worthless soul, my friend. Now let me see what hand you hold.'

"After that night the *Frau of Haarlem* never was heard of again, but they say that somewhere the captain and his mate are still sitting in the lugger's cabin, and the infernal game goes on night and day, and the mate's eyes are always on Jan van Steen, who would like to die and cannot."

I must do Mr. Weston the justice to say that he told this grewsome story with a good deal of dramatic power and with excellent effect, and while he was speaking you could have heard a pin drop in the room. The captain, whose pipe had gone out, sat staring with his mouth open and his eyes fixed upon the speaker, and Victory had risen from her seat at the window and come forward into the room, where she stood motionless, her two hands resting upon the table. I was myself at once shocked and fascinated, but I could not help thinking that for some reason Mr. Weston had told this story very largely for my benefit. He had more than once addressed me directly, and at a particular point in his tale had looked at me with significant meaning. At the same time I did not believe that he knew anything—indeed, it never occurred to me that he could—regarding the tragedy I had myself witnessed or my own doubts regarding it, but I could not help wondering at the points in common between the two stories and the particular emphasis he laid upon them. It was probably, nay, certainly, a mere coincidence, and it was only my fears that could transform it into a parable. He himself had intensely enjoyed relating it, and appeared pleased at the effect he had created.

"With your leave," said the captain after a pause, during which he had been moving uneasily in his chair. "I won't believe a word of your story. 'Tis the most unnatural ghost ever I heard of."

" In what way does the gentleman displease you, sir ? "

"God bless me," cries the captain, "I don't mind a fine, healthy, natural spirit, do you see ? But a dead man without a soul is no more a ghost than I am a boatswain's mate. There, there, Victory, you had better see that Sparling brings up the supper."

"Mr. Weston has not frightened me," she said with some eagerness, "and I should like to hear the end."

"There is no more to tell that I know of," said Mr. Weston bluntly. "Mr. Cassilis agrees with me that the story is pretty complete as it stands."

"But the mate was not really dead, you know ? "

"On my conscience you credit me with too much knowledge. I think he must have been."

"That is a woman all the world over," said the captain. "She won't hear of me killing a grub on my roses."

"Van Steen deserved no sympathy at any rate," Weston said, "and I should know, for I dealt with him once or twice myself. By the way, Mr. Cassilis, has my friend Will made his appearance yet ? "

"Not so far as I know," I answered shortly.

"And you think he will?"

"I cannot tell.　I trust he may."

"Both Heronford and yourself were very fond of his brother."

"We should not care to hear that any misfortune had happened to him."

"It would break both your hearts if it did."

"You know more about Mr. Cassilis than either Lord Heronford or myself," I answered shortly, and merely in a little burst of temper.　But my words had an effect that I had not foreseen.　He turned suddenly upon me with a red and angry face, and quite forgetting where he was broke into a fine round oath.

"What do you mean, sir?"

"I mean," I answered, in no way put out, "that you were his friend and confidant and knew his secrets better than any man alive.　I should have thought if he had reasons for disappearing that you would have been in his confidence and could probably have told us his whereabouts without much difficulty."

"Oh! you thought that, did you?"

"Mr. Weston thinks he is dead, Mr. Cassilis," said Victory gravely.

"I am sure of it," he said firmly.

"Then you must have some reason for your knowledge."

"My reasons are my own.　There are people who gave my friend a bad name, but there may have been reasons for that, too.　But for my part I say that he was a better man than his brother or—others I could name. He gave himself no airs and affected no sanctimonious virtues, dam'me. He may have loved a bottle like other gentlemen. He could sing a good song, tell a good story, and perhaps loved a pretty face too well for his own comfort. But other people have done that, Mistress Victory. There was no harm in that."

"I have nothing to say about his character," I said with rising heat, "and I have never cared to discuss it."

"And now one must not, for Mr. Weston says—" Victory added and stopped.

"Mr. Cassilis knows he had enemies who would have liked very well to see him out of the way. When I left him he was going to see one of them, and nobody ever set eyes on him again."

"And that was the reason why you told us the story of Jan van Steen, Mr. Weston?" Victory said quietly.

"Upon my soul, I think it was," he cried with a laugh.

But whatever he knew more, whether much or little, and I had now begun to think he knew much more than he had said, it was impossible to draw him an inch further. He saw that he had awakened my curiosity and alarm, though I had done my best to conceal it, and he appeared for the present quite satisfied with this result.

Nor could I understand for what reason Victory had turned the conversation into this channel with quiet persistence, and showed so much anxiety with regard to the fate of Mr. William Cassilis. It was not, I was certain, merely feminine curiosity. Knowing her, or thinking I knew her, so well, I saw in her eyes and manner a deep and serious earnestness, and an anxiety for which I was unable to account. I own it set me thinking. Mr. Weston was my enemy, and as he very well knew, up to this time, my unsuccessful enemy. I had reason to know that he was unscrupulous, and in this case there were grave motives for his employing that vice to my disadvantage as his rival. Was it possible, I asked myself, that he was endeavouring to connect the disappearance of his friend with myself, or to suggest that I had aided Lord Heronford to accomplish a terrible and awful crime? His language, no doubt, had been vague and mysterious in the extreme, but his manner conveyed a thousand times more than his words. There was accusation almost in the way in which he had addressed me, and he had seemed to me to say that he could tell a great deal more if he pleased.

But here, I need not say, I felt no alarm; it was elsewhere that my dread began to take root and grow. What knowledge had he of the actual facts? Was William Cassilis really dead, and had Weston become possessed of the secret of which I had believed myself the sole depository? Jan van Steen and the murder on the cliffs! That story was no mere coincidence; it led straight to the scene that I had witnessed. And how had he learned? Had he also been an eye-witness, or—so nimble are our thoughts—had he himself taken part in the drama, and were his own the guilty hands? If that was the case it might be possible in this way to account for the disappearance of the body which had so staggered and perplexed me.

But then—in a word I was quite at sea, and on every side there were such perplexities and difficulties that I knew not what to think. Still there was no doubt that my enemy held the clue in his hands wherever it led, and Victory knew that as well as myself, from whatever quarter she had gained her knowledge. Could she have imagined, I asked myself, that having reason to hate my lord's brother, I had lent myself to a plot against him? To-night she had treated me with coolness, almost with coldness, and had listened to Weston's calumnious tale almost with eagerness.   She had spoken to Mr. Weston as though a confidence had been already established between them, and almost as if they shared a secret together.

Such feelings upon my part placed me altogether at a disadvantage, and while the squire of Langston plunged riotously through jest and anecdote, I sat in a moody silence nursing my own gloomy thoughts.   It had been my intention to overstay him, but he seemed certainly in no hurry to take his leave, and treated me rather as the intruder who forced myself upon an unwilling company, while he himself was the welcome and honoured guest. The captain was altogether unconscious that we were not the most harmonious party in the world.   He rallied me upon my reserve, told his old stories with his old unflagging spirit, and lighted his pipe that was always going out a hundred and odd times.   Jan van Steen had interested him a good deal more than William Cassilis, and for Mr. Weston he thought him an excellent companion and the best of good fellows.

But for my own part I could bear it no longer without exhibiting some of the annoyance which I felt, and, as it was already growing late, I rose up to take my departure. I was greatly surprised when Mr. Weston rose almost at the same moment and declared that it was time for him to be going.

"Mr. Cassilis has been asleep and dreaming about ghosts," he said without looking at me, "and, faith, I feel as if I might see them too. I'll see him over the running water at any rate."

While he looked for his riding-whip and bade the captain good-night hilariously Victory, who had all the night been in very high spirits, drew me a little aside in the most natural way and without attracting attention.

"I think I have found out something, Jack," she whispered. "Do not say anything, and remember above all things you must not quarrel, and, Jack—do not think foolish thoughts. Good-night, Mr. Weston, and a pleasant ride."

With that she disappeared.

Mr. Weston and myself went down the path together till we came to the gate where his horse was tied that had been standing for I don't know how many hours. He said nothing till he unhitched the reins, and then throwing them over his arm, and with his hand resting on the cropper of the saddle, spoke to me in a voice greatly altered and almost in what I might call his natural tone.

"I'm damned if I don't think myself a good Christian after all."

"I am glad," I said, "that you have done something to merit your own approval."

"Oh! you speak like a book of bishop's sermons. But I have shown that I can forgive my enemies at any rate."

"You mean, I suppose," I said temperately, "that you have forgiven me?"

He flung out a wild oath.

"You struck me on the face, Mr. Prim; you knocked

me down before I could defend myself, and there were fifty people there to see it done. You knew I couldn't call you out or treat you like a gentleman ; you knew that, by ———"

"Well, sir ? "

"Well, sir ! I put my affront in my pocket, for there was nothing else I could do, and ———"

"And you forgave the offender ? "

"Did I ? That will depend on how he conducts himself."

"Oh ! I thought you said you had forgiven him. We may as well be plain with one another, Mr. Weston, and I shall ask you to be more explicit. I cannot understand your language."

"I can speak plain enough when it serves my purpose. You must give up coming here—that is my first plain point."

"I cannot quarrel with its plainness. May I ask the reason for this extraordinary request ? "

"Because I will have it done."

"That may be quite satisfactory from your point of view, but I am afraid it is not equally satisfactory from mine. I fear it will require a stronger reason than that, Mr. Weston, to induce me to comply with your demand."

"I have held my tongue so far, but I think I can show you that I am able to back my will with something stronger. Murder is not a very nice thing, Mr. Cassilis."

"It is a very ugly thing, Mr. Weston," I answered calmly.

"Heronford and yourselves should know. You thought you were safe, and there was no one loved a fine night but yourselves. And Will Cassilis has gone on a visit to his friends, has he? A long visit, Mr. Cassilis, and an old friend; but you will think over what I have said and let me know when you have made up your mind. I should like to see you hanged very well, but at present there are some things I should like better. Don't take too long in thinking over it, for I haven't a great stock of patience. Good-night."

I did not attempt to detain him. He threw his leg over the saddle, gave the horse a cut with the whip, and left me standing looking after him in dismay and confusion. There was no doubt my enemy held my secret in his hands, and the story of Jan van Steen was only a parable.

CHAPTER XII

I HAD a suspicion which amounted to certainty as to who first set the rumour afloat, but it was not long before it was everywhere bruited that Lord Heronford had killed his brother. It was said that he had flung him over the cliffs, and such details were added as left no doubt in my mind that the original author of the story was in full possession of the facts. There were complaints, not indeed loud, but widespread, for men still spoke with reserve, that justice should long since have been placed on the track of the criminal; and it was declared that only Lord Heronford's position had hitherto prevented the necessary inquiry from taking place. Of course my lord had no opportunity of hearing what was said regarding him, but the same reticence was not observed with me, and this dreadful story met me at every turn.

But the care which I took to prevent my lord from hearing the gossip of the world was unavailing. One afternoon in my absence he received a letter, delivered by a stranger to one of the servants, and written in an unknown hand. Believing that it was upon a matter of mere business, with which he now never troubled, he laid it carelessly aside unopened to await my return, for such things at this time fell altogether upon my shoulders. It so happened that I had been to Fareham to see Mr. Stone and did not return till much later than usual. I found my lord sitting up for me in the Book Room, where a fire had been kindled, for the nights were growing chilly, and a single candle burning upon the table which surprised me, for my lord was like his father and loved plenty of light. Though there was a book upon his knee I do not think he had been reading, and he was glad to see me when I came in.

"You are a late traveller, John," he said without rising. "It must be nearly midnight."

"It went twelve as I came through the village," I answered. "I was unable to see Stone till five o'clock, and we had a good deal of business to discuss. The leases at Appleby expire at Martinmas. But I had hoped that you had gone to bed."

"I am a bad sleeper and was looking forward to a talk when you came back. But I daresay you are tired."

"Not in the slightest. There are only two or three accounts I want to verify before I forget them, and then I have finished. It will not take me more than a moment."

"There is no end to business in this world," said my lord with a sigh.

I went to the table for the purpose of lighting another candle when my eye fell upon the unopened letter lying among my papers where my lord had thrown it. I took it up and was about to open it when I caught sight of the superscription, and I stopped short.

"You have not read your correspondence," I said.

"No, I have other uses for my eyes, and it is generally troublesome. Who is the fellow now?"

"I do not know; the hand is quite strange to me."

"Trouble, I am certain. Let me hear what he says."

I broke the seal and opened the paper without any premonition of evil, but the moment I read the first line I saw that the accusation had come home at last, and that here in its full details was all the hideous story set out with cruel and vindictive circumstance. I stood holding the letter to the light with my eyes glued to the page, and all the while my mind was doing a twofold work. I could not help reading the words, and while I read I clearly followed their meaning, but all the time I was wondering in what way I could prevent my lord from knowing what I read. I knew that he was sitting watching me with a quiet, settled smile upon his face and without any foreboding of the truth; I could feel his eyes upon me. But strive how I might I could not conceal my agitation. I saw that my hands were shaking, and I knew that the blood had left my cheeks.

The moment that I had feared had come at last, and it was through me, who would have done anything to spare him, that he was to hear what the world was saying. The brutal words that I read rang in my ears and swam large before my eyes. I read them twice over, and then feeling that I must face the ordeal, flung the letter upon the table carelessly and reached for the books I wanted. But though he had said nothing he had noticed my agitation, and I had aroused his interest. He was evidently waiting for me to say something, but for my life I could not find a word to utter. I opened my book of accounts and appeared to be seeking for the figures that I wanted. He allowed me to go on until I seemed to have finished, without saying a word, and I began to think that perhaps the danger was past. But I was mistaken. When I had done and closed the book he rose in his chair.

"The letter seems to have given you annoyance," he said, "or perhaps as usual you wished to spare me pain. Are the duns knocking so loudly at the door?"

"It is nothing," I answered.

"Nothing! The writer has a good deal to say."

"The writer does not generally spare his reader," I answered, with an assumption of cheerfulness. "This has answered itself. Shall I tell you what Stone had to say about Appleby and the new leases?"

"Presently. But first let me see that unpleasant letter. Perhaps I should have opened it myself. You are doing too much for me, and one is only young once."

"I should prefer, my lord, that you did not read this letter."

"No! That is very like you, John. And yet you said it was of no importance."

"At least it requires no answer."

"Then I think I can bear it with equanimity. I should like to see it."

"My lord," I cried, taking a step forward, "I beseech you leave it in my hands. The villain who wrote it wished nothing better than it should come under your eyes. That was his object and I would not help him. Indeed you must not read it."

"I understand," he answered calmly; "I think I understand. But we cannot put off the evil day. It must come in spite of ourselves. I must see what the writer has to say concerning Richard, Lord Heronford."

" But, my lord ———"

" Why should you fear for a few words more or less ?
If they are true there is nothing here that can surprise me ;
if they are false they cannot injure me."

He rose from his chair and walked steadily to the table,
though I would have stopped him if I dared. He took up
the letter where I had thrown it, and sat down in the
seat I had quitted that he might take advantage of the light.
His thin white hands were quite firm and his face was unruffled only for the little frown between his eyes. Then he
began to read and I stood watching him, following his gaze
as he went down the page and turned the leaf. He read on
steadily without a pause until he came to the end, and I
almost breathed a sigh of relief when he had finished, so
great was the strain upon me. He laid down the letter
without a word and looked up in my face. I did not
speak but I am sure he knew all that I would have said.
But all the time I wondered at his apparently perfect
self-possession.

" I would give a good deal to know who is the writer.
It is a person of some education ; he writes with force
and clearness."

" He is a pitiful villain," I said indignantly.

" Ah ! Do not judge any man harshly or hastily ; he
probably believes that he writes the truth, and he has not
hurt me. But ———"

I stood silent.

" I would have spared you. And," my lord went on,
" he writes as if he had seen everything, heard everything,
knew everything. He speaks like a—a man's conscience.
It is a pretty tale he tells, John, and hangs together

wonderfully.   You have not heard anything like it before ? "

" My lord," I cried, now almost glad to get rid of my
secret, " I have heard it all before."

" And you did not tell me ? " he said reproachfully.
" That was not like my friend.   But it is as well to hear
what the world is saying."

" The world is a liar," I cried.   " Why should I carry
its slanders to your ears ? "

" Ah ! why indeed ? "

Lord Heronford began to walk up and down the room,
his face hidden from me in the shadows, but I could not
notice any signs of agitation about him.   There was certainly none in his voice.

" From whom did you first hear this—this wretched
story ? "

" The first hint came from Mr. Weston, of Langston,
but since then ——"

" Yes, he was my brother's friend, his close associate.   I
have sometimes wondered how much he knew, but I think
he does not know—everything.   Had he known he would
not have spared me—Good God ! I say me—so long.

" But," cried my lord, " I had almost forgotten.   You
yourself were on the cliffs and saw the deed.   Will you
accuse me too ? "

" If I had only seen," I cried.

" Then I should indeed have had a faithful witness.
Not even a suspicion, John ? "

" My dear lord," I groaned, " you see my heart.   Have
I not known you for years—the truest, tenderest friend,
the faithfulest brother, the kindest heart in all the world ?

Suspicion! I would ten thousand times rather doubt myself. I would not even have believed the witness of my eyes."

He seemed pleased with my warmth, and held out his hand, which was burning hot.

"It is a good thing for a man to know that he has one friend. I have one faithful friend at least."

"Lord Heronford needs no friend but himself," I said gravely. "My lord, you will help me to stamp out this accursed falsehood? It has begun to grow without cause, and the longer you remain passive the harder it will be to trace the first slanderer. I think, nay, I am sure, I can find the author, and if you will give me leave ——"

"You must do nothing rashly. Suppose—I say suppose—the story here were true?"

"My lord, for God's sake, do not speak like that."

"Ah! but we must look on every side."

"I could never suppose it true."

"I do not mean as the writer puts it—a deliberate crime brooded over for days, weeks, months, wrought out with cold and devilish malice—not that, thank God, not that, but something that might seem the same to the world, something reaching almost to the same black guilt, something almost as horrible, unnatural, and ghastly. I seem to myself to have been waiting patiently for this, and it has come at last. The writer, though he did not mean it, has proved himself my friend. It is better that you should hear the truth from me, for I know now that I am standing on the edge of the precipice."

"Tell me nothing," I said, "that gives you pain."

"Ah! though you loved me, I have seen your own

fear in your face, which you would not admit or acknowledge to yourself. It will give me ease to tell you. I thought I was strong, and I am only a child."

He sat down on the chair beside me and took up the letter in his hand.

"This cur says I feared and hated my brother. He was right and wrong, for he does not know me. I feared his passion, his selfish temper, his shameless disregard of my name and his, and I feared his knowledge of my own shame. But God knows I did not hate him. We were brothers, and he could not help himself, for he was only as he was made. You have yourself seen how he used to treat me, but you did not know the half. The half! You knew nothing."

"I have seen," I cried, "how much you have borne with him."

"Never as I should have borne—I confess my fault. But the story goes far back—for years and years of watchfulness—almost to my youth. There was a time in my life when I was mad as a man is mad when God has forsaken him and the fire of hell is consuming his heart. I had squandered the present, mortgaged the future, spent every farthing I could raise, till I was weighed down with a load of debts, and still my lusts were not satisfied, my passions were not slaked, and my soul still kept calling out for more. Good God! it is a fearful dream now. A madman panting after his hot sins. I recollected nothing but the fierce delights I hungered after. I forgot that I should some day have to pay the penalty. And I have paid it."

Alas! I could see that he was paying it now.

" There was a little while that my better angel fought with me, and I was almost saved—almost—and the end was worse than any man could guess. One wicked night did it all, and in the morning there were ten thousand pounds—a debt of honour—that I a pauper must pay. I was mad—I know I was mad—and never thought of what I did. To pay that debt I, who was a gentleman, sacrificed everything that should be dear to a man—love, honour, happiness, peace, good name. And before I knew where I was standing I had become a criminal for whom there was no retreat or safety. That was the fate of Richard Cassilis, the future Lord Heronford, at twenty-five. I do not wonder that you shrink from me."

" Before God, I pity you with all my heart."

" I wonder will you pity me when you know everything. There were reasons, there still are reasons, why I guarded that secret from the knowledge of the world—from my brother, from you—and hoped it should never be known till I was dead. I was not afraid to meet the punishment I deserved, but that punishment would not have fallen on myself alone. It was not even the honour of Heronford—who am I that I should talk of honour ?—but through my attainted blood the punishment would have fallen on one I love better than myself. It will not be long till you know what I mean—I cannot, I dare not, tell you now."

" Tell me nothing," I cried, with almost a glimmering of the true light breaking in on me at last and a new love surging in my heart, " tell me nothing you do not wish me to know."

" Ah, John ! you have been in the place of a son to me

—I have sometimes almost thought you were my son. But what would become of him if his father's crime were blazoned to the world ? Let the secret lie till I am carried yonder—I who am tired of living. In the escritoire you will find the full history and all the proofs complete—everything in order, not a document missing. As my executor you will have little trouble in proving your—my fault. The world will talk for ten days, and then all of Richard Cassilis and his sins will be forgotten."

He sat watching me with an unwavering look that took its steadfastness not from courage but from the weary resolution of hopelessness. The candle that now burned dimly with a long wick left his face in the shadow, but I could see his eyes.

" That was the first step," he went on after a long pause, " and it has led us here. My father knew, and it embittered his last days, but pride, not love, kept him silent, and I hoped that there was no other person had any suspicions of the truth. I think—I am sure—that was so for some years, and how the clue first came into my brother's hands I cannot tell. But I think it was by some foolish and reckless words I spoke on the night, you remember, before Mr. Earnshaw left Heronford. But he grasped the truth, and from that hour till he disappeared I had not one moment's rest or peace. I am sure he took a pleasure in torturing me, and a hundred times threatened to denounce me. But the proofs were not all to his hand, and he was not certain where his own interest lay if my sin was discovered. That was my only hope of safety, but I knew how treacherous and insincere that hope might prove.

"I was at the mercy of a drunken brawler, who was bound by no restraint of feeling, no pity, no honourable shame. I waited to hear my secret from Weston's—from a hundred lips; I listened for the sharpening of the sword of justice, and I trembled for the destruction of my hopes—my hope that I might die before it came. All the time I paid him for his silence he taunted me with my dishonour, and yet, as heaven is my witness, I never thought or dreamed that I should raise my hand against him. You remember the night upon the cliffs. I am not sure now whether he was alone, but he must have been watching and waiting for me—it was no wish or will of mine that I should meet him. I was patient with him beyond the endurance of a saint; I listened to his threats and reproaches, and I thought that I had no spirit left to stand up against him.

"But at last he threatened not me but another whom it was my duty to protect, and then for the first time he stung me to defence and retaliation. But not in that way—God knows not in that way. I spoke wildly, madly, and then I raised my arm to warn him—only to warn him, not to strike him. But it was in anger—almost in hatred. He was afraid of me, for he was always a coward; but he need not have feared me, for I would nor have hurt him for the world—not for the world. You saw it all—I see it still. He had forgotten where we were standing, and he stepped back to avoid the blow he feared. I could not believe that he was gone, but I knew it in a moment, and I know it now. I know what Cain felt when the blood of Abel cried to him from the ground. You do not speak to me."

"I was thinking, my lord," I said.

"Thinking?"

"I was thinking whether Mr. Weston was with his friend, or does he only guess."

"What does it matter now?"

"I think it matters a great deal. I find it very hard to put my thought in words, but I know now, indeed I always knew, there is no guilt upon your hands. 'Twas a terrible, a deplorable accident, but that is quite a different thing. And I am sure Mr. Weston could not have witnessed what I saw. My lord, I will fight him and the world with his own weapons. I am glad I know everything."

"And you do not shrink from me?"

"Neither I nor any honest man," I answered with emphasis. "Why should I or any man for what was no more your fault than it is my own? 'Tis your own kind heart and tender conscience that have distorted this lamentable deed till it has put on the face of guilt. 'Tis the mind that makes the guilty man; you could not help it; your hands are clean."

He caught eagerly and hopefully at the comfort in my words.

"You think that; indeed, you think that! But I should have borne with him for I was wiser, older, stronger; I should have yielded ——"

"Years ago," I answered, "you should have ceased to bear with him for he was not worthy of your kindness. This is a time when we can only afford to speak the truth even of the dead. He was a bad man, and he met a just end. It was the judgment of God."

" Upon us both," cried my lord bitterly.

" I think indeed upon both of you. But we cannot alter the past; regret is the amendment of fools, my lord; we must face the future. I shall speak only once of the secret that you have kept so long. I think now I dimly guess its nature, and, guessing that, I am certain your brother made no confidant, and shared his discovery with no accomplice. With his own hopes he would have feared to do it, and upon your death he may have looked either to destroying the proofs of which you have spoken or finding them defective. I think, I am sure, that secret is safe. For the other, my dear lord, we can both face the world bravely, for we know that you are innocent. Mr. Weston has guessed part of the truth—and how small a part—for he is keen-scented and quick, and would not hesitate to piece the lie to serve his purpose. Perhaps, indeed, he was waiting—I have it now," I went on with a sudden inspiration; " it was he who removed the body—I could swear it. That morning I saw the lugger that he sails in Carnforth Bay, and he has lain by till he can strike us both. I never guessed till now. But he has lain too long."

" Ah, John !" says my lord, " I like to see the light of battle in your eyes. It gives me courage."

" My lord, we will fight this fight together."

He held out his hand to me.

" If we did not stand together, who should ? " he said softly.

Our eyes spoke what neither of us dared to put into words.

" If we did not stand together, who should ? " he repeated, still holding my hand in his. "I hope some day you will altogether forgive me."

"We will try to bear the burden together," I said steadily, "and if I had known earlier ——"

"Ah! if I had had courage—you will find it all—the long, shameful story—locked up there, and you will then know how much I have suffered. I could not bear to read it again—I could not look at it. Take the key; it contains your birthright and my—legacy. You are now the proper guardian."

"Let us live as we have lived," I said. "It is better that we should wait."

"No, no," he cried, "I am already easier to know that you share my secret. It has crushed and broken me."

I took the key from his hand without any further protest. Then he did what he had never done before; he placed his two hands gently on my shoulders, and drawing me toward him kissed me twice upon the forehead. Neither of us spoke a word, but the silence was more eloquent than any words of ours. I could only see him dimly through the midst of my own tears.

"And now, John, will you help me to my room?"

I took up the candle without a word and gave him my arm. He placed his hand upon it, and I felt how it trembled. The fire had long since gone out, the room was full of quivering shadows, and the midnight silence caught up the faint echo of our footsteps as we moved to the door. That was concealed by a curtain of tapestry, and I was surprised to find that it lay slightly open, yet I was almost positive that I had closed it carefully after me. Though I did not suspect there might be any eavesdropper, I was annoyed at this, and was angry with myself that I had not been more careful. But I am sure my lord did not notice anything. I threw the door wide open and we paused for a moment on the threshold, the candle that I carried giving forth a faint, yellow light, and the long corridor with its many doors stretching before us from shadow into darkness. I do not quite know why I halted; it may have been merely instinct; it may have been the warning of a finer sense than any appreciated by the understanding. But I stopped and felt a little shiver of nervous apprehension too vague to put into words. I could not understand or explain it, but my mind had been excited and I was full of fear and foreboding. I listened with all my ears; I endeavoured to evoke some palpable form from the grey shadow and further gloom. My lord caught a glimpse of my irresolution.

"What is it, John?"

"Nothing," I answered. "Nothing—stay, did you hear that?"

I could have sworn I heard the sound of someone breathing softly, and a moment afterwards the fall of a footstep as of a person walking with great gentleness. Surely it could not have been merely fancy, and yet it might have been! It was long since I had felt in the same way before; not since the days when my boyish mind had played in my loneliness with the phantoms of the night, and the superstitious terrors of childhood had encircled me with their appalling reality. I thought I had entirely outgrown the feeling and that it had lost its hold upon me, but every moment I felt that horrible dread grow more and more acute. My lord caught my alarm, and we both stood listening.

" There is someone here," I whispered.

" I do not think there can be."

" I am sure of it. There it is. Listen."

Again I distinctly heard the sound of footsteps, and not very far from where we stood. The candle only illumined a few yards round us, and I held it up above my head as I advanced half a dozen paces forward.

" My God ! " I cried, " who is it ? "

My heart had almost stopped beating in my bosom. I stood paralyzed with terror. I could not have moved to have saved my life. My eyes were fixed with the paralysis of perfect fascination. At first it was a mere motionless shadow, only a little denser than the shadow in which it stood. A shape so vague and indistinct as hardly to be discerned. And then it seemed to grow out of the shadow and to gather form. And then before I knew—almost before I had time to realise the fact—a grey figure with a white face—I could only see the colour, it was so faint—moved rustling past me and disappeared into the darkness. It was hardly seen before it was gone, and yet to look back on it it seemed to have been there a lifetime. I could not resist the impulse. I heard my lord give a little gurgling groan behind me as I leaped forward in pursuit, but only the stout wood-work of the door against which I stumbled met my hands.

Then the awful sense of the supernatural, blind and unreasoning, again overcame me. The old story of my childhood flashed back upon me, and struck me with the cold horror of it. I turned round to where my lord was standing with a fixed terror in his eyes.

"You saw it too?" he gasped.

"Yes, yes!" I cried involuntarily, "the Grey Countess! My lord, I could not have believed ——"

"No, you did not see the face?"

"I did not. No."

"Ah! I knew you did not. My God! you did not. But he will not let me rest. He is following me from the grave."

"Who is following you?" I cried.

"Oh God! My brother has come back. It was his face and eyes."

"You fancy that, my lord."

He turned upon me almost with a certain fierceness, shaken as he was.

"Fancy! Did we both fancy that we saw that cold shadow rising out of nothing and passing into nothing? Are your own lips white, and are your own hands shaking for a mere fancy? We both saw it with our living eyes, but the message was for me alone. I am not mistaken; I know the truth. My brother has come back."

"I thought," I said doubtfully, "I heard the sound of footsteps. Perhaps we are both mistaken."

"Help me to my room, John. I am sure it was a message for me, and I must obey it."

Whether it was that my own nerves were shaken, or that I was impressed by his terror and the midnight silence of this remote and gloomy corridor had affected me, I cannot tell, but for the moment he almost won me over to his belief. When I felt his hand in my own, bathed with cold perspiration, and saw his white stricken face, I almost looked for the reappearance of the apparition. Once a door slammed in a distant part of the house, and I started so violently that the candle had almost fallen from my hands. Nor was it till we reached my lord's room, where there was a bright fire and the full, pleasant shine of two burning lamps, that I was able to shake off my horrible panic. My lord sank into a chair by the bedside, and I poured out for him a quantity of spirits in a glass, which I compelled him to drink. But I could see that my medicine failed to touch the deep spring where his malady had its rise ; his broken and diseased mind failed to respond to my words of encouragement, and nothing that I could say had any effect in rousing him. Now that the first sudden shock of fear was over he desired to be left alone, like a man altogether abandoned to his despair and beyond the reach of hope. And after I had done all that was in my power I left him unwillingly.

That night Lord Heronford had his second seizure.

CHAPTER XIII

THIS second stroke by which Lord Heronford was smitten was far more grave and serious than the first, and it was thought that he could not possibly recover. When the servant had entered his room in the morning he had found him lying close to the door quite unconscious of where he was, and only able to move his limbs as an infant does apparently without conscious volition. His powers of speech were completely paralysed, and he lay with his eyes wide open and meaningless. I had never seen anyone in this condition before, and I thought it a picture infinitely pitiful. At one sudden and swift step the man's mind had relapsed into the perfect blank of first childhood, and his look was that of the infant that looks with wonder that is hardly wonder on the scene of his new arrival. He recognised no one, but with the same vacant look his eyes followed us as we moved through the room. I had immediately sent post for the medical practitioner at Fareham, but on his arrival he admitted that he could do nothing but make some trifling suggestions for the apparent comfort of the patient. He held out no hope of my lord's ultimate recovery, and though he did not say so in so many words, I could see he thought the case beyond recovery.

I sat with my lord during the entire morning and afternoon, for I felt that now a new duty had been imparted into our relationship, and I was jealous that anyone should take the place which I felt to be imperatively mine. Madam Cassilis had shown a good deal of concern—more than I could have expected—and had proved herself of great use in the sick-room in our early trepidation and confusion; but she had not ventured in any way to interfere with me, nor had she shown any desire to usurp my place. I think her grave anxiety for her brother had for the time banished all lesser considerations, and it was not until the evening that she found time to make clear her feelings toward myself and her view of the general situation.

I had been able to find a very excellent nurse, and I was engaged in giving her some trivial directions, when Madam Cassilis came softly into the room and waited with perfect composure until I had finished.

" I should like to speak with you, Mr. Cassilis, on an important matter if you can spare the time," she said coldly and with a glance at the sick-bed. " Lord Heronford is still unconscious and does not seem to have moved."

" He is still unconscious," I answered gravely, for I saw the look that was not at variance with the tones of her voice; " and I am quite at your disposal."

She made no reply and I followed her out of the chamber. She did not speak till she reached the room she used as a boudoir, and which I had never been in but once or twice a long time before. She threw open the door and entered, turning up the lamp which was burning on the table.

" Close the door," she said sharply, and turning round with swift decision; " I have a good deal to say to you."

I obeyed without saying a word, wondering upon what ground and for what cause she intended to do battle with me, and now resolutely determined in so far as I was able to allow her to have her own way. Since the revelation of the previous night I had acquired in a way not very explicable a new self-respect, which rendered me more enduring and patient. With my new knowledge I could not help feeling some sympathy toward her; her attitude was feminine and natural; and it was only just that she should imagine my government of the sick-room to be a usurpation of her own right and inheritance.

"You are aware, Mr. Cassilis, that there is no hope my brother should recover. In case he dies I suppose you have formed some plans about your future?"

"I have not yet lost all hope," I answered. "There is plenty of time to think about the future."

"You have sense enough to see—you were never wanting in sense—that his death will alter your position."

"It must necessarily make a considerable number of changes. But I still cling to hope."

"You know very well what I mean. I have no desire to hurt your feelings, but you cannot then remain in this house. My brother had reasons for treating you as a member of his family, and perhaps for holding you before them all. But on his death you will be a stranger and less than a stranger, and you can understand that it is impossible for me to tolerate you here. Your—your relationship to the family would entirely prevent that. I think it is not unlikely my brother may have made some provision for you, but if that should not have been the case I—well—I can spare you enough to push your fortunes respectably abroad."

"You are very good," I said, thinking what an ocean of surprises lay before her, "but I have reason to know that provision has been made for my future. Lord Heronford has given me to understand as much."

"I might have known that," she answered sharply; "unlike my brother William, you were always wise in your generation. I do not wish to be hard upon you, but you know what I think of you. You came between my brothers; you came between my brother and me, and robbed me of his confidence. I have had more reasons than one to regret you ever came into this house——"

"I could not help my birth, madam——"

"Your birth!" she cried scornfully; "you had no birth."

"I had at least the misfortune to be born," I answered, smiling gravely.

"It was a grave misfortune for all concerned—for my brother, for me, and for yourself, if you do not change your mind and habits. You are not used to be blind in other things, but you never seem to have known your true position in this house and in the world."

"It is not very long since I have learned."

"Ah! you have learned. I hope it has taught you humility."

"It has taught me that among other lessons; I hope it will also teach me to practice justice and to show kindness."

She seemed to think there was an implied rebuke in my words, as, indeed, perhaps there was.

"You were always a saint and martyr," she said scornfully. "I have sometimes wondered where the Heronford blood came in.   Perhaps ——"

" Perhaps, madam ? "

" No. We will not quarrel. My brother was satisfied, and there was a time when he knew his own business. I merely wished to warn you that when he died you must prepare to leave Heronford at once. You had better make your preparations, for I do not wish to seem to deal too harshly with you."

"I am afraid," I answered, "I am not in a position to appreciate your kindness. But I think I will wait."

"You think you can set up your will against a defenceless woman ? Very well, we shall see. If my brother William were alive ——"

"I have had one friend all my life," I interrupted gravely, "and you may be certain I shall endeavour to carry out his wishes. I am sure I know his mind."

" Take your own course," she said, "you know what is likely to happen, and you cannot blame me. I will not call the servants to put you out, but there is one thing on which I will insist so long as you remain under this roof."

" And that, madam ? "

" You shall not enter my brother's room. That is my place, and you have no more right or business there than one of the grooms from the stable. It is monstrous ; it is wicked to think that you of all the people in the world should stand at his death-bed."

For the first time I was pained by her speech, and I knew that upon this ground, at least, I was largely, if

not altogether, in her power.   If she had been anxious to
wound me, and yet I am not sure that that was really her
purpose, she could not have adopted any more effective
means.

"You surely do not mean that?" I said.

"I will take means to prevent it.   Is it a fitting thing
that the memory of a man's sin—oh! I can speak plainly,
Mr. Cassilis—should stand at his bedside when he is
dying?   And what are you but that memory?   For the
time, at least, I am mistress here, and I will not have it."

"I am afraid," I said, "I cannot make you understand,
but surely love gives me the right which you deny me.
Lord Heronford loved me like a son."

"And I loved my brother, sir; I was proud of him; I
hoped for a great career for him, and he wasted his life
miserably among shadows.   His conscience was too
tender, and I am certain—I am certain—it was you who
played the part of ghost.   A pretty ghost!   It was you
who wrecked his life; he cried over you like a woman
crying over her—faugh!   I have had enough of this disgrace, and will now have matters in my own way, when
it is too late."

"I cannot oppose you, but you will regret the step you
intend to take."

"At any rate I will not discuss my regrets with you,
Mr. Cassilis.   I shall endeavour to choose another confidant, and you now know my wishes.   I think we have
finished.   You can go."

And in this way I was dismissed without being able to
make any further protest.   Though I had been treated,
as I felt, with great injustice and want of consideration, I

must admit that I was rather grieved than angry. I was able to put myself in madam's place, and I could not but feel she was able to justify herself in taking the course she had adopted. Having no suspicion of my real place in the house, she had looked upon my presence so long as I could remember as an insult to herself and a disgraceful incumbrance upon my lord, and I am sure she had imagined my influence had been a hostile one, and had helped to shut her out from her brother's sympathy. With no clue in her hands to account for my lord's actions, she had watched our growing familiarity with pain and disgust, and had now taken the earliest opportunity of manifesting her feelings.

I went down to the Book Room and tried to lose myself over a volume that I took up, but I could not read. My feelings were too much moved, my thoughts too clamorous.

There was no book in the world at this moment had grip enough to hold my mind. My lord was dying! In that room looking out over the lonely sea and cheerless downs the curtain was falling upon the last scene of another tragedy. For twenty years the dead hand had guided the living spirit, and now it was all nearly over. The grey evening of a grey life was settling into night. Another man might have risen and defied himself and the world, and drunk the cup of life with its coarse and vital pleasures to the end, but my lord's nature had not the strength for this. A certain tenderness, a weakness of will, a want of robust and virile strength, had left him a prey to his fears, and his strong emotions, finding no outlet in his life, had lain hidden in his bosom, gnawing and stinging there. I could not bear to think of that life of broken purposes, humbled pride, and solitary conflict.

I was so agitated that I rose and walked up and down the room, shaken by the storm of emotions my train of thought had raised in me, and after a while my eye chanced to light on the escritoire at the end of the apartment. I suddenly stopped, overtaken by a temptation that in the end I found irresistible. I could not help myself; I yielded almost with a sense of shame. I had my lord's word that the proofs were here upon which my whole future depended—my honour, my name, my inheritance, my whole future life. I did not doubt his word—not for an instant—but I knew his careless habit in regard to papers, and I knew that if one simple link were missing the whole chain of proof was broken. If he were mistaken —if he had overlooked some vital point, I could find no means of repairing that, and there was a sudden end to my cherished hopes.

The fear grew upon me as I stood swaying, and, as I say, in the end I yielded to the impulse. But it was almost with a sense that I was violating his confidence that I fitted the key into the lock and opened the drawer. It was with the sense that I was guilty almost of sacrilege that I untied the ribbon that bound them and spread the papers before me. The secret of a man's life that he had guarded fearfully from the world! I sometimes even now wonder whether I was wrong in doing what I did, and even now I have not solved the doubt. My lord had desired the papers should remain undisturbed till his death, though not in so many words, but I knew that that was his wish. And yet, upon the other hand, a great wrong

might be inflicted which he most of all would have regretted, and if a portion of the chain of evidence were
wanting it might still be repaired should he regain consciousness.   And above all I alone should see them, to
whom they would tell no new story and who already
knew their history.

I entirely forgot myself in the perusal; I forgot my
doubts and scruples, and sat, absorbed in the recital of the
pitiful narrative.   In one thing I had been quite wrong.
However careless my lord had been in other matters, here
he had been rigorously exact.   He had forgotten nothing ;
he had omitted nothing.   There was no flaw in the proofs.
They admitted of no doubt, and were clear and intelligi-
ble to a degree.   He had taken pains that there should be
no difficulty regarding them, and upon the wrapper that
enclosed them was written in his fine, legible hand the
words, *The Confession of Richard Cassilis, Lord Heronford*,
with the date.   The documents were arranged in their order.   There was first the certificate of marriage, which
set out that Richard Cassilis was married to Gertrude
Wiltshire, in the parish church of Soame, in the county
of Herts, and was signed by James Dempster, vicar of the
said parish.   There was a number of letters from the young
wife that were very painful to read, and which spoke of her
husband's desertion, and her fears for the child of which
she was about to become the mother ; and immediately
after followed the certificate of the baptism of this child,
which took place at the parish church of Chelsea.   I found
the letter which the late Lord Heronford wrote to his son,
and which showed that he was in entire possession of all
the facts.   I could almost hear the old lord speak as I

read it. A Cassilis, he wrote, might be mad, but he always went to the devil like a gentleman. He had never heard of any that had been hanged, but it seemed that his son was about to bring the fashion into the family. Nothing would give him greater pleasure if it could be done without the world knowing it. Bigamy was a novel crime in the annals of Heronford, and his son had added graces to the act none but himself could attain to. He had betrayed an angel, who had the bad taste still to love him, villain as he was, and the writer ended by saying that it would be his care to provide for the future Lady Heronford and her son.

But the paper which most interested me was the declaration of my lord himself, which had been written out at great length and apparently not very many weeks before. It had been written with great care, for there were many erasures and interlineations, and certainly with no intention of sparing himself or of extenuating his conduct. The facts were nearly all as I had already supposed them to be.

He began by stating that it was while he had been on a visit to Sir Onslow Gresham at his country place in Hampshire that he had first met my mother. Her father, who had been a retired captain of foot, had recently died, and she was at that time residing with an aunt in very straitened circumstances. At first he had looked upon it merely as the case of a rustic beauty and her town admirer, and had hoped for an easy conquest, but he found himself altogether mistaken, and in proportion as the lady repulsed his careless advances he fell more and more deeply in love with her innocence and beauty, until at last he was prepared to make any sacrifice and at any cost. But under the circumstances an open marriage was impossible. At the first intimation of such a step his creditors would have pressed their claims, and his father would at once have ceased to furnish him with supplies. Nor did he fail to add that shame and fear of ridicule had a share in persuading him to the course he adopted.

A secret marriage was resolved upon, and when my mother left her home it was believed by her friends she had fallen a victim to the advances of an unscrupulous lover. No one knew or suspected the real state of affairs. The only witnesses to the marriage were the verger and his daughter, whom Lord Heronford believed to be still alive. From that day my mother never saw nor communicated with her friends again, and followed her husband to London, where she remained in perfect retirement. Then followed the usual course of such unhappy marriages. If the young husband was not soon tired of his wife he was not long in seeing at what cost he had gained her, and the allurements of his old life irresistibly drew him back within their vortex. I do not think he had at first any deliberate intention of abandoning her and of denying this marriage, but for some months he only visited her rarely, and at last suggested she should return to her friends.

It is impossible to say how matters might have ultimately resolved themselves, but the crisis was accelerated by one evening's play. Already nearly bankrupt by his extravagance the misguided young man one unlucky night rose from the card-table with a loss of twelve thousand pounds, which he had absolutely no means of discharging. His friends knew his condition; the most disgrace-

ful form of ruin stared him in the face; his resources
were at an end; his credit was exhausted. And just at
this time an unfortunate providence stepped in to assist
him. Mrs. Carteret had recently lost her husband, who
had left her the bulk of his fortune. Before her first
marriage, which had lasted only three years, she had had
a tenderness for my lord, and even during her married
life had remained upon very friendly terms with him. At
this juncture in his affairs she wrote him the letter of a
woman whose heart has taken possession of her judgment—a letter in which she laid her hand and fortune at
his disposal. The temptation was too great for the
already-drowning man. The irretrievable step was taken,
and they were married within a fortnight.

It was not till nearly a month afterwards that my lord
saw the young wife whom he had forsaken. He made
no attempt at disguising his conduct; he threw himself
upon her mercy and declared that his life was in her
hands, which was, indeed, the case. The interview must
have been a very painful one, and it was the last time
they met. It was only after the birth of her child that
my mother was impelled to take the decisive step which
led her to Heronford, and it was perhaps the wisest step
she could have taken. But her heart was broken, and I
do not think she was ever happy again. It was a fortunate thing that Mrs. Carteret—she was never Mrs. Cassilis—died a few years afterwards without leaving any
family, and had it not been for myself there was left no
memorial of this crime which had wrecked two lives.

In the margin there was a note which explained a
matter that I had never been able to understand. Before

the death of his second wife my lord had made a restitution of that portion of her fortune which had come into his hands, and the sacrifices he had made to achieve this had contributed largely to his present embarrassments. The one desire now remaining to him was that his son might have a happier life and a more prosperous lot than had fallen to his father. He had done him a wrong for which he could never forgive himself, and he now left himself with his sins and follies in the hands of the great Judge Who sees the hearts of all men, and measures out their portion of reward with justice and mercy.

There were some other letters, carefully marked and numbered, which formed a running commentary upon the narrative, and it was a long time before I had finished their perusal. When I had done I tied them up once more as I had found them and restored them to their place in the drawer of the cabinet, which I locked, and then withdrew the key.

CHAPTER XIV

A WOMAN'S WISDOM

MR. WESTON's visits and insinuations were not long in bearing fruit. Captain Blythe was perceptibly troubled in his mind, and met me with far less of his boisterous frankness than he had ever before exhibited.

Though there was no failure of kindness upon his part, I felt that our intercourse was to some extent strained, and that there was something upon his mind of which he felt himself ashamed. This was not so manifest that it gave me ground for asking for an explanation, but I felt that a barrier of suspicion and restraint was growing up between us at which he chafed as much as myself. Mr. Weston's visits were now of daily occurrence, and were so timed that we never met. But it was perfectly evident to me the course which he was pursuing. He had ceased to annoy Victory with his importunities and, instead, was making court to her father, who had conceived an admiration for what he considered to be his outspoken honesty and rough heartiness. He had won upon him completely, and I felt that in proportion as he obtained an ascendancy over him I was declining in his favour.

I was sure that Mr. Weston had managed to insinuate some suspicion in regard to my share in the disappearance of William Cassilis, and by hints adroitly dropped had implied that that had been carried out for my interest and with my connivance. I did not know what he had said or how far he had gone in making this charge, but the captain was the least suspicious of mortals, and it must have taken a great deal to alter his feeling toward me. Nor could I quite understand the attitude that Victory had assumed. She had formerly shown her aversion toward Weston in a way that was not to be misunderstood, but her manner had now become frank and friendly toward him, and she had ceased to make him the object of her quiet and playful wit. She had entirely lost the fears she had at first entertained regarding him, and went so far as to encourage his visits. I own that there were times when I imagined her conduct was the result of waywardness and coquetry, but even then I never doubted her fidelity toward myself. Sometimes, also, I thought I detected in her an increased seriousness that was quite new to her, and this especially after Lord Heronford had been struck down.

Her father had entirely ceased to make enquiries after my lord and would change the subject in an awkward manner when his name was mentioned, but Victory showed a quickened curiosity, and returned to the subject again and again. I was not in the least afraid that Mr. Weston might injure me in her esteem or supplant me in her affection, but I honestly own that I was jealous when I saw that he was rapidly taking my place with Captain Blythe, and I more than once made my complaint to Victory about it. But it seemed to afford her amusement, and she only smiled when I expressed my fears. "The compass is out of order, Jack, and my father is only waiting till it points north again. Have a little patience; I am sure it is coming round. You see he is so honest himself that he thinks no one can be a rogue, and he cannot understand Mr. Weston's stories. I know he is more unhappy than yourself."

I found the captain in a very ill temper and complaining
of the pain in his timber leg, which usually troubled him
when matters were not going to his mind.   It was evident
that he was not overjoyed to see me, for he was more pro-
fuse than usual in his greeting and more pressing in his
hospitality—the manner in which he was accustomed to
show his uneasiness.   When I sat down opposite to him
he was not very sure how he should treat me.   The suspicion he had begun to entertain about me was struggling
visibly with his old affection, and after wringing my hand
very warmly he had suddenly relinquished it as though
ashamed of his warmth.   I affected at first not to see
his embarassment, but talked vaguely on a hundred trivial topics, until at last I determined at once to bring
matters to an issue and find exactly the ground of difference between us.

"I hope I am wrong, sir," I said, "but I think you
are not pleased to see me.   You would prefer that I
stayed away altogether."

"God bless my soul, John Cassilis, what makes you
think that?   Has the little baggage been talking?   Have
I said anything?   Ay, I'll warrant I have, for I'm a bad-
tempered man when the wind is between east and north,
and it never blows from any other point nowadays.   Or
perhaps it's the schnapps—I'll give up the schnapps and
try a larger dose of tobacco.   You shouldn't mind what
a one-legged old mariner says when he gets into the doldrums."

"It is not what you have said, sir," I answered.   "It
is what you have not said."

"Then I can't please you any way, my lad.   You are

worse than my old lieutenant in the *Hecate*; he couldn't sleep afloat, for he wanted a four-poster, and he couldn't sleep ashore, for he wanted a hammock, and between the two it was twelve years since he closed his eyes."

" I used to think you were my very good friend, sir."

" And you thought rightly, but it doesn't always blow a twelve-knot breeze, and, egad, John, I am just now in a flat calm, and that's the truth."

" Will you tell me what is wrong ? "

The captain rose from his seat and, hobbling to the mantel-shelf, reached for his tobacco-pipe. This was always a sign of mental agitation with him, and I knew that he was endeavouring to make up his mind to say something which he thought might give me pain. He turned sharply round and looked at me gravely.

"I'm a dismasted old fool," he said, " and you are worse than I am to heed me. Let us go on as we have been going, and we'll fetch port at last somehow with the help of God."

"You are trying to spare my feelings," I answered, " but I should like to get back to our old footing as soon as we can. Captain Blythe, I know very well what is the matter. You have been listening to stories about me, and you are not willing to tell me what you have heard."

" Stories, my lad ? "

" Stories, sir, grave calumnies, lying slanders. I know what the world has been saying in general, and your friend Mr. Weston in particular."

" Now that I think of it," said the captain, with a futile attempt at diplomatic evasion, " I have heard something, but ——"

"And you believe it?"

"Believe it!" cried the captain excitedly, and I think he was glad of the opportunity of losing his temper. "Believe it! Before God, sir, I am a gentleman, an officer, a man of honour. Had I believed it do you think I would have admitted you into my house, shaken you by the hand, permitted you to speak a word to my little girl who imagines, like every woman who ever wore a petticoat, that the sun rises and sets on the man she wants to marry? By heaven! sir, you do not think I have so far lost my self-respect, and forgotten what I owe to myself and the service? Yes, sir, I have heard stories, but I don't turn my back on my friends because the world is talking, and I don't believe them guilty because the old wives are wagging their tongues."

"At least I am glad you do not think me guilty," I said.

"I wouldn't," said the captain, "believe the verdict of any twelve men between this and the town of Plymouth. But it is not that. I am in swithers, John, and that is the truth of it."

"In what way, sir?"

"Well, you see, 'tis one thing to believe a man guilty; 'tis another thing to prove him innocent. If it were only a matter of friendship, do you see, I would double shot my guns, run up my ensign, and clear my decks for a close engagement. But there is something more than that. I must think of the little woman—of her before everything. She must not marry a man who can't hold up his head before all the world with a name as clean and sweet as her heart. I don't mind your birth the value of a straw —a good man is better than an earl; I don't mind that

you should be poor, but dam'me, John, I do mind that the
world should be able to talk about Victory's husband."

"Then the world is a liar, Captain Blythe," I cried
hotly; "I care nothing for the world."

"Nor I, my lad—not the value of a straw, nor does any
man who is worth his rating, but a woman is different.
Now what has become of William Cassilis? Tell me
that."

"I wish to God I knew," I answered.

"Is he alive or dead? What do you think?"

"I believe that he is dead."

"Then you have some reason for thinking that? You
know what people are saying, and what they will go on
saying till we come to the truth. I liked Lord Heronford myself, but Weston says ——"

"Mr. Weston has concerned himself a good deal about
the matter. I should like to know what Mr. Weston says."

"Oh! you must not quarrel with Weston, he is a good-
natured, honest fellow who can keep his mind to himself,
and is very friendly toward yourself. And—and to tell
you the truth, John, I promised in a way that I would
not discuss the matter with you or mention his name one
way or other. He did not want to hurt your feelings."

"He is very careful of my feelings," I answered bitterly;
"but he has managed to poison you against me at any rate.
And I am powerless, sir. This abominable lie I can meet
nowhere face to face. I can find no one who will openly
accuse me; I can find no one even to tell me with what
I am charged. I had no grudge against William Cassilis;
I had nothing to do with his death, and I had neither
hand nor part in it. You believe that, sir?"

"As I believe in my own existence, my lad. But ———"

"But what, sir?"

"They say you had something to gain by his death, and that Lord Heronford and his brother were on the worst of terms."

"I had nothing to gain by his removal," I answered, "as you yourself will discover, and Lord Heronford is now lying at the point of death and is unable to answer for himself."

"It is all a tangle," said the captain despairingly, "and from my heart I am sorry for you, John. But ———"

"You have had enough of me, sir."

"That's not fair, lad, and you know it. Enough of you! I would give my right hand to see you again with a clear course and a soldier's wind. If it were not for what Weston said— There—there—I am talking again, and upon my word I don't think he said anything after all. But you must find William Cassilis, alive or dead."

"And in the meantime you would prefer that I did not come to Carnforth? I know you don't want to hurt me."

"No, no. Come with a thousand welcomes; I am always glad to see your face. But—you know I am a plain man, John—it will be only fair to Victory that you should sail off a little, do you see, till things come right. We both love you, and the clouds will break, never fear."

"I may speak to Victory, sir, before I leave?"

"To be sure you may. Tell her all your troubles, and everything I said. She is a sensible little woman and will give you better advice than I could, and, John—don't hurt her more than you can help. God bless me, I thought when I had given up the sea I had done with trouble."

The captain made a pretence of pulling down the blind, upon the ground that the sun was shining too strongly for his eyes, but I could see that he was a good deal affected by our interview and would willingly bring it to a close. I was sure that he had not said all that he had at first intended to say, but he had said enough to show me that Mr. Weston had to some extent succeeded in turning his stout old heart against me, and that I might prepare for a still greater coldness between us. It was so unlike him to alter his views upon any matter, and especially to change in his affections, that I felt a stronger argument than that of mere general rumour must have been used in effecting this alteration. But it was useless to question him, and at the moment it was impossible for me warmly to urge my complete innocence. My knowledge made me feel that I was almost a partner in the deed, and robbed my vindication of myself of much of its force and warmth.

When I left him I found Victory waiting in the garden with her hat on and dressed in her rough walking-dress. She had not been present at any time during my interview with the captain, and I was not sure whether I should be able to see her before I left. But she had evidently been waiting for me for some time, and was apparently in a very serious mood.

" I know what you have been talking about," she said. " And I am going to walk with you to the top of the downs."

" Then you are not yet ashamed to be seen walking with me ? "

" John ! "

" Oh ! I am quite serious, Victory. Your father thinks

—I do not know what he thinks—but he told me almost in so many words that I was not fit to be your lover."

" My father is a dear old—goose, John, but there is not another gentleman like him in the world."

" I am sure there is not," I answered heartily, " though he has almost ceased to be my friend."

" I am sure he did not tell you that. I know in his heart he loves you like a son ; if he pained you, he pained himself as much, and what is more, he did it for your good."

" Would it be good for me that I should lose you ? "

" Well—perhaps, but you have not lost me yet. Oh ! you will not get rid of me so easily, and then, being only a woman, I do not think I could give you up, even for your good."

" At least you do not believe these stories ? "

" When a woman has given her heart to a man she is ready to believe all the evil she hears about him. You think that, John ? Then you don't know what a woman's heart is made of."

" I used to think I knew your heart."

" Oh ! but you do not. I hardly know myself. When her love is in danger it wakens the savage in her nature. She is ready to watch and plan and fight, and she feels almost that she could lie for him. I haven't done that, but—almost."

" I do not think I want you to fight for me," I said reproachfully.

" And if I did not, who should ? You think I am a poor fighter ? Well, we shall see, and you—you are too proud to fight for yourself. Now do not speak to me, for I want to put my thoughts in order, and then you will see how wise I am."

She trudged along by my side, her sweet brows puckered in a little frown, and never speaking a word. We walked along the wet sand together, where a recent gale had scattered patches of tangled sea-weed, and then climbed the hill until we reached the sea of purple heather that grew upon the downs. Here upon a great stone she sat down and made a place for me beside her.

"Now," she said, "I am quite ready for the debate. And before we begin I want to say two things."

"A hundred, if you please. I am listening, Victory."

"Firstly, I am a very wise woman for my years, and you are a very silly fellow."

"Both are admitted," I answered. "And now to the next."

"Secondly, I should like you to—kiss me, Jack."

Her sweet red lips were smiling, but her eyes were serious.

"That is your way. I did not mean that you should kiss me more than once. But at any rate the conference is opened and we can proceed to business. The trouble has come that I looked for, John."

"Yes, the trouble has come, but I know that I could bear more than this with you by my side."

"I do not want you to bear it; I want you to face it and—overcome it. A man should not rest on his innocence when his enemies are trying to injure him."

"But I cannot find my enemies," I cried despairingly. "I can meet no one who will tell me of what I am guilty. I only know that there is a hideous story in the air. It meets me everywhere, but only by insinuation. It has reached your father's ears, and even you have heard it."

"I could not help hearing it. You do not think I would have listened willingly. Is there anything you would like to tell me, John?"

"There is nothing I can tell you but that I am wholly innocent."

"I do not need that you should tell me that. But I have been thinking—night and day I have been thinking—since I first heard the beginning of the tale, and I have been piecing so many things together. In some things I may be wrong, but in others I know I am right. You will hear by-and-bye how I know, but love is a wonderful prophet, John, and I can see now the whole way to the end."

"It seems to me to be a very long way."

"Perhaps it is not so far as you think. Now let me begin at the beginning, and do not interrupt me till I have done. Lord Heronford and his brother have been living on bad terms for a long time—I can't help your family secrets—and a little while ago there was a great quarrel. I am not sure what it was about, but I have a suspicion. But that does not matter. Then something dreadful happened, and Mr. William Cassilis disappeared. What became of him? Lord Heronford would have liked him out of the way, and John Cassilis was Lord Heronford's friend and confidant."

"Victory!"

"Oh! you must not interrupt me. I am sure Mr. William Cassilis was a very bad man, and you did not love him either. On the night he disappeared you were at Carnforth till nearly twelve—you see I remember, and have been weaving the threads—and an hour afterwards there were three people on the cliffs. Lord Heronford, his brother, and my sweetheart, John Cassilis. Were they all all together? I think not at first."

" In God's name, Victory," I groaned, " how did you find this out ? "

" Oh ! then I am right," she cried with animation, " I was not sure that you were there. Now what happened ? Words only or blows—blows, I am sure, for John Cassilis has been changed ever since, and Lord Heronford had reason to think his brother was dead. He searched for his body, but he could not find it. Now why could he not find it ? "

" It is an awful mystery," I said.

" We are still travelling on the dry ground," she cried. " Oh ! my poor John, why could you not have given me your confidence ? You did not find him because you did not search in the right place."

" What do you mean ? I do not follow you."

" Have you never thought there might have been a witness ? Have you never wondered how the story grew ? Have you never asked yourself why no magistrate — Mr. Weston is a magistrate."

" You are torturing me, Victory. Tell me everything."

" And you told me nothing. Oh, John ! If you had told me ! You remember Mr. Weston's hints—those little sly hints that cut both of us like a knife, for the story was growing then, and I had heard it. I thought at first it was all false, but Mr. Cassilis did not come back, you had changed, and the story grew and grew. I told you that a woman could fight for her lover and could almost lie for him. John, I have lied for you, and Mr. Weston thinks that I love him."

She laid her hand, hot and trembling, upon mine.

"Yes," she cried, "he believes I love him, and I hate myself when I think of it. John, I have allowed him to kiss me for your sake. I paid the price, but I have won the game."

I looked at her in wonder.

"I felt that it was he who had first set the story in motion, and I knew that he was holding something back. I would have found it out if it had cost my life. I laid a trap for him, John, and he fell into it; he never suspected me. I was only a fickle girl who had found a new lover and discarded her old one. And then little by little he told me the tale, and oh ! my dear, how I hated him while he told me. I felt like Judith with the head of Holofernes.

" His servant had gone that night to Heronford with a letter for his friend, and not finding him at home was returning by way of Carnforth. On the cliff road he heard the sound of quarrelling, and coming quietly along he saw Lord Heronford and his brother and someone he thought was yourself. At first he was not sure, but in the end he recognised you. He did not know who struck the first blow, but in the end William Cassilis was driven to the verge, and with one cry went over. Lord Heronford instantly rushed back toward Heronford, but you, the cooler villain, waited to see that he was dead. And Mr. Weston has spared you for my sake, John.

" The servant brought the story to his master, who told him he was dreaming and threatened him with a horse-whip. But he has proved a better friend still, for he has sent the man out of the country where no one will be able to find him, but not before the fellow had time to tell the tale to a friend in the stables. But Mr. Weston thinks nothing can be done now. For my sake he has refused to take any steps himself, and since I have given you up he has no enmity against you. If I had not given you up ——"

" If ——"

" Then I am afraid the servant would have come back. You see, John, the matter is very simple."

" But it is a tissue of lies from beginning to end. Victory, I must tell you everything, though you may not believe me."

" You must tell me nothing," she cried impetuously. " When I gave John Cassilis my heart I gave him my life and my faith. Do you think I believed this or any story about you even before I knew it was a lie? Do you think I did not see that Mr. Weston wanted to play upon my love and fear for you? Do you think I would believe anything to the discredit of the man I love? But you were in danger: I thought I might help you, and I know I have helped you."

" Your faith and love have helped me," I said gravely. " But, Victory, you cannot understand till you know the truth. Since William Cassilis is dead ——"

" How do you know that he is dead? "

" I have grave reason for knowing that he is dead."

" And I have excellent reason for thinking that he is alive."

I rose to my feet in such a tumult of bewilderment as kept me silent for a minute. She was so confident; there was such a dancing look in her eyes and triumphant smile upon her lips that a sudden flash of hope illumined my heart. I would have given the world to be assured of the truth of this.

"You are not playing with me, Victory?" I stammered. "If it were true and my lord could have heard that news ——"

"Wait until you hear," she cried. "I could not understand why Mr. Weston should have spared you if he had had it in his power to injure you, and a chance word he dropped first set me on the right track. I knew that he wanted me to believe the worst about you, but if he had wanted to shield you he would not have set the country talking. And then I knew that a great part of his story must be a lie—the part in which I was most interested. At first I could not tell where the truth lay until I heard the story of the ghost."

"Mr. Weston told you that?" I cried. "How did he know of that?"

"A man is blind when a woman can see with ease. Because he had already learned from Mr. Cassilis. When I asked who had told him the story I read the first hint of the truth in his face, and I have been following the truth ever since. I could almost have enjoyed seeing him fall into the little pitfalls I laid for him, if I had not been ashamed of myself. But I learned the truth, and, John, I have seen Mr. Cassilis myself."

"A living man!" I cried.

"Alive!" she answered with a gentle scorn. "As much alive as you or I. One night last week—Thursday it was—Mr. Weston told my father that a friend was waiting for him with his horse beyond the village, and he could not stay. You know my father's habit. He would have this friend sent for and would take no refusal. There was something in Mr. Weston's answer that awakened my curiosity, and I made up my mind to satisfy myself. I promised Susan a new bonnet to go with me, and we got as far as the bridge when her courage failed her. I had to go on alone, and though it was dark I saw enough to be sure that my suspicion was right and Mr. William Cassilis was still alive."

" This is the best news I ever heard in my life. Oh, the pitiful villains! And you are sure you were not mistaken?"

"I am as certain as that I am living. He took care that I should not have more than one glimpse at his face, but you have noticed the way he rides. John, it was Mr. Cassilis."

" But you have said nothing to your father?"

" The dear, old, gallant, loyal blunderer. He is the last person who must hear it until Mr. Cassilis makes his bow to the public in person. On the first hint he would rise up in arms and take Mr. Weston by the throat, and after that we might have long to look for the missing Mr. Cassilis. And who would believe that I was not mistaken? Only my father and yourself. It is you who must find him, and now you know where to look."

" Oh!" I cried, " if we had only known this before! What agony and suffering it would have saved my lord, whose grief has killed him. The lying, wicked knaves! If you knew it all, Victory; if you knew it all!"

" It was of you that I was thinking, John; it was for you that I was fighting."

" Greatheart, the gallant soldier," I cried, pressing her hands to my lips. " You have, indeed, seen where I have been blind. If that cruel villain is above ground I will find him."

CHAPTER XV

JOHN CASSILIS PAYS A VISIT

THE country round Langston was very different at the time of which I write from what it is at present. Now the people are honest, thrifty, and industrious; there is a good market in the village, several excellent schools, and a constable, who gives his time to the cultivation of roses. Then the people had the worst reputation in the world. When they were not drinking at the " Thatched House " they were helping to run the smuggled goods ashore, and there was hardly anyone for seven miles round who was not in some way connected with this pernicious traffic. The half-yearly fair was an orgie in which lives were habitually lost, and it was seldom that the offender was brought to justice.

It was the day following the news of Victory's startling discovery that I found myself at the " Thatched House," the only inn in the village of Langston. That news found me at first bewildered and incredulous; it was so unexpected, so unhoped for, that I could hardly at first believe it; the malice and heartlessness that underlay it staggered my credulity. But the more I thought over all the circumstance, and especially upon Victory's unequivocal conviction, the first faint hope grew into positive certainty and assurance.

Early the next morning I had visited the cliffs and again carefully examined the scene of the accident, and I found that at this point some fifteen feet down there was a projecting ledge on which a quantity of dense brushwood was growing, and a young ash quite strong enough to bear a man's weight.   As far as this ledge the cliff did not run quite perpendicular, and from this point it would be perfectly practicable for one with some degree of safety to make his way back to the top.   I wondered that this had never occurred to me before, but I was so certain of the fatal termination of the tragedy that I had never looked for any other issue.   But I felt now that by a miraculous good fortune the body had fallen upon the ledge, and had been sustained by the brushwood that had its roots deep in the crevices of the cliff, and that probably William Cassilis had lain here for some time stunned and unconscious.

Whether Weston had been in the neighbourhood awaiting the result of the interview I was not certain, but certainly either he or someone in his confidence had seen what had occurred and had come to the assistance of the fallen man immediately after I had left.   As to the mind that had planned the scheme of the disappearance I had not very far to seek.   If left to himself William Cassilis, in his vindictive hatred, would at once have raised an outcry, or would have endeavoured to exact compensation in some manner equally effective.   But his friend had turned the incident to serve his own purpose, and in fact had nearly succeeded.   What arguments he had used I do not know, but certainly, so far as Lord Heronford was concerned, no plan could have been adopted that would have caused him greater suffering and anguish.

But this was not the main motive for the design, though it probably formed a part of it.   I had been present and my lips were sealed ; if I was not an accomplice I might easily appear one, and had no means of clearing myself of the charge. With that weapon Weston could strike me at pleasure, and for my lord's sake I dare not retaliate. By this means he would be able to clear a successful rival from his path, and after he had succeeded William Cassilis could then return to life with any story he might choose to invent. The scheme was simple in its diabolical cunning, and if it had been carried out with care and vigilance it is hard to tell what the result might have been. But William Cassilis was hard to hold, and Weston had found it impossible to enforce a rigid seclusion upon him. I was now assured that Victory was not the only one who had seen him; my lord and myself had seen him in the corridor at Heronford, and whether or not it was a wicked jest, we had met face to face the man whom we would have given the world to know was alive.

After I had perfectly made up my mind as to the certainty of the discovery I did not quite know what was the wisest course to take. I had a great mind to go over to Fareham to consult with Mr. Stone upon the subject, and it might have been well that I had, but I had a strong disinclination to lay all the facts before him, and I was naturally desirous of making the discovery myself. I felt pretty confident that Mr. Weston had no suspicion of the failure of his plans, and I hoped that this easy confidence might beget some further carelessness.

In this mind I drove part of the way to Langston, and then dismissing my conveyance I walked to the " Thatched House," where I resolved to spend two or three days. I was altogether unknown here, and I suppose there was nothing in my appearance that called for comment, for I seemed to escape all observation, and the story that I told appeared to be received quite readily.   All the enquiries that I made, and they were made unobtrusively, were entirely barren of result.   I hung round the little quay and chatted familiarly with the fishermen; I affected to drink in the evening in the corner of the common room, and listened to secrets that were once illumined by a flash of knives, or I lay in the shrubbery round Langston Priory and watched the doors and passage to the stables. But I could discern nothing that afforded me any satisfaction.   No one appeared to know anything about Mr. Weston's household, or if he did was equally averse to discussing the matter with a stranger, and certainly I myself saw nothing that awakened the slightest suspicion.

I had imagined that it would be easy for me to pick up some clue, but at the end of the three days I was no wiser than I had been at the beginning.   I was then more than surprised to receive a polite notice to quit.   I had thought I had secured a good friend in the landlord for I had been free with my money and had given very little trouble, but I now found that for some reason he was tired of my company.   He had formerly been butler at the Priory and had lost an eye in that dangerous service, but though crapulous in his manner he was at bottom a good-humoured fellow, and would not have done me an injury without some provocation.

"You'll not be staying much longer in these parts, I reckon," he said, with his amorphous smile and his blind eye beaming upon me with mellow benevolence.

"I am sure I don't know," I answered.   "I haven't quite made up my mind."

"For a young gentleman that has to earn his living

you must have a deal of spare time on your hands, Mr. Brown "—this was the travelling name I had assumed— " not but that you are a good customer and easily satisfied. But I'm thinking you had better make up your mind while you have a whole skin. You see there are times when a change of air is good for the constitution."

" I didn't think I had offended anyone," I answered, " and I am certain I am not in the slightest danger."

" Oh ! you're sure of that, are you ? I don't say that you are and I don't say that you're not, but I'm not going to take the responsibility of the doubt. You can see for yourself that they're a quiet people in these parts till the drink is in them, and then they take queer fancies about strangers. Now they have begun to take fancies about yourself, and in general there's no Christian burial in the parish since the curate went to Bramston."

" I suppose you are serious," I said, " but I must say I have seen no sign of ill-will since I have been here."

" Oh, never a sign. You never would till you wakened up in glory with a hole in your back as deep as a well."

" It is too preposterous. What do they suppose I am ? "

" Well, I haven't quite got the rights of it yet. Some of them say you're a gauger and some of them say you're a bailiff, but the most hold you're a Frenchman because you cut your words small and won't drink spirits. No, no, Mr. Brown, I'm sorry to lose you, but you'll have to be packing and let us get back to a quiet life."

" Oh ! " I answered, smiling, " I have no desire to disturb the peace, but surely you will not turn me out this evening ? It is a long way to the next inn, and it promises to be a wet night."

"I think I can do with you another night if you keep to your own room and don't show yourself too much in public.   But I'll have to answer for your conduct, and your thirst for information has got me into trouble already."

He delivered his last words with a snap which showed me two things: that this was a real and substantial grievance upon his part, and that he was desirous of bringing an unpleasant colloquy to a conclusion.   I was fain to be content with the further indulgence he showed me, and though I was not altogether satisfied with his explanation, I felt that after all I was merely losing time in the manner in which my search had hitherto been conducted, and that I must adopt some other course if I hoped for immediate success.   I thought over the matter for a long time after I had retired for the night, but I could think of no feasible plan that would bring me any nearer my end, and at last I made up my mind that I must consult with Mr. Stone and, putting so much of the story before him as I might think necessary, rely upon his riper and practical judgment and experience.

This was the resolution with which I fell asleep, but in the morning I awakened with a new and bolder plan fresh and fixed in my mind.   This was nothing less than personally to call upon Mr. Weston and charge him boldly with the conspiracy into which he had entered.   Looking back upon it now I cannot possibly see what I thought to gain by adopting this course, but my impatience was so great that I wanted matters hurried to a crisis.   I admit I did not see the danger involved in this or the possible advantage I might give my enemy in showing him his scheme was suspected if not discovered; but, indeed, I did not

weigh the consequences at all, for no sooner had I conceived the design than I resolved to put it in execution.
I do not think I was foolish enough to imagine that I
would be able to extort a confession, but I probably
trusted to the chapter of accidents, which is sometimes
more fruitful of results than the wisest and most deliberate counsel.

Langston Priory stands in the dip of a wooded hill that
bounds the view upon all sides but that of the sea, of which
you might almost catch the fresh, salt smell upon a day
when a landward breeze is blowing strong. Several miles
of park lie between the house and the coast road, and the
avenue which winds with many sweeps and turns, though
narrow and ill-kept, through a dense growth of noble trees,
gives one the idea that the extent is even greater. The
place showed no sign of care, but everywhere rather of
neglect and decay. The entrance gate was in ruins and
the lodge deserted; in the avenue great trees that had been
uprooted by the winter storm lay just as they had fallen,
almost obstructing the path on which the grass was growing in long and tangled patches. The house was larger
and more imposing than Heronford.

A considerable portion of the abbey still stood in excellent preservation, but the grandfather of the present
Mr. Weston had added a great range built in the Italian
manner, an undertaking which had almost impoverished
him, and which he had left still incomplete. Neither of
his successors had attempted to complete the work he had
left unfinished, and the house now stood a memorial of
extravagance and folly. But I can give you no idea of the
appearance of neglect and ruin that the place presented.

The windows along one entire side had either been boarded up or were closed with shutters; the grass was growing upon the drive till it could hardly be distinguished from the turf, and the gardens with their forlorn groups of statues—fauns and nymphs and neglected gods—were rank and overgrown with weeds.

I rapped at the main door until I was tired, without being able to make anyone hear me, and then I walked in the direction of the stables, where I knew that I should find someone to answer my inquiries. I was not mistaken in this. I found an ostler crossing the yard and very intent upon his work; at sight of me he almost dropped the bucket he was carrying.

"Is Mr. Weston at home ? " I said civilly.

" Anan ? "

" I am anxious to see Mr. Weston," I repeated. " Shall I find him at home ? "

" Noa; 'tis too early for squire. Ye had best not wait for him. He wooant see you, I'm thinking."

" But my business is of importance."

" So is hissn, I reckon. You do'ant happen to know squire, mister, nor dogwhip nayther," and he laughed as though he enjoyed the jest.

" I know Mr. Weston very well," I answered, " and look here, my man, if you will find him for me you shall have a couple more of these. Perhaps," I added, " he has visitors with him ? "

The fellow looked at the crown I gave him, holding it in his open palm, and then he bit it with his teeth.

" Noa, noa," he said with a roguish look, " I do'ant answer no questions about squire's business, but ye'er a civil-spoken gentleman enough, and its odds—not a parson, eh ?"

"I am not a parson," I laughed.

"Nor a Revenue man ? Squire's death on they."

"Not even that."

"Then he may see you, though you do'ant look his sort. But I wo'ant answer for squire of a morning, and ye'll best give him soft side of your tongue if ye want to come soft wi' him. Ye're warned fair."

"I'm prepared even to take that risk."

"Well, I'll take the liberty of putting you into th' gun room. There's only poor doitered Sir Archie there wi' his whamlaries, and he wo'ant mind ye."

"Sir Archie ?"

"Ay, squire's brother—soart of innocent. An ye're sure ye're not a gauger ?"

On my reassuring him he led the way across the yard and up a short flight of wooden steps that hardly hung together. Going down a narrow hall we came to a door, which he flung open without ceremony.

"Veesitors to see ye, Sir Archie."

He almost pushed me into the room, assured me hurriedly that he would do his best to find his master, and then closing the door behind him turned the key in the lock and left me there a prisoner. I thought for a moment that I had fallen into a trap, but knowing that my visit was quite unexpected, I assured myself that the fellow had only taken this precaution upon his own responsibility.

The room was so dimly lighted by one window at the end where I was standing that at first I could not see the other occupant. But when I grew accustomed to the gloom, and took in my surroundings by degrees, I was overcome with no small degree of astonishment. There was a number of fowling-pieces and three braces of silver-mounted pistols arranged on a rack near the door, but the rest of the room contained as curious a medley as could be imagined. A mangy fox was snarling and snapping in a wooden cage; half a dozen white rats stopped to look at me with their pink eyes, where they fed from a stone trough in the centre of the room; and a couple of owls sat blinking on the branching antlers of a stag over the fireplace. A litter of lurcher puppies were disporting on a rug of bear's skin, and a little grey monkey, very quaint and hideous, was perched tailor-wise upon the table among a heap of bottles and broken plates. At one side against the wall was a magnificent mirror, reaching from the floor to the ceiling, but the glass was starred and cracked in a hundred places as though it had been done with a hammer. The chairs, which were originally covered with silk or tapestry, had been stripped or broken, and a beautiful Italian cabinet, that must at one time have been of great value, was used to store a number of pairs of boots and other miscellaneous lumber.

At the other end of the room, and as though occupying the place of honour, was a carved lectern, which I had no doubt had originally been brought from the abbey. On this was seated a huge jackdaw that at the time I entered was in a state of great excitement and anger, and was flapping his close-cut wings with a rancous clamour. A man was standing before him in a brown coat with wide skirts that reached nearly to his heels, and was engaged in tempting him with some food that he would hold within his reach and then suddenly withdraw. I thought at the moment that I had never seen a more repulsive-looking object than this individual, but in a little while my feeling of aversion was turned into pity. His hair grew very long and apparently never received any attention, while his hands and face were indescribably dirty. His eyes had a wild and vacant stare in them that sometimes narrowed into a look of animal cunning; his forehead was bulging and projected; and his thick, blubbering lips emphasised the narrow and retreating chin. One shoulder was a little higher than the other, and altogether I thought he might very well have passed for a Caliban without his malice and ferocity, though with a certain freakish mischief.

He stopped in his occupation when I came in, and stood looking at me with a mixture of curiosity and alarm. The jackdaw flapped heavily on to his shoulder but he made no attempt to dislodge it, and the bird sat there, thrusting out its neck and apparently scolding me. The odour of the room was intolerable, and the din at first so great that I could hardly make myself heard.

" Your favourite does not seem to care for strangers," I said in a conciliatory tone, seeing his look of trepidation.

" Eh ? Ay ? " he queried in a thick, indistinct voice.

" I like birds myself. You seem to be fond of them."

" Jeremy is not well. It is one of his bad days. He is always ill when he fasts. Jeremy is no saint. Are you Jeremy ? "

He held up his finger to the bird that suddenly became quite motionless, and then reproduced his tone so exactly that I was almost certain it was he himself who had spoken.

" *Damnation !* "

His master, apparently delighted with the answer, burst into a hoarse, broken laugh that stopped as suddenly as it began.

" Ho! Ho! Jeremy is the wisest bird in the world. He can tell what you are thinking about before you open your mouth. Eh ! old Jeremy ? "

" He has learned bad habits. He should not swear."

" The gentleman says you should not swear—not even in Lent—Lent, Jeremy. But we could tell him a secret, old bird. He would swear himself after seven hundred and fifty black years with only Sir Archie of all the round-bellied old fellows to keep you company. Seven hundred and fifty years, with never a prayer for the good of your soul, and the devil sitting bolt upright in your coffin and playing at marbles with your round old skull."

" *My head aches*," croaked the bird.

" His soul is uneasy," said Sir Archie gravely ; " he is always like that when he thinks of it. Would you like to know his history ? "

I assented solemnly.

" Jeremy was not Jeremy in those days. He was the Abbot Ambrosius, and wore a ring like a bishop, and had two hundred jolly old monks to say the Aves and drink with him when he was thirsty. And I was a lay brother and dug in the garden, and looked after the poultry, and sometimes held Jeremy's horse when he rode to see his brother at Fareham. He was a great man in those days —weren't you, Jeremy ? But the devil got among the monks, and Jeremy listened to the devil and there was an end of it. He was to live to Domesday and never quit the Priory as long as he lived. A bad bargain, old Jeremy, and the lay brother had the best of it."

" *Hold your tongue, fool !* " cried the bird, and this time the voice was not Sir Archie's voice.

" He is always like that when he thinks of it. He used to have a good temper, but seven hundred years have broken it. And then it breaks his heart to think what the Westons have done to him. I am Sir Archie Weston, you know."

I nodded sympathetically.

" I never could understand how that came about ; that was the most curious part of it. But George is all right. There is no doubt that he is a Weston."

" *D——— the Westons !* " croaked the jackdaw.

" You hear him now ; that is right, old thunderstorm. He does not love George ; you know him ? "

" You mean your brother ? "

" There is only one George—my brother George. Ah ! he is the only Weston that ever I could bear, and he is so strong and tall and beautiful—like an angel in a picture. He hates Jeremy, but he bears with his temper for my sake, and George is very good to Sir Archie—you can't think how good. I couldn't live without George."

The tone of honest affection in the midst of his aimless, maundering babble struck me, and I was certain that it could only have been waked by the remembrance of kindness. I could not help thinking a little better of Mr. George Weston.

" I am glad," I said, " that your brother is kind to you. I am sure he is a good brother."

" Those are his puppies," he said, pointing to the rug.

"They don't understaud him as well as they understand me, but then I have learned the language, and I love them better. I suppose I was something else before I became Sir Archie, and that is how they know me. I can tell you it is a great thing to have been something else."

I am sure I pitied him from my heart, and I felt that I could do nothing but acquiesce in his mood.

"You must be very happy," I said, "with your family of pets."

"None of them ever troubles me but Jeremy, and that is because he knows so much more than the rest. George does not like them, but he bears with them because they are mine. You don't happen to know William Cassilis?"

I started at the sudden question, and then answered —

"Yes, I know William Cassilis."

He came close to me and laid his hand on my arm with a look of great cunning, in which there was mingled a sense of satisfaction and enjoyment.

"Sir Archie and Jeremy know all about it—they are not sleeping. Ah! but I am not sure of you. It is a secret. Ho! ho! A secret! You are sure you can keep a secret?"

"I can try if you will trust me with it."

"But you haven't seen Simpson yet? Simpson is my fox, and is quite a gentleman. You must ask him whether he is better."

"But about William Cassilis?" I said gently.

"Ah! yes; I was forgetting him. Sir Archie is not the only one who is dead and walks up and down when he should be lying in a lead coffin, and have a stone with his name cut on it, and a little house all to himself with the worms and black-beetles to keep him company. I can't make out what William Cassilis is now, but I know he is dead and they haven't buried him."

"That is wrong," I said; "but how do you know that he is dead?"

"Oh! I know. Archie knows. Did I not hear George tell him that he was the maddest dead man he ever saw in his life? You know all dead men are mad?"

"I suppose they are when they come to life again."

"That must be the reason," he said with a sagacious air. "If they would only remain dead they never would have a pain in their head. I have sometimes pains in my head."

"I am very sorry to hear that. But you are forgetting William Cassilis."

"I don't know why everyone when he dies should come to live at Langston unless William Cassilis is right and it is really hell, you know. He came here when he died, and he has been walking about ever since and playing cards, and—but I was telling you about Simpson. You can see that his leg is nearly broken ——"

"I see that he has been badly hurt."

"William Cassilis did that. George gave him to me when he was only a little cub, and I suppose he misses the fields and his little brothers, and the earth with the bracken brown and green about it, and his temper is not good. Last night—was it last night, for I always forget ——"

"That will do, my dear Archie, I will tell this gentleman the story myself."

I turned round and found the door open and George Weston standing close at my elbow.

CHAPTER XVI

I suppose I was too much interested in the unconscious revelations of the poor imbecile to hear the sound
of the door opening, and I was vexed that we should have
been interrupted so inopportunely, but I hid my embarrassment and returned Mr. Weston's stare with a cold
and distant bow. At first he paid no more attention to
me than if I had not been present at all, but turning his
back upon me went over and laid his hands with a rough
friendliness on his brother's shoulders. I imagined it was
their morning greeting, for Sir Archie's dull hanging face
was lighted up with a broad smile, and he mumbled some
words that were quite inarticulate. There was no doubt
he was unfeignedly glad to see my enemy.

"How is the poor head this morning, Archie? The
monks have been quiet, eh? and Jeremy has been a good
bird?"

"Jeremy has said his prayers and my head is better.
I have told this gentleman about Jeremy. Why has he
come to Langston?"

"To catch rats, Archie, if he can find them. Never
mind, we will set the dogs on him if he gives us any
trouble, and we will show him the way we hunt vermin.
Go into the stable and see how the horses are getting on,
and in the afternoon you and I will look after the badger.
I want to talk to this gentleman now."

He laid his hand affectionately inside his brother's arm and drew him to the door, while Sir Archie followed him, apparently perfectly satisfied with his assurance. When the door was closed and we were left alone he turned round on me with a face instantly lighted by the passion of hate and resentment.

" By ——, you'll rue this. What the devil has brought you here ? "

" I have come here to see you, Mr. Weston," I answered coolly, though I thought for the moment he was going to strike me.

" Oh! you have come here to see me, you sneaking cur ? You weren't content to spy on me at Langston, Mr. Brown, when with a word from me you would have been tossed into the quay or sent a longer journey than you might have a taste for. I might have forgiven you that. I might have let you go to the devil in your own way, but you weren't satisfied with that. You must come here to pry into my secrets, to dig up my family skeletons, to—who brought you into this room, you ——? "

" If all your secrets were as much to your credit, Mr. Weston, as the one I have discovered here, you would not have been troubled with my presence. I have thought better of you since I have learned it."

" Who wants you to think well of him? By Heaven, I had rather have your ill-opinion than your good. I want no man's good opinion—least of all yours. I'll know who brought you into this room, and if I leave a whole bone in his body my name isn't George Weston. Have you rubbed up your dull wits ? Have you found out what you wanted ? Has that poor innocent satisfied you that he is no wiser than yourself with more excuse for his folly? You were well-matched; yes, you were well-matched."

"*A precious pair, George*," croaked the jackdaw, that all the time had been sitting on the lectern watching us out of his wicked eyes.

"Hold your tongue or I'll wring your neck, you old devil!" cried Weston. "Now, Mr. Brown or Mr. Cassilis—one name is as good as the other—what have you come here to say to me?"

"I have not come here to quarrel, sir."

"Only another lecture on deportment—I thought as much," he said with a sneer. "I don't forget that you were not always so peaceably inclined, and if I bore with your blow then it was for purposes of my own. But I haven't forgot it, and will cry quits if we both live long enough."

"I am ready to give you the satisfaction of a gentleman for my conduct."

"A fine gentleman! It doesn't please me to stand up to be shot at—that's not my way. I'll fight you with my own weapons, and when we have done I'll get more satisfaction than I would ever get, in attending your funeral. That's my notion of honour in fighting a gentleman like you."

"You have strange notions of honour, Mr. Weston."

"Well, I don't change my name, and lie in a pot-house for the end of a week to see how my neighbour's smoke is blowing—my honour doesn't take that turn. I'm sorry now that I let you off so easily and only asked you to change your lodging. I should have called 'shark' and let the lads treat you in their own way. I'll do it yet, I will, by ——"

"Then this was another polite attention of yours. It did not occur to me."

"I suppose I should have sent you a polite note of invitation, and asked you to come and share our festivities at the Priory. Archie and you would have got on very well together. But we have had enough of these civil preliminaries, and I don't want to lose my temper. May I take the liberty of asking on what errand you have come to see me, for you are an intolerable time in getting at the essentials?"

"My errand is a very simple one, Mr. Weston, and can be spoken in a word. I have come to ask you to restore Mr. William Cassilis to his friends, for by this time the farce is nearly played out."

His astonishment was so well counterfeited—the blank look, the start of surprise, the unconscious pause—that had I not already perfectly known the part he was acting I should have been staggered by his manner. That could not have been excelled by any actor upon the stage, and only wanted an audience less incredulous than myself to have rendered it perfect.

"Dam'me, the farce is only beginning. But I can't have understood what you want with me."

"I have spoken plainly ; you understand me perfectly. If you think to deceive me in this way once for all I tell you plainly you are mistaken, for I know ——"

"That I was so fond of honest Will Cassilis when he was alive that I couldn't part with him now that he is dead and gone. It seems I have founded a museum and turned a collector of curiosities. I have seen the thing done—labelled in spirits and a stopper on the bottle—and Will Cassilis is to make a specimen. If he were alive he would enjoy the joke with any man I know, but since he is dead it can't tickle him now. Upon my word I don't understand you, Mr.—is it Brown or Cassilis ? "

" Is it still necessary to endeavour to keep up this deception, sir ? Was it last night you played at cards with him, or did you see him this morning ? If you will be good enough to bring him here I should be happy to tell him what I think of your conduct and his."

" I see," he sneered, " that we are beginning to arrive at an understanding, though you have a confounded way of arriving at your meaning. You do not mean that I have the custody merely of his honoured bones ; I am supposed to produce him alive."

" That is exactly my meaning, and no one knows it better than Mr. Weston."

" This is a better joke than the other, and that was hard to beat. I see now what brought you to Langston and set you prying into every hole in the village, though for my life I couldn't understand it before. Your conscience is troubling you, Mr. Cassilis; the ghost has got into your brain. I'm told you have seen the ghost."

" I have no doubt your friend has told you the whole story."

" Oh ! he has, has he ? Come, sir, we'll beat about the bush no longer. I wonder at your assurance. Do you think that I am a child to be taken in by this cock-and-bull story ? "

"We both know that William Cassilis is alive and in this house at this moment."

"I know that you are standing before me with a rope round your neck if I chose to speak the word. I know that if I did my duty as a magistrate I should make out a warrant for your committal, and see you conveyed safe to Fareham gaol. And you come to me with your trumped-up story—to me, by —— who saw with my own eyes—you have the truth now—your master and yourself do my unfortunate friend to death. You would make a fine show in the cart together, and I don't know why I don't see you both upon the road."

"Shall I tell you the reason, Mr. Weston? Because you might find it difficult to produce the body. Knowing what you appear to know you will now find it difficult to explain why you have remained so long silent, but I am glad to think I should have had so excellent a witness on my behalf had things turned out differently. I am sure you would have spoken the truth, Mr. Weston."

"I'll speak the truth yet, happen what may, and then you can tell your story to a judge and jury and see whether they will believe you. Do you want a warrant to search my house, to examine my servants, to twist the words of my unfortunate brother to the tune of your midsummer madness? Oh! this is too much, by —— The confederate who stands by and watches the deed done when he feels that his neck is in danger comes here to try to shift the charge and close the witness' mouth against him. I know your tricks; I see through your scheme, but it won't do with me. No, no, Mr. John Cassilis, you must try some other plan."

"You mean, then, to persist in your denial at all hazards?"

"I mean to see you hanged as high as Haman."

"It is idle for you to talk in this way.   You have yourself admitted to me even now you saw what occurred. If William Cassilis had been killed no one knows better than yourself it would have been merely the result of a deplorable accident in which I had neither hand nor part. But you know and I know that he was not killed, that he is alive at this moment, and that you are keeping him in hiding to serve your own ends and answer your own wicked purpose."

"Fine words!   You would find it hard to prove that."

"I think I have found the means of proving it nevertheless."

"Let me hear your proofs.   An idiot and a ghost?"

Though he spoke contemptuously I saw that I had awakened his interest, and he was anxious to know the extent and source of my knowledge.   I was almost upon the point of allowing my feelings to get the better of me and giving him the information he sought when I restrained myself.

"I shall produce my proofs at my own time and in my own place, and even you will be compelled to confess their sufficiency.   I own that I did not come here out of any spirit of friendship or good-will toward you.   You have tried to injure me; you have injured me, and I may have given you some cause for your hostility.   I admit that and I do not regret it; I should do the same thing again under the same circumstances.   But that is not everything.   I have not come to you on my own account, for you will see that I shall fight my own battle in a different way; not on my own account, nor thinking of my own advantage. I implore you on behalf of an innocent man whose heart has been broken, whose spirit has been tortured, who has been hounded to death by this cruel plot of which I alone am the object, to give him some hope and let him have some peace before he dies. There is no need to disguise from you that Lord Heronford imagined he was the cause of his brother's death. Is he to die with this black shadow lying upon his death-bed when a word from you will remove it? It were only common humanity to cease to persist in it."

"Upon my life, Mr. Cassilis, you have missed your vocation in the world; you have some skill in the use of language. But might I not suggest that if I am guilty of all you say, that it would be an easier and plainer course to produce your evidence than to try to extort a confession from the criminal? Come, come, sir. You need not harp upon that string; I am too old for cheap pathos. You and I have tried conclusions together and I have had the best of the argument. You thought a fox-hunter couldn't fight; you imagined because I loved a bottle better than books that I had no wits. You were good enough to declare war against me; well, sir, you declared war, and I imagine I have had a good deal the best of you in the battle of Carnforth. That is the whole situation."

"Is it necessary, Mr. Weston, that we should touch upon that subject?"

"No, not now, for I think I have effectually done your business there. I would only remind you, Mr. Cassilis, that even a prize-fighter can love a woman as well as a troubadour, and perhaps go a little further in his rough way for her sake."

"And I am to take it as your final answer that you will still persist in this persecution?"

"You are to take it for my final answer that you are a fool to suppose that I will give up the advantage I have gained, and that I should be a greater fool still if I did. And now, Mr. Cassilis, I have only one word more to say. If my lamented friend is not dead I shall take care to see, as far as you are concerned, that he is as good as dead. You came here to see me on my own ground—first to threaten, and when that failed then to wheedle. Very well, I haven't done with you. You say that you will fight me in your own way; so will I, and I will give you a lesson you will never forget as long as you live. I will take off the gloves and show you how easily I have been dealing with you so far."

"Threatened men live long, sir; at least, we need not wrangle further. Even for your own sake I am sorry that you have not seen your way at least to do common justice."

"Well, at any rate, I will do it now."

He went over to the window and, throwing up the sash, called to someone in the courtyard, upon which the window looked. Never having had any doubt as to the length to which his violence was capable of carrying him I expected nothing less than that he was about to resort to physical means, and I looked hastily round for some means of defence in case it should come to the point of resistance. With that view in my mind I edged nearer the arms rack; he glanced round, and seeing my movement burst into a roar of laughter.

"You needn't be afraid, Mr. Cassilis. It has not come to that yet, though it may. Simon!"

I heard the sound of footsteps under the window.

"I want a couple of men to go into Langston. They are to drive the gentleman who has come to see me, and they had better take the light cart. Hurry them up. Now, Mr. Cassilis," he continued, turning round to me, "you see I have been providing for your comfort. I hope you will see your way to accepting my kindness; if you do not I am afraid I shall have to use force, and they will drive you whether you will or no. The next time you visit Langston Priory I shall not be at such trouble to provide for your convenience."

"I have not the slightest objection to your driving me to Langston," I said, looking at him firmly, "and there is no need for you to threaten me. I am not at all afraid."

"Fools never do fear," he cried with a laugh, as he threw open the door. "Now, Mr. Cassilis, the cart will be ready in a moment, for my fellows never lose time when I am near them. You see they are nearly ready."

We had come out into the bright sunshine of the court-yard and stood watching the men yoking a high-spirited mare in the cart. They were stout, honest-looking fellows, who, though handy enough, seemed to me to savour a good deal more of the sea than of the stable, and I remembered that Weston was generally supposed to have a closer connection with the free traders than it might have been convenient for him to have publicly known. However, I did not think he now intended me any foul play, but merely wanted to see me safely off his premises, and

I was preparing to get into the cart when he laid his hand on my arm.

" Before you go there is something more that I should like to say to you."

" Well, sir ? "

" It was merely that I never could understand why my poor deceased friend was so bitter against you. It is a curious coincidence. By the merest accident I discovered that only this morning, and I am glad I did not know earlier. I loved Lord Heronford so much that in showing my affection for him I might have done yourself some service. But all is well now, and I hope you will find everything right at Heronford, only you might have been as profitably employed looking after your interests there as uncovering my nakedness here. Good-morning, Mr. Cassilis."

The mare plunged in the shafts two or three times, and then settling steadily to her collar we were carried rapidly down the drive, and in a quarter of an hour I found myself again before the doors of the " Thatched House."

CHAPTER XVII

I HAD certainly no reason to congratulate myself upon
the result of my visit to Langston Priory ; indeed, when
I looked back upon it I came to the conclusion that I
had been hurried into the commission of a grave folly.
I had to deal with a vindictive and unscrupulous enemy
who had been bold enough to avow that he had not yet
satisfied his enmity, and had boldly declared that he was
preparing to strike another blow. I was not a step
nearer the solution of the difficulty ; I had learned nothing of importance, for the rambling talk of the poor
imbecile had told me nothing of which I was not already fully assured ; but, upon the other hand, I had
voluntarily and of my own motion informed the con-
federates that their scheme was discovered, and that by
some means I had gained possession of their secret.

When I thought over the result of my visit there was
another matter that troubled me a good deal. I had not
failed to notice the look of triumphant malice with which
Mr. Weston had closed our interview, nor the significant emphasis he had laid upon his last words. It was
impossible, in part at least, not to understand what he
had meant to convey. By some means he had learned
the secret which my lord had guarded so jealously, and
which there were so many reasons for keeping inviolate
till his death. At first I supposed that William Cassilis,

who had apparently withheld his confidence from him so long upon that subject, had at last been induced to admit him fully into his discovery, but his language conveyed more than that, and carried with it a warning which struck me with dismay when I began to consider it. That warning had not been directed toward Lord Heronford, against whom he had, indeed, obtained a powerful weapon, but toward me, who could not possibly be injured by the disclosure. It imported something more than a mere discovery—that had carried with it a power to strike directly at myself or there was no meaning in his language.

But how? By what means? All at once a series of possibilities presented themselves to my mind, which grew upon me with a heightening feeling of terror until I felt my heart knocking in my breast. Was it possible that by some means my precious papers had fallen into his hands, and that while I was pursuing my foolish and fruitless enquiries he had succeeded by some means in obtaining the sole evidence of my birthright? I had imagined the papers were perfectly safe; I had felt the most absolute security in the fact that their existence was known only to my lord and myself; it had never occurred to me for a moment that any attempt would be made upon them, or that the place where they were deposited would be discovered.

But I remembered all the circumstances now, and I exclaimed upon myself for a blind and heedless fool. Upon that very night when these precious documents had been intrusted to my keeping William Cassilis had been at Heronford; nay, more, he had been upon the very

threshold of the room in which my lord and I were sitting. I remembered now the circumstance of finding the
door open that I had supposed to be shut, and it was
possible for him to have overheard every word we had
spoken. I had been carried away by my idle fears that I
had myself afterwards laughed at, but the real significance
of the apparition had never struck me until now. In his
father's time William Cassilis had been accustomed to
come and go in that great house without anyone being
the wiser of his presence, and upon this occasion, led
probably by some freakish fancy, he had revisited the
house where he was supposed to be dead. It was such an
adventure as would appeal to his malignant nature, and
how could I now doubt that he had heard and seen everything that had taken place between my lord and myself?

If my presentiment was well founded this was the
position in which I was placed, and the mind is so constituted that this new calamity completely dwarfed for
the time all my other troubles and centred my hopes and
fears entirely upon myself.

The coast road from Langston to Heronford runs
through the village of Carnforth, where it makes a detour
of several miles, skirting the base of the hills that there
rise against the sea, and joining Leyton and Amberley in
the chain of communication. When I was deposited at
the door of the " Thatched House " my conductors un-
yoked the mare from the cart and sat down to a can of
beer in the common room, keeping their eyes, as I felt,
on me all the time. I do not know whether they had
been able to communicate with the landlord without my
seeing, or whether he already had his instruction, but he

seemed perfectly to understand the situation, and treated me very dryly and with the scantiest hospitality. I had called for some luncheon, for it is a walk of nine miles to Heronford, and there is no other house upon the road where it would be possible for me to get any refreshment; but he seemed unwilling at first to supply my wants, and demurred to serving me. However, after a little insistence upon my part I at last got what I wanted, though I found that my morning visit had entirely robbed me of an appetite. But when I came to pay my modest bill he spoke out his mind very plainly.

"I'm glad to see you'll be for the road back, Mr. Brown, and I hope you'll put out your right foot first. I told you before in a friendly way that Langston wasn't a healthy place, and if you take my advice it'll be a long time before you pay us a visit again."

"You seem to be an honest fellow," I said, "and I should like to know what you have against me. I haven't grumbled over your charges, and when a man keeps an inn he usually likes to see his guests coming and not leaving him."

"Oh! I'm not saying that I am different from other people, but there are guests and guests. I've nothing against yourself; you seem to be an honest, harmless sort of gentleman, but I can't afford to let you in, and the next time you come round these ways my orders are to show you the other side of the door."

"That is plain spoken at any rate. But I understand your position. I know you are Mr. Weston's tenant."

"I am nobody's tenant but my own, thank God, for my wife who came from Amberley way had a little fortune of her own, and ready money isn't so plentiful in these parts now that it isn't welcome. But they are all Mr. Weston's men hereabouts, and we must live on good terms with our neighbours. You don't think that Mr. Weston would interfere with my customers, the Lord love you—not he—he is the most open-handed gentleman in the world—but folk here have a suspicion, somehow, that you and he aren't friendly, and that's enough. It's as much as my house is worth to serve you, and though I'm sorry for it, I can't do it again."

" I'm sure I don't complain in the least of your treatment ; I shouldn't like to think you had suffered on my account."

" Oh ! it's all right now that you are going, and if you will take the advice of a friend you won't come back to Langston till you have made your peace with some people we won't talk about. At any rate, I would rather you didn't come to the ' Thatched House.' "

Of course I was perfectly aware that it was due to Mr. Weston's interference that he had already turned me out of his house, and it was the same influence now which led him to look so eagerly for my departure. But I was unable to find fault with his loyalty where his interest was so deeply concerned, and when I took my road homeward, to his evident satisfaction, we parted on perfectly amicable terms. The two men who had accompanied me to the " Thatched House" had evidently not entirely completed their instructions when they set me down before the door of that primitive hostelry. After I had gone some distance on my way I turned round and saw them watching me from the hill above Langston, until I finally lost sight of them at the turn of the road. But I took this only for a piece of Mr. Weston's bravado, though, indeed, my mind was at the time so fully occupied by other subjects of interest that I did not give the circumstance so much thought as I might otherwise have done.

As you know the road from Langston makes a long elbow at Carnforth before it reaches Heronford, but there is a shorter way, usually taken by those travelling lightly like myself, across the sands and along the beaten road by the cliffs. The way ran, indeed, it still runs, for I can see it as I write, through the meadow by the captain's garden and past the gate that leads to his house. There were several reasons why I was at the moment unwilling to take this way, for I had not the heart just now to see either Victory or her father; but my anxiety to verify my fears was so great that I did not care to lose time in taking the longer road, and I accordingly leaped over the stile and made my way through the meadows. I hoped for the first time in my life that I might be able to pass the house unobserved, and I thought for the moment I was about to succeed. Though the door lay open there was no one in the porch, and the little garden was deserted but for the presence of the *Saucy Arethusa*. I passed the gate with the feeling that I might never enter it again and reached the bridge, where I stopped for a moment to look back at the house that I loved, and the shady garden where my happiest hours had been spent.

I stood looking back on it all for a moment or two, and then lifting my knapsack, that I had rested on the parapet of the bridge, turned away and began to resume my journey. But I had hardly gone more than a step or two when I heard my name called behind me, and turning round saw Victory running swiftly down the walk from the house, her shining brown curls uncovered, and her red stockings twinkling under her white dress.

" Jack! Jack ! "

I again set down my knapsack and waited where I was standing till she came up to me. Never had I so wanted to take her in my arms and pour out all my trouble to her patient, loving ears.

" Well, madcap," I said gravely, holding out my hand as she came up, " I see that it is not possible for anyone to pass your door without discovery."

" You have never tried to do that before, Jack."

" But it is different now."

" Is it different ? Shall I go back ? "

" It would be far better for yourself, Victory, that you did. A poor beggar like me has no right to mix you up in his troubles or ask you to take a share in his misfortunes."

" Of course you have no right. Do you think a woman ever loves a man when he is unfortunate ? "

" Well ——"

" Or do you think she loves him better when he has trouble that he can share with her ? What do you think, Jack ? "

" I think you are far too good for me, Victory."

" And I think you are a very foolish lover. If I were a man I should love differently—perhaps. But I am only a very foolish girl, and—I see by your face that you need comfort, Jack. Tell me what is wrong ; I was not mistaken ? "

" Everything is wrong, but you were not mistaken.

There is no doubt that William Cassilis is alive and may be found at Langston."

"Oh! I was sure of that; I was sure of that," she cried joyfully. "Then everything is right and you have found him, as I knew you would."

"I have bungled everything from the beginning, and I am further from the end of the difficulty than I was when I started. I have learned nothing; I have not gained a shred of proof that people would not laugh at, and I have thrown away the advantage that I had at first."

"But the great thing is that he is alive. We are strong in that, dear; we can afford to wait."

"Your eyes shine like stars of strength, Victory. Perhaps I should have waited. But you don't know everything."

"I know, sir, we must fight our ship to the last plank," cried the sailor's daughter, "and then, Jack, we can go to the bottom together, but not till then. Now tell me all the foolish things you have done."

It gave me heart to see her steadfast eyes, and hear the ring of loyal faith in her sweet voice. Beginning at the beginning I told her how I had gone to the village of Langston, and how probably during my whole stay there Mr. Weston was aware of the inquiries I was making; how I had at last recklessly made up my mind to visit the Priory, and of all that had taken place there down to Weston's final threat that he had not yet exhausted his enmity against me. But I carefully avoided making any reference to the further direction my fears had taken, or to that new misfortune that threatened me with ruin even after this horrible accusation had been satisfactorily cleared up. She listened to me without interruption until I had finished, and then she stood for some time without speaking, apparently considering seriously what I had told her.

" I think you did what I should have expected you to do," she said at length ; " it was not perhaps very wisely done, but it was honest and courageous. How can he do you any further injury ? "

" That is not my secret, dear, and I cannot tell you yet. But perhaps it was not altogether an idle threat—he may have had it in his power to do me a serious injury."

" But not in a way that would strike at your character or good name—not that ? Then we need not care ; let him do the worst he can. But, John, I can see one thing."

" What is that ? " I asked.

" That we are not strong enough to win this fight ourselves. You must have the advice of someone who has more experience, and someone who, perhaps, does not love you as well as I do. He will be able to see more clearly."

" There is only one person I can think of who might be able to assist me. I mean Mr. Stone, the lawyer at Fareham, who is my friend, I am sure, and a very honest man."

" Then you must lose no time in seeing him, and in the meantime I want you to promise me one thing."

" If you do not ask too much."

" It is not a great deal—only that you will not run any risk till you have succeeded. I am beginning to grow afraid ; I am sure you are in danger."

" I thought that you had all the courage, Victory. What is the danger that you foresee ? "

" I have more courage than wisdom," she said, " or I

could help you better. But I am sure the man who tried to kill your good name would not hesitate to attempt your life. Tell me this," she cried suddenly, " is there anyone who would gain anything, or thinks he would gain anything, if you were removed ? "

I hesitated before I spoke and then I answered —

" Perhaps—yes."

" Ah ! I thought as much—I was sure of it. And you think there is no danger—you think it is only my fear for you when I say I am sure that there is ? You will promise me to be careful ? And listen, John ; you will promise to let me hear from you every day or I shall imagine they have succeeded ? "

" That will be an easy thing to do, I can promise that. What would your father say if he knew you had such thoughts about his friend ? "

" A woman's instinct is clearer than a man's reason, and you must not laugh at me. I feel that you are in danger."

" The danger, Victory, is not of the kind you think, but I promise to be careful. And you still love me though I have not succeeded ? "

" Love is only itself, and doesn't ask whether you have succeeded or failed."

When I had left her and was once more on my way home I asked myself whether such steadfast faith, such sweet unflinching loyalty was not in itself compensation enough for any suffering that I might endure or for any prospective loss I might sustain.

But I did not share her fears for myself that there was any personal violence to be dreaded at the hands of my enemies. If they had succeeded in accomplishing what

I feared, they had already done as much as malice could
suggest, and had nothing or little to gain by taking me
out of the way. On my lord's death I would be as
powerless as if my proofs had never had existence, and
any claim that I might be foolish enough to make would
only recoil upon my own head. I felt, indeed, that
neither Weston nor his less capable confederate would
hesitate at any step, but I was secure in the feeling that
personal injury to myself, while it was fraught with possible danger to them, could be of no great advantage,
and that was my best security.

I had hardly entered the main hall of Heronford and
made a hurried enquiry as to the condition of my lord
than Madam Cassilis came to meet me, looking, I
thought, worn and haggard. I imagined afterwards she was
relieved to see me, but she did not seem to notice my
formal greeting and spoke with her usual brusqueness.

"You have been travelling, I see, Mr. Cassilis. I
thought we should not see you again."

"But you see I have returned, madam."

"I am not blind, sir. You care a great deal for your
—master. You have been absent for three days."

"But, madam, I hope you will remember your instructions. I could not quarrel with them, and I am
glad to hear my lord is better."

"Who told you that he is better? I cannot see that
he is greatly changed, but I do not think he suffers."

"I suppose I need not ask," I said. "Will you permit me to see him?"

"Not a moment if I could help it, for I am frank with
you, but my lord wishes it, and that is enough. You had

better see him at once, for he appears to care less for his sister than for his—" and without finishing the sentence she turned abruptly upon her heel and left me. Without waiting a moment I ran to my lord's room, and finding the door closed knocked softly. The nurse whom I had left in charge opened the door, and upon seeing me expressed her delight in a whisper.

"I'm glad you are come, sir. He has been calling for you for two days, and I am sure has been fretting his heart out. It has been 'John, John,' all the time. His eyes are shut, but I don't think he is sleeping."

I stole on tip-toe into the room and took up my place at the foot of the bed. My lord's white face was sunk among the pillows and his eyes were closed, but his face did not wear any further sign of suffering than that it was shrunk and wasted. When I had seen him before he had been respiring heavily, but he was now breathing softly. The light in the room was quite dim, for the blinds had been drawn, and I stood watching him where I stood at the foot of the bed for some time. After a little the nurse came up and joined me, and then I think she made a little noise, for he opened his eyes. At first though he had been staring at me steadily he did not appear to recognise me, for he made no sign and the expression upon his face did not alter. I imagined that if in my absence he had regained consciousness his mind had again relapsed into the blank into which it had fallen, and I stole quietly round to the side of the bed and took his nerveless hand in my own. But I found that his hand returned my pressure, and bringing my face close to his own I heard him whisper, though with great difficulty and with a catching in his throat, "John, John." I found that this was almost the only word he could utter; and that though his mind was now clear on one side he had altogether lost the power of motion, and that a paralysis nearly as complete had fallen upon his speech.

I sat down upon the bedside and remained for some time in silence, holding his hand in mine. I cannot tell you how I knew, yet I was certain he was glad to see me, and that he was happier now that I had come back. I had longed for the moment when he could again understand me, and now that the time had come I was almost afraid to break the news to him that was trembling on my tongue. Yet I felt whatever happened he must hear the good news before he died, and that joy is a medicine that seldom kills. I therefore motioned the nurse from the room, and waiting till she had closed the door behind her I bent over him and kissed him on the forehead.

"You can hear and understand me, my lord?"

A lingering pressure upon my hand was the only answer.

"I am going to make you very happy," I said. "You must prepare yourself to hear good news—wonderful news—and I am not sure whether you can bear it."

He turned his dull eyes toward me and gazed at me with a fixed look; I wondered whether he perfectly understood me.

"You can hardly believe," I went on, "what I have to tell you, but it is true, perfectly true. There is no more doubt about it than that I am sitting here beside you. Think, my dear lord, of what I know you would like best in the world. It is that; it is that I have to tell you. Perhaps we had better wait till you have thought what the good news is likely to be, for I fear you cannot bear it now."

But I saw that he understood me perfectly. He drew my hand closer to him, and again, with the catching in his throat, he called out my name.

"If I thought you could bear it," I cried. "It is almost too good for you to believe it. You have been made to believe a lie, and I have discovered the truth—I and another. Can you not guess what that truth is? You remember the night we were together in the Book Room and what we saw there—that was a part of the lie, but it began before that. It began—" I could never understand or explain it; you may remain incredulous and declare that this is only an idle story, but so surely as I write, as I was speaking, my lord sat upright in his bed and gazed at me with widening eyes, from which the dull, heavy stare had completely disappeared.

"My dear lord, you have been punished for nothing. Your brother is not dead; William Cassilis is alive and well."

I had broken the news to him far more abruptly than I intended, for I saw the effect I had already produced. But I thought now that I had killed him. His body seemed to relax; he dropped my hand that he had still been holding, and he made a violent effort to speak that fell into a little choking gurgle. Then quite plainly and altogether in his natural voice he called out "Thank God!" and fell back upon his pillows. I ran hastily to the door and called to the nurse, who had been waiting in the corridor. For a moment we both thought he was dead, for he made no response to our efforts to revive him, and then gradually his eyes opened and he raised his hand.

CHAPTER XVIII

A BLOW IN THE DARK

WHEN I left the sick-room I had the satisfaction of knowing that the news which I had broken so unskilfully had done Lord Heronford no injury. On the contrary, the first shock, which had produced an effect so extraordinary, had seemed rather to have quickened his faculties and to have supplied a healthful stimulus. I have, indeed, since heard of cases in which a sudden shock has given the paralytic a complete command over his useless limbs, but though nothing of that kind happened here, a slight, if transitory, improvement was certainly noticeable. I was, however, forbidden the sick-room when it was thought further excitement might prove injurious to the patient, and I was now at liberty to pursue my enquiries upon that subject which had caused me so much uneasiness and distress.

I suppose years afterwards one likes to dwell on his former weaknesses and his serious follies with a mild complaisance, whether because we have a secret sympathy with folly, or because we are pleased to think we have outgrown our weakness. I can now recall with a smile the subterfuges I adopted to gain a few moments respite before I entered the room where I felt my fate was to be decided. One moment I was flattered with the hope that I was the victim of my own unfounded fears; the next I was plunged in the most profound despondency, and between fear and hope I hung vacillating, hardly daring to take the decisive step that was to resolve my doubts. I lingered on my way down the staircase and stood halting in the corridor, and when I came to the door I walked two or three times past it before I ventured to turn the handle. When I had thrown open the door I stood with a beating heart upon the threshold; so far as I could see nothing had been disturbed, but everything was as I had last left it. My papers lay in order upon the table; the silver candlesticks did not appear to have been moved; and the books of account which usually lay upon the escritoire were in their usual position. When I noticed this last circumstance I gave an audible sigh of relief; I could almost have cried out with joy; after all I had been pursued by a shadow and tortured by my own foolish fancy. I was at last able to breathe freely.

I was so certain now that all was right that I did not at once make any closer scrutiny, but sat down at the table thinking how different my state of mind would have been had my fears been well founded.

It was at this moment that by some chance my eyes fell on a handkerchief lying close to the escritoire. I do not know what possessed me but I rose from my seat, and walking across the room lifted it from the floor. It did not belong either to my lord or myself; it was too fine to have been the property of a servant. Then I turned it over and examined it; embroidered in one corner were the letters "W.B.C." At the sight I turned hot and cold in the same instant. My hand trembled so much that I could hardly take the key from my pocket, and with difficulty was able to fit it into the lock. But

I could not turn the key at all. I imagined at first that it was my excitement that prevented me, but I was very soon convinced that the lock had been tampered with. Then I saw that the wood had been split near the hinges, and hastily taking hold of the lid that came off easily in my hands. My worst fears were realised. A single glance showed me that—my ruin was complete! The other papers did not appear to have been disturbed, or if they had, had been laid back again in their place as though the thief had lingered over his work, but the packet was gone. I knew that I need search for it no further; I knew where it had been laid before my lord had handed me the key; and, alas! I was only too certain where it had gone. I let the lid fall from my hands with a crash; I was paralysed by the blow, and stood staring at the wreck before me like one distraught by his grief.

Still you must not think that after the first stunning moment I was so beaten to the earth that I resigned myself to the worst or resolved hopelessly to abandon the field to my enemies. Perhaps it was partly resentment, partly pride, but I was determined that I would not surrender, even to this blow, until I could fight no further and had exhausted every means. But what was I to do? To whom should I turn for assistance and advice? The very nature of the papers prevented me from publishing my loss, or giving my full confidence to any one with whom I was acquainted. Unless I extended that complete confidence I felt that I could not hope for help; my own knowledge of the perpetrators was founded upon the secret those papers contained.

But it was impossible for me to rest, and my thoughts

turned instinctively to Mr. Stone, in whose prudence and common sense I had the utmost confidence, and who perhaps might be able to assist me with his advice. I had no sooner thought of him than I made up my mind not to lose any further time. Late as it was in the afternoon I resolved to ride at once to Fareham, and put the matter before him as fully as I dared. I had no idea what advice he could give me or what assistance he was able to render, but I felt that if any one could be of use it was he, and at the worst I would lose nothing by seeing him. Accordingly without losing any time I had my horse saddled, and in about a quarter of an hour was in the courtyard booted and spurred for my journey. It happened to be John Transome, a great favourite of mine, who was holding my horse, and he expressed his surprise that I was riding so late and asked whether he would sit up for me.

"I am afraid you must, John," I said as I took the reins in my hand, "for I cannot be back much before midnight. I am riding to Fareham on a matter of business and may be detained an hour or two."

"If you are coming back to-night, sir, you will have to be careful. It is likely to prove a very black night and there won't be any moon."

"Old Whitefoot could find his way back alone," I said. "I am quite certain to be back to-night."

The steady old horse must have wondered what new and evil spirit had entered into his master, for I certainly did not spare him, and when I got to Fareham he was covered with a lather of foam. It is eighteen miles from Heronford to Fareham by the high-road, but though I

travelled faster than I had ever done in my life the way
had never seemed so long. It was not that I was anxious
to finish my errand, or that I was likely to gain much
when it was finished, but in my present state of mind I
felt the absolute necessity for doing something, and in
some way or other that I was losing what might prove
precious time.

It was already dark when I got to Mr. Stone's door,
and having tied my horse to the railing, I went up the
steps and plied the brass knocker three or four times without compelling any answer. This was so unlike the
methodical little bachelor's household ways that I began
to think there was no one within, when the door was
opened by a comely maid servant whose cheeks were very
red, and who seemed not a little confused at my summons.

"Is Mr. Stone within?" I said.

"He is not at home, sir. He left the house at six."

"When do you expect him back?"

"I don't know, sir; I am not sure. He goes usually
to the vicar's in the evening, but he went off in the gig."

"And you have no idea at what time he will return?"

"No, sir, I can't say; but, perhaps, sir, that is ——"

"Well?" I asked.

"Perhaps, sir," she said, with what I thought was a tell-
tale blush deepening on her cheek, "you would see John
—John Vanney—if you would not mind. John——"

"I will see any one," I said, "who can tell me what
I want—John Vanney or any one else."

I followed her into the dining-room feeling terribly depressed by my disappointment, and a few minutes after
she had left me a young man made his appearance, whom

I thought I had seen once or twice in Mr. Stone's office. He had evidently made a very hurried toilet for the mark of the wet brush was apparent on his hair, and for a moment he seemed almost as self-conscious as the maid had done, but he was not so long in regaining his natural confidence. He was afflicted with an atrocious squint, but appeared very good-natured, and was certainly not wanting in a moderate amount of self-possession.

"I am Mr. S-S-Stone's clerk, sir. P-p-perhaps you r-remember to have s-seen me?"

Some of his words he took with a gallop, running them into one another, and others he took with a little gulp, but upon the whole his rate of progression was slow and exasperating.

"Yes," I said. "I remember you. When shall I be able to see Mr. Stone?"

"Upon my w-w-word I don't know, M-M-Mr. Cassilis. He's g-gone to make old M-Mrs. C-Cooksley's will, and I d-don't think he'll b-be back m-much before morning."

"I am sorry to hear that," I said. "I wanted to see him upon important business."

"I b-beg your p-pardon, Mr. Cassilis, b-but is it about the n-new leases, sir? You may not t-think it b-but I know as m-much about them as M-Mr. Stone. He t-trusts me with everything."

"It is not about the new leases. I want to see him on quite a different business."

Notwithstanding his unpromising appearance, Mr. Vanney showed a natural aptitude for his profession.

"N-not the new l-leases, sir? I b-beg your pardon. I b-believe I understand. We heard L-Lord Heronford was ill. I d-do that b-business regularly now, M-Mr. Cassilis, and my c-con-v-vey-ancing is n-nearly as good as M-Mr. Stone's. If the m-matter is urgent I c-can go with you m-myself, and you may be s-satisfied that the d-devises, b-bequests, and limitations will be q-quite correct."

"I don't doubt your knowledge, Mr. Vanney, but I won't trouble you. My business was with Mr. Stone, but since he is not likely to be home to-night I suppose I must wait until the morning. Will you be good enough to tell him that I shall be with him at eleven o'clock to-morrow, and that it is of the utmost importance I should see him?"

"I will c-convey your m-message to him, sir, and I am s-sorry that I c-can't be of no use to you. You will be s-staying in Fareham to-night, sir?"

That was my intention when I unloosed my horse from the railing where I had tied him, but I do not know what caused me to alter my mind. I had thought of putting up at the "Green Man" to save myself the fatigue of riding back the next morning, and I had even ridden some way in that direction, when I suddenly touched Whitefoot with the spur and turned his head in the direction of Heronford. Life is made up of these impulses, and I have sometimes found that the burden of the future turns on such undetermined acts.

When I left Fareham behind me the night had grown very dark, with a heavy mist rising that threatened to settle into rain. But I did not trouble about the darkness, for my horse was very surefooted and there is a fine broad road all the way to the hamlet of Amberley West, where you turn off the high-road to Heronford. On the whole

I rather enjoyed the solitude and darkness, and the time passed much more quickly than it had done on my mad gallop to Fareham. There was something congenial to my mood in this midnight isolation, but, indeed, there was no health in my thoughts, and none of that steady fortitude with which a man should face the frown of evil days. My mind was still so agitated that the course of my thoughts would not run clear, but was lost in the tumultuous riot of my emotions and passed into gloomy despondency.

As I came through Barstowe I heard a clock strike eleven, and I quickened my pace a little until I came to the turn at Amberley West. There rather a curious incident happened which did not strike me as being of much significance at the time, but the meaning of which I discovered afterwards. As I turned into the narrower road a man upon horseback, apparently coming from the opposite direction, though I had not heard the sound of the hoofs, suddenly shot out of the darkness and almost touched me before I was able to rein in my horse. I could not see his face, nor did I think he could see mine, but before I could utter a word he had wheeled round and galloped back in the direction in which I was going. I called after him, but he returned no answer, and I smiled when I thought he had probably taken me for a highwayman, though such romantic personages were even at that time seldom to be met on our roads. It never occurred to me that he had any design upon myself, and in the end I ceased to think about the incident.

But I soon came to see that the adventures of the night were not over. There is a long hill with a sharp turn near the middle as you come up to Heronford, where one must necessarily travel slowly. As I came toward the foot of this hill I thought I caught sight of a light upon the road, stationary at times and then moving with a fitful, irregular motion. Folk generally retire early to rest in this neighbourhood and I could not imagine what was wrong, especially as I soon heard the sound of voices raised either in distress or anger. I was armed only with my heavy riding-whip, but I pushed on more rapidly, and soon came near enough to see that this light was carried by a man who stood in the centre of the road. There were a couple of horses standing near him, and close by the hedge I saw a heavy chaise, the near wheels of which had evidently left the track and gone into the ditch. I thought at first the chaise had been overturned, and when I came close I reined in my horse and asked what was wrong. At that moment I saw another man close to the carriage and apparently endeavouring to move the chaise into the road, but his efforts did not seem to meet with much success. This man raised his head where he was stooping beside the wheel.

"It's easy to ask what is wrong," he answered in a surly voice, again resuming his task. "I'd be more thankful if you'd step down and give me a hand. There's a lady inside that is nearly frightened to death."

"She is not hurt, I hope?"

"More frightened than hurt. What's the use of talking?"

"Not much," I answered pleasantly, "but I'll give you what assistance I am able. If we can't manage it I can bring you help in a few minutes."

I dismounted from my horse thinking that at least I had

to do with a very ill-tempered fellow, but feeling concerned for his passenger. I left Whitefoot standing perfectly steady on the road and went over and joined the man at the chaise.

" You can't see what you have to do in the dark," I said. " Bring over the light and let us see exactly what is wrong."

The man came a little nearer with the lantern, and when I saw how matters stood a dark suspicion flashed upon my mind. There was nothing to prevent the horses drawing the chaise out of the few inches of ditch into which the wheel seemed to have slipped; the accident had been planned; the men were either laughing at me or had acted with some much more serious intention. I instantly drew back and caught my riding-whip firmly in my hand.

"What game is this you are playing? " I cried. " There is nothing wrong here, and ——"

Someone had been struck—a crashing blow on the head—struck in the dark and without warning—a murderous blow that rung with a dull thud in my ears. Had the earth suddenly become blood red, and was it I—I, John Cassilis—who was catching at the empty air and had called out once with that thrilling, stifled cry for help? I was not sure; I did not know; and then I became unconscious, and for a long time remembered nothing more.

CHAPTER XIX

THE BIRD IN THE TRAP

I DO not remember how long I remained unconscious,
but it must certainly have been for some hours. I have
a confused and indistinct recollection of the rough jolting
of the chaise, and of being carried between a couple of
men into a colder air that set my head throbbing. But it
is all a painful dream, and I think that no sooner did I
begin to come back to consciousness than I would swoon
off again, for I had little broken gleams of remembrance
shut in as suddenly by the blank of forgetfulness. The
first thing I remember perfectly was lifting my hand to
my head and finding it clotted with blood. I recollected
then that something unpleasant had happened, but at first
I imagined that it was someone else and not myself who
had suffered. It could not be myself for I felt no pain,
and though I had a feeling of languor I was almost happy.
But gradually my thoughts became clearer; it was my own
blood that I felt, and myself who was lying at my length
in a bed of rustling straw; it was I who had been struck,
and—immediately the whole circumstances were present
to my mind. I did not know whether my life had been
aimed at, but certainly whoever used this violence had
been indifferent regarding the consequences. The scheme
for removing me had been deliberately planned, and there
was no doubt who were the authors of the design or of
the object with which it had been accomplished. I had
been struck down cruelly—relentlessly—and wherever I

might be I was still in the hands of my assailants. And whither had I been carried? What was the place of my imprisonment? I raised myself on my elbow in the straw and looked round me; then I fell back upon the bed with a kind of groan.

It must have been now some hours after daybreak for three separate shafts of grey light streamed through as many little grated windows or apertures high up in the wall near the ceiling. The room in which I lay was evidently a kind of cellar, the floor of which was considerably lower than the surface of the ground. The walls were apparently very thick and were built of rough stone, down which here and there poured a little trickle of perspiring damp. The door was reached by means of a flight of stone steps, and upon every side of me were piled up casks and puncheons from which there came a sickening smell of raw spirits, and over which I could hear the scurrying rats. The floor was paved with broad stone flags, and, so far as I could see, the ceiling was composed of the same material, but I noticed that in the centre of this was a wide wooden trap, by means of which entrance could be gained from above.

Had I been carried back to Langston? or was I confined in some secret hiding-place of the free traders? Was it intended by my captors that I should be left here to die? or, if not, what more dreadful fate was in store for me? There was no possibility of my being traced; it would even be days before I should be missed at all. Missed! There was probably no one who would do more than coldly inquire after me, and then turn away satisfied with the answer that I could not be found. Not Victory—no, she was different—and if the loyal old captain only knew the truth ! But he would probably never know the whole truth now.

At first when I recovered consciousness my mind was quite clear, but it cannot have been long before the fever supervened and I was entirely prostrated. My head was wracked with pain; I was consumed by an intolerable thirst, and in my delirium I was carried through interminable caverns of ice and pressed down under suffocating avalanches of snow.

I had no idea how long I lay in this condition; it seemed to me that I passed through months of torture, though I discovered afterwards that I cannot have spent more than four-and-twenty hours in this way. As I lay turning on the straw I imagined that occasionally someone raised my head and gave me a drink from the pannikin that was lying at my side, and more than once I imagined that the trap-door in the ceiling had been raised and that someone had remained there staring at me with fixed and wide-opened eyes. As my fever abated and I came back to myself I thought it very likely that in the first matter I had really not been mistaken, but the latter I set down to mere delirium, and convinced myself that it was altogether a hallucination.

It must have been drawing toward evening for the light in the cellar was growing fainter, when I heard the sound of the door being unlocked, and presently someone came cautiously down the steep flight of stone steps. I looked up eagerly, and in the darkening twilight saw a man carrying a platter and a jug, which he set down close to me. I sat up in the straw, but it was too dark to see his face.

"I am glad," I cried, "to see the sight of a fellow-being. For God's sake tell me where I am and how long I am to be kept in this dungeon."

"Till the master can do better for you. You feel more comfortable? I'm glad you can talk now. I thought you were going safe to Davy Jones."

"Yes, I feel better," I said, "but am weak as a child."

"Sakes, you have bled like a pig; but that won't hurt you, and you'll feel your feet under you in no time. The master hits hard when ——"

"Who is your master?"

"You must ask no questions, but I don't mind making you a bit comfortable if I can. Is there anything more I can do for you—a rug or a blanket?"

"Yes," I said, "it is cold; but I don't mind the cold. There is something you might do for me that I should like far better, and you will be well paid for it."

"What might that be?"

"If you will carry a message for me ——"

"It can't be done at no price. I don't say that I'm not sorry to see a gentleman down on his luck, and I wouldn't mind being friendly, but here you are and here you must bide till further orders. Take my advice and just make yourself as easy as you can, for if you once cross the master you won't go much further, and you may fare a deal worse."

"I don't see how I can be much worse. Tell me one thing—am I in Langston Priory?"

"You may spier at me till Doomsday, and as long as I'm here you'll get a civil answer and decent victuals, but you'll get no information. I'm not responsible for the bringing of you here, but I am responsible to see that you don't get out."

"At least," I said, "you will take a message for me to your master ?"

"Eh ! I would like to see myself trotting on any such fool's errand. Man, if I begun to carry messages to him I know what answer I'd be like to get. No, no, I'll just keep on the safe side of him for your sake, and I'll bring you down a blanket and a bit of a light to pass the time, though with the rats running about you'll have no want for company."

The man was evidently disposed to be friendly toward me, but was not to be shaken in his dogged honesty to his employer, and could be prevailed on to give me neither information nor assistance.

He went away, and in a short time came back with a blanket and a ship's lantern, which he set down on a cask beside me. Nor did his little attentions cease here. With more skill and tenderness than I could have expected from him he examined and bound up my wounded head, and then arranged a pillow for me. It was, perhaps, only a touch of common humanity that prompted him, but his spontaneous kindness affected me.

"If I am ever able to thank you," I said, "I won't forget what you have done for me."

"Hoot! Hoot! it's just nothing at all. You're not the value of a pin the worse, but you should thank God that He made your skull so thick when He fashioned you. A good thick head is a gift in some parts, and it has just stood your friend here. I'll be wishing you a good-night, and when I come down to see you in the morning I'll be finding you jumping about as merry as a grig."

He again passed up the stone staircase and secured the door carefully after him, leaving me with the light burning and a good deal easier in my body. I lay back on my pillow watching the dull yellow gleam, and listening to the occasional drip of damp in the further corner. After a while the rats that had been disturbed by my gaoler's entrance began to come out of their hiding-places again, and sat watching me with their bright, inquisitive eyes till they had become accustomed to my presence, and fearlessly resumed their gambols. I thought that sleep was impossible; I own that I should almost have been afraid to resign myself to slumber if I had thought it could have visited me. A thousand hideous suggestions presented themselves to my mind that I could not banish. If I had dared I should have liked to put out the light and shut out the sight of the dreary stone walls and the grey rats that tumbled over one another on the floor.

At first every sense was awake to its full stretch and span; I was alive to every sound; but gradually I began to grow drowsy, and though I struggled against the feeling as long as I was able I fell into a troubled and broken sleep. But it must have been deeper than I had imagined, and have lasted much longer. Indeed, it must have continued several hours. I awakened with a cry, and started up on my couch. The lantern had gone out and it was as black as midnight. The hoarse, eldritch scream of laughter that had awakened me still rang through the dungeon and echoed upon every side of me. I could not tell from what quarter it had come, but it continued long after I had risen to my feet and stood listening to it with a beating heart. There was no meaning in the sound—it was wild, hoarse, discordant beyond description. I tried to pierce the darkness in vain, but nowhere was there a ray of light to be seen. And then the mad laughter died away as suddenly as it had commenced, leaving me again alone with the intolerable silence.

I found myself trembling in every nerve; I could think of no explanation of the sound. It was impossible to imagine that my enemies had added this further torture to my suffering, unless indeed they had desired to drive me mad. Surely their fiendish malice could not have driven them so far as that; and yet what other solution was there of the mystery? If I could only have seen what I had to face I felt that I could bear anything with equanimity; but the expectant fear that lives in darkness laid entire hold upon me. I stood listening for a repetition of the sound; I sought to catch the faintest whisper or movement—there was only the silence of death about and around me.

Further rest was now altogether out of the question, and never in my life did I long so eagerly for morning. I thought it would never come, and when at last the sickly grey dawn began to creep through the little windows I welcomed it as the coming of a friend. As that kindly light grew and broadened I could see nothing in the cellar to account for what I had heard; nothing appeared to have been moved or disturbed, and certainly the door had never been opened or I should have heard it.

I suppose it was about eight o'clock when my gaoler

of the evening before made his appearance with my breakfast. I found him a thick, low-set, sturdy fellow, who
appeared to have something of the sailor in his carriage,
though his dress was rather that of an honest countryman.
His face was very good-natured, and a white scar across
his cheek gave his countenance rather a humorous turn.

"I told you you'd be right as a trivet this morning and
could put your pins under you like a Jack marine.
Hope you slept well?"

"No," I said, "I have not slept."

"No? I am sorry to hear that. But then I always
think myself the rats are uncanny bedfellows. For my
part give me a sonsy ——"

"It was not the rats," I said; "I don't think I should
have minded the rats so much. Have you no idea of
what disturbed me during the night?"

"Unless, maybe, it was the old chaps —— No, I
don't think they would trouble you now, they have been
so long under. I never saw any sign of them myself.
You had company then?"

I told him how much I had been alarmed and what I
had heard, and I could see that he was thrown into
genuine perplexity at the news, and perhaps a little stirred
by superstitious fear. It was evident that he had no ink-
ling of the source of the disturbance, and if a trick had
been played upon me he was certainly not a party to it.

"I think you must have been dreaming," he said; "a
knock on the head like this gives one queer fancies, and
I'll take my oath that nobody got out or came in since I
turned the key in the door last night myself. I don't
hold by spirits myself, leastways unless they run in this

shape, though I'm not saying that such things haven't been seen by a time. There was my own aunt by marriage, old Judy Pentreath, saw the corpse-light the night Simon went under in the old *Fly Away*—but then she was a Cornish woman, and that doesn't count. No, no, mister, you may take it from me you were dreaming, though if you weren't— Gosh, I should not like to spend a night here myself, and that's the truth of it."

"I am sure you wouldn't," I said, "and think of my case."

"That's between you and the master," he answered, "and I can't interfere. You mustn't try on any of your soft sawder with me for I can't and won't listen to you, but as I say, in the way of my duty, I'll do you a good turn if I can."

"You are a good fellow, and I am glad to have your good-will. But you haven't thought you are helping to commit a felony."

"As like as not," he answered imperturbably, "but I always leave the thinking to the master, and it saves me a world of bother. But I'll leave you to your breakfast, for I'm sure there'd be more trouble still if I listened to you."

It was evident that he was still a good deal alarmed by my communication, for before he left me he made an examination of the cellar so far as he was able, and as he went out I saw him shaking his head, though whether in doubt or in pity I did not know. I did not think I could have eaten at all, yet when I began I found that I was able to make an excellent repast, and felt a great deal the better for it. At least my captors did not intend that I should starve to death. My meal consisted of a rabbit pie excellently flavoured, sweet butter and bread, and a jug of generous beer, deliciously cool and refreshing.   Certainly it gave me fresh spirit, and for the first time I began to investigate more closely the place of my confinement. I dragged a couple of casks under the window and, setting the one upon the other, clambered up by means of the iron bar across the aperture till I was able to look out.   But my view was bounded by a sloping bank of earth and a dense growth of laurel trees that grew upon it, very high and luxuriant.   I remembered that at one side of Langston Priory there was just such a growth of laurels, and I had now no doubt, if I ever entertained any, that that was the place of my imprisonment.   But there was no possibility of escape in this way, for the window, even if unguarded, was too narrow to admit my body, and the wall was built of massive single stones that could not be dislodged.

When I had again descended to the floor I examined the walls where the boxes and casks left me room, but I could find no other door than that which was reached by means of the stone steps.   This door also I had the curiosity to examine, and I found that it must have been of extreme age, but was so closely studded with great nails and strips of iron as to be almost composed of metal.

I sat down upon the lowest step that led to this door, and by the mearest chance my eye happened to light upon the trap in the ceiling, the existence of which I had altogether forgotten.   It flashed upon me at once that it must have been by this means that my mysterious visitor of last night had succeeded in alarming me.   There was a ring in the centre of the wood by means of which the trap could be let down from the inside, and I resolved to take an early opportunity of examining it, for I could easily reach it in the same way that I had reached the window.   There was no definite thought of escape in my mind, as I was sure that every possible means had been taken to prevent that, but I was visited by faint and shadowy gleams of that hope that keeps a man's spirit and heart alive.   Something unforeseen might happen—I could hardly tell what.   Whoever had opened the door might leave it unsecured imagining I could not reach it, or after all I might find the means of prevailing upon the good-nature of my gaoler, whose sympathy I already seemed to have won.   At any rate, whatever fate was in store for me, it was hardly likely that I should be kept here long, and in the turn and change of fortune —

Surely the trap had moved; surely the heavy frame had changed its position; surely I now heard the sound of footsteps on the floor above!   I sat motionless, filled with expectation, and almost, I confess, with dread.   It was not merely fancy; my senses had not played me false. I saw the trap-door slowly raised and a bright ray of sunshine streamed in from above.   Finally the trap fell back with a clang, and a moment after there appeared at the opening the face that I imagined I had seen in my dreams.   At first the round, staring eyes did not see me; then they met mine.   No sooner had that happened than the loud wild laughter that had so alarmed me before again broke out.   But there was no terror in it now; everything had been satisfactorily explained to me.

"Ho! ho! ho!   The bird's in the trap."

It was the voice of poor Archie Weston.

CHAPTER XX

THERE was a touch of grotesque humour in the situation which might have appealed to me under different circumstances. I had been almost frightened out of my wits; I had racked my brains to think of a possible explanation of the sound I had heard, and here in a moment I found that I had been driven to terror by the vacant laugh of a harmless imbecile. But it was not the incongruity between my alarm and its cause that appealed to me now. I was filled with quite a different feeling. The walls of my prison were so thick, the window and door so strong and securely guarded, that escape seemed hopeless, but here was at last perhaps a loophole that offered some opportunity for hope. My enemies had certainly never foreseen or imagined this visit. Whither the trap-door led I did not know, but I felt that it probably led toward freedom. If Sir Archie had managed to escape observation and find his way hither, I thought it not unlikely that I might be able to make my exit by the same means and equally avoid detection. This was my first thought, and it was with this rising hope that I rose from my seat and softly called out his name.

He lay looking at me with an expression in which cunning and triumph were blended, but at first, though I spoke to him several times, I could not get him to return me any answer. He still laughed occasionally; not, however, in the same boisterous, strident tones, but almost under his breath, and raising his head at times as though he were afraid of being detected. I was anxious not to alarm him, and I did all that I was able to show him by my manner that he had no reason to fear me. He regarded me like an animal, at once curious and alarmed, but by degrees he appeared to grow more confident, and allowed me to come close under where he lay.

"We are old friends, Sir Archie," I said, "and how is the jackdaw? Will you bring him to pay me a visit?"

"It is too dark in the priest's hole for Jeremy, but I want to see the little grey fellows running about and frisking their long tails. Ho! ho! I often come here to watch them but they never think I can see them in the dark. They come out of the hole under the window and they go pop—pop—one after the other."

"Will you come down and see them?" I said. "They are quite friendly now and I have seen them all."

He drew back with a little shudder.

"Archie's legs aren't long enough and he doesn't like the dark. And it's cold there, very cold. I don't like the cold."

"Then you are right not to come down here."

"I should like to come down," he went on, nodding his head knowingly, "if it weren't for the dark. I know there are spiders down there—great fat fellows with long legs—black-beetles, and little things I can't see that go tick-tick. But I daren't—I daren't. It is the place where the damned are locked up."

"Then," I said softly, "you must help me to get out."

"No, no, I know all about you—you must never

come up again.   George says you are better dead.   But Archie is sorry for you.   Is your head better ? "

" My head aches as badly as your own does sometimes, Archie.   I am sure you wouldn't keep me here if you could help it."

" If I thought you wouldn't hurt Archie—but I can't, for George would be angry and I won't offend George."

" But he need never know," I urged persuasively ; " and listen, Archie, I have been here ever so long, and I can tell you all about those little grey fellows that you like to watch.   There is one that must be at least a hundred years old he is so wise, and he limps a little as if he used to go on a crutch ; and there is another—   Oh, I shall tell you all about them.   And I want to hear more about the jackdaw and the owls and the fox and whether he is better."

" Simpson is dead," he cried.   " The devil killed poor Simon."

" I am sorry to hear that.   You must be very sorry to lose him."

" I will kill this devil," he cried passionately.   " I hate him !   I hate him !   Do you think you could help me to kill the devil ? "

" Perhaps—I do not know."

" I am waiting till I get a chance, but he is strong and cunning.   If I could only catch him when he is asleep !   If you saw this devil you could tell whether you could help me ? "

" We might be able to do something together.   But you must not let anyone know."

" Archie is very wise sometimes," said the poor creature, shaking his head, "and no one knows that he had found out the priest's hole. But I will show you the devil, and then you will be able to say whether you are strong enough. You must not move till I come back."

He raised himself up from his prostrate position and stole away so softly that I could not hear the sound of his footsteps. I had no idea what object he had in view nor what wild scheme was working in his confused mind, but I knew that such a mind as his often shows great power of secrecy and cunning, and I hoped there might be some advantage in the secret he seemed anxious to share with me. I remained standing where I was, and it was not more than two or three minutes till he returned in a state of great excitement.

"Ho! ho!" he cried, "I can show you the devil, but you must come up softly and make no noise. And you must only come up for a minute for George would be angry, and you know I wouldn't vex George."

No sooner had I found that my appearance would not alarm him and that he would offer no opposition than I began to arrange the means of ascending through the trap. This was very easily done. By placing half a dozen of the smaller casks on end I formed a secure and stable structure upon which I hastily clambered, and then pulling myself up I scrambled on to the floor above. On my sudden entrance Sir Archie appeared a little frightened and seemed inclined to fly, but I speedily reassured him and we again became very friendly. The apartment in which I found myself was quite bare and ruinous and seemed to have been formerly used as a little chapel or, indeed, may have been the refectory in former times. The roof was very high and arched, and the row of windows, which were now unglazed, were of what I suppose is the Gothic shape and placed high up in the wall, and certainly far beyond my reach. There was one doorway at the further end with a great deal of grotesque carving about it, and excepting this there was no other means of exit. These general features I observed at the first hurried glance, but I was now more anxious to retain Sir Archie's good-will and avoid giving him any cause for alarm.

"Now," said I, "you see you have no reason to be frightened at all, and I am going to help you if I can. I will follow wherever you may lead me, but remember, you must take great care that no one may see us."

He regarded me with a very knowing look and laid his finger on his lip.

"Wait till you see. Ho! ho! no one would think of it," and then he went on as though he were imparting a secret of importance, "I found it one day when I had lost old Jeremy, and the sly fellow was trying to get back to his old haunts. But I kept it close for the rogue's sake, and now I will let you see the devil through it."

Taking me by the arm he drew me to the door, which I found led upon a narrow corridor with windows like those in the apartment we had quitted and built upon the same level. At the end of this passage were half a dozen steps, and after we had ascended them I found myself in a little gallery, round the entire circuit of which there ran a stone bench. In the wall opposite where we had come up there was a small aperture about a foot in diameter, but very skilfully masked, and which I failed to see until Archie drew my attention to it. It had formerly been covered with an iron grating of some sort, for I saw the marks in the stone where the clamps had been fixed, but these had long since disappeared, and it was now merely filled with rubbish. By standing upon the stone bench we were able to reach it very easily, and Archie, putting in his hand with great circumspection, cleared away the material that choked the aperture.

"Now," he said, "look down and see the devil for yourself. You needn't be afraid, for I have watched him a hundred times."

I do not know with what object this post of observation was originally planned, but certainly nothing could have better answered its purpose. I could see every corner of the room into which I looked, and I could equally hear every word that was spoken. But certainly since either the wakeful abbot had spied upon the erring brethren, or the host had overlooked his suspected guest, none of the watchers had ever been filled with livelier emotions than I experienced at that moment.

Mr. George Weston stood with his back to the fire of wood that burned in the grate, and at the moment when I first saw him was speaking his mind with great plainness and emphasis. Sprawling over the table near him with a look half indifferent, half sulky, and perhaps one part drunk, was Mr. William Cassilis himself. Weston had evidently not long returned from his morning ride, for his boots were bespattered with mud and he still carried his riding-whip, while I thought his companion seemed only lately risen from bed.

"Dam'me, you drunken brute," Weston was saying, "you would spoil all with your folly? What more do you want than the snug quarters you have here, where you can drink yourself to death if you please, and my company when you are sober? I'm d——, but I wish I had never had anything to do with you, for I feel as if the noose was round my neck already. There's a hue and cry raised over the country already, and there's one person at least imagines I have had a hand in it. We managed the affair cursedly ill between us. The old horse got home without his rider in the morning, and they found the fool's hat and whip on the road. What was it to me which of you won in your sparring match? What have I to gain whether he elbowed you out of Heronford or no? I was an idiot to mix myself up in it, and if I hadn't hated the supercilious cur so much I would have seen you both to perdition before I moved an inch. But I am in it now, and if you think I am going to let you hang me with any of your foolish tricks you don't know George Weston."

"That's all very well and I don't want to quarrel, but how long do you mean to keep me mewed up here in this cursed old ruin? I must get out I tell you, or I will go mad. What with the blue devils and the drink and that jibbering idiot ——"

"You had better leave my brother out of the question," cried Weston angrily, "and remember, at least, that he is my brother, whom I won't have ill-treated. But you will stay here till you have served my purpose, and till I can see my way to let you go with safety to myself. We are both in the same boat, but don't forget that I could hang you with a word. Robbery, Mr. Cassilis; burglary, Mr. Cassilis; attempted murder, and if you had struck a little harder — Oh, no! I can't afford to let you swagger to Heronford yet. Your business is not finished and neither is mine."

"It is all your own business," cried William Cassilis, "and I know very well why you want me shut up here. I have got all that I wanted."

"But I have not, and that is the more important matter of the two. My dear Will, you must try and be reasonable."

"Reasonable! I have done all that you wanted me, and upon my soul you forget, Weston."

"What do I forget?"

"That when Heronford dies, and he can't live long now, I'll be the biggest man in the county. I will, by ——"

Weston laughed.

"You can't get that out of your head for a minute. And who has made you? Who put you in the way, and put the cards in your hand that won the game? But don't be too sure, Will; don't crow till we have finished."

"What more have we got to do? I have the papers ——"

"You forget that we haven't yet got the person most interested in them out of the way. I have no liking for murder, though I think there is a friend of mine who would hardly have hesitated even at that. It's an infernally ugly word, and perhaps I don't hate your nephew enough to give my friend a free hand. No, no, I don't say that you meant anything by that blow on the head— but we must arrange things differently."

"Arrange things as you please, only see that he doesn't come back to give me trouble."

" I don't think," said Weston, " that he will give you much trouble when we have finished with him. I have told them to take good care of him, but I have been considering matters, and I think a sea voyage would be good for his health."

" The longer the better, and if the vessel founders ——"

" I am afraid I couldn't afford that even for your sake, my dear Will, but I'll wager that I manage without going so far as that. The heir would hardly be pleased if he knew how I had arranged for his comfort."

" You'll arrange both of us beautifully before you have done," cries Will with an oath.

" I am more concerned for myself than for you at any rate, and I propose for my own good to ship your relative to the West Indies. There are some sugar plantations there that I think would suit him, and some friends of mine who could show him how to work. One thing is certain, the sooner we wash our hands of him and his affairs the safer I shall feel."

" I should like to see the nigger among the canes with all my heart," said Will heartily, " but can you manage that ? "

" There's nothing easier. The *Swallow* will be off Langston to-morrow night if the weather holds, and Claude Slingsby will carry him safe to Havre. If he escapes the cruisers he will reach port safe, and if he doesn't escape the cruisers ——"

" Ay, if he doesn't ——"

" Then your Christian prayer will be answered and he will go to the bottom, for Claude is not the man to give up his ship while two planks hold together. Once in

Havre there will be no difficulty, and then Mr. Cassilis will have some chance of becoming—the greatest man in the county. But look you, Will, until I give you leave I won't have you trapesing over the country like a resurrected ghost, and while you are here I will have you keep your drunken hands off Archie and his playthings. You may treat your brother as you please, but, dam'me, for my part I was born with some natural affection, and I won't have it."

"You think you have me under your thumb," cried Will, "but I will have you know ———"

"I have your worthless life in my pocket, and if it weren't for one thing I would have your relative out of the magazine and send him riding back to Heronford to his books and his meagrims, but we can't afford to go back. But look here, sir, never forget this for a moment," and Mr. Weston advancing to the table struck it heavily with his riding-whip; "I am the master here; you are mine, soul and body, my property, my goods and chattels; and if you venture to raise a finger in opposition to my wishes I will teach you a lesson you won't forget. Oh, no! I don't want to quarrel with you—you are not worth quarreling with—but you had better remember my words for the future."

"You are always riding me too hard, George, and you know very well that this was your scheme, and you wanted the young fellow out of the way as well as I did. Maybe you haven't your own ends to serve— maybe ———"

"Maybe you would like to see us both go to pieces and this precious coxcomb come sailing in before us after all ?

I was a fool to bring him here—as great a fool as yourself —and I won't be easy till I see him out of this house. That damned fellow Stone, of Fareham, has been making enquiries, and I think somehow he has got upon the right track, but who put him on the track I can't imagine. Now you know the truth, and you can say whether I have any reason for my temper."

"Stone would do me an ill-turn if he could."

"Then don't give Stone an opportunity of falling across you.   The first time you move out of this house you will find him at your elbow and then farewell to Heronford, and look out for another chapter in the Newgate calendar and a bran new ballad all to yourself."

With these words Mr. Weston flung out of the room and left his associate to meditate upon the unpleasant truths to which he had just given utterance.

During all this time I had overheard the conversation with difficulty for Archie had manifested a great deal of impatience, and had continually interrupted me by his interjections.   His hatred of William Cassilis was so great that it seemed to have overmastered his dread, and I was afraid lest he might give way to an outburst, which would have the effect of leading to our detection.   I found it necessary to endeavour to quiet him from time to time, but it was impossible to turn him from the one thought that had seized hold upon his mind.   I had promised to help him to remove the devil, and between us we must devise some means for that object.

When George Weston had left the room I leaped down from the stone bench on which I had been standing, and Archie caught hold of my arm.

"You saw him—the black devil? You are not afraid of him?"

"No, Archie, I am not afraid of him, nor need you be. I don't think he will do you any harm."

"You don't know him, but I do. The devil always leaves a black mark wherever he touches you, and look here. What is that?"

He pulled up his sleeve and showed me his arm where the skin was discoloured about a crown-piece in extent, or perhaps a little more.

"What is that? He caught hold of me, and his fingers burnt me then. Oh! I could feel them burning me. Which do you think is the best way to kill the devil?"

"I don't know, but we must think of a plan. But before I can do anything you must show me how you came in here. When we are once outside——"

He looked at me with a leer of great cunning.

"When the bird gets out of the window he flies away home to his nest. No, no, you must stay with Archie now, and perhaps some day he will show you when the wicked old devil is dead. And the devil's secret too; he knows his secret."

"You must show me now or I shall not be able to help you. I think I can promise you, Archie, when I get out that he will not trouble you much longer. I can find a way to drive him out of Langston Priory."

"You are sure of that? If I thought you could——"

"Trust me, and remember I am always your friend." He hung for a moment doubtfully, but at last, with one furtive glance at my face, he seemed to have made up his mind and turned back into the passage through which we had come. When we reached the chamber into which I had first ascended I thought that he was playing some elfish trick on me for he stopped short and burst into a fit of vacant laughter. So far as I could see the only means of exit were the trap-door and the door through which we had just come.

"They say Archie is a fool, but all your wise men couldn't get out of this but myself. Let me see if you can find the way."

"It won't do for us to lose any time now, Archie. We must make haste if you want me to help you."

"Ah! I knew you couldn't. Your wits must be a thousand years old before they could find it. Now see how easily I can do it."

At the further end of the apartment the wall was covered by a thick curtain of ivy, which had originally grown from the outside through the window but had now struck its roots into the wall within and entirely hid it. Archie walked straight across the room and surveyed the dense screen for a moment without speaking; then with an agility which I could not have expected he seized hold of the thick tendrils and swung himself into the foliage. When he had clambered about ten feet from the ground he suddenly stopped and, dividing the branches with his hand, disclosed an opening quite large enough to admit a grown man with ease. He appeared greatly delighted with his performance, and manifested his pleasure in his own peculiar way. I was about to follow him when his discordant laugh suddenly ceased. He gave a little cry and sat with his eyes fixed on something behind and beyond me, apparently at once deprived of all power

of motion. I turned swiftly round and knew in a moment that my hope of escape was dashed to the ground.
Just as I was about to raise myself from the ground I
saw a rough head appearing above the trap, and in another moment my gaoler had leaped upright upon his feet
and was hurrying toward me. He had drawn a pistol
from his breast, and as he came up presented it at my
head.

"I don't want to shoot you if I can help it, but if you
stir hand or foot I'll do it. Stand back, sir, I tell you.
I have only to whistle to bring up half a dozen more,
and you'll find them rougher than I am."

My first impulse was to make a struggle for the liberty I had so nearly gained, but I saw that he would keep
his word if I moved, and there was no means of defence
within my reach. There was no help for it; I was
powerless to resist, and I yielded with the best grace I
could assume.

"If you had given me ten minutes more," I said, "I
should have been on easier terms with you, and if you
will now lay down your weapon ——"

"My business is to keep you safe, and I think you
have given me a poor return for my kindness. I'll keep
a sharper eye on you for the future, and for you, Mr.
Archie, I'm of opinion the master wouldn't be very
thankful to you if he knew what you were trying to do
for him. Now, sir, we'll march, if you please."

CHAPTER XXI

My hope of escape cannot have been excessive, for though I felt my disappointment, yet it was not to such a degree that I was greatly affected by it. It is true that I was disappointed, but all through I had felt in some way that my luck would be too great to escape so easily; and, besides, it might be some comfort to know the worst that could befall me. I had at least been freed from the torture of anticipation and suspense. But comfort! To drag out my years in a gang of slaves chained to a life of drudgery and wretchedness; to pass without a word out of the life and knowledge of those who knew me and the few who loved me; to go on living and yet to die more certainly than if the grave had closed over me—this was the fate for which I had to prepare myself, and the lot to which I had to steel my heart. I could expect no mercy; I could hope for no reprieve. My enemies had gone too far to turn back now without destruction to themselves, and to keep themselves safe it was necessary that my sacrifice should be completed. Yet the mind is so curiously constituted that I had some little sense of satisfaction in knowing their intentions and reading the hidden working of their hearts. I had indeed paid a terrible price, but I had learned everything, and now knew with certainty all that I had hitherto desired to know.

But there was one matter from which I was able to

derive some hope, however faint. My friends had already discovered that I was missing, and had begun an active search on my behalf. I could see that Weston was in a condition of great disquiet regarding their enquiries, and I was certain he must have had some further reason for his uneasiness than he had stated to his friend. I knew that Stone was keen, energetic, and loyal, but without some clue to guide him it was more than probable his labour would be only thrown away. Without the knowledge which only Victory or myself could impart he could never guess or imagine my fate, or the person into whose hands I had fallen.

But Victory—upon her and her alone could I rely if I was to be saved from this future worse than death, and I felt the most implicit confidence in her clear intelligence and unfailing instinct. She had warned me of the peril that I had treated with contempt; she had seen the danger with which I was menaced and to which I had been blind; and now I felt assured when the moment of trial came she would act with promptitude and wisdom. She knew my faith in Stone; she knew that I had intended to ask his advice, and I felt almost certain when the news of my disappearance first reached her she would at once find the means of communicating with him. It was evident that he was already so warm upon my track that Weston was frightened and anxious to have me disposed of elsewhere, and there was still a chance, however slight, that my friends might reach me before I was carried on shipboard, whither it would be impossible to follow me.

Morgan, my gaoler, was determined that I should not make an attempt to escape a second time, or if I did make the attempt he would be present to witness it. However much he disliked the task he made up his mind to stay with me during the day, and although he was not quite so friendly as he had previously been, I still found companionship in his presence, and he helped to relieve my loneliness. At bottom I am certain he was a kindly, honest fellow, but his devotion to his master, which was not unmingled with fear, seemed to possess him entirely, and prevented his natural instincts from finding any outlet. He seemed to think that I had shown myself ungrateful for his former kindness, and that my abortive tempt to escape had been an injury especially directed toward himself, who would have suffered most had that attempt proved successful. This was the entire burden of his complaint against me, and this complaint he reiterated again and again.

"I did all I could for you," he said more than once; "I made you comfortable with good victuals and a bed that might do a prince, and I treated you like an honest shipmate who wouldn't get a poor fellow into trouble. And that's your way! that's my thanks! when you get my back turned to slip your cable, and leave me here to tell the master that you had fooled me with your tricks. Did you think, mister, what would have happened to me?"

"I am afraid," I answered, "I never thought about you at all. You are a good fellow, Morgan; I am sure they have kept you in the dark. This is a matter of life and death to me. I think you know who I am. Do you know why I am here? Do you know what your master intends to do with me?"

"Some tomfoolery about a woman, I suppose? The

wenches have a deal to answer for in this world and the next, and the master would give his soul for the blink of a blue eye—God bless them! But I heern them say you are going to make a trip with the little spitfire, and Captain Claude—I wish ye luck with him. Thunder! he's a daisy."

"I was certain you did not know everything. What would you say to the West Indies, Morgan? Would you rather die at once here than be tortured to death there?"

He whistled and looked at me curiously.

"The West Indies! I thought Captain Claude was the worst of it, and to my mind that was bad enough, for I made a voyage with him once myself. But the West Indies! What have the master and you been up to?"

"I'll tell you, Morgan," I cried eagerly, seeing at last a distant hope of winning his sympathy. "I'll tell you, and when you have heard——"

"By —— you'll tell me nothing. I won't listen to you. My business is to keep you here and not hearken to stories, but, mate, I'm sorry for you, and that's the truth on it. The West Indies! Phew! I don't wonder you were so eager to levant with Sir Archie. I declare to God I forgive you, but I'll see that you don't do it again."

"But, Morgan," I went on, "that is not even the worst of it."

But he interrupted me again.

"Best or worst, I can't help you. If you were bound for a hotter port still I'd do the same, little as I liked it.

I can only wish you a good voyage, and hope that it may turn out better than you think for. I wish you hadn't told me for I don't like the thought of it, and I've taken a fancy to you though you did try to get me into trouble."

I suggested that at least after I had been removed he might carry a letter for me, but he demurred at once.

"No, no; I thank God I can neither read nor write, and I don't know what you might put upon the paper. I'll make you comfortable as far as I can, but more you mustn't expect, and now, if you please, we'll try the other tact in our talk, for we have sailed this one as long as I have a mind for."

I felt that if Weston was as well served by all his servants as by this one my chances of escape were not great, and during the two days that Morgan spent almost entirely in my company he never altered in the attitude of stubborn fidelity he had assumed, and the blunt yet not unsympathetic denial he gave to all my attempts to secure his friendship. He certainly did not like his task, nor during the whole time was he quite free from a certain superstitious expectation regarding the vault in which I was confined. It had formed part of the Old Priory, and it appeared there was a current tradition, which may have been well or ill-founded, that it had formerly been used as a burial-place for the more exalted brethren. I found that Morgan's first affected indifference toward the supernatural was not long maintained, and in a short time he was regaling me with tales so weird and ghastly that my gloomy prison seemed to myself still more hideous and uncanny. He evidently believed every word he spoke, and at times I almost fancied he was listening for the dead abbot's footsteps on the stairs or watching for the hooded procession of cowled figures moving to the strains of a ghostly Kyrie Eleison.

I could not help listening to his stories, sometimes I listened in spite of myself, but for the most part my mind was in a state too troubled and agitated to lend him a serious attention. The minutes seemed interminable; I counted the crawling hours; and as the second day wore on I resigned myself altogether to despair, and for the first time felt myself completely broken and unmanned. I do not know that I had found any definite hope. I do not know exactly in what manner I had expected Providence would interfere on my behalf, but I was unable to realise that at the last moment I should not in some way be snatched from the horrible fate that was impending over me. Now, however, as the daylight passed and the evening shadows closed round me, a dull, blind, hopeless feeling, that was not resignation, took possession of me. My hope was dead; I was beyond the reach of help; I could only bow down my head and let the storm pass over me. The cup of life, with its almost untasted sweetness, was lying broken at my feet.

There may have been some who would have faced the situation with more courage and constancy—perhaps there were, but I think my feelings were natural and not altogether ignoble. I was still suffering from the effect of the injury I had sustained; I could do nothing to help myself, and there was now no hope that any help or assistance could reach me. I had imagined that in the rough justice of the world wrong might sometimes triumph, but never wholly nor for long; now, however, this comfortable doctrine failed to afford me consolation, for I saw the unrighteous triumph and the innocent trodden under foot, and I lost sight of the landmarks of my faith in a sense of crushing defeat and overwhelming despair.

It was the night of Friday, and must have been between nine and ten o'clock, or perhaps a little later. I was beginning to think that the summons I had been expecting would be deferred for another day, and Morgan was making his preparations to spend another fearful and uncomfortable night in my company. He had trimmed the lantern afresh, which he had set on a cask near him, and was making a frugal supper of coarse bread and cheese when there came an imperative summons upon the iron door, so sudden and loud as to cause us both to start where we sat.

"Good Lord!" Morgan cried. "What is that?" But he did not venture to move.

A moment later the knocking was repeated and I heard an angry voice demand admittance. In an instant Morgan leaped to his feet, ran up the stone steps, and unlocked the door which swung inward. I had risen from the box on which I had been sitting, knowing that the fateful moment had at length arrived, and I endeavoured to repress the throbbing of my heart that laboured loudly in my bosom. For a moment a grey mist swam before my eyes, but presently that cleared away, and I was able to see a cloaked figure coming down the steps and a bright light behind the open door. I waited without moving where I had risen, and when Mr. Weston, for it was he, came close to where I stood he raised his hat and bowed to me with a cruel mocking laugh in his eyes that I have never forgotten.

"Good-evening, Mr. Cassilis," he said; "I hope honest Morgan has made you comfortable?"

I remained silent.

"You do not appear to have cared for your quarters—perhaps you are right. They are damp certainly, and dark, and the view is not extensive, but they are roomy and commodious. But we can't get all we desire in this world, and it wasn't quite convenient to lodge you better."

"You are in a position now to say what you please, sir."

"Ay; I am glad you have come to that comfortable frame of mind. If you had always been of that way of thinking it wouldn't have been necessary for me to take so much trouble to show you that I like my own way. I am going to change your lodging, Mr. Cassilis."

"I am quite aware of your intention," I answered; "I need not ask you to show me any mercy, but I would remind you that though it seems to be your turn now, mine may come some day."

"Oh! I'll take the present and let you make what you can of the future. I'm a dangerous person to offend I think you will admit now, especially as you seem to know my intentions."

"It is a long way to the West Indies, Mr. Weston, but men have been known to find their way back."

He looked at me in astonishment.

"By ——" he cried. "Morgan, you have been blabbing. I'll ——"

"Morgan has told me nothing," I interposed, "and I

do not think it necessary that you should know how I have learned. But I warn you that so surely as you live, William Cassilis and yourself will yet have to reckon with me for what you have done."

"Threatened men live long," he laughed. "By the time that you come back you will find some changes, Mr. Cassilis; and then, you know, you may never come back at all. I think that is much more likely myself. You were once good enough to knock me down and I supposed you wondered why I did not shoot you. You know now, and every day you live you will know better. It did not suit me to give you the satisfaction of a gentleman, but I have squared our account in such a way that I don't think the balance is on your side now."

"Yes, you have proved yourself a generous enemy."

"Have I not ? " he cried with a sneer. "I have given you good measure, pressed down and running over. Will you dance at the wedding, Mr. Cassilis ? "

I suppose I should not have spoken the words but I could not help it; they were forced from me.

"I may yet live to see you hanged, Mr. Weston."

"Who knows ? " he answered with a shrug of indifference; "though if that happened I shall be the first gentleman of my family who has met his deserts. By the way, there are some fine secrets in the Heronford family. Had I known them sooner I might have dealt with you differently."

"I am satisfied that you have dealt with me after your nature. Even in seeking this interview, Mr. Weston, you have tried to show me that you could not help yourself. Is it necessary that you should prolong it ? You have now done your worst; you have enjoyed your triumph, and I am ready to show you that I can bear even more than this with the courage of a gentleman."

" By ——, Will would like to hear you crow like that; but you were always good at crowing, even when we thought you only my lord's bastard. I wonder will you crow as loudly six months hence. By that time the merry wedding bells will scarce have finished chiming. I see that touches you," he went on, stepping back; " you have not yet gained sufficient command over your temper, and there must be no further breach of the peace—oh, no, we cannot afford that. Morgan, see if the cart is ready."

" Ay, ay, your Honour," said the willing and obsequious servant, who immediately ascended the steps and left Weston and myself standing facing one another alone in the cellar.

" Now, Mr. Cassilis," Weston said, seating himself coolly beside me, " you see, however much I hate you, I am not in the slightest degree afraid of your violence, though you cried me for a coward through the country. You believe I am a coward ? Very well. You think I'm a fool ? Very well. You have had the satisfaction of calling me both. And now let us see what is the price you have paid for that indiscreet indulgence of your passion and vanity. First, I have assisted that very unworthy gentleman William Cassilis to make sure of your inheritance— you are *filius nullius*, Mr. Cassilis. Second, I am going to marry the young lady with whom you are in love—you had an excellent taste, Mr. Cassilis ; she has the sweetest figure and loveliest face in England. Third, I intend to send out a tombstone to the Bahamas—is it the Bahamas ?

—to record your virtues. Fourth—there is a fourth, fifth and sixth, if I haven't forgotten them. You remember Humpty Dumpty—a case very much to the point ?

> "' All the king's horses and all the king's men
> Couldn't put Humpty Dumpty together again.'

Perhaps you never understood the meaning of the lines before ? "

He had advanced his face quite close to me, a lurking light of triumph in his eyes and a cruel smile upon his lips. At that moment I thought of the tortures which the Indian warrior inflicts upon his captive—the taunts, the insults, the vindictive mockery which precedes the torture of the stake, and I knew that the same savage instinct now filled his bosom and had inspired his speech. I could hardly understand such malignant hatred; it seemed to me almost to approach to the verge of madness. I had imagined before that he was merely a bully and a coward, but though we were now alone he sat quite close to me, unconcerned and triumphant, and even seemed to court a display of violence upon my part. At the moment, indeed, some vague thought of resistance occurred to me, and I do not know to what lengths I might have been tempted, but before I had formed any definite resolution the opportunity passed away. At this point Morgan threw open the door and came down the steps, apparently dressed for a journey.

" Is all ready ? " Weston asked, rising to his feet.

" Ay, ay, sir. The cart's here."

" You have seen that the men are armed ! It may be

useful. Now, Mr. Cassilis, I will have to trouble you. Your own naturally excellent judgment will suggest to you that it is best to come quietly ; should you be disposed to act otherwise I have no doubt Morgan will deal with you as gently as possible under the circumstances, but he sometimes forgets himself, and I should not like to answer for the consequences."

I rose to my feet without making any response.

" That is right. Permit me to lead the way. I assure you it is not every gentleman who is afforded an opportunity of seeing the world without incurring expense."

CHAPTER XXII

THE FIRST BOW OF CAPTAIN CLAUDE SLINGSBY

WHEN we got into the open air I found a fine clear night with a wide glitter of stars and a new moon lifting its thin crescent above the woods. The faint odour of the grass and foliage was inexpressibly sweet to me; the cool air, that carried on its wings a distant fragrance of the sea, revived me like a charm, and I drank it in like one suffering from a consuming thirst. It blew upon my face like the breath of a lover; it kissed my parched lips and caressed my brow that ached and throbbed with an intolerable pain. How cool, how sweet it was, the blessed breath of that starry autumnal night! I had not known how weak and ill I was; I had hardly noticed the foul and sickening atmosphere of the loathsome cellar in which I had been confined, but as I came out into this clear brilliance of stars I felt as though I had awakened from a nightmare horrible beyond words.

Two lanterns had been lighted and were placed upon the grass hard by the path that ran past the door, but their light was hardly needed. I was able to see everything quite plainly. Upon one side the wall of the Priory rose dark and silent; upon the other there was a little sweep of lawn enclosed by a dense growth of timber, above which, as I have said, the moon was lifting her sickle of silver. A horse harnessed to a light cart stood a little distance away, and behind them another horse bridled and saddled. There were already two men seated in the cart, but I could not see their faces, and another held the saddle-horse by the head. I could hear the faint click of grasshoppers in the grass, and now and again the solitary note of an owl wakeful under the moon. Weston stopped to lock the door behind us, but Morgan advanced to my side and laid his hand upon my arm. It may have been to some extent a precautionary measure upon his part, unnecessary though it was, but at the same time I think he desired in his rough, yet kindly way to offer me some assistance.

"Keep up your heart, Mr. Cassilis," he whispered. "You may be down on your luck now, but 'tis a long lane that has no turning, and mind this—don't run across Captain Claude if you can help it. The master is purgatory, but the captain is simple ——"

"That will do, Morgan," said Weston, coming quietly behind us. "You need not give the captain a character at present. Mr. Cassilis can form his own judgment; and now look you—you must see that Mr. Archie gets into no trouble till I come back. I think there is one of his old fits coming on him and you may have to lock him up, but if you hurt him I'll—you know what I will do. He doesn't get on well with Mr. Will and you had better keep them apart."

Morgan hastily relinquished my arm and fell back without a word. Whatever Mr. Weston's faults might be, he certainly had the art of keeping his servants in an excellent state of discipline.

"Now, Mr. Cassilis," Weston continued, "I am sorry that I must trouble you, but we have very little time to lose. I intend to see you as far on your journey as I can, and will do myself the honour of riding with you to Langston. Here, Dick, help this gentleman into the cart."

I shall never forget this drive so long as I live. My senses were preternaturally acute ; every trivial incident, every sight and sound, is engraven in my memory. I could not bring myself to believe that even at the last moment there would not be a miraculous interposition of Providence upon my behalf. While the mare plunged through the darkness, and her ringing hoofs struck fire from the stones, I listened for the voices of my friends, and I was tempted, fruitless and foolish as I knew it to be, to call out loudly for help. The two men sat so closely upon either side of me that I could scarcely stir ; I could barely see the road where it wound in the darkness under the gloomy shadow of the trees, and I could only hear Weston's voice in front when he called out some word of warning or direction, but I could see neither the horse nor the rider. Occasionally we came upon a little open space, where I caught sight of the cold calm stretch of stars and the silver arc of the autumnal moon, but for the most part we were whirled rapidly through almost un-broken darkness.

At last we came out upon the high-road, and here for some reason our pace became slower, and Weston drew close to the cart and gave some directions in a low tone, which I only caught indistinctly. When we came close to the village of Langston we halted abruptly and turned down a broken, narrow lane that ran directly to the sea. Here our progress was necessarily slow, and I thought several times we should have stopped altogether, but all at once I caught the sweet breath of the sea, and the silver waters of the bay lay before me reflecting the brighter glory of the sky. We were not more than a hundred yards from the beach when we climbed the abrupt crest of the little hill.

Never was there a scene wilder and more picturesque. A mile away on the rocky promontory that is called the Blind Man's Head a solitary fire had been lighted, and the golden trail of light lay trembling on the sea. Hard by us on the beech another great fire swirled and roared, and a dozen or twenty men were hurrying here and there in the broken shadows. Some distance from the shore a schooner lay with her tapering masts clear against the moon, and a light burned brightly on her deck. A boat was passing from the schooner to the shore, ploughing a furrow of phosphorescent light on the dark, starry bosom of the sea, and the rowers were singing some wild sea-song in excellent time as they bent over their oars, but I only remember the chorus —

> "Oh! the brandy, the brandy, the brandy and the rum!
> We'll bring the lace ashore for the girls that we adore,
> And we'll drink till the morning come."

The men upon the beach were busily engaged piling the square boxes and casks upon half a dozen carts, each of which was drawn by a couple of horses, and were evidently working with a will, for they never paused in their task. I had known that the entire population along the coast was in sympathy, if not in active alliance with the free-traders, but I own I was astonished at the recklessness and audacity of these proceedings. I could see that most of the men were armed, and I was sure that they were prepared to fight if necessary. The ordinary feeling of antagonism between those who break the law and those whose duty it is to guard and protect it, had been deepened into one of intense hatred and desire for revenge by a recent affray in which a number of lives had been lost. It was now quite apparent that the smugglers were in sufficient force to repel any attack that might be made upon them, and it may have been for this reason that they neglected to take the usual precautions they were in the habit of adopting.

Mr. Weston halted his horse for a moment alongside the cart in which I sat, and having directed the men to remain where they were, rode down to the beach, where the boat had just landed as he arrived there. At this point it was almost as clear as noonday, for it was close to where the great fire was roaring, and I could easily distinguish the faces of the sailors as they unshipped their oars and sprang knee-deep into the water. One man still sat on the boxes in the stern-sheets with his cloak drawn close about him.

"Ay, that's him," said the man on my right hand; "Captain Claude's a dandy; you may take your oath he won't wet his feet. That will be the last of the cargo."

"Old Harry's his own cousin," the other answered with evident conviction. "He's got the devil's luck, but there's nobody would dare to do it but himself, and as fine-mannered as a lady. Did you ever hear him talk?"

"I don't hold by his manners, but I allow he's a good sailor and can handle his ship with ever a man from Langston to the Ness, but for all that I wouldn't sail under him for a keg of diamonds."

" They say there's a fortune for the king's officer that can catch him, but there'll be two moons in the sky before they do that. There they are now; the master could hitch him under his arm and carry him to the Priory like a bundle o' silk."

In the meantime the sailors had drawn the boat higher up on the beach, and one of them taking the captain in his arms had carried him ashore and set him down on the dry shingle. Weston dismounted from his horse, shook him warmly by the hand, and the two retired to a distance where they walked slowly together arm in arm, apparently engaged in an animated conversation. I watched them walking up and down, and I felt certain that I knew what formed the subject of their deliberation. They walked in this way for nearly a quarter of an hour, and then I saw Weston halt and hold out his hand. But Captain Slingsby merely raised his hat, and then the two men walked leisurely toward where I was standing. As he came close to me I saw Captain Claude distinctly for the first time. He was of quite diminutive stature—not more than five feet four in height—and his face was as smooth and delicate as the face of a girl, with the most dreamy and melancholy eyes in the world. He had now divested himself of his cloak, which he carried over his arm, and I could see that he wore fine silk stockings and great silver buckles, while his blue coat and crimson vest fitted him with exquisite neatness. I imagined at the time that he was quite young, but I found afterwards that he must be at least fifteen years older than I had first supposed him. When he smiled he showed the whitest and most regular teeth, of which he was inordinately proud, and I never knew him that he did not carry a jewelled snuff-box in his hand.

"This is the gentleman who is going to sail with you, Captain Claude," Weston said as they came up. "I hope you will make him comfortable."

"On the honour of a gentleman," the captain answered with a little lisp, which I soon discovered to be a pure affectation. "I am profoundly pleased to make your acquaintance, Mr. Cassilis. I have no doubt we shall find ourselves the most excellent friends in the world."

"I presume, sir," I said, "that Mr. Weston has told you I am his prisoner and how he kidnapped me? It is hardly necessary to continue this farce."

"A little misunderstanding," said Captain Claude, waving his hand airily; "a disagreeable necessity which sometimes arises in the noblest families—a trifle, it's hardly worth one's while to mention. My dear friend, you need say no more. Permit me to offer my profound commiseration. Believe me, I am your most obedient servant."

"I am glad to hear it," I said bluntly. "Then I am sure you will assist me to return home."

Captain Claude's laugh was as low and sweet as a silver chime.

"'Tis a monstrous pity I did not know your wishes earlier—a thousand pities—on the honour of a mariner. It would have been so easy; I should have enjoyed your society at Heronford; I love the amenities of a noble house. I regret, Mr. Cassilis, I am bound by the promise I have rashly made—I regret, nay, I am overwhelmed with remorse."

He spoke so simply and naturally that I could hardly

imagine that he was playing with me, and that he was not perfectly sincere. But Mr. Weston's laugh was the best commentary on his speech.

"Your friend," I said, "appreciates your humour better than myself. I know it is useless to appeal either to your pity or your sense of fair-play."

"I am sure I have not been misinformed," he answered still in the same tone; "Mr. Weston, of Langston, would be the last person in the world to deceive his friend—positively the last. I understood that you wished to see the world, that you were desirous of perfecting your education by travel; in a word, that you wished to make the *grand tour*, and that it was to be my honour and felicity to see you take the first step. On my faith, a delightful prospect. Is it not so, Mr. Cassilis?"

"No one knows better than yourself," I answered. "I do not doubt you will carry out your instructions."

"I assure you to the last point and nicest shade—a gentleman has no alternative. I have promised, Mr. Cassilis; I am bound by my word. As a gentleman you would not have me break my word?"

"From what I have heard of you I am sure you will keep it."

"Ah; you pay me a delicate compliment—a charming compliment. Mr. Weston, our friend appreciates the situation. Had I known earlier that you had such strong objections to the voyage I should not have consented to receive you—my better feelings would not have permitted it. I cannot bear to see my friends unhappy."

"Captain Slingsby is a gentleman of sentiment," said Weston with a sneer.

"It is the air I breathe," cried the captain, with a nice flourish of his handkerchief. "I live for love and friendship. Do not misjudge me, Mr. Cassilis; pray do not misjudge me, it would make me the unhappiest of men. I would not hurt your feelings for the world. But duty is imperative—duty and honour."

"And Mr. Weston agrees with you. I assure you, sir, I already know the fate that is in store for me, and I am afraid I am in no position to appreciate your fine language."

"Ah! do not say that. That would indeed be an unfortunate circumstance. I merely desire to pave the way to an abiding friendship. I anticipate many delightful evenings in your society unmarred by recrimination and reproach. We will rise above the narrow feelings of self-interest; we will forget our selfish fears; we will drink the undiluted nectar of friendship. Judge no man harshly, Mr. Cassilis, and especially a poor sailor whose coarse and halting speech is always doing wrong to his tender heart."

His gravity was absolute; he spoke with the emphasis and deliberation of profound conviction.

"I have no doubt," I said, "you will carry out your instructions. You will do justice to your reputation."

"Ah! my reputation—the breath of a cold, unfeeling world. You are sneering, Mr. Cassilis; you show me the false reflection of my face in the glass of groundless slander. That is nothing, sir. It is true I am beyond the law and the dogs of justice are laid upon my track. And then? There are good laws and bad laws; I solemnly revere the good and just as solemnly despise the bad. My conscience is above the law; it makes its own. A free trader—a smuggler—a contrabandist ? Words, only words. I pour wealth into the bosom of my country; I increase its commerce; I enlarge its knowledge, and improve its taste. So far I am the benefactor of my kind, and hope for my reward in the applause and admiration of posterity, and in that proud confidence I despise the slanders you have heard."

"Mr. Cassilis will know the full extent of your perfections before you have finished with him," laughed Mr. Weston.

But the captain turned upon him fiercely.

"You be——, sir. My remarks we not addressed to you. Yours is not the example I should follow ; yours is not the appreciation that I seek. My misfortune makes you my employer, but my deserts prevent me from making you my friend. Remember that, Mr. Weston, and remember that I will tolerate no impertinence from any country squire from Land's End to John o' Groats. Remember that, and be —— to you."

But Weston refused to see any cause for quarrel, and shook his head with an appearance of rough good-humour.

"We won't quarrel, Claude—at least, not till we have squared accounts. You are as full of fire as a flint and always had a blind eye to my graces, but I admit that you are the prince and pink of mariners. There goes the last of the cargo—a good one and safely landed. I can hear Swain swearing by this time how we have hoaxed him. When do you get under weigh ?"

"When the Lord pleases, my bucolic friend," answered the captain, who had not yet quite recovered his equanimity. "If you will come aboard with myself and my excellent compeer, Mr. Cassilis, you may have an opportunity of observing the dangers of my calling."

Mr. Weston laughed.

"I wouldn't sail with you, you little devil, for the wealth of the Indies. What do you mean ?"

"Your keen senses will observe," said Captain Slingsby with a well-marked lisp, which for some minutes had disappeared, "that it is now a flat calm. We brought the last of the breeze with us, and upon my honour I believe—nay, I avow, I was the d—est fool under heaven to come in here in weather like this. The *Spitfire* is somewhere on the coast, and should she manage to stumble upon us here there is a chance that we may find ourselves full-fledged angels, beating the nebulous ether with post-mortem pinions. You see I cannot surrender with grace, for I have a constitutional and natural objection to being hanged in the vulgar manner which is now the fashion."

"Then I'll pray that you may have a breeze before morning."

"With your permission I should prefer that you permitted matters to take their natural course ; your interference is unnecessary. However, if you are unwilling that Mr. Cassilis should undergo the risk, he may remain ashore and wait for more propitious circumstances. You will observe that I am acquainted with his Majesty's brig *Spitfire* and her captain. I know that the one has a consuming and unnatural desire to put an end to my little ventures since the accidental explosion of my long gun which carried away an infinitesimal portion of his rigging, and the other when it comes to reaching has decidedly

the heels of us. You are aware that I dislike fighting,
Mr. Weston, but I fear, alas! I am convinced, that disagreeable alternative would be forced upon me should
the *Spitfire* find me here. Mr. Cassilis as a non-com-
batant ——"

"He will be delighted to see how you handle your
ship, Claude," Weston answered with a laugh. "He
wouldn't miss the sight for a thousand pounds. There's
no doubt it's cursed weather and this would be an ugly
place to be caught in, but I hope you'll get a breeze from
the land before morning."

"Should it prove otherwise, my good friend, I think
you may bid farewell to your share in the little *Swallow*,
and for Claude Slingsby—gentle Claude Slingsby—he
will never run another cargo ashore or watch for the
signal fire from Blind Man's Head. One splendid moment, sir, one moment worth a life time, and then it will
be all over. The sun will set, the wind will blow, the
tides will flow and ebb, but only a lingering memory will
tell how Claude Slingsby fought his ship and went to
Davy Jones like a good sailor and a loyal gentleman."

The little captain had taken off his hat and stood bareheaded with his clear, soft face and shining eyes turned
to the light. His voice, that had grown for the moment
deep and musical, vibrated with emotion, and though I
saw a certain grim humour in the situation, I felt not the
slightest inclination to smile. But Weston was evidently
more familiar with his moods and manner.

"You always croak like a frog, Claude," he said. "I
have never known you yet that you were not on the
point of a glorious death, and that drunk or sober. The

Spitfire will no more catch you this time than she has at any other for the last four years, and if she did, why, man, you can't expect Nature to stand still at the catastrophe."

Captain Slingsby bowed with a frigid politeness and replaced his hat on his head.

"I look for neither sentiment nor regret at your hands, sir. You remain as you were quarried, uncouth, unhewn, unpolished—but you are for the time being my employer, and be —— to you, sir. Our interview has lasted too long; I will bid you adieu. And look here," he cried, turning round, "you —— lubbers, get that gentleman aboard the boat, and ——" —I will not repeat his profanity—"if you don't hurry, you swabs, I will break every bone in your —— bodies. Hurry along now; lift you feet; show your heels. Why the —— do you stand like a pair of moonstruck calves? Don't I speak plain enough?"

I was beginning to understand why men were afraid of Captain Slingsby. I had never seen a man more wholly possessed by a demoniac passion, and that by an instantaneous change. His lisp had vanished; the soft and melancholy look had passed from his face. His form seemed to dilate; his eyes blazed and his voice rang out hard and clear. And yet there was no cause for this passionate outburst; it was so sudden and unaccountable that I was lost in amazement. But I was left no time for speculation. The two men, who had remained in close attendance upon me all the time, caught hold of me by the arms and hurried me to the boat before I could utter a word of protest.

By this time the shore was almost deserted. The carts and horses had disappeared in a file along the road over the sand-hills; the fire upon the beach was burning lower like a great eye of light in the darkness, and only the boat waited for the captain and myself, moving uneasily as it lay almost aground in the lazy tide. I was bundled into the stern, though with no great violence, and I now saw that the crew was fully armed. They looked at me curiously for a moment, but no one made any remark, nor had I any cause to complain of their treatment, though I confess their appearance was not such as to inspire me with confidence. A more forbidding set of ruffians I thought I had never seen in my life, but whether it was the proximity of their dreaded captain or the usual discipline to which they were accustomed, no crew in any king's ship could have sat more silent and impassive.

I watched Weston and Captain Slingsby still walking up and down in the wavering shadows of the fire, and saw the former stop once or twice to laugh at something his companion had said. He was evidently in very high spirits, a state of mind to which the successful landing of the cargo and the removal of John Cassilis may both have contributed. Then they came slowly down to where the boat was lying, Mr. Weston with his hand resting upon the captain's shoulder.

"It is farewell at last, my gallant captain," Weston said. "I wish you a good voyage and never a ship on the sea but yourself. Good luck."

The captain lifted his hat slightly, and wading through the water stepped into the boat beside me.

" Good-bye, Mr. Weston. The devil and I will carry out your instructions between us, and if I should happen to visit him this trip I will convey to him your respectful compliments and inform him that you will not be long after me. Good-bye, my flower of brimstone, and now you —— get me aboard in a twinkling for I must change my stockings or I shall catch my death of cold. Look alive, you ——"

He leaned back in the stern-sheets with an air of extreme languor and drew his cloak closely about him, nor did he speak a word till we were alongside the schooner. Then he turned to me.

" This is my poor ship, Mr. Cassilis. As companions in misfortune, the quarry of a cruel fate, I shall endeavour to make you comfortable during our temporary sojourn together. May I ask you to step aboard—a poor and narrow dwelling-place, but large and wide enough for the sweep and play of noble spirits."

One of the men laughed behind him but the captain was perfectly grave.

CHAPTER XXIII

IT was a night of breathless calm when we came aboard the *Swallow*. The tender crescent of the moon lay like a fairy pinnace in the western sky, and the stars were dying out in the wide sweep of the stirless sea. The fires upon the headland and the beach were now only little points of faint light in the darkness; there was no movement in the deck under my feet.

Captain Slingsby with infinite grace of manner drew his arm within my own and brought me to his cabin, where a supper was already spread upon the table. Nothing would have surprised me regarding this remarkable man, but I was certainly unprepared for my surroundings, the like of which I had never seen before. The cabin was not very large, but it was brilliantly lighted by a silver lamp of beautiful workmanship which hung from the ceiling. At one end a massive crucifix was placed upon the wall, and beneath it was a small *prie-Dieu* with a number of candles fixed in silver sconces. At the other side was a bookcase filled with books bound in bright, red leather, and beside this there was a guitar in a greenbaise cover and several musical instruments in a rack. The tablecloth was of a snowy whiteness, and I noticed that nearly all the appointments were of silver.

The captain threw aside his cloak as we entered and bowed me to a chair.

" Make yourself at home, my dear friend," he said with an engaging smile, " and forget the unfortunate cir-

cumstances under which we are compelled to meet. Forget and be happy. With your permission I shall retire
for a moment. My delicate constitution requires that I
should change my stockings—a weakness I could never
overcome—but that being done I shall rejoin you in a
moment."

When he returned I observed that in the meantime
Captain Claude had not been forgetful of his personal
appearance. He had newly arranged his hair, which was
naturally very luxuriant and glossy; a slight touch of
rouge had brightened his complexion and added roses to
his cheeks; a fine diamond sparkled in his bosom, and
the fingers of both his hands—small as a girl's—were
covered with brilliants. He carried a cambric handkerchief which he pressed occasionally to his lips with the
air of a *petit maître*.

" Now, my dear Mr. Cassilis, with your permission we
shall have supper," he said, taking the chair at the head of
the table and touching the bell; " a swinish but necessary
meal. I find it clouds my understanding and darkens my
more delicate perceptions, but if we are indeed spirit we
are also flesh—alas ! flesh and blood. Though I dislike
supper I cannot afford to dispense with it. We must
humour our fallen nature. Chicken, Anthony, and tongue
garnished with the classic parsley," he continued as the
steward entered, " and, Anthony, cheese and butter for Mr.
Cassilis. And, my excellent Anthony, the water for myself
and wine—two bottles of the green seal—for my respected
guest. When you have done that you may go to —— in
double quick time for Mr. Cassilis and myself intend to
have a night with the Muses and the elder Gods. And,

Anthony, tell Mr. Peacocke I want a word with him now. Pardon me, Mr. Cassilis, but one must attend to business."

A moment or two afterwards the mate and steward entered almost together.

"Ah, Peacocke, I sent for you. We have made a good voyage of it, but we must get out of this. No one knows why better than yourself."

"I own I am growing uneasy, sir."

"You have very good reason, Mr. Peacocke," the captain laughed pleasantly, "for you will infallibly be hanged if we are taken—most unpleasant operation. You must get every rag on the schooner with the first breath of air and we must take our risk of the tide; for I had rather go on the rocks than sail into Execution Dock. Do not hesitate to call me should you want me."

"Ay, ay, sir."

"And, Peacocke, you had better see that the carronade is got ready; and, Peacocke ——"

"Sir."

"Have an eye to the smallarms and see that the cutlasses are in order. My fellows are apt to be careless, and a good edge, Peacocke, is an excellent thing both in steel and an appetite."

"Ay, ay, sir. There is nothing more?"

"I think not. Ah, yes, leave the case-bottle alone till we are going into action or get into port and then you may drink yourself drunk with my full authority and permission, but not a drop till then."

"Very well, sir, I shall observe your instructions."

"An animal, Mr. Cassilis," the captain continued when the mate had retired, "a very useful animal and an excellent seaman, but no companion for a man of breeding and sentiment like myself. That is the curse of my calling, sir. I must rejoice among barbarians and live among savages, and the fine and delicate flowers of feeling and fancy wither away without appreciation. I may work with men like Weston and Peacocke, but how in heaven's name can I confide in them or make them the partners of my heart?"

"And yet Mr. Weston has shown that he has a good deal of confidence in you," I said gravely. "Will you allow me to tell you what you are doing for him?"

"Ah! better not. Rather let me help you to a wing of this most tender chicken, and try a glass of that wine of France in which the spirit of the vine is dancing like sunshine. I drink water myself, but that is merely a weakness against which I have been fighting all my life. Always avoid unpleasant topics while you can and make the most of the shining hour. There was a poet once—Horatius Flaccus—whose Latin I have forgotten, though it was whipped into me till I ran away to sea, but I have never forgotten his charming philosophy. Ah! Mr. Cassilis, remember Horatius Flaccus—you also are a scholar—and tell me what you think of my wine."

"I may seem ungrateful," I said, "but I am afraid I am unable to forget my situation. I cannot forget what I have come through: I cannot forget you are carrying me into slavery—that you are carrying me into a life worse than death. It is enough almost to unsettle my reason when I think of it."

"Then why think of it at all, my poor friend," said the captain soothingly. "Believe me I deplore the circumstances as much as yourself, possibly more, but upon my honour as a gentleman I am in no degree to blame—it was not and is not my fault. I have kept my word all my life; I have never varied from it to the value or breadth of a hair; I have sailed in the eye of duty as to a point of the compass. In a moment of weakness—are the angels themselves exempt from weakness?—I gave Mr. Weston my word of honour—yes, sir, my word of honour—that I would carry a passenger for him to Havre —that pleasant town on the sunny shores of France. I knew nothing more than that, and indeed I cared for nothing more. I was paid for my promise, which meant with Claude Slingsby the full performance of his contract. And yet, believe me, I would not cause you pain for the world."

"Can you not put yourself in my place?" I cried. "And the crime——"

The captain smiled and waved his handkerchief airily.

"Crime is only the creature of the law, and like the king I am afraid I am above the law. The law has no terrors for me, Mr. Cassilis, and no claims upon me. I would not violate my conscience or prove false to my word and my friend for all the laws of Europe."

"I think you have a heart somewhere, Captain Slingsby," I cried despairingly. "Will you permit me to tell you my story?"

"I am all heart, sir," he answered, apparently flattered, "and that is why I am now captain of the *Swallow* and not flying the flag of an admiral, as many a worse man is doing. Endeavour not to pain me too much and I will hear your tale."

He poured himself out a glass of water and settled

himself in his chair with the look of a martyr. I did not quite understand him; I was young, and hoped that I might touch him and win his sympathy, and in that hope I began my story. I was terribly in earnest; I felt that my fate was depending on the issue, and I watched his face with my heart in my eyes. At first he was listless and indifferent, now and again sipping the water in his glass with an air of apathy, but gradually I saw that he was growing interested, and finally I knew that I held his sympathy in my hand. That knowledge inspired me. I pictured the hope and joy that were growing in my life —my sweetheart's love and beauty—the unmerited injury my rival had inflicted on me—the sufferings I had endured—the awful fate that was in store for me, and when I had finished I saw without astonishment that there were tears in his eyes. He was as much moved as myself. Then he rose to his feet, and leaning across the table held out his hand to me.

" My poor friend," he cried, "as heaven is my witness I pity you with all my heart."

" I knew," I said, " I should win your pity. You did not know the truth."

" The truth! I knew nothing. On my oath, as a gentleman, Weston is nothing more or less than a double-dyed villain."

" He has certainly treated me villainously."

" He has treated you like a scoundrel. And the tall, sweet girl with the shining eyes and lips like Cupid's bow —Mr. Cassilis, he will break her heart—I am certain he will break her heart. Good God, sir, the devil made a world in which such things are possible."

"At least you are now glad that you listened to me?"

"I shall regret it as long as I live."

"Regret it?"

"Do you think I shall ever get your cursed story out of my head? Do you think I am a mere block—a creature fashioned without a heart and a beast born without a conscience? Do you think that I can go through life with equanimity, knowing that I have made myself the tool of this designing knave, who should be a gentleman and is merely an unwhipped rogue? Ah! Mr. Cassilis, I shall regret the night I met you so long as I live."

"But," I said in astonishment, for I had believed I had made him entirely my friend, "you will not permit him to carry out his wickedness? You will save me from the fate he had in store for me? I am surely safe in your keeping."

He threw up his hands with an air of extreme dejection.

"I am powerless, sir—powerless to help myself or you. What can I do? What would you have me do? Mr. Weston is a rogue, but he trusted me—he confided you to my hands. I gave him my promise; I took his filthy pay, and under these circumstances, if the whole future of my life was passed with broken hearts and every heart my own, I could not withdraw a step but go right on to the place of torment that is prepared for me. I have broken every law, divine and human, but I have never broken my word."

He spoke with an air of indescribable pride, and I saw in a moment that I had been speaking to ears as deaf as Weston's own. Whatever else might happen I need look for no help from Captain Slingsby.

"I see," I cried, "that nothing I can say will alter you."

"My mind is fixed, Mr. Cassilis, as the pole star. The situation lies, so to speak, in a nutshell. I do not love my task, but it is my duty to carry you to Havre, and carry you to Havre I will if God's winds and the king's enemies permit. But that need not prevent our being and remaining friends. Why should it? We are both the victims of adverse circumstances—I of a rash and hasty promise, you of a bad man's enmity. I do not upbraid you that by your means I am doing an act of grave injustice and cruelty, nor need you reproach me that I lend myself to that act. Rather let us forget it for the time and make the most of the shining hour."

He drew the cork from the bottle and filled my glass with an appearance of great cordiality.

"We have had enough of the past, Mr. Cassilis," he said; "let us talk of the rosy future."

"Ah! the rosy future!" I cried bitterly.

"Or rather let us talk of supper," he answered, seeing my meaning, "which you have still left untasted. I remember the time I could not eat myself, but now I think there is no chance or change in this changing world that could rob me of my appetite. I am not perhaps what you would call a religious man, but I am something of a theologian and have a taste for divinity. I believe most strongly in the decrees of Providence, and am certain you cannot alter them by forbearing to dine or sup."

"I am in no position to quarrel with you, Captain Slingsby; I will do whatever you desire."

"Ah! that is a more hopeful frame of mind. Now a little more chicken and a glass of the sunny south. Ah!

Mr. Cassilis, I have an idea that you may never see Havre after all."

"What do you mean?" I cried eagerly.

" I am the victim of presentiments," he said dreamily. " The airy voices of the future have whispered in my ear from childhood, and misfortune has always knocked a warning note at my heart before she dealt her crushing blow. It is probable there may be a fight this trip, Mr. Cassilis," he went on softly, " and it is possible that the *Swallow* has made her last voyage. I have had something like that in my mind for the last two days, and yet you see I can make my supper with a hearty appetite."

" And what will happen then?" I asked with curiosity.

" Ah! what indeed? There is a little breeze from the south—an air soft and tender as a maiden's breath— the *Swallow* hardly stirs—the sky is blue and cloudless —and suddenly the air is filled with shouts and cheers, the flash and smoke of guns, and someone cries that the *Swallow* is sinking by the head. The bottom is yellow sand and shells, Mr. Cassilis, and the bones of Claude Slingsby and his gentle mariners will lie there side by side till the trumpet of the judgment."

I know that I can only give you a faint idea of the man, and I certainly cannot describe the air with which he spoke these words or the tone that he used. He seemed to me to be almost dreaming with his eyes open, but he spoke like one speaking under a sense of profound conviction, and describing what he actually saw pass before his eyes. A prophet in a blue coat and crimson vest, with rouge on his cheeks, rings on his fingers, and the smooth unlined face of a boy may seem a curious spectacle, yet its incongruity, strange as it may seem, did not strike me, and I treated him with a perfectly serious attention. At first sight, you would have thought Captain Slingsby an object meant for ridicule and the provocation of laughter. His precise and finical manner, his affected lisp, his splendid dress and diminutive figure, his absurd speeches and florid language were all in the true comedy manner, and yet I should never at any time have thought of laughing at or with him. These things were, it seemed to me, merely a transparent mask that never hid the real man. At the most unexpected moments his true nature would flash in his eyes, and when you would look to see him soft as silk you would find him hard as iron. The man fascinated and bewildered me. His mind made as many leaps and changes as a harlequin, and yet he was always so demoniacally in earnest that he only impressed you with wonder and curiosity.

He now described the fate of the *Swallow* with the earnestness of one who was watching the scene unrolled before his eyes, and from that he passed to the subject of dreams and visions. This was evidently a favourite topic with him. He narrated a hundred instances of his own power of second sight; he recounted the miraculous dreams that had warned him of impending dangers; and spoke of the spirits that seemed to be his constant companions. I never spoke a word but sat and listened to him, fascinated by his shining eyes and eager, animated face.

Then he waved his hand airily, and laughed a pleasant approval of his own power of narrative.

"You are a companion after my own heart, but I

weary you, Mr. Cassilis.   I like to ramble through this fairyland of wonder, and look through the prison bars of the unseen.   I never rest; I never tire; I could fly forever with the spirits through the infinite of space.   The world does not know Claude Slingsby.   You think me a strange being ?"

"I have met many men who are different."

"Why, that is a wise and harmless answer.   But you think I am a bad man.   I have treated you like a pig.   Oh! you need not answer me, I know your mind."

"I am not sure that I know my own mind regarding you."

"No?   Then you must go to bed and think me over. I have taken you to my heart, Mr. Cassilis; I have numbered you among my friends.   Your eyes please me; your ingenious youth has won my sympathy; you are honest, sincere, generous, and unfortunate.   *Meliora probo*."

He rose from the table and going to the other side of the cabin took the guitar out of the case, and coming back resumed his seat.   For some time he did not say anything, but sat fingering the strings with his head a little bent to one side.   Then he looked up at me with a look which seemed to me almost shy and apologetic.

"I know you are tired out," he said, "and so am I, but this is my own best friend, and I have a habit—a foolish, harmless habit—of forgetting my fancies for the night in the music that I love.   If you do not mind, we will perform our devotions together, and then you can go to bed and dream of Claude Slingsby knocking in vain at the gates of Paradise and all the angels weeping because they cannot take him in."

Without waiting for my answer he settled himself in

his chair, and after striking a note or two began to sing in
a low tone, but very sweetly and with great expression :

> " Mother of God ! there is sorrow
> And anguish under the sun,
> And the tears are wet on our faces
> Till the night of travail is done.
>
> " Mother of God ! on thy bosom
> I would lay my burden of fears,
> And thou who in life felt the burden
> Wilt dry the trace of my tears."

There were some other verses which I do not remember, but certainly no man could have thrown greater
pathos and meaning into the words he sang. His breast
shook with his emotion, and for the second time I saw the
tears in his eyes. Then he rose hastily and, catching my
hand, pressed it in his own.

" Forget my folly, my dear friend, and think of me as
I would be, not as I am. You will sleep with an easy
conscience and rise to the joy and glory of a new day.
Where the —— is Anthony ?   Here, you —— scab,
show Mr. Cassilis to his berth and —— to you."

It was a long time before I fell asleep, for I was weary
almost beyond the healing of sleep, and the figure of the
little captain and the sound of his voice kept dancing in
my brain and linking themselves fantastically to the chain
of my own misfortunes. Then somehow there came a
welcome oblivion, though I remember to have heard indistinctly the creaking of the winch and the measured lilt
of voices and the rattling of the anchor chain. I do not
know how long I slept, but when I wakened the sun was
high up in the heavens and the *Swallow* was rolling un-

easily in the measured swell. I rose hastily and was proceeding to dress when the man Anthony came into my
cabin with a basin of hot coffee.

"The captain's order, sir," he said. "I was to make
you comfortable, and see that you had your breakfast."

"I am obliged to him and you," I said, feeling that I
should make as many friends as I was able. "I have
been quite comfortable, and we seem to be making a quiet
passage."

"The Lord love you," he cried, smiling at my igno-
rance, "we have hardly stirred. There is not as much
air as would cool your porridge. And I beg pardon, sir,
do you know the captain at all?"

"I met him last night for the first time."

"Then I would advise you to give him a wide berth
this blessed day, that's all. He's been raising hell since
daybreak, and if he's pretty free with his tongue more by
token he's very handy with a marlinspike. He don't like
the weather and he don't like the coast and he don't like the
Spitfire that's been trying for us since Adam was a boy.
I think 'twas that brought him in, and I know now he's
sorry he was tempted, and, Lord! to hear him! I never
seen him so bad before."

"Then there is a chance of the *Swallow* being taken?"
The man looked at me significantly.

"No more chance than of your flying ashore, sir.
That's not Captain Claude's sort. We'll all go to the
bottom first like a snug ship's company. But you'd better
have the coffee now, and I'll get you a rasher for your
breakfast. I beg your pardon, sir, you won't forget not to
meddle with Captain Claude while he's in his tantrums.

I'm sure he'd be sorry afterwards if anything happened to you."

After I had breakfasted, which I did quite alone, I climbed the companion ladder and came upon the deck. I was amazed to see that we were certainly not more than two miles from the shore, and I could observe every object upon the land with the utmost distinctness. We were just outside the horn of the bay, and I could see the long sweep of cliffs running to where they are shut in by St. Dunstan's rock to the southward. The sea rolled in a long, greasy swell; there was not a breath of air, and the white sails only stirred with the motion of the vessel. Though the sun was somewhat obscured by the autumnal mist, it was already very warm, and there was everywhere the promise of a day of intense calm. It seemed almost like an answer to my prayers, for I knew now that my one hope of safety, slender as it might be, depended on the coming of the *Spitfire*.

One man stood idly by the tiller, and two or three others lay sprawling forwards, but Captain Claude had almost the entire deck to himself. He paced up and down like a wild animal behind the bars of his cage, his head bent forward and his hands folded across his chest. He was dressed with quite as much care as he had been the evening before, but I noticed that he was now armed, and that a pistol-butt projected from his pocket. Remembering the steward's warning, I went over to the bulwarks upon the other side and stood there watching the long line of cliffs, but the captain seemed not to have noticed my coming and to be altogether unconscious of my presence. The only sounds I could hear were the occasional creaking of the blocks and the quick, sharp tread of the captain as he paced the deck. I had no desire to go below again, and while my eyes rested on the line of cliffs that shut in Carnforth Bay, I felt that the last link was not yet broken that bound me to those I loved.

An hour or more passed in this way when I heard the hurried tread of the little captain close behind me, and turning round I saw him standing regarding me under his brows. I lifted my hat without a word, but he did not seem to notice my salutation. He was evidently labouring under intense excitement, for his lips were twitching and his eyes were ablaze with an inward fire.

" You are familiar with the Word of God, sir ? " he cried.

" I believe I am," I answered quietly.

" I thought as much," he said with a sneer. " Then you must have heard of Jonah who made himself snug in the stomach of the whale. I'm tempted to look out for another miracle."

" Why, sir ? "

" Why, sir ? Is this weather natural ? Where's the —— breeze that should be bowling the *Swallow* merrily out of danger ? Who keeps me rotting in this cursed calm, the like of which was never seen since the beginning of the world ? You, sir—you're my Jonah—my —— snivelling, sanctimonious, unsophisticated Jonah, and by —— I'm tempted to let you try your luck with the fishes. I'm sorry I ever saw your face, your —— smug, freezing, indigestible countenance. Go below, or I fling you overboard."

I verily believe he would have been as good as his

threat, but I had no desire to continue the altercation, and I turned away and went down the companion without a word. I sat down in the cabin and took a book out of the case, but I could still hear Captain Slingsby pacing the deck, which he continued to do with brief intermissions all through the morning and afternoon.

Anthony brought me some dinner, which I ate alone, and I then continued to read until it became too dark for me to see longer. The captain made his mid-day meal upon the deck, and so far as I could see there was no change either in the weather or his temper. I began to hope that I would end this long day altogether by myself, but after Anthony had lighted the lamp, and I was again settling myself to my book, Captain Claude came in and sat down beside me. I laid down my book and waited for him to speak.

"I am a brute and a fool, Mr. Cassilis," he said. "I am ashamed of myself, and have come to beg your pardon."

"It is granted at once," I said; "you have not hurt me."

"But I have hurt myself. I cannot help it; I may do it again. It is not I who speak, but the devil. I am glad you did not answer me."

"It seems a pity," I said, "that you should let the devil speak for you."

"A thousand pities, but it is so. I won't trouble you again, Mr. Cassilis. The devil and I will keep clear of you for the future. Use my cabin as if it were your own, make yourself comfortable, and don't be afraid that I will break in upon your meditations."

"But I cannot do that, Captain Slingsby. And I have quite forgotten your hasty words."

" 'Tis all the amends I can make you, but don't think I am virtuous enough to deny myself anything for your sake. I deny myself nothing; I couldn't rest to-night in a bed of down. I must be moving, man; I must keep stirring or I shall go mad. Don't you see that I'm caught in the trap of my own making—I who was wary as a fox and slippery as an eel. The air is coming up from the southward now, and do you know what that will bring?"

I shook my head.

" Death, sir—death to you and me and every man jack aboard this tidy craft, for the *Swallow* will go to the bottom with her sails standing and my flag flying at the main-mast as if I were an admiral of the blue. And that is why I ask your pardon, Mr. Cassilis, and so bid you a very good-night." He held out his hand to me, which I could not refrain from taking, and with a muttered word or two, which I could not catch, he left me to my solitude.

I do not think I fear death more than other men, and I am sure, in comparison with the fate in store for me, I should willingly have chosen that alternative, but I own the little captain's words almost stopped the beating of my heart. He spoke in a tone of positive assurance; he seemed as certain of the future as if it were already an accomplished fact. Under other circumstances I should have looked for the coming of the *Spitfire* with joy and hope, but I was now assured that in that event Captain Claude would keep his word and would blow up his vessel sooner than surrender. He had already made up his mind that he could not escape, and I now understood him well enough to know that it was not his own fate that troubled him, but the thought that he was beaten at the game in which he felt he had no superior. The vanity of the man stood out conspicuous even in the moment when he thought he was face to face with death.

I turned the pages of my book, but I felt that I could read no more. I was like a man lost and groping in the darkness who suddenly comes upon a blind wall and can turn neither to the right hand nor the left. There seemed to be no hope for me anywhere, and yet the distant perfume of life and love—alas! no longer mine— was inexpressibly dear and sweet to me. I had only begun to taste of the cup when it had been dashed from my hand. And yet at that moment I made up my mind to face the future with courage and resolution, and if I was indeed to die then to go out of life like a gentleman and a Christian in charity and at peace with all mankind.

The hours that I spent this evening alone were certainly unpleasant, but I am sure they were not unprofitable and they have since exerted a silent influence on my life and character. It is not necessary that I should carry you into all the secret chambers of my thoughts, but when I rose up I felt like a man who had gained a new access of strength from some hidden source and who feels that after all death is not the worst thing that life has power to bring us.

I lay down in my berth without divesting myself of my clothes for I thought there was no possibility of my falling asleep. For a minute or two I lay listening to the swish of the sea against the *Swallow's* sides, the straining of beams and the creaking of blocks—for a minute or two —and then quite in an instant I fell into the deepest, sweetest and most dreamless sleep I ever enjoyed in my life. It was not late when I retired to bed and I must have slept for many hours—many hours, for the sun had dawned when I awakened in the grey cold light.

I sat up with a sudden start; for the moment I was all abroad. Where was I? How had I come here? What sound was it that had awakened me and still echoed in my ears? I sat up and listened. In an instant I remembered everything. The wind had come at last for my cabin was now at an angle and I felt the *Swallow* slipping through the seas like a thing alive. But the sound—a crash like the headlong ruin of a falling tree? and then it came again, but now I was awake and in a moment I knew its meaning. I leaped hastily from my bed and sprang to the door. The moment that Captain Slingsby was looking for had arrived and the *Spitfire* had fired her first salute. Oh! I knew by instinct the sound that tore asunder the silence of the dull grey morning with its reverberating thunder. And it was not distant but near at hand.

I dashed through the empty cabin without waiting to think, and sprang up the companion-way to the entire disregard of my neck in my blind haste. When I got upon the deck I found it was blowing freshly, a cold, steady wind though the ragged mist still lay in blurred masses to the eastward where the newly risen sun glowed like a dull red fire. The *Swallow* had every inch of canvas set and was laying down her shapely bows to the leaping waters that hissed round her. The entire crew were lying under the bulwarks—all but the captain, who stood at the tiller bareheaded with his long fair hair tossed by the wind and such a look in his eyes as I shall never forget; his mouth was open and showed his white teeth; his cheeks were flushed but now with no unnatural tints;

his frail, diminutive figure swayed with every movement of the schooner.   Yet even at the moment I felt that his was the soul that inspired the flying vessel and that all depended on his indomitable will and fearless courage.

The shore was not now in sight, but about four hundred yards away on the weather beam—and I saw it with a leaping of my heart—there rose a ghostly fabric of canvas looming through the thin mist.   Captain Claude never turned his head toward his passing foe but kept his eyes fixed on the drawing sails.   But the sight of the brig fascinated me.   Every moment she seemed to me to be drawing nearer and nearer, and every moment I watched to see the spurt of fire lighting up the greyness of the haze. For a time I could not withdraw my eyes; and then I saw the flash of another gun; I heard the hissing of the iron messenger, and the green water was tossed into white foam a few yards astern.   Captain Claude turned his head for the first time, and laughed pleasantly.

"He has got our range now," he cried.   "He means business, Mr. Peacocke."

"I am afraid he does, sir," answered the mate, who was crouched near where the captain stood, "and he has the legs of us."

"And the body and the head, but not the heart, Mr. Peacocke.   They won't say we did not die game.   And now, sir, we must not let him have it all his own way.   See what you can do with the carronade.   You can take your time; there is no hurry for we have all eternity before us."

The mate made no response, but rose to his height and —it is wonderful how trivial incidents impress the memory —stopping to spit contemptuously over the bulwark, lounged slowly forward.   I saw from where I stood a little crowd gathered round the gun and the tarpaulin covering withdrawn, and then one ran to the galley and presently returned with a light in his hand. Captain Claude put down his helm and altered the schooner's course.

"Don't fail to give them our compliments, Mr. Peacocke," he shouted. "Now, old sure and steady."

Almost simultaneously came the deafening roar of the gun and the shock that shook the *Swallow* from stem to stern and for a moment seemed to stop her flight.

The captain had turned his head a little to watch the effect of the shot and then he waved his hand delightedly.

"Hulled by the living thunder! Try him again my prince of Trojans. Never mind his blank body but show us the daylight through those cursed long spars of his. Ah! good-morning, Mr. Cassilis. You will be in at the death after all. 'Tis a fair hunting morning, and you are not going to Havre this cruise. Ho! ho! we are booked for a longer voyage—the dismal Acheron and the lonely Styx. What do you think of Claude Slingsby as a prophet now?"

"Upon my word I think you are mad," I said bluntly. "This seems to me a midsummer folly."

At this moment the *Spitfire* had answered the *Swallow's* gun, and a great, ragged hole had been torn in the mainsail almost above my head.

The captain glanced coolly at the sail.

"This is growing pleasant. I avow they are most pressing in their attentions. A little lower, Mr. Cassilis, and you would have solved the great mystery. Mad! You think I am mad? Very well, sir. Upon my honour I believe you are not very far wrong, but I am sorry we have not time to discuss the subject fully. Now, Mr. Peacocke, we shall try our luck again if you please, and be —— to them. By the immortal gods we'll weather them yet."

The effect of the *Swallow's* last discharge was plainly seen. The *Spitfire's* topmast had been shot away, and hung a ruin of ropes and canvas, while almost at the same moment we glided into a thick belt of fog that completely hid her from our view. Captain Claude gave a little cry of delight and again altered the *Swallow's* course. The mist was so close about us that I could not even see the schooner's bow, and the wind was still blowing freshly.

"If it holds," cried Captain Claude joyfully, "we'll sail them round this glorious world of God. Give us an hour of this and they won't catch us in a century. How. do you make Dunstan's holy light, Mr. Peacocke?"

"South by south-west, captain," said the mate bending over the compass. "I wish they would give us another gun."

"To be sure you do, my gentle Peacocke, but Seymour's not such a fool as to set our course for us. Keep the men quiet forward, and listen with all your ears for the dropping of a pin on the starboard side. If the fog holds thick enough I am going to teach them a lesson they'll never forget in their lives—if the fog don't hold, do you know what will happen, Mr. Cassilis?"

"I think I know," I said.

"They'll blow us out of the water, and then hey for the mermaids and their combs of gold! That's the truth of it. I think a couple of cable lengths would draw us slap aboard them now. Ah! did ye hear anything?"

But I heard nothing. The fog hung thick and cold about us; the *Swallow* like a leaping greyhound, shouldered her way through the freshening sea, and Captain

Claude stood erect with his head thrown forward listening for every noise. The minutes seemed to me to pass
like hours, and there was no change. The only sound
that I could hear was the leaping of the waves round the
bow, and the swish of the heavy sea. The men never
moved or spoke where they leaned over the bulwarks
listening and watching. I felt my heart beating with the
excitement, and I could hardly breathe. Was it ten minutes or ten hours that had passed in this way? Once I
thought I heard the sound of creaking spars and of a
chain rattling, but I may have been mistaken for Captain Claude neither moved nor spoke. Then the mist
began to lighten, for I could see clearly from one end of
the *Swallow* to the other.

The next few minutes are now in my memory like a
dream. The fog had changed into wreaths of writhing
mist; the round, red sun flashed out above the bows, and
suddenly bearing down upon us loomed the towering
fabric of a noble ship.

"Steady my lads all!" cried the captain. "Ready
with the gun, Mr. Peacocke?"

And then I heard a voice hailing us, a clear, ringing
voice that spoke above the sudden clamour.

"Surrender, you fool! or I'll send you all to the bottom."

"Surrender be damned!" cried the captain. "Sink us
if you can, you infernal son of a sea-cook. Now Mr.——"

But the words were never finished. There was a sudden
crash, a jagged flash of dazzling flame, and the reverbera-
tion of ten thousand thunders. I was caught by the
throat and whirled into space like an eddying straw,
stunned and crushed and choked. But then there was a
great, silent darkness and I remembered nothing more.

CHAPTER XXIV

THE LIGHT AT THE END OF THE JOURNEY

WHEN I came back to consciousness there was a grey, wavering light in the little cabin where I lay. At first I thought I was lying in my own bed at Heronford, and it was a long time before I could piece the fragments of my mind together and think collectedly. Then gradually and little by little the stray gleams of memory brightened and widened, and I began to remember what had happened. I was still on board the *Swallow*, and the steady, swinging motion that I felt was the movement of the vessel.

After all Captain Claude had eluded the imminent peril with which he was menaced when I was struck down, and I was still his prisoner. His dexterity and courage had stood him in good stead, and he had escaped where escape had seemed impossible. My own position was unchanged. The hopes—faint as they were—that I had of the *Spitfire's* coming had ended in nothing—the last chance of rescue had disappeared.

I tried to raise my arm, but I found that I was unable, and my head was racked with an intolerable pain. I remembered now—I had been wounded by the falling of a spar when the mast had gone by the board. That last scene rose vividly before my eyes—the great grey mass lifting itself out of the waters, the swift leap of flame, and the hopeless ruin of the *Swallow's* deck. And yet we had escaped! It seemed impossible, and as I tried to fancy how it happened, the darkness again overtook me and I lost myself among the shadows.

I was awakened by the sound of voices, and I opened my eyes dreamily. The pain in my head no longer troubled me, and my intolerable thirst was gone. At first the voices sounded as if from an infinite distance, and I had no curiosity to hear the words or know who were the speakers. I was drowsy and contented and had no desire to be disturbed. But gradually the voices became more distinct, and as I listened a feeling of interest grew in me.

"The seven sleepers of Ephesus were nothing to this young gentleman," said a mellow voice with a clink of laughter in it. "He's been asleep two days by the round face ov Apollo, and Venus her sweet self couldn't get a word out ov him. But the fever's gone, glory to God, an' we've rejuced the inflammation to the natural condition entirely. It'll be his head that's troublin' him now."

"And the salt water, doctor. He had a good dose of that."

"The salt water never hurt anybody yet unless by way ov the sea-sickness, an' that used to play the juice with meself. Ah! me good sir, good morning. It's meself is glad to see you so fresh and smiling after all."

"Where am I?" I said.

"Afther a little nap of twenty-four hours and three-quarters, be the same more or less, you find yourself on board his Majesty's brig *Spitfire*, under the treatment ov a poor surgeon's mate by name ov O'Brien, and, please God, there's no harm done in the world."

The news wakened me into a new life. In a moment I was wide awake, and a great rush of joy filled my heart.

" The *Spitfire !* " I cried.

" Ay, sir, that's the name of this blessed old hulk, though I'm told by all accounts you have some reason to give thanks to the same, and it's not for me to take away her character."

" You are telling me the truth ? "

" I was born in Ireland, me dear boy, and never told a lie since I was a baby but wance, and that was an accident. You'll see for yourself in a day or two."

" And the *Swallow* and Captain Slingsby—I thought —"

" A dream, an ugly, good for nothing dream. I've dreamt about them meself. I dreamt we met the little devil on Tuesday morning, and more by good luck than good guidance we gave him a belly full. Never a man wanted it more and deserved it better. He's the only man in the world, and I'm a good Christian, that I'd have seen hanged with a heart and a half. Dream away, sir, and dream that the *Swallow* has carried her last cask of brandy—it was the beautiful stuff by all accounts—and that the little rogue in the blue coat will never stick a knife in the back of an honest man again. For they went down together, and he cheated the gallows after all. And now let me see your arm, and I'll try and make you a little more comfortable."

" Ah! I see I have been hurt."

" You have the luck of St. Patrick's great aunt, who had a saint for her nephew. What's a little knock on the

head, a broken arm, and an infinitesimal derangement of
the nervous system when you might have been in purgatory these two days past. Let me tell you, Mr. Cassilis, there were only three ov you saved, and the other
two by the same token will be hanged because they hadn't
the luck to be drowned."

But, indeed, I felt that I could not be too thankful for
my good fortune, and that I could never be sufficiently
grateful to that merciful Providence which had snatched
me from death and a fate still more awful. Only two
others and myself—Peacocke was one of them—had escaped the general destruction which had overtaken every
soul on board the *Swallow*, and I had been picked up
clinging to a floating spar—dead rather than alive. But
indeed, as I learned, it was only by the merest accident
that the *Spitfire* had arrived upon the scene at all, and I
heard with astonishment that this happy event was due
to the captain having received the afternoon before a note
signed by my friend, Mr. Stone, of whose existence he
had never heard, and whose communication he at first
regarded with suspicion. At first, knowing Captain
Slingsby's way, he had thought it only another ruse, and
had made up his mind to pay no further attention to it,
but at the last moment he had altered his resolution and
got a fortunate slant of wind northward.

Certainly I was now overpowered with kindness. Captain Seymour and the surgeon were continually at my
bedside, and the latter promised that in a few days I
should be on my feet again, while the former declared—
by this time he had heard a good deal of my story—that
I should be landed nowhere but in Carnforth Bay. You

can imagine how eagerly I looked forward to that event, and to the moment when I should rap at the cottage door and take my sweet love again in my arms, for I felt like one newly risen from the dead; I had been lifted out of the blankest despair ; I was about to be restored to love and happiness. I pictured over and over again the look upon my sweetheart's face, and I heard her cry of joy as she flung her arms about my neck and hid her face on my breast. It seemed too great happiness to be real, and sometimes I began to think that I was dreaming again.

Upon the subject of Captain Claude, Seymour and I could never agree. Though he had intended to do me a great wrong he had treated me not unkindly, and I had imagined that he had once or twice displayed the vestiges of a better nature. But the captain of the *Spitfire*, who had known him for some years, had not a word to say in his favour, and certainly if all the stories I heard were true, I had reason to congratulate myself upon my treatment. It appeared that he had been born of a good Devonshire family, and had originally been in the royal service. He had been dismissed his ship and had disappeared—report said he had tried his fortune on the Spanish main—but at any rate he was not heard of for a good many years. Then he reappeared in London, where he swaggered for some time as a man of fashion, until he was involved in a serious murder in a Covent Garden coffee-house, and, being tried upon the capital charge, narrowly escaped with his life.

It was after this he became the owner or part-owner of the *Swallow*, and for six years he had laughed at all attempts to capture him. There was no free trader on the coast so daring as himself; he fought with a rope round his neck, and occasionally added piracy to his other avocations. He was as careless of his own life as he was of the lives of his companions, and seemed as greedy of danger as if he loved it for its own sake. The long list of crimes of which he was accused—and of some of them he was probably guilty—found me lost in wonder that a body so frail and slight could have been animated by so much energy, for he never seemed to have rested. But of that other side of his nature, with its sentiment and softness, no one seemed to have the least suspicion, and I found it difficult to get credit for my narrative. Even yet I cannot tell what he was—whether a good man gone wholly wrong, or a bad man with a distorted and glimmering perception of better things.

The surgeon found me an excellent patient, and in a day or two I began to mend rapidly; indeed, on the third day I had recovered so far that I sat up for a little while and made no doubt that I should get ashore by the end of the week. I had written a letter to Mr. Stone and another to Victory, but from neither had I yet had a reply. Both letters were very short, and merely assured them of my safety, but in Mr. Stone's letter I added the request, knowing his energetic nature, that he would take no steps in regard to the punishment of my enemies until I had first communicated with him. Upon this matter I had not made up my mind, though I am afraid I am like most other men who do not care to suffer serious injury without retaliation.

But there was another thought working in my mind. I now held the lives of Mr. Weston and his accomplice in the hollow of my hand, and it occurred to me that I could now make that important circumstance the means of obtaining possession of the papers of which I had been robbed. I felt sure that when he was driven with his back to the wall, Weston would no more hesitate regarding the sacrifice of his confederate than he had hesitated to destroy myself. How this desirable end was to be accomplished I did not yet see clearly, but I was pretty sure that with Stone's assistance I should be able to attain it. It would be no great advantage to me to punish the offenders—I am afraid in any case I would never have made a persecutor—and on the other hand there might be an enormous gain to be derived from present forbearance. I was afraid that Mr. Stone, by his excessive zeal, might precipitate the catastrophe, and I couched my request to him in language as strong as I could command, and obscurely hinted at the urgency of the cause.

I think there was reason in this view, but you will see in a moment that it never became necessary for me to pursue it, and that that retributive Providence which follows the footsteps of the wrongdoer wrought for me, and administered the last justice in its own inscrutable way.

It was two days after this that I came upon deck for the first time, and though I still felt a little distressed and shaken, I was able to walk about with the help of my kind friend the surgeon's arm, and felt that I was no longer an invalid. Still, it did not require very much to tire me, and after the lapse of a quarter of an hour I was very glad to return to Captain Seymour's cabin, where I had sat every afternoon for the last three days. Here, with the stern windows open, and the warm autumnal air blowing sweetly through, I was able—the captain having gone ashore on some business—to indulge in quiet meditation, with occasional snatches of refreshing slumber. I must have slept longer and more deeply than I imagined. I never heard the captain's gig coming alongside, I never heard the door of the cabin thrown open nor the familiar ring upon the floor; but I was first awakened by the call of a loud and cheerful voice —

"Come aboard at last, Jack, my boy."

I opened my eyes with a start, and looking up saw Captain Blythe standing beside me with both his honest hands held out to me and a look of joy written on his face. For the moment neither of us said another word, but he caught hold of my outstretched hands and pressed them in an eloquent silence.

He drew out his red silk handkerchief and rubbed his forehead, and blew his nose vehemently. Then he looked at me with misty eyes.

"You have had the devil's own time, my lad," he said at last with a sympathetic ring in his voice.

It was so like an echo of the sweet, old days that I could not help laughing boisterously.

"I have had my adventures ashore and afloat, sir," I said; "as many as would fill a book. But I am as a man famished, and you must tell me the news first. Is all well? How is Victory and my—— Lord Heronford? Tell me everything."

"All goes cheerily, Jack, now that we have got you safe in port. Lord, man, what a fright you gave us to be sure! And I never could have thought that Weston would have played the rogue as he did. I'll tell you the truth, Jack, I will, by ——. I thought at first you had slipped your cable and taken French leave of us in the dark. I have been thinking since I could never look you in the face again."

"Never fear, sir," I said, "we will soon forget that. But Victory ——? "

"There is no wonder in the world like a woman," said the captain profoundly. " The little baggage is a witch, and knew everything as if she had read it in a newspaper. I can't tell how she found it out, but there it was—as plain sailing as if it had been laid down on a chart. When the news first came she was under sail in two minutes, and where do you think I found myself? "

" I think I can guess, sir. I remember we spoke of Mr. Stone."

" Not by a long way. Under the guns of Madam Cassilis, and let me tell you the storming of Carthagena was nothing to that. It was after that we saw Stone, and I have had enough of Stone to satisfy me for the rest of my life."

" But he is a very honest man," said I.

" There is very little honesty goes to the making of a lawyer, but I admit that his port is the very best I ever tasted in my life, and I could almost, God forgive me, forget his calling for its sake. I have eaten and drunk Stone for a week, but he's your good friend, Jack, and I wish him no ill."

"I am sure you do not," I said smiling.

"No, no, don't mistake me. I admit he ruffled me ; he trod on my toes, and kept driving me out of my course,

but I don't cherish any feeling about him—not a grain.
I don't like a man who cries ' pooh, pooh,' at every turn,
but I can forgive him if his heart's sound. And the little
girl and he seemed to understand each other. At any
rate, they ran you straight home to Langston."

" By that time I had gone," I said.

The captain nodded.

" It's a very strange story," he said, " and the strangest
part to my mind is in the end of it. I did you a terrible
wrong, my lad, and I am not sure that I can ever forgive
myself for it. You see I had begun to doubt you—well
hardly that but as bad—and Weston's tales had set me
thinking, and I am sure that William Cassilis was dead.
I thought you knew something about it, and I didn't like
it—it was a bad business, and I didn't see my way clear.
Well, well, when you disappeared I own I thought for a
while there might be something in it, Jack. I wouldn't
speak evil of the dead if I could help it, but when I think
of it that man's villainy takes away my breath."

" The dead ! " I cried. " But you know that William
Cassilis is as much alive as you or I."

Captain Blythe looked at me in momentary wonder,
and then he went on.

" I was forgetting that you had no news. It is a strange
story, Jack. You are sure you can bear to hear it ? "

" I can bear anything," I cried, " but this suspense.
What have you to tell me ? "

" We were too late," said the captain solemnly, " to be
of any use to you, but we were in time enough to see the
corpse of William Cassilis sent home to Heronford."

" What ! " I cried rising slowly to my feet.

"That was Mr. Stone's doing, and I suppose he did it wisely. We had got a search warrant or some document of that kind, for Victory had found a man out of Weston's stables who was ready to depose on oath that you were in the house. Well, we lost no time, but you were gone, and a just God had dealt out his punishment before we got there. You never knew that Weston had a younger brother—a poor, half-witted creature whom he kept closed up and treated, I'm told, well enough. It seems while William Cassilis was in Langston he never would let the poor idiot alone, but tormented and worried him as he did every living creature that came in his way. Once or twice Archie—that was his name—had turned on him and Weston was afraid there might be mischief between them, for he had left orders that he was to be looked after. I suppose they had set a bad watch or none. At any rate they found the part of the house where Cassilis was lodged all in a blaze and the idiot and him there together. They couldn't reach them, and I'm told it was an awful sight. They fought together with the flames roaring behind them, they fought on the window, and they fought on the stone coping ; but the idiot never let go his hold, and they came crashing to the ground together."

"Both dead?" I asked breathless, thinking of poor Archie's fears and threats.

"The poor innocent was breathing, but William Cassilis never moved or spoke again—his neck was broken and he was dead. Stone thought, for your sake and his brother's, the world should know all about it, and he was buried yesterday morning in Heronford churchyard."

" And my lord—does he know ? " I asked.

" He knows nothing, I'm told. They say he may live
for twelve months, but his mind is gone and he's a mere
child. He was a fine man, was Lord Heronford : I never
saw a handsomer, but I suppose it was this trouble has
told upon him. All the world knows now that we did
him a terrible wrong."

I had never seen my good captain so eloquent or so excited, and he had not yet half finished his narrative ; but
the tidings I had already heard was too much for me and
I believe I fainted. At any rate the surgeon who was
hastily summoned induced my visitor to retire, and I was
left alone with my news. You can easily understand that
it was a long time before I could fully realise it. It had
come so suddenly and unexpectedly ; it was so horrible in
its details, that my mind at first could hardly grasp it. The
actual fact of that terrible death-struggle filled me with
horror. It almost softened my feelings toward the wretched
man who had pursued me with malignant hatred, and had
inflicted upon me a wrong so grevious. I could easily
imagine what had happened. I remembered with what
hatred Archie had watched his tormentor, and had waited
for an opportunity of retaliation. The animal ferocity
of the imbecile had been awakened, and he had planned
his revenge with instinctive cunning and certainty. I
pictured again and again that awful scene, and I could not
help feeling that William Cassilis had brought about his
own punishment and prepared his own end. And when
the first sharp edge of horror had become dulled, I thought
of my dear love who had never lost faith in me, who
had never wavered or doubted, and who with all a

woman's splendid heart and courage had laboured toward my safety. My dear blind old captain might doubt, but Victory had shown herself a true woman to the end. Heaven bless those dear eyes that saw so clearly. Heaven shield that tender heart that beat so faithfully.

It was nearly a week after this that the chaise I had taken at Colehaven deposited me at Heronford. I must admit that I was touched by my welcome for I had never dreamed that I had come so near the hearts of my people. They showed their delight in a hundred ways, and had I not prevented it would have taken the horses from the carriage and drawn me in triumph to the door. I found then that many trivial nameless acts that I had done were remembered, and if old Transome blubbered upon my shoulder and spoilt my coat, I am sure I forgave him with all my heart and almost hugged him in return. I felt that I was indeed again among my friends, and their kindly feelings found a responsive echo in my own breast and filled my own heart. But this was not the only surprise in store for me ; there was another still greater and more startling. Madam Cassilis was standing on the steps to receive me clad in deep mourning. I noticed that her face was drawn and aged, and perhaps she had lost a little, but not much, of her stateliness. But I thought notwithstanding her outward coldness of manner that her eyes were not unfriendly, and certainly she had never before addressed me in the same tone and language.

" You are welcome home, Mr. Cassilis."

She held out her hand to me, and permitted it to remain in mine perhaps a moment or more longer than was neces-

sary.   Then our eyes met and at the altered look in them
I started with a sudden thought.   Had she learned?   Had
my lord told her?   But in an instant I knew that was
impossible.   Then she turned in her old hard manner.

"I know you are ill and tired, I will not detain you,
but I have a duty to discharge, and shall not keep you
long.   Can you spare me a moment?"

"Certainly," I said.   "I have ceased to feel tired
since I entered the gates."

"Yes, they are glad to see you," she said with a contemptuous shrug.

I remembered the last time I had stood in madam's
boudoir, and the hard and, as I then thought, unfeeling
manner in which she had treated me.   But now a wonderful change had taken place in her.

I am sure she was not sorry to see me; there was not
the faintest trace of condescension in her manner; she
regarded me as an equal, and, I thought, seemed almost
afraid of me.   She turned round and faced me with her
hands resting upon the table behind her.

"You have always thought me a hard woman," she
said, slowly.

I was silent.

"Yes, a hard woman, and perhaps an unjust one."

"I do not know," I said.   "I speak honestly; I have
always thought you acted from a sense of duty."

"Yet one may do that and act wrongly."

"It has happened before," I said.

"It has happened now," she answered quickly.
"John Cassilis, I never thought I should live to beg
your pardon.   Yet it has come to that, and I have the

pride left to humble myself before you. I beg your pardon with all my heart."

" For what reason ? " I said, almost doubting my ears.

" Because," she cried, and I can hear her speak the words yet, " it is the duty of the women of Heronford to honour the head of the house. Wait," she went on, " you will know in a moment. My brother William was not a good man, and I am sure he intended to do you a great wrong. But in death he made amends for the injury he would have done, and this was found upon him when he was brought here. You are the proper guardian of these papers and the secret they contain."

She placed the little packet in my hands and I knew it in an instant. It seemed never to have been opened, but was tied with the same string as I had last seen it. She watched me as I held it before me.

" Open it," she cried impatiently. " Open it and read."

" I need not do that," I said. " I have seen it before ; I know the contents."

" Then you knew —— "

" Yes, madam, I knew everything."

" And you never spoke."

" The secret was not mine alone."

" I think," she said, and I knew how much it cost her to speak the words, " there are good days in store for Heronford. Will you let me take you to your father's room ? "

Many years lie between that time and this—many happy years that love has filled with music and hallowed with the richest blessings. I have seen my sons grow up round me and heard the prattle of my grandchildren filling this old house with joyous echoes. And the old lady who sits yonder with little Ally's golden head upon her knee—her head is as white as my own, and she moves out into the sunshine when it is warm against the southern wall, but I can still see in her eyes the spring-time and sweetness of a love that time has never weakened, and death will only make the stronger. Ah! My Lady Heronford, I can still hear the laughter of the old Victory, and see the gay and cheerful courage that shone in the eyes of my brave old captain's daughter. Him we buried full of age and honours, but I think his fighting spirit is not dead, for there is another Blythe of his blood and mine who has heard the thunders of Trafalgar, and saw the great captain fall in his hour of victory. I have another neighbour now in Langston Priory. Mr. Weston has long since gone to his own place, and his deeds have followed him. For myself I let him go his own way, and if I did not forget, at least I forgave him the wrongs he did me; and he met his final punishment, as often happens in this world, not at my hands, but his own.

THE END.